THE DOCTOR'S DIAMOND PROPOSAL

BY

ANNIE CLAYDON

This is a work of fiction. Names, characters, places, locations and incidents are purely fictional and bear no relationship to any real life individuals, living or dead, or to any actual places, business establishments, locations, events or incidents. Any resemblance is entirely coincidental.

Published in Great Britain 2016
By Mills & Boon, an imprint of HarperCollins*Publishers*
1 London Bridge Street, London, SE1 9GF

ISBN: 978-0-263-92628-6

Our policy is to use papers that are natural, renewable and recyclable products and made from wood grown in sustainable forests.
The logging and manufacturing processes conform to the legal environmental regulations of the country of origin.

Printed and bound in Spain
by CPI, Barcelona

Dear Reader,

Science fiction has taught us that using time travel to meddle with the past isn't always the wisest course of action. One small thing changes and it sets off a cascade of alternative realities, any one of which might have unintended consequences.

When Alex and Leo first meet they're dressed up as space travellers from their favourite TV show. That meeting sets a chain of events in place which reverberates through their lives, and when they meet again the night that they shared together all those years ago has become an irrevocable part of who they have both become.

It's an often-posed question. What would you do differently? But, although it's always good to learn from the past, it's not something that any of us can change. The present might be fleeting, and the future unknown, but that allows us the great gift of hope. One of the things I most enjoyed about writing Leo and Alex's story was seeing Leo gradually turn away from his past and learn to hope for a better future.

I hope that you enjoy Alex and Leo's story. I'm always thrilled to hear from readers, and you can contact me via my website: annieclaydon.com.

Annie x

To my wonderful editor, Nicola Caws.
With grateful thanks for your guiding hand on this journey.

Books by Annie Claydon

Mills & Boon Medical Romance

Stranded in His Arms

Rescued by Dr Rafe
Saved by the Single Dad

Snowbound with the Surgeon
Daring to Date Her Ex
The Doctor She'd Never Forget
Discovering Dr Riley

Visit the Author Profile page at
millsandboon.co.uk for more titles.

Praise for
Annie Claydon

'A compelling, emotional and highly poignant read that I couldn't bear to put down. Rich in pathos, humour and dramatic intensity, it's a spellbinding tale about healing old wounds, having the courage to listen to your heart and the power of love that kept me enthralled from beginning to end.'

—*Goodreads* on
Once Upon A Christmas Night...

CHAPTER ONE

Ten years ago...

THE PARTY HAD got off to a slow start, but by eleven o'clock the house was packed with people and Leo Cross was beginning to feel hot and uncomfortable in his costume.

It had seemed like a good idea at the time. *Orion Shift* was less of a TV show to the six medical students who shared the sprawling house in West London and more of a Friday evening ritual. The one hour in the week that didn't belong to study, girlfriends or the urgent need for sleep. So what better way to celebrate their third year exam results than decorate the living room with as much tinfoil as they could get their hands on and suspend inflatable planets from the ceiling?

Dressing up as the crew of the interstellar spacecraft *Orion Shift* had been the next logical step. But a hot summer's evening wasn't really the time to be wearing a heavy jacket with a high collar, and Leo was beginning to wish that personal temperature regulation fields really had been invented.

A girl in blue body paint and a leotard sidled up to him. 'Captain Boone! You look particularly delicious tonight.'

'Maddie. How are you doing?'

'You want a Tellurian cocktail?' Maddie draped her arms around Leo's shoulders. Clearly she and Pete had been arguing again. It was only a matter of time before the inevitable reconciliation, but at the moment Pete was on the other side of the room taking a great deal of interest in a red-haired girl dressed as a Fractalian hydra and Maddie had clearly decided that she was going to give him a taste of his own medicine.

Leo disentangled himself from Maddie's grip. 'No. Thanks, but...' *Just no.* If Pete and Maddie wanted to play games that was fine, but Leo knew better than to get involved.

'Leo...!' Maddie stuck out her lower lip in a disappointed pout as he retreated quickly through the press of people.

He pushed his way to the kitchen, avoiding the usual group around the beer keg, and slipped outside into the back garden, sighing with relief as the warm breeze brushed his face. The paved space at the back of the house was packed with people, drinking and talking, and Leo made good his escape, dodging across the grass and into the pool of darkness that lay beneath the trees at the end of the garden.

He bumped into something soft and sweet-smelling and saw a flash of silvery-green luminescence. A shadow detached itself from the other shadows and stumbled into a pool of moonlight. It was Lieutenant Tara Xhu to a T.

'Another fugitive?' A smile played around her lips.

'You could say that. So how did you manage to make it out of there?'

Tara—or whatever her real name was—shrugged. 'I'm not sure. I've only watched one episode, and that was to get the costume right, so I don't really know what Tara's strategy might be.' Her mouth twitched suddenly into a flirtatious smile. 'So you're Captain Boone?'

Leo's eyes were beginning to adjust to the darkness and the more they did so, the more he liked what he saw.

She was dressed all in black, thick leggings, boots and an off the shoulder top that followed her slim curves and displayed the green scales which spread across Tara's shoulder. A fair replica of an immobility gun was strapped to her thigh and twisted metallic strands ran round her fingers and across the back of her hands. Her dark hair was streaked with green and anchored in a spiky arrangement on the top of her head with Tara's silver dagger pins.

Leo had been in love at first sight before, but suddenly the other times didn't seem anything like the real thing. She raised one jewelled eyebrow and Leo realised that his gaze had been following the path of the scales that ran down the side of her face and neck and disappeared beneath her top.

'Um... Great costume. Your scales look...really lifelike.' Captain Thomas Boone would undoubtedly have managed something a bit more urbane, but then he had more experience of the galaxy than Leo.

'Thanks. Iridescent body paint. I felt a bit of an idiot on the bus, on my way here.' She grinned at him and moved back towards the old picnic bench which stood under the trees. 'So are you really escaping something, or do you just want some fresh air?'

'A bit of both.' Leo sat down next to her, stretching his legs out in front of him. This replica Tara had a lightness about her movements, a kind of joy about her, which broke through the warlike quality of the real Tara's appearance. Even though she was sitting a good two feet away from him, Leo could almost feel her warmth.

'You live here?'

'Yes.'

'Then you must be a medical student.'

'That's right. Starting year four in a couple of weeks, so this'll probably be the last party we have for a while.'

'I hear it's a tough year. An interesting one, though...'

That was exactly how Leo felt about it. He knew that his clinical attachment was going to be hard work, but he couldn't wait to start putting all that he'd learned into practice. 'What do you do?'

She shrugged. 'Nothing at the moment. I'm just back from a year in Australia.'

'Yeah? What's it like?' All Leo wanted to do right now was sit here in the darkness and listen to her talk.

She laughed. 'Bit too big to describe in one sentence. I loved it, though.'

Leo imagined that she'd taken every moment of the last year and squeezed the very most out of it, in the same way that she seemed to be draining every drop of potential from these moments. It was infectious.

She was fiddling thoughtfully with the bright silver strands across the back of her hand. 'Did you always want to do medicine?'

'Yeah. My uncle's a doctor, and when I was nine I saw him save someone's life. That settled it for me, and there's never been anything else I wanted to do.'

She nodded quietly. 'So you have a calling. A mission in life.'

Sometimes, poring over his books late at night, it didn't seem so. But Tara made it all sound like something special.

'Yeah. Guess I do.'

'I'm still looking for mine. There are so many possibilities and I don't think I can settle on just one. So I'm going to be helping out on my dad's farm for the next year while I think about putting in my university applications.'

'You'll find the right thing.' Leo applied all of the weight of his twenty-one years to the problem. And all of the certainty from the last five minutes, that whatever she decided to do she'd do it wholeheartedly.

'I suppose I will.' She seemed to ponder the idea for a

moment, then smiled suddenly. 'Nothing like mucking out to concentrate the mind on your aspirations for the future.'

'Would you like me to go and get you a drink?' Leo hoped she'd say yes. That they could continue this conversation alone, out here, rather than going back to the heat and noise of the party.

'Thanks, but no. I tried one of those blue cocktails and it was too sweet.' She hesitated, then seemed to come to a decision. 'That coffee bar around the corner. Think it'll still be open?'

'It's open all night.' Sweet promise stirred in Leo's chest.

'You fancy making a break for it, then?'

Theirs weren't the most outlandish costumes amongst the coffee bar's customers that night, but she had still tugged awkwardly at her green hair and silver jewellery. Leo had laughingly persuaded her to stay just as she was, saying that since he was dressed as a spaceship captain, it was practically expected that his First Lieutenant should be accompanying him.

They'd talked all night, fuelled by coffee and then ham and cheese toasties at three in the morning. At six, she'd refused to allow him to see her all the way home and he'd had to content himself with walking her to the bus stop.

'May I call you?' Leo made a silent wish that the bus wouldn't come just yet.

'I was hoping you would.' She smiled at him, reaching into her jacket for her phone and reeling off the number. Leo repeated it over in his head, his fingers shaking unaccountably as he pressed the keys. He hit dial, and her phone chimed. Even her ringtone seemed fresh and full of joy.

'That's it.' She rejected the call and gratifyingly saved his number.

'Lieutenant Tara.' Leo grinned, spelling out the words

as he typed them into his phone. 'What's your real name, though?'

'Alex...' She turned as a bus drew up at the stop. 'This one's mine. You will call, won't you...?'

'Yes.' Leo wondered whether it would be appropriate to kiss her goodbye and decided that he'd already missed his chance. The night had been perfect as it stood, a meeting of minds that had nothing to do with any alien powers, and when he kissed her he wanted enough time to do it properly. She got onto the bus, pressing her ticket against the reader, and turned to wave at him.

The bus drew away. Calling her now would be too soon. He turned to walk back home, and his phone buzzed.

May we meet in other worlds.

Her text mimicked Tara's habitual farewell.

And get some sleep.

Leo grinned, texting back his reply, watching until the bus turned a corner and disappeared.

He called that evening and she didn't reply. Perhaps she'd decided to have an early night. The next day she didn't reply either.

Leo counted the number of calls he made, knowing that each one would show up on her phone. Half a dozen was beginning to look a little stalkerish, so he sent a text instead.

No answer. He left it a week and called again, leaving a carefully scripted voicemail and resolving that if she didn't reply this time he'd take the hint and give up. Clearly, the gorgeous, vivacious Lieutenant Tara had decided that, of all the glittering possibilities she saw ahead of her, he wasn't one of them. It was time to retreat gracefully and get on with thc next chapter of his life.

CHAPTER TWO

Time warp to the present day...

ALEXANDRA JACKSON WAS shaking as she walked across the large marble-clad reception area of the hotel. The receptionist gave her directions to the coffee lounge.

'Oh, and where's the ladies' room, please?' She still had ten minutes to spare, and her heart was beating like a hammer in her chest. She needed to calm down.

'Through there…'

Alex followed the receptionist's pointing finger, ending up in a tastefully decorated ante-room that was larger, and rather smarter, than her own lounge. Sitting down, she closed her eyes, concentrating on deep, slow breaths.

Leo Cross. She'd thought about him a lot in the last ten years, certainly more than one night in a coffee bar would warrant. Maybe because of what had happened on her way home. The car that had swerved across the road and hit her, after she'd got off the bus, had changed everything.

Alex had wondered whether, by some chance, he might be one of the unending stream of doctors who stopped by her hospital bed, but he never had. She'd lost her phone and when her parents brought her a new one the number was different. In any case, what would he want with her now?

All the same, the memories of Leo's slightly awkward charm, the shining passion with which he'd talked about his ambition to become a doctor, had still lingered. Like a touchstone that stayed with her through the long months of convalescence, learning to walk again with a prosthetic leg, leaving home for university… Leo's commitment, his absolute certainty that he had a calling in life, had spurred her on. If he could do it, then so could she.

She'd hung onto the dream as long as she could, imagining Leo as some kind of white knight, a public health crusader—a starship captain, even. Nothing less would have been enough for Leo. But then she'd been brought back to earth with a bump.

Seven years after the night she'd met him, she saw Leo's name in the papers. Not believing it could be him, she'd searched the Internet for a picture. And there he was. The newest TV doctor, charming and urbane, who made an appearance at all the right parties. It seemed that the Leo she'd met had lost his ambition to change the world, and cashed in on his melting blue eyes and blond, handsome looks.

She'd thought about contacting him, but what would she say? That she'd held him in her heart for all these years until he became an ideal, rather than a blood and bone man? Perfect was best left where reality couldn't tarnish it, in dreams and the imagination.

But now Leo Cross had something she wanted.

Alex zipped up her bag and stood, straightening her jacket and smoothing her trousers. He wouldn't recognise her, nor would he remember. She could start again and pretend he was a completely different person from the one she'd met all those years ago.

As she walked into the coffee lounge she saw him immediately, sitting in one of the easy chairs grouped around each table. He still took her breath away. His hair was shorter and neater but still gave his face an almost angelic quality, even though the softness around his eyes had gone. He was dressed impeccably, a dark suit with an impossibly crisp white shirt and a subtly patterned, expensive-looking tie.

Everything about him screamed celebrity: the winter tan, the way the waiter knew exactly who he was and where he was sitting when Alex said who she was there to meet. She wondered whether the air of gravitas, lent by the pile of papers on his knee that were currently taking his full attention, was for her benefit and dismissed the thought. She was the one who needed to impress him, not the other way around.

He looked up as she approached, the sudden flash of uncertainty in his eyes giving way to recognition. Then he sprang to his feet, his papers dropping unheeded onto the carpet.

'Lieutenant Tara!' His smile was just as melting as it had ever been and the shock of being recognised and suddenly catapulted backwards in time left Alex momentarily at a loss. 'As I live and breathe… How are you? What have you been up to?'

'I think you know already. That's my PR bundle you've just dropped on the floor.'

He put two and two together with creditable speed. '*You're* Alexandra Jackson?'

'Yes. Only I prefer Alex…'

'Fewer syllables to contend with?' Leo's quiet, understated humour had remained intact, at least. She grinned up at him stupidly, a mixture of pleasure and panic rendering her silent.

'Did you know it was me?'

It was somehow engaging that he could even entertain the notion that someone could forget his smile. 'Yes. I didn't think you'd remember me.'

'Well, it's good to see you. I'm afraid I haven't had a chance to go through all the material you sent yet.' He bent to pick up the papers, shuffling the disorderly pile and laying it on the table.

She'd read every word of his PR material. Top of his class at medical school, and now practising as a GP in central London. An advanced diploma in counselling, and membership of a long list of professional bodies. Co-hosting a radio phone-in had quickly led to his own show, which aired three evenings a week, and then TV appearances, a couple of bestselling books and patronage of various health initiatives. On its own that was impressive, but if his social life was even half as interesting as the papers would have everyone believe, it was practically superhuman.

'So...' He gestured her towards the armchair standing opposite his. 'Shall we get down to business?'

'Yes. That would be good.' That was what she was here for. Not to spend the time gawping at Leo's smile.

'Right, then.' He seemed impatient now to start and Alex dumped her coat and bag onto an empty chair, sitting down quickly. 'I'd like to be honest with you about why you're here.'

That would be good. Alex nodded dumbly.

'Only I need your confirmation that this information will stay confidential. It'll be public knowledge soon, but I'd prefer it didn't come from anyone connected with us.'

'I understand. I won't say a word.'

'Thank you.' His stern look promised all kinds of retribution if she did. 'As you know 2KZ, the radio station I work for, holds an annual charity spotlight during February. And your charity applied to participate in that.'

'Yes. We were told before Christmas that our application wasn't successful.'

'It wasn't.' He paused to let that particular defeat sink in. 'But the charity we chose has had difficulties. We stuck by them for as long as the allegations were unsubstantiated but, now that they are, we have little choice but to look elsewhere.'

'And we have another chance?' Alex wondered which charity it was, and what the allegations were, but Leo's measured professionalism made it clear that he wasn't about to divulge that information.

'We considered abandoning our plans for this year completely, but we feel that a new charity, which we can investigate thoroughly for any sign of irregularity, would be an appropriate fallback position. The format would be slightly different—we'll be doing informal phone-ins instead of a series of pre-recorded programmes, because of the time factor. Are you still interested?'

Alex swallowed. 'This is a big project for us and it'll take a good proportion of our resources if we get involved. Can you tell me how far down the list we were?' Her feelings about being told that they were second best were irrelevant, even if Leo could have put it a little more tactfully. But she did need to know that 2KZ were interested enough to present her charity properly, and that they weren't just filling a few spare hours in their programming schedule.

'No. That would be inappropriate. But I can assure you that we're fully committed to going ahead with this and that I believe you're a good fit for the project. And I do need your answer now.'

In other words, she had to trust him. The old Leo would have been a lot easier to trust than this new one. But Alex knew she'd have to be crazy to pass up a chance like this.

'Yes, we're interested. Thank you. This is a wonderful opportunity for us.'

He dismissed her gratitude with a practised smile, a flip of his finger bringing a waiter over. 'Shall we have some tea? The Darjeeling, I think…' The waiter began to scribble on his pad.

She'd never been here before and had no idea what to

order. All the same, Leo had left her to choose for herself at the coffee bar. Alex supposed that it had been a bit more straightforward then—coffee or tea, with or without milk. But it seemed that everything had been a bit more straightforward that night.

'That sounds nice. But I'd prefer Lady Grey if they have it.'

The ghost of a smile flickered around his lips. 'Lady Grey it is.' He looked up at the waiter. 'A pot for two, please.'

'Sandwiches or cakes, sir?' The waiter's gaze turned to Alex as Leo deflected the question her way.

'No, thank you. Not for me.' Dealing with Leo was taking all of her concentration. She wasn't sure she could manage cake crumbs as well.

Leo was shuffling through the papers in front of him on the table. 'Right. So your charity is called Together Our Way?'

'Yes.'

'No acronyms? Something a bit more snappy?'

'No.' Defiance bloomed suddenly in her chest. If they were going to do this, she was going to have to learn to stand up to Leo's steamroller tactics. 'We like to be referred to by our full name because it's the way we do things.'

'Yeah, I got that. And you're…' He caught a sheet from the pile which Alex recognised as her own CV. 'A qualified physiotherapist, and you founded Together Our Way to help young people with disabilities participate in sport.'

'Yes. I've brought some photographs with me that I think best show…'

'Later, maybe. I'd like to ask a bit about how the charity's run first.' He didn't even look at the pile of photos that Alex had pulled from her bag. 'From what I can see here, you're managing on a shoestring. You work three days a week as a physiotherapist and you don't take a salary from the charity. And you just have one part-time paid employee, who called me back yesterday to arrange this meeting. From what Rhona says, she seems to be doing rather more than I'd normally expect from a part-timer.'

'When people give us money, they want to see it spent on our core aims, not our running costs. We have an arrangement with Rhona that suits us both—she has family commitments and we give her very flexible working hours, and in return she's very committed to us. And we have a network of very enthusiastic supporters.' Alex had photographs of them as well, but she doubted that Leo would want to see them.

He nodded. 'And you have your own office?'

'Yes. It's a loft room. The law firm that owns the building wasn't using it and they let us have it free of charge.'

'That's good of them. And what do you do for them in return?' His eyes seemed to bore into her, both tempting and cajoling at the same time.

'The senior partner's son takes part in one of our training programmes.'

'And this boy—he fulfils your standard criteria for this service?'

Anger seized hold of her. Alex knew the exact position of the photograph in the pile, and she snatched it out, dropping it onto the table in front of Leo. 'He was born without the lower part of both legs. Like most five-year-olds, he loves running and playing football. His name is Sam.'

Leo glanced down at the photograph, his face suddenly softening. As he reached out to touch it with his fingertips, Alex saw the melting blue eyes of the young man she'd once met.

'It looks as if Sam's pretty good with that ball.'

'He is. What he doesn't have in speed, he makes up for with tactics.'

'Well, I hope I'll get a chance to see him play.' It was just a glimpse of compassion—a brief acknowledgement that Leo really did understand what Together Our Way was all about. But it was enough to stop Alex from giving up on him completely and putting her involvement in this project up for review.

And then the moment was gone. The tea arrived, and Leo took that as a cue to resume his questioning. The way the charity was run. Exactly what they spent their money on. How many volunteers they had, how they dealt with Health and Safety. He was nothing if not thorough and, although Alex struggled to keep up with him, he seemed content with her answers.

'And now that I know all about you—' his smile became melting again '—it brings me to the question of 2KZ's planned involvement.'

Maybe he'd been a little hard on her. There was actually no maybe about it, but Alex hadn't let him walk all over her and Leo respected that. And the delicious surprise of seeing her again…

Had been shockingly tempered when he realised that she had been through so much in the last ten years. An accident, losing her leg. But she'd turned that around. And, out of respect for her, he'd concentrated on her achievements.

If it had been anyone else, he would have allowed the personal to oil the wheels of the professional. But Alex clearly didn't want to put their relationship on that level. She hadn't called him back ten years ago. And even though she'd known it was him, she'd left it to her assistant to call him and arrange this meeting. Leo wasn't prone to holding grudges, but that looked like a pretty definite expression of intent.

He'd reacted like an iceman, shrinking from a flame.

Ill-prepared, because of an emergency with one of the patients at his GP's surgery, he'd asked the questions he needed to ask and kept his feelings to himself.

And his feelings weren't a part of this equation. If Together Our Way was slightly amateurish in its approach, its heart was quite definitely in the right place. It was an organisation that his show could make a big difference to, and Leo seldom turned down a challenge.

'As I said, the spotlight we're proposing is a little different from the one first offered.' This was the sticking point. 'The intention now is that I'll be hosting a representative from Together Our Way as a guest on my medical phone-in show, once a week during the whole of February. I'm assuming that it will be you?'

Panic flared in her eyes, and Leo felt another little piece of him melt in response. Clearly the idea that she'd be talking live on the radio hadn't registered with Alex the first time he'd mentioned it.

But she rallied beautifully. 'Yes. It'll be me.'

'I'm trying to get some ten or fifteen minute slots on our Community Affairs programme in addition to that. That'll involve me spending some time with you, and seeing your work first-hand. I assume you have no objections to that?'

'We'd welcome it. What do you have in mind?'

'I'll be making reports, and probably writing a few articles for our website. And there'll be an outside broadcast...' He fell silent. He could see from her face that Alex had an issue with that, and he waited for her to put it into words.

'Would you be happy to fit in with our way of doing things? Our first priority is the young people we serve, and if we needed to change that emphasis to accommodate you we'd have some difficulty.'

She'd have no *difficulty* in changing; she just wasn't prepared to do it. Good for her. 'We'd be there to observe.

Low-profile isn't my usual approach, so I'll be giving those muscles a little much-needed exercise.'

Her pursed lips reminded him of a severe version of a kiss. 'That's part of what we do. Help exercise under-used muscles.'

'We'll stay flexible, then.' He imagined that Alex was just as used to acting on her own initiative as he was, and that might be interesting. Even so, it was time to flex the muscles he *did* use regularly and remind her who was in charge of this project.

'2KZ has broadcast to the whole of London for more than thirty years now. Interviews with young people appeal to our listeners and we know how to do them appropriately and with all the necessary safeguards and permissions. We give our listeners what they want, and outside broadcasts are very good for ratings.'

Another disapproving look. Maybe he needed to mention that ratings weren't just a number on a spreadsheet; they represented hearts and minds. She might deal in hearts and minds but she couldn't reach them without his domination of the ratings lists.

Despite all that disapproval, she came to the right decision. 'That sounds excellent. As long as our young people are properly supported and safeguarded, I think an outside broadcast would certainly be something we'd be keen to do.'

'Good. Anything else?'

'Yes, would you mind if we featured the spotlight on our website?'

'We'd welcome it. We can provide you with artwork if that's of any help. I'll have our in-house designer get in touch with… You have a web designer?'

'That's me, actually.' She shrugged. 'I'm afraid it's not very professional. One of those standard template designs…'

He'd looked at her website briefly and had been very

favourably impressed. 'If you like, I can set up a call with our designer. She's got a lot of experience with liaising with other organisations we partner with, and a conversation might be helpful.'

'Thank you. I'd be grateful for any suggestions she has.' Alex paused, squeezing her hands together. She seemed to have something else on her mind.

'If there are any other issues, now's the time to raise them. We have a very tight schedule on this.'

'I've never been on the radio before…' And she was clearly terrified at the prospect.

'That's what I'm there for. I ask a few questions, to steer things in the right direction, and step in when you dry up…' He couldn't help smiling when Alex's eyebrows shot up. 'Everyone dries up first time. It's expected.'

'Right. I'll try not to do it too much.'

'Be yourself. Don't think about it too much; just say what you want to say. There's a seven second broadcast delay, which allows us to catch anything too bad before it airs. It's supposed to be so that we can cut any profanity, but it works pretty well if you suddenly find you've forgotten what you were about to say.'

'I won't forget. This is really important to me, and I want to do it well.'

Leo nodded, taking a sip of his tea. 'That's exactly what I wanted to hear. Hold that thought and you'll be fine.'

He seemed to have loosened up a bit, which was good, because the giddy chicane of Leo's questioning, and his efficient, autocratic way of doing things, had left her almost weak with exhaustion. He took a thick card from his jacket pocket and handed it to her.

'Here's my number. I dare say that our PR department will be bombarding you with all kinds of details that don't really matter. If you want to cut through all of that, give me a call.'

Alex looked at the card. It was printed with Leo's name and a mobile phone number. She'd never met anyone who had personal calling cards before. 'Thank you. But I don't want to bother you…'

'You won't be. It's always better to sort things out direct, and we don't have any time for messing about.' His gaze raked her face but he said nothing more. Perhaps he'd called her, ten years ago. Maybe she should explain why she hadn't called back, but Alex couldn't think of a tactful way to approach that conversation.

'Yes. Thank you. Can I give you my number?' Alex rummaged in her bag and found the box of cards with the charity's contact details, scribbling her own name and mobile number on the back and handing it to him.

'Thank you.' He glanced at the card and put it in his pocket, seeming to relax a little now that the business of the afternoon had been despatched. 'It's good to see you again, Alex. If I'd known it was you, I'd have come in costume…'

'Then I'd have had to do the same.'

His lips twitched into a smile. Pure, seductive charm, which rushed straight to her head. 'That would have been the one and only thing which would have persuaded me to leave home looking so outrageously foolish.'

Alex had rather liked outrageously foolish. Clearly Leo didn't any more.

'It's just as well you didn't know, then.'

She grabbed her bag, wondering if she was supposed to leave now, and he stood immediately. Leo was done with her now, and about to move on to the next thing on his agenda.

It wasn't until she was walking away that Alex realised that there was one thing he hadn't asked, one thing he hadn't done. Her CV stated quite clearly that losing the lower part of her right leg in a car accident and her subsequent rehabilitation had inspired her to study physiotherapy and then to found Together Our Way. But, even though his questions had been searching and thorough, he hadn't brought the subject up, nor had his eyes wandered to where the prosthesis was hidden beneath the fabric of her trousers.

She should be pleased. Alex sometimes had to struggle to get people to see past her accident and the loss of her leg, and that was exactly what Leo had done. It was chastening, though. He might have remembered her, but it seemed he cared so little about her that he hadn't even mentioned it.

Leo watched her go, wondering if the tremble of his limbs was some kind of delayed shock. The last time she'd walked away from him, he hadn't seen her for another ten years. He had no doubt that this time would be different, but he still couldn't help feeling that he wanted to call after her.

But running after Alex was a very bad idea. She was committed and clever, and the amount she'd achieved in the last ten years was nothing short of extraordinary. When she smiled at him the warmth in her eyes was mesmerising, reflecting all the possibilities that he no longer had it in his heart to believe in. Ten years ago, he'd been as much in love with her as it was possible to be after only one night together, but now love wasn't on his agenda.

The memory of the night they'd met, the dizzy rush of blood to his head, the tingle as all his senses went into overdrive, almost overwhelmed him. But all that was in the past. He just couldn't contemplate a relationship, that bond that required his full commitment, his full attention.

He looked at his watch and signalled to the waiter for the bill. He'd have to leave now, if he wasn't going to be late for his next appointment.

Leo stood, stretching his limbs. There really was no choice about this. If he pulled out, then 2KZ had no other suitable applicants who could respond at such short notice. If she pulled out, then Together Our Way would lose a golden opportunity to increase public awareness about their work. And if his association with Alex didn't look as if it was going to be all plain sailing, then he'd deal with that as it happened.

CHAPTER THREE

LEO KEPT HIS PROMISES. A letter, confirming what they'd discussed, arrived at her office the next morning. When the negotiations over the outside broadcast had stalled, he had called and spoken to Alex about it, then gone away and sorted the whole thing out within ten minutes. He was perceptive, intelligent and he made things happen.

She listened to his radio show without fail, telling herself that the sound of Leo's voice was an incidental pleasure and that preparing herself for what was to come was the real object. The on-air version of Leo was slightly different from the one she'd met, still astute and probing but not so confrontational, his gentle charm putting people at ease and encouraging them to talk.

Afraid to trust in either the public face or the private one, she left most of the liaison to Rhona, picking up her normal duties in return. Two weeks, a week—and then there was no avoiding it. Everything was arranged, and the following Monday saw the first of her guest appearances on the Dr Leo Cross medical phone-in show.

Alex had arrived at the radio station at six, two hours before the show was due to start. Half an hour had been taken up with a short induction from one of the production assistants, and then she'd been taken to an empty studio to have a look around. Leo was due to arrive at seven, but Alex was reliably informed that he was always late.

'What are you reading?' She'd given up looking at her watch and was sitting alone in the restroom, trying to read, when she heard Leo's voice.

'Oh… It's the latest thing apparently, for teenagers.' She tilted the cover towards him and he nodded. 'I like to keep up. It's actually pretty good.'

He smiled, and suddenly warmth zinged in the air between them. He was dressed in jeans and a dark blue sweater that looked far too soft to be anything other than cashmere. However hard Alex tried to look at him dispassionately, he still took her breath away.

He slung a leather jacket down onto a chair and sat down. 'How are you feeling? Nervous?'

Sick with nerves. That must be probably pretty obvious. 'A little…'

'You'll be fine. Once we get started, the hour will go too fast and you'll be wanting more time.' He was leaning towards her, his elbows on his knees. This was clearly Leo's pep talk for beginners and, strangely, it seemed to be working. Now that the dreaded time had come, and he was here, she felt better about everything.

'So… What are we going to say?'

Leo shrugged. 'No idea. I'll introduce you, we'll take a few calls and we'll talk. That's the thing about phone-in radio—there's no script.'

'You like that? The uncertainty?'

He grinned. 'Yeah. Keeps me on my toes. You'll be just great, trust me. And if you're not, then I'll just interrupt and steer things back on course.'

'Right. Thanks.' She'd rather be just great, and not need Leo to save the day. But then that might be a bit too much to ask on her first time.

The door burst open and Alex jumped as the production assistant who'd showed her around popped her head around the door. 'Leo… Fifteen minutes.'

'Okay, thanks. We're ready.' He turned to Alex as the door closed again. 'Just relax. It's a conversation between you and me. Concentrate on that, and the one person out there who's listening.'

'One person?'

'Yeah. Just visualise someone you know, and talk to them. You'll be surprised how well that works.'

'I'll try.' Alex wondered who Leo visualised. Maybe he'd been doing this long enough not to need anyone. 'Was it this nerve-racking for you? Your first time?'

He shook his head. 'Nah. I didn't have any nerves left to be racked. I was so numb with fear that you could have knocked me over the head with a brick and I probably wouldn't have noticed. And I wasn't tipped in at the deep end, like you. I'd been volunteering on a student helpline for years, and done some spots on local radio in connection with that.'

'That must have been pretty tough. Manning a helpline at the same time as you were studying and working at the hospital.' Leo hadn't said anything about a helpline ten years ago, and Alex had thought they'd talked about almost everything in their lives.

'It was something that meant a lot to me. You make time for the things that are important.' His face seemed to harden a little, as if the memory was difficult.

'And you've stayed here. Even though you're on TV now.' It seemed a little odd that he should hang on to this, when he obviously had other opportunities. Leo didn't seem the type for sentimentality.

'Yeah. I like talking to people.' He shook his head, as if to clear it, and then grinned. 'You'll see.'

He ushered her through to the studio, giving her time to get settled. The producer hurried in, putting a few sheets of paper in front of him, and then the call for silence and the 'On-Air' light glowed red.

She hardly heard the music that heralded the start of the show, hardly saw what was going on around her. Then she felt Leo's fingers brush the back of her hand. His gaze caught hers and he smiled, then started the introduction.

'And tonight I have Alex Jackson with me. She's the founder of Together Our Way, a charity which helps young people with all kinds of disabilities participate in sport…' He glanced down at the paper the producer had put in front of him and frowned suddenly. 'Alex is going to be on the line with me here, and so if you've got any questions for her then you know the number to call…'

The jingle for the phone number started to play and Leo took the opportunity to scrunch up the paper in front of him, tossing it towards the control room. It bounced off the glass and dropped to the floor and then suddenly, seamlessly, Leo was talking again.

'To start us all off, I'm going to ask Alex a few questions about Together Our Way. And, just in case anyone accuses me of monopolising her time here, she will be right here with me every Monday for the next four weeks, as part of our Charity Partnership Project…'

Suddenly his gaze was on her. The smile on his lips, the look in his eyes, said that he was talking just to her. 'Alex, how long since you founded your charity…?'

He'd given her an easy one to start with. 'Five years.'

'And in that time you've made yourselves felt. How many sports fixtures are you planning next month?'

'We have eight. But our own sports meetings are just the tip of the iceberg. We've been working with schools and clubs, advising them on how their sport can be fully inclusive, and we've developed a training day for group leaders. Mostly, though, we work with the young people themselves, to help…'

Suddenly, her mind went blank.

'I imagine that there's a bit of confidence-building to

be done.' Leo's eyes were suddenly warm and soothing, dark as a blue Mediterranean sea.

'Yes, that's right. Many of our young people need assistance with special equipment or training, but it's also a matter of showing everyone what's possible.'

'So you're out to capture hearts and minds?' Somehow, he made it seem as if it was *his* heart and *his* mind that were the ones in question and that they were just waiting to be captured.

'Yes. I think that's the aim of any charity, isn't it? Money's vital to us, of course, because we couldn't do what we do without it. But hearts and minds are just as important.'

'And I see that the charity's run on a shoestring, so all the donations you receive go straight into your work.'

He was feeding her lines, bringing up all the points that Alex wanted to highlight. She smiled a thank you. 'Yes, that's right…'

Alex felt as if she'd run a marathon. It had only been an hour, but she was exhausted, her heart thumping in her chest. All the same, Leo had been right. She was eager for more, and had been disappointed when he'd announced that this was all they had time for tonight and handed over to the next presenter.

'Did we speak to everyone?' Leo had said that there were callers waiting but Alex had been unable to gauge how many, or whether they'd been able to speak to them all.

'There are always people who don't get through. Some of them try again.' Now that they were off-air, Leo seemed suddenly more guarded.

'But… They may be in trouble. They might need someone to talk to…'

'Yeah, a lot of them do. We have procedures to deal with that. You needn't worry about that side of things.'

She couldn't—wouldn't—let him give her the brush-off like this. 'I'm… I'm sorry Leo, but that's not the answer I'd hoped for.'

Alex was expecting some kind of reaction; Leo clearly wasn't used to being challenged by anyone around here. But she hadn't expected a smile.

'What answer were you hoping for, then?'

She took a deep breath. 'That there's some way that I could get back to the people who didn't get through.'

He leaned forward, flipping a switch on the console in front of him. Alex's headphones went dead and she realised that, even though the sound engineer in the control room seemed to be paying no attention to it, their conversation could be overheard. She slipped the headset off and laid it down.

'The call-handlers take names and numbers from everyone, and they always ask what the caller wants to say.'

'And they make a note of that?'

'Yes, they do. And they pass the list on to me.' That seemed to be the end of it as far as Leo was concerned. *He* was the trustworthy one, the one who got things done, and he was ready to steamroller over anyone who questioned him.

Maybe she'd deserved it. Maybe he *had* called her all those years ago, and he still remembered that she hadn't called him back.

'Look, Leo. I think there's something… We need to clear something up.'

'What would that be?'

He gave so little. It was questions all the way with Leo, and she was starting to wonder whether he wasn't hiding behind them.

'Did you call me after the party?' Alex wondered how

he'd like a taste of his own medicine, and answered his question with one of her own.

He seemed surprised. 'I'm not sure I remember.'

'Why don't you try?' If this issue was getting in the way of the work she was committed to now, she wanted an answer.

'I said I would.' His slight shrug seemed designed to imply that it really didn't matter all that much to him. 'But that's the way it works. It's a lady's privilege not to call back.'

He flashed her his most charming, roguish smile. That alone probably made the chances of any woman not calling him back extremely slim. Or maybe it was just Leo's way of changing the subject.

'Since you won't give me a straight answer, I'll assume that you *did* call. And I've been wanting to tell you that I'm sorry I didn't get back to you, but I really couldn't. Something happened on the way home and…it was impossible.'

She had his full attention now. Leo couldn't hide the surprise in his eyes. 'What happened?'

'I…' Alex gulped. It was all such a long time ago now and it ought to be irrelevant, but it wasn't. A rap sounded on the glass that separated them from the control room and she jumped.

'I'm sorry.' Leo snapped suddenly into professional mode. 'The producer's here, and I need to have a word with him. Would you mind waiting?'

Alex nodded and he swung to his feet, striding to the door and closing it behind him. He reappeared on the other side of the glass, where a man was waiting for him.

Leo's back was turned to her but the man was glancing at her, even though Leo was obviously talking to him. Curiosity got the better of Alex and she reached for her headphones, flipping the switch that she now knew controlled the sound between the control room and the studio.

'It's not acceptable, Justin.' Leo's voice rang in her ears.

'I really don't see what the problem is…' Alex saw Justin spread his hands in a gesture of puzzlement.

'Well, there isn't any problem because I'm not going to do it. I won't introduce Alex Jackson as a *disabled person.* She has a disability, and she's open about that, but I'm not going to read out an introduction that makes it seem as if it's the most important thing about her. She's here to talk about her charity, which, by the way, is all about encouraging young people to see past their disabilities. *And* educating others to do that too.'

Alex's gaze moved to the screwed up ball of paper on the floor, which Leo had tossed at the glass. He'd moved past it so smoothly that she'd hardly realised he had a problem with it.

'Okay…okay.' Justin's tone was conciliatory. 'It was an error of emphasis, I'll grant you that. No harm done, though…'

'Only because I didn't read the introduction out. I want to hear all the trailers for the show, because I don't want Alex or her charity misrepresented.'

This was almost too much. Leo was fighting her corner without being asked, but just knowing how she'd feel. A thrill of warmth for him clutched at her heart and Alex wondered whether she should go and retrieve the paper, to see what had been written. But then she'd have to take the headphones off, and she wanted to hear this.

'We'll email the sound files through to you. Anything else?'

'No. I'm grateful you're addressing the issue with your customary effectiveness.' Leo's tone had relaxed into lazy charm. 'Actually, there is one more thing. Thanks for all you did to help make this evening happen. It's been a good night.'

Justin seemed to heave a sigh of relief. 'Yep. Nice chemistry in there, Leo. And the caller rate went through the roof…' Justin's gaze flipped towards Alex and Leo turned. When he saw her, his lip curled imperceptibly.

She reddened and took off the headphones, putting them back onto the console. Perhaps he'd think she was just trying them on.

Leo had followed Justin out of the control room and when he appeared at the door of the studio again he was holding a manila envelope.

'Your car's waiting.'

And he thought he was going to slip away now? 'No, Leo. I'm not going anywhere until we finish…what we were talking about.'

'I thought I'd catch a lift with you. The car's a lot more private.' He walked across to the console and, too late, Alex realised that she'd forgotten to cut the sound in between the control room and the studio, and that voices were whispering out of the headphones.

He reached out, switching the sound off again. Then he turned, leaving Alex to grab her coat and handbag and follow him out of the studio.

Leo wondered whether letting sleeping dogs lie was the best option. It probably was, but he knew that wasn't what he was going to do. Not many people questioned his decisions and, while it came as no surprise that Alex bucked that trend, it was unexpectedly like a breath of fresh air.

She settled herself on the wide leather seat in the back of the car, and Leo got in beside her. The driver confirmed the address with her and the car slid smoothly out onto the road.

'This is nice.' She stretched her legs out in front of her, smiling. Clearly she was attempting to disarm him before she started on the next onslaught. He wondered briefly if she knew how much damage her smile could do to a man.

The lights from the street outside were sliding across her face, giving it an almost ethereal quality and it was an effort to stop himself from staring at her. Alex was even more perfect than when he'd first met her. Or maybe he'd just become more of a connoisseur of perfection and learned how to appreciate it better.

He pressed the control button and the glass partition behind the driver's seat slid upwards. Not that the driver probably cared two hoots about their conversation, but the gesture wasn't lost on Alex and her cheeks reddened.

'What happened?' It was probably something stupid—she'd lost her phone or met an old boyfriend on the bus. But Leo had learned the hard way that hoping for the best didn't always mean that the best was going to happen. He had to be sure.

She ignored the question. That usually annoyed him, but Alex did it so blatantly that the assertive twist of her mouth was enchanting.

'I want to thank you. For standing up for me… I mean the charity. And our aims.'

'That's what a good host does.'

'I know. But it doesn't always happen, and… Thank you. You're a very good host.'

People said that all the time, but on her lips the compliment warmed him. Despite that, he still hadn't forgotten what he wanted to ask her…

'What happened? On your way home.'

'I had an accident. I lost my phone.'

'What kind of accident?' Something tingled at the back of Leo's neck. That instinct, honed over years of listening to people, told him that whatever she was about to say next was important.

'I got off the bus and crossed the road…' She paused for a moment, as if the memory was a difficult one.

Leo was trying not to put two and two together and

make four. Hoping that the almost inevitable conclusion wasn't the right one, this time.

'And…?'

'I was knocked over by a car. Drunk driver. I woke up in hospital and my phone was… I don't know where it was. It was gone.'

A great wave of horror seemed suspended above his head, just waiting to crash down on him. 'This was…' He couldn't even say it. His finger twitched, gesturing towards her right leg.

'Yes. My right foot and the lower part of my leg were completely crushed. The only way I'd ever be able to walk again, or be pain free, was for them to amputate below the knee.'

The full horror of it washed over him in a suffocating wall of guilt and remorse. 'Alex… I'm so sorry. If I'd known…'

'You couldn't have known.'

All he could think about was the trail of small events which had ended in this one great one. If he'd only done just one thing differently…

'I should have seen you home.' He remembered that he'd offered and that she'd told him no. If only he'd insisted. If they'd even just argued about it, and she'd missed her bus and had to wait for the next one…

'What would you have done? There were witnesses and they said that the car swerved right across the road and hit me. There was no getting out of the way.'

'I might have helped…somehow.' Anyhow. If all he could have done was just hold her hand, then he would have done it with every ounce of his strength. But he hadn't been there for Alex, and then six months later he hadn't been there for his brother either. The thought seemed to be literally eating at him, taking great chunks of his flesh and leaving him quivering with shock.

Her gaze searched his face. 'You would have put me back together again? That was beyond anyone.'

He couldn't answer. Didn't have words to tell her how sorry he was—for all she'd been through, and for his part in it.

'Do me a favour, eh?' Her voice was soft and he felt her fingers brush his arm. Clawing him back from the memories that swirled in his head.

'Yeah?' Anything.

'I've given up on the *what if* because the past can't be changed. I prefer to concentrate on *what is*.' She shot him an imploring look. 'Please...'

It was an effort to smile, but if Alex could do it so could he. 'You've got it.'

There was one thing he could do. The only thing that made him feel any better about having let his brother down were the people he could help now. Leo guarded that role jealously, never letting anyone else get in the way, and no one ever asked about the call-backs that he made after each show. But Alex had.

He slid the manila envelope across the seat towards her.

'What's this?' She touched it lightly with her fingers, seeming to know that it was something important.

'It's the list of people who didn't get through to the show. Names, numbers and I ask the call-handlers to find out whether they would like a return call if they don't get through.'

'And you were going to tell me about this?' She narrowed her eyes.

'I don't usually volunteer the information. But you did ask.' The envelope lay between them, Alex's fingers at one end of it and his at the other. As if neither of them could quite bring themselves to let go.

'So...when were you thinking of calling back?'

'The call-handlers have told everyone that it'll be tomorrow, late afternoon. I have a surgery in the morning but I'm usually finished by about three o'clock.'

She nodded. 'If you want a hand… Actually, I think I'm going to insist on helping.'

He felt his lips curl into a smile. 'You're free tomorrow afternoon?'

'Yes. I usually work Wednesday to Friday at the hospital, but I'm taking some time off over the next few weeks. I can be available any time.'

He was suddenly almost breathless. It was as if they were making a tryst. More than that, because this would require his full attention.

'You'll be at your office? I can come to you, and we'll go through the list together.'

'That sounds good. Although you might like to bring a scarf. The heating's on the blink again.'

'Sounds delightful. I'll be there at about half past three.' He pushed the envelope another inch towards her. There was a copy back at the radio station, but it still felt difficult to give it up. 'You take this. But don't call anyone until I get there…'

She grinned, stowing the envelope in her bag. 'I imagine they've been told that they'll be hearing from you, not me. Don't worry, I'll wait.'

Before he got the chance to change his mind, the car drew up outside a block of solidly built flats, set back from the road behind a curving drive. Leo made to get out and she laid her hand on his arm.

'I think I can make it on my own.'

She knew just what he'd been thinking, and Leo jumped guiltily. He'd made the promise, but it still wasn't easy to stop thinking about all the things that might happen to her in between here and her front door. 'I dare say you can. But…'

Alex chuckled. 'I know. A gentleman always sees a

lady to her door.' She got out of the car, bending down before closing the door. 'I'm no lady. I'll see you tomorrow.'

Leo begged to disagree. He watched her as she smiled at the driver, giving him a wave and a nod of thanks. She was every inch a lady.

'Wait...' The instruction was unnecessary, as their driver seemed as unwilling to go before Alex was safely inside as he was. She opened the main door and then turned, flapping her hand as if to shoo them away, and, without any reference to him at all, the car pulled out onto the road.

Leo kicked the door closed behind him. The car had retraced its route, driving back into town to the flat that he kept for weekdays, ten minutes' walk from the radio station.

The flat was quiet and dark, shadows slanting across the floor. He fixed himself a drink and, without taking his coat off, slid back the large windows and walked out onto the roof terrace, set seventeen floors above the ground and commanding a view across practically the whole of London. Alex was out there somewhere. One of the lights shimmering in the distance was hers.

He moved closer to the glass barriers which stood at the perimeter of the terrace and a gust of chilly air hit him full in the face. Leo shivered. He had no right to wonder what she was doing, or to wish that he could be doing it with her.

Leo Cross. Never there when you needed him.

He hadn't been there for Alex. To the extent that he hadn't even known that she'd needed him. But he'd known that his brother needed him. He'd known that Joel was under stress, that his first job after university hadn't turned out quite the way he'd wanted it, but Joel had seemed a lot better, and promised Leo that he was handling it. Leo had returned from a weekend away to find that his brother hadn't been handling it at all.

His father had been waiting for him, gently breaking the news that they'd lost Joel. An overdose of prescription drugs. Maybe it had been a mistake.

Leo had doubted that. Joel was his twin, and he knew him almost better than he knew himself. And when he'd finally been able to get a couple of moments alone he'd found the missed calls on his phone. Joel had called him on that Saturday evening.

The brothers used to joke about missed calls. Once meant: *I'll catch you later.* Twice: *Call me back.* Three times: *Call me back now.* The five missed calls on Leo's phone had spoken to him loud and clear. *I'm in trouble. I need you, Leo...*

He pulled his phone from his pocket, scanning it. There was a text from his mother, saying she'd heard the show tonight, and automatically he hit speed dial.

'Hi, Mum…' Leo smiled into the phone, knowing that even if it was forced, the smile would sound in his voice. 'How are you doing?'

'Oh, darling! Exhausted. I went shopping with Marjorie today…'

'Yeah? Find anything nice?'

'Of course we did. You know Marjorie. I heard the programme tonight.'

His mother could always be relied on to give him an honest assessment of his performance. 'What did you think?'

'Good. Very good. I was very impressed by that young woman…'

'Alex?'

'Yes. She sounds as if she's a force to be reckoned with.'

'She is. She's very committed.'

'That came over. And she sounds nice with it.'

'Yeah. She's nice too.' Leo took a sip of his Scotch.

'Pretty?'

'No. More beautiful, I'd say.' Leo chuckled. His mother's wish to see him settled down with a nice girl, preferably one he *hadn't* met at some glitzy party, was never all that far from the surface.

'That's nice. And she'll be back next week, will she?'

'You were listening, then…' Leo laughed as his mother protested. He knew well enough that she always listened. 'In which case you'll know that we're holding quite a few events over the next couple of weeks.'

'Well, I hope you enjoy them. What's that funny noise…?'

'Wind, probably. I'm on the terrace.'

'What on earth for? You'll catch your death of cold…'

'I just wanted to clear my head. I'm going inside now.'

Leo had accepted that, faced with the loss of one son, his mother could be a little over-protective about the remaining one. The least he could do was go along with it; there was little enough else he could do to ease his parents' agony. Apart from keeping quiet about the five missed calls. If his parents wanted to believe that Joel's death had been some kind of horrendous accident then he couldn't rip that shred of comfort away from them.

He slid the balcony doors closed with a bump and threw himself down onto the sofa.

'You sound tired, darling.'

'Long day. I'm about ready to turn in now.'

'Well, don't let me stop you. Goodnight.'

'Yeah. Speak soon, Mum.'

Leo ended the call, staring for a moment at the screen of his phone. Joel's number was still on there, transferred from one phone to another, over the years. It was stupid, really, but it reminded him why he did what he did. Why the radio show was so important to him. He hadn't been around to help Joel, and the only thing that made that agony a little easier to bear was the hope that maybe, as a result of something he'd done, there was another family out there who hadn't had to grieve the way his had.

And now Alex. He'd let her down, as surely as he'd let Joel down. But there was one very big difference. There was no possibility of going back and helping Joel. But Alex… She had a future, and he could do something to change that.

Putting his glass down on the small table beside the sofa, he walked into the bedroom, picking up the key to the gym downstairs. Hard physical work would calm his mind and help him think straight. And he needed some ideas about how exactly he was going to make things up to Alex.

CHAPTER FOUR

DESPITE HAVING VOWED that Leo was going to have to take the office as he found it, Alex had been working hard since lunchtime, tidying and vacuuming the small space, cleaning the windows and putting the two most comfortable chairs on either side of her desk. Rhona was working at home today and she had the place to herself.

Her thick sweater and sheepskin boots were just about keeping the cold at bay, but she couldn't expect Leo to freeze. When she left the office door open, some of the heat from downstairs percolated upwards and the electric heater in the corner was making some difference. By four o'clock it might be warm enough to think about taking her scarf off.

Finally, she put the envelope on her desk, still sealed. She'd wanted to look inside, but wanted even more to show Leo that she understood that he'd trusted her, and that she'd taken that seriously. Sitting down, she surveyed her handiwork. The place didn't look too bad at all. Apart from Rhona's mug… Alex got to her feet, grabbing the mug from the tray and hiding it in her desk drawer. Leo didn't need to come face to face with a row of stick figures demonstrating the fourteen most popular positions from the *Kama Sutra*.

'You call this accessible?' He appeared suddenly in

the doorway, tall and lean, dressed in jeans and a heavy sweater under his jacket.

'No. We call it cheap.' She returned his grin. He must have walked straight past the receptionist downstairs, found his way to the lift and then up the flight of narrow stairs on his own. Breezing in as if he owned the place seemed to come as second nature to Leo.

'I brought provisions.' He set a brown paper carrier bag down on the desk.

Alex peered into the bag and drew out a large polystyrene container, peeling back the lid. 'Don't tell me you made this yourself.'

He chuckled. 'What do you think I am? Of course I didn't; I stopped off at a place I know.'

'Who just happen to do the best French onion soup in town?' It smelled gorgeous.

'Debatable. They're in the running, but tell me what you think.'

She fetched paper napkins for the crusty, fresh baked bread and Leo tore open the manila envelope. They reviewed the list while they ate.

'That's a good question…' She tapped the paper with her finger. 'I should have said a bit more about how we weight our races so that everyone has a fair chance.'

'He's a regular caller. I'd be surprised if he doesn't call again next Monday; I'll let the call-handlers know we want to talk to him.'

'Can you do that?' Alex had supposed that everyone just waited in line.

'We do it all the time. It's a radio show; we balance the calls to provide the best broadcast we can…' He caught sight of Alex's frown of disappointment. 'Don't do that to me.'

'What?'

'That disapproving face. Look, I know what you're thinking...'

'No, you don't.'

In the sudden silence, Alex could hear the chair creak as Leo leaned back in it. 'You're thinking that this is all about heightening awareness and reaching people who need the service you offer. Not about making good listening while people do the washing-up.'

That was exactly what she was thinking. Maybe not quite in those words; Leo had put it much more succinctly than she could have done. 'And if I was thinking that?'

'If you were, I'd tell you that my world's different from yours. For me, it has to be all about ratings, and making sure that the show's popular enough to survive. Being realistic is what makes me good at what I do.'

Why did he have to do this? Every time Leo did something nice, he devalued it, pretended that it was all self-serving. Or maybe he was just being honest. Maybe she was just looking for something in him that was no longer there.

'So you're really just a cynic?' He wasn't. She knew he wasn't, or what would he be doing here, calling people back? Why had he guarded the list so jealously?

'Yeah.'

'I don't believe you.' Alex felt herself redden.

'That's because you're an idealist.' He reached into his jacket pocket, pulling out his phone and propping it on the desk between them. 'Which is what makes you so good at what *you* do, and exactly why you're the best person to help me with these calls.'

Perhaps he'd gone a little too far. Alex had seemed ready to shake him, until she heard what she wanted to hear. But that wasn't what Leo was prepared to give.

It would be so easy, so very pleasurable, to indulge the

connection between them. To reach out and touch her, knowing that their hearts weren't so very different. He wanted that, and he had a good idea that Alex did too, but if he felt her softness he'd be unable to stop.

He'd been this way before, and recognised the signposts. Love affairs which bloomed briefly and then faded, as it became all too obvious that even when Leo was physically present, his mind was elsewhere. In the end, he had resigned himself to the fact that short-cutting the process, and keeping his relationships with women strictly on the level of a friendship, saved a lot of heartache all round.

A love affair with Alex might be very sweet, but it would inevitably be short. And Leo needed time. Time to help her dreams for the charity come to fruition. He was there to be used, and the sooner he convinced her that he owed her that, the better.

She didn't press her point. Almost as soon as he'd dialled the first number, she was smiling again, ready to talk. He grinned at her, leaning over to speak into the phone.

'Hello… This is Leo Cross. Is that Nina?'

There was a long pause. 'Yes…'

'You called my radio show yesterday evening, about your nephew, John. He has cerebral palsy, and you'd like to know what opportunities there are for him to play football.' It was always good to give people a few details, just to reassure them that this wasn't a hoax call. 'I have Alex Jackson with me…'

'You do?'

Alex leaned over towards the phone. 'Hi, Nina.'

'Leo… Thank you for calling. I didn't think you would. I'd love to talk…'

'We're here to listen. Tell us about John…'

It had taken three hours to work their way through the list. Longer than usual, but then last night's show had been popular. Alex had done most of the talking, and Leo had taken the opportunity to watch her. She didn't so much speak into his phone, but shone into it. He wondered whether little trails of light would leak back out of it when they were done and he put the phone back into his pocket.

'Last one?' She consulted the list. 'What does that star by her name mean?'

'Under eighteen. Look, it says she's seventeen.'

'Right. But she's old enough to consult someone medically on her own if she wants to.'

'Yep, but not necessarily on the radio. We need parental consent for under sixteens, and if they're sixteen to eighteen we have an extra duty of care.'

Alex nodded, grinning. 'So let's fast-track this one. I'll get stroppy about a seventeen-year-old calling a phone-in show because she needs help and then not getting to speak to anyone. You'll tell me you have some kind of procedure and she's been well looked after. Then I feel like an idiot.'

'She'll have spoken to a counsellor. But you're not an idiot.' Alex's stubborn belief in him was beginning to grow on Leo, and it was becoming harder to cling to the reasons why he shouldn't believe in himself.

'That's that dealt with then. She's definitely a pink.' Alex had used pink highlighter for follow-ups, green for everyone who hadn't requested a call, and yellow for those who'd raised important issues that she'd like to talk about on the next programme. The list was beginning to resemble a Neapolitan ice cream, and Leo wondered whether Alex would like the Italian ice cream parlour in Knightsbridge. He saved that thought carefully as he dialled the mobile phone number.

'Hi, this is Leo Cross. Is that Carys?'

Alex had leaned in a little closer to the phone with each call they made. This time her hair brushed his cheek, and Leo shivered. The sound of an alarmed squawk came from the phone, and when they both jumped he caught the faint but alluring scent of her perfume.

'Carys…?' It was an effort to keep his voice steady.

A pause, the sound of a TV in the background.

'I can't talk…' The words were whispered down the line.

'Okay, that's fine. Would you like to talk another time?'

'Yes. Please… I want to…'

The hairs on the back of Leo's neck prickled. He'd worked on helplines for long enough to know when someone really wanted to talk, and he guessed that the girl needed to do so in private.

'What time's good for you, Carys?' Leo looked at his watch. 'Would you like me to call you in an hour?'

'Yes. Thanks.'

'That's no problem. I'll call you at eight, and if I don't get through to you I'll try again tomorrow.'

'Yes. Good. Thanks.'

The line cut before Leo could say anything else and he looked up into Alex's gaze.

'What do we do now?'

He smiled. It was so easy to smile into her honey-brown eyes, and when he did so he always saw some spark of a response. 'I'll wait and call her back in an hour.'

'Is that going to be okay? You're not meant to be anywhere else, are you?'

Actually, he was. The solution which presented itself curled its way around his mind, beckoning him to at least ask. 'I have a drinks party in Hampstead but if I go home now and change, then I can call Carys and then leave straight away. If you'd like to come back with me, we can talk to her together. If you're not busy tonight.'

'No… No, I've got nothing on. Are you sure that's okay?'

'It's fine. And it's starting to get cold in here anyway.'

The encroaching chill of the evening was finally making itself felt, despite the portable radiator. 'I'll drop you home afterwards; it's not far out of my way.'

'If it's no trouble… It sounds as if Carys wants to talk.'

'Yeah, it does.' Leo rose from his seat, stretching. 'Let's go then.'

His car was parked outside the office on a meter. Alex was no connoisseur of cars, but this one had the kind of shine that made the paintwork seem almost liquid under the streetlights. And she recognised leather seats when she saw them.

'This is where you live?' He drove into the entrance to an underground car park, beneath a glass-clad tower block, less than half a mile from the radio station.

'Yes.' He slid into a parking bay and switched off the engine, leaning towards her slightly. 'Fast-track. You wonder why I came all the way to your place last night and then back again and I point out that we had some unfinished business to talk about and that the car was the best place to do it. You see my point, but think I'm an idiot.'

When Leo was in this mood, he couldn't fail to make her smile. 'I don't think you're an idiot.' Alex got out of the car before she could betray what she really *did* think.

The flat was gorgeous. On the top floor, the city lights spread out behind floor to ceiling windows. The seating area was designed to impress, with a huge glass-topped table between black leather sofas that were long enough to lie down, stretch right out and still not be able to touch both ends.

Red leather armchairs gave the room a pop of colour. Diamond-shaped bookshelves, where the books were stacked in a zigzag pattern, a touch of class. A huge abstract painting on one wall, swirling blues and greens, was the only thing that didn't seem to conform to rigid straight lines.

He helped her out of her coat, throwing it down on an armchair and dropping his own jacket next to it, then dumping his keys on the coffee table. Clearly the almost obsessive tidiness of the place had more to do with who-ever cleaned it than it did with Leo.

'This is beautiful, Leo. What a view...'

'Yeah. I took one look out of the window and knew I had to have this place. The view's different every day, and I never tire of it.'

Alex wandered over to the window, drinking in the panorama of London at night which lay beyond the roof terrace. 'It's wonderful. Very tidy.'

He grinned. 'I don't get much time to make a mess. I only stay here during the week, when I'm in town.'

'And at weekends?'

'I have a house down in Surrey, but it's a long drive after working in the evening. Make yourself at home.'

It wasn't that easy to make herself at home in a place that so obviously wasn't one. 'I'm torn between the view and the sofa.'

He chuckled, moving one of the red leather armchairs over to the window. 'Here. Best of both worlds. Would you like something to drink?'

'Do you have any juice?'

'I expect so. I'll look.' He turned, trekking across the enormous room to a doorway which lay at one side of it. Alex flopped down into the armchair. Leo's apartment had told her nothing about him that she didn't already know. Beautiful, well thought out and sophisticated, it betrayed no clue as to the real nature of the man who lived there.

His interior designer had told him that the space by the window was for circulating during drinks parties, and the seating area was for sitting. Leo usually conformed to those instructions but it was typical of Alex that she should subvert the plan within two minutes of arriving here.

He found an unopened carton of juice in the fridge and poured two glasses. Moving a side table over to where Alex was sitting, along with a chair for himself, he wondered why he'd never thought of doing this before.

She'd stripped off her heavy sweater and scarf to reveal a thick checked shirt and she was rubbing at her leg fitfully, her hand slipped down inside her boot.

'Okay?'

'Yeah. My phantom foot itches. If I rub the other one, it usually goes away.'

She'd talked about her leg on the show, fluently and without any embarrassment. But Leo had left the subject alone when they were off-air, leaving Alex to dictate what was said. Mentioning this small detail seemed like a breakthrough of some kind. Not a big one but the beginning of some kind of trust.

'You get that a lot? Phantom pain?'

'No, just occasionally. And it's more of a sensation than a pain now.'

'And rubbing the other one works?'

'It seems to. Fools the brain into thinking you're doing something about it.' She grinned at him. 'It's a trick they taught me in rehab.'

Leo hesitated. In any other circumstance this would be crossing the line he'd drawn for himself. But if he concentrated on the medical aspect, tried to learn a little about what worked and didn't work…

'I do an outstanding foot massage.' It was just a matter of not succumbing to temptation and getting carried away.

She flushed a little, snatching her hand out of her boot. 'Outstanding sounds…a bit like overkill. A bit of a rub is enough.'

Maybe that was what friends really were for. Stopping you when you were about to rush headlong into a mistake. And right now it felt as if there was no *just* about this friendship. It had the potential to be as big and beautiful as the glittering panorama they sat beside.

He should leave her alone to rub her leg in peace if she wanted to. Leo looked at his watch. Another twenty-five minutes before they were due to call Carys, which would give him time for a shower that was cold enough to bring him to his senses. 'I'll get going, then. Are you okay here, or can I get you anything?'

She shook her head, motioning towards the window. 'No, I'm fine. I have company.'

CHAPTER FIVE

IT WAS LIKE sitting in a sparkling bubble. She could see the city below her but she couldn't hear its din. The air outside had to be freezing but she was warm and relaxed. Leo would be taking a shower around now but, in the substantial structure, she couldn't hear the sound of water running.

Just as well. She didn't want to think about him in the shower, emerging from the shower… Anything even remotely connected with showers was way out of line. The idea of his touch, let alone what a massage could do, had made her feel giddy.

Alex slipped her foot out of her boot, closing her fingers around it and rubbing gently until the phantom feeling in her other leg subsided. The high tone of a phone penetrated the wall of silence and she ignored it. Leo had kept checking his phone, seeming anxious about missing the call, and it was no surprise when the tone cut off abruptly and she heard the muffled sound of Leo's voice from the bedroom.

The conversation seemed to be taking a while. She looked at her watch. Another ten minutes before they were due to call Carys. She couldn't hear his footsteps on the thick carpet, but the sound of his voice seemed to be getting closer.

'Carys… Would you like to talk to Alex? I can pass the phone over to her if that's okay with you…?'

Alex twisted round in her chair. Carys must have picked

Leo's number up from the call he'd made earlier, and not been able to wait for him to call her back. Suddenly, the whole world seemed to tip in a dizzy, vertiginous burst of rapture.

Leo's hair was wet from the shower, spiking on the top of his head as if he'd just rubbed it hastily with a towel. Perhaps the one that was currently wound around his slim hips, and the only thing he was wearing. She'd imagined that his body was perfect, but it was so much better than that. Strong, well-muscled, with smooth tanned skin. *Perfect* would have been an understatement.

And the best thing about it was that he was entirely unaware of it. Leo was concentrating on the voice on the other end of the line, and nothing else seemed to matter to him. Innocent as the day he was born, and yet far more delicious.

'Okay. Would you like me to call you back…? Yes, I'll do it straight away and then put you on to Alex. All right…'

Leo walked over to where she was sitting, which was just as well because Alex was paralysed with something that felt suspiciously like lust. He was focusing on his phone and she took the opportunity to give him one last look. *Fabulous*. He moved so well, the right mix of control and almost animal grace.

'It's Carys. Will you have a word with her while I get dressed? She lost her leg six months ago and she needs to talk…' He switched the phone to loudspeaker and put it down on the side table next to her. Alex caught the scent of soap and skin, and swallowed hard.

Six rings and then the call went to answerphone. Leo shook his head, cursing softly. 'Come on, Carys. Answer—I know you're there…'

He bent over, stabbing the phone with his finger and redialling. He was so close, one hand on the arm of her chair, and, although she was staring at the phone, the curve of his bicep nudged into her peripheral vision. But all he seemed to care about right now was that Carys hadn't answered her phone.

The line connected and Alex heard the sound of breathing. Leo smiled into the phone.

'Hey, Carys. Thought I'd lost you for a moment there. Are you still okay to talk?' His voice was friendly, like a concerned big brother.

'Yes… Sorry…'

'No problem. I know this is hard for you. Alex is with me now, and I think it would be great if you two talked a bit.'

'I'd like that…' Carys's voice quavered down the line.

'Hi, Carys. Alex here. Thanks so much for getting in touch with us.'

'Alex…'

Carys sounded as if she was crying now, and Alex leaned in, closer to the phone.

'I was wondering if I could tell you a bit about myself.' Carys didn't answer and Alex's gaze found Leo for a moment. He nodded her on. 'Okay. I lost my right leg below the knee when I was nineteen, in a car accident. It's a lot to cope with, isn't it?'

'I feel as if…all the things I wanted to do…'

'Yeah, I know. I felt like that too. And everyone says that you can still do them, but they don't know how hard it is, do they?'

'No. I keep falling flat on my face.'

'Has your physiotherapist taught you how to fall without hurting yourself…?' Alex almost didn't notice that Leo was moving away now. She concentrated hard on the phone, listening for Carys's reply.

Leo scrubbed the towel across his head and flattened his hair with a comb, then reached for his clothes. Dark trousers, a dress shirt. He'd leave the bow tie until later. Slipping on his socks, he picked up his shoes without even inspecting their shine, and walked back into the sitting room. Alex was still talking to Carys.

He hung back for a moment, just listening. Alex was articulating all of the feelings that Carys had told Leo about, letting her know that she wasn't alone. Just the right balance of understanding and hope. Somehow it touched him, in a way that he'd felt nothing could ever touch him again.

'I'm worried about my dad. He was driving, and we had an accident.'

Alex's face was fixed in an expression of intense concentration; she was staring at the phone. 'And how do you feel about that?'

'I keep telling him it's okay and it wasn't his fault, but he doesn't listen. Last night I heard him and Mum arguing again, and he was crying.'

Leo almost choked. Carys hadn't told him that, and if she had he wouldn't have known what to say. Because last night, sweating hard in the gym, he'd found tears in his eyes, thinking about all the *what ifs* that Alex had told him he shouldn't think about. He walked silently over to his seat by the window and sat down.

'Carys, it's really good that you're talking about this. Does your dad talk to anyone?'

'I don't think so. He and Mum are divorced.'

'Okay. I'm going to suggest something, and I want you to tell me if you think I'm on the right track. You've got a lot to cope with at the moment, and you can't help your dad as well. But there are lots of people who can. We have a families group, and they're really friendly. Might he come to something like that?'

'No, I don't think so. He says that he's okay, and that I'm the only one who matters now.'

'Well, I disagree. I think that both you and your dad matter, a very great deal.' Alex shot Leo a glance. Just one moment, but it seared through him, as if she were talking to him, not Carys.

'I asked him if he'd bring me to one of your meetings, the ones you were talking about on the radio yesterday…'

'And how does he feel about that?'

'He said it sounded like a great idea. But… I don't know if I can do all the things that you do…'

Alex chuckled. 'The whole point of it is that it doesn't matter what you can or can't do. We'd love you to come and just watch, maybe meet a few people. Some of us might be able to do a bit more than you, and some not so much, but it's all about valuing each other for who we are.'

'I'd like that.'

Carys's voice was steadier now, her manner more self-assured. Alex had given her something that Leo couldn't, a practical way forward, and the courage to take it.

'Okay, well, why don't you think about it, and I'll call you tomorrow. We can talk about what you want to do a bit more then, if you like.'

'I can't always talk… My mum doesn't know I'm calling…'

'In that case, do you want to text me? Whenever you like. I'll call you back.' Alex took her phone from her pocket. 'I'll text you now, so you've got my number.'

'Yeah. Thanks.'

Carys recited her number and Alex sent the text.

'Okay, I've got it. Will Leo be there? At the race meeting?'

'The one on Saturday? I think so.' She looked up at Leo and he nodded in confirmation.

'Is he as good-looking as he is on TV?'

Carys apparently thought that, since he'd said nothing

for a while, he wasn't there, and Alex grinned suddenly, holding up one finger to silence him.

'I wouldn't like to say. You'll have to tell me what you think.'

Was that a giggle on the other end of the line?

'He's nice to talk to. I'll text you tomorrow, yeah?'

'Yeah. I'll be waiting to hear from you.'

They said their goodbyes, and Leo slumped back in his seat. Alex was smiling.

'What? Don't look so crestfallen; she said you were handsome.'

'Right.' Leo wondered whether Alex agreed with the assessment, and wished he had the nerve to ask her. 'Reduced to a piece of eye candy while you do all the meaningful work.'

'I'm not proud. If I need eye candy to get to speak to someone, I'll take whatever opportunities I can get.'

'Ah. And you call *me* a cynic.' Leo couldn't help smiling. It was Alex all over, not caring how she got her opportunities, but grabbing them with both hands.

'No, I think you called yourself a cynic. And I think it was a very nice compliment. Carys obviously felt at ease with you, and that helped her talk about the things which mattered to her. You have a problem with that?'

'No, no problem at all.' He bent down to slip on his shoes and tie the laces. She was flushed with success and so, so beautiful. Perhaps…

Leo wondered how long it would be before he stopped hesitating over asking the simplest, most innocent things. Persuading himself not to overthink them might be a good start. 'I don't suppose you'd like to come along tonight? There are going to be some interesting people there.'

If she'd just stop blushing every time, it would make asking easier. 'I don't think I'm dressed for it.'

Alex would outshine every woman in the room, whatever she was wearing. But he had to admit that she might *feel* a little out of place in jeans.

'Telling you that you'd make the whole room look overdressed isn't going to work, is it?' Leo took refuge in the charm that everyone expected from him, which Alex clearly didn't take all that seriously.

'No. That's a bit over the top for my liking.'

'We could swing past your place and you could slip into something suitable…' He laughed as she pulled a face.

'I'm not slipping into anything. Apart from my pyjamas.'

'Okay.' He wasn't sure whether it was a relief that she'd turned him down, or a disappointment. 'Don't suppose you're any good with a bow tie, are you?'

'Why? Surely you've got the hang of that by now.'

'It's my policy never to tie my own bow tie when there's a lady present.'

She rolled her eyes. 'Sounds a bit risky to me. What happens if they want to strangle you with it?'

Leo hadn't really expected Alex to fall for that one either, but it was becoming increasingly compelling to watch her not falling for his charm. He walked back into the bedroom, smiling.

Ever resourceful, Leo seemed to have solved the problem of whether or not he was going to watch her up the drive outside her block of flats. Instead of stopping on the road, he turned in and brought the car to a halt a dozen feet from the main door.

'I'll see you tomorrow afternoon, then?'

'You're coming?' She'd given Leo a copy of her calendar for the next month, but Alex hadn't thought he'd bother with an after-school session.

'If you don't mind. I'd like to see some of the training that goes into the event days.'

'You'll be very welcome. But I have to warn you that it's unlikely we'll get much of an audience. That kind of thing has very low ratings…'

He narrowed his eyes momentarily, then brushed the dig off. 'I'll survive. I might be a little bit late, depending on whether my surgery runs to time or not.'

'Right then. See you tomorrow. At whatever time you get there.'

She got out of the car and Leo turned in the driver's seat. He looked stunningly dapper in his dark suit and bow tie and now that Alex knew exactly what lay beneath his white dress shirt, there was an edge of hard craving to go with it. She almost wished that she could have said yes to tonight.

There was a small problem, though. Leo seemed to assume that she could just pop home and shimmy into a little black dress, but she didn't have anything that even approached that in her wardrobe. And, more to the point, she hadn't quite found that place where she could turn up at a social event on Leo's arm without feeling that made them more than friends. The *interesting people* would have to wait until she was more sure of herself.

The thought made her close the car door behind her with rather more vigour than she'd intended. Alex bent down, pulling her face into a foolish grin, and gave him a little shrug, as if she hadn't banked on her own strength. He waved her away from the car and when she stepped back it slid away.

'So. What's he like, then?' Rhona was busy taking off layers of clothing, to reveal a bright, ebulliently patterned dress. The heating engineers had been in first thing this morning and the radiators were pumping out heat, to the point that the windows had started to steam up.

'He's…complicated.'

If Alex had thought about her answer for more than five

seconds, she would have known it would be like a red rag to a bull. Rhona pounced on the word.

'Good-looking and complicated. Sounds like the answer to a maiden's prayer.'

'Says the woman who's engaged to the most uncomplicated guy I've ever met.' Tom was solid, dependable and clearly just as head over heels in love as Rhona was.

'I didn't say that *complicated* made him a keeper. Where's my mug?'

'Here...' Alex reached into her drawer and held it out. 'Sorry. I tidied up a bit.'

'I thought the place looked a bit stark.' Rhona's idea of tidy was being able to see over the top of the piles of files, magazines and paperwork on her desk. But it was organised chaos and she could pull exactly the right thing from the pile at exactly the right time.

'You should see his flat. The only thing out of place in it was me.'

'You went to his flat?' Rhona grabbed her mug and sat down at her desk, clutching it. 'Do tell. Is he really a blond?'

'Of course he is. He was blond when I met him the first time.'

'So you got close enough to look at his roots, then?' Rhona grinned.

'I don't need to look at his roots; I know a natural blond when I see one. Just take my word for it.'

'Okay.' Rhona leaned back in her chair. 'Natural blond, *very* handsome, complicated. Tidy flat...although I don't necessarily hold that against him. Anything else?'

'Very good at what he does.'

'Aha! So you like him, then.'

'He's...got a lot of charm. And he's tall.' Alex decided to leave the bit about the great body out. Rhona was going to want a full description, and she'd been trying to forget all about what Leo might, or might not, have been doing with his great body last night. This morning's papers had pictures of a very famous, very beautiful woman walking down the steps of a smart-looking building. Holding tight to the arm that Leo had offered Alex last night.

'And… Come on, Alex, you always go for the serious guys. Ever thought of a quick dalliance with someone who'll leave you with a smile on your face?'

'Leave me? You're seriously suggesting I go out with someone who I know is going to leave me?'

'Yeah. Don't knock it. He crashes in, rocks everyone's world and then leaves again. Five minutes of feeling good and then he doesn't look back. You need to waste your time with a few like him, before you can work out who the right guy is.' Rhona's thumb gravitated to the band of her engagement ring in the way it always did when she talked about the *'right guy'*.

Alex sighed. Leo was already rocking her world, and the experience wasn't altogether positive. He was charming, unpredictable, those flashes of commitment and compassion just enough to keep her wondering. Just enough to make her believe that there was more to him than met the eye, and that maybe he just needed someone to bring that out in him.

'I don't want someone who'll leave me. And I can't just tap him on the nose with my magic wand and get him to change. What's the first rule in the book? You think you can change them, but you can't.'

'True enough. So ten minutes of magic is out, then. I bet he'd make it interesting…'

Alex *knew* he'd make it interesting. And she'd thought about it—who wouldn't? But if the last ten years had taught her anything, it was to focus on the goals that were possible, not the ones which weren't.

'There's no point in wasting your energy going after things you can't have.'

'Your famous single-mindedness?' Rhona grinned. 'You *can* take some time out from that, you know.'

'What for? Life's beautiful. Why fill it with the things you know aren't going to work out?'

Rhona thought for a minute. 'Dunno. You've got me there. Want some coffee?'

'Yes, thanks. And thanks for the chat, Rhona...'

Rhona rolled her eyes but said nothing. There was nothing *to* say. It was all very clear in Alex's mind. Leo was handsome, complicated and wouldn't know what to do with a relationship if it smacked him in the face. And he wasn't the one she wanted.

CHAPTER SIX

BY THAT AFTERNOON the picture in the paper—the one Alex was ignoring because it was none of her business—had done its work. Nudging at the jealousy centres in her brain. Telling her that all the good she thought she saw in him was just her imagination, and stamping on any notion she had of trusting Leo any further than she could throw him.

It had taken her three months to get a permit for the teachers' car park, but when she arrived Leo's car was parked in one of the spaces reserved for the Year Heads. When she inspected the windscreen, there was a note on the school's headed notepaper giving him temporary permission to park there and when she shouldered her bag and walked towards the gym she saw Leo, wearing a fur-hooded parka, standing on the frozen ground by the entrance, talking to the headmistress.

Typical. Was there no one on the planet who was immune to Leo's charm?

'And Together Our Way provided training for your staff...?'

'Yes, we have a two-day workshop every summer, in the holidays. The first one was just for our staff, but last year we invited PE staff from schools all over the borough.' Belinda Chalmers was justifiably proud of the initiative her school had taken.

'And has this impacted the culture of sport in the

school? As a whole?' Leo was absorbed in the conversation and hadn't noticed Alex standing behind him.

'Have you ever seen the winners of a race turn round to cheer the losers on to the finish line? I hadn't, before I went to one of Alex's race meetings, but now the idea's caught on and it's something a lot of our children do.'

'Impressive. So the kids with disabilities aren't just struggling to keep up. They've been leading the way.' As usual, Leo's questions had led him to the very heart of the matter.

'Exactly.'

'And you take children from all over the borough? Not just this school?'

'Yes. But we don't have enough places for all of the children who want to come. Even though we have a new gym building, we only have so much space and equipment. And there's a very high ratio of trainers to children during the sessions, so we're limited by that as well.'

'I wonder... Do you think I might do a telephone interview with you for my show? It would be great to get someone who understands the wider impact of the work that Alex and her charity are doing.'

'Of course. I'd be very happy to talk about it.'

'Fabulous. I'll give you a call tomorrow if I may, and we can set something up.' Now that he'd finished with the questions, he finally noticed Alex's presence and his face broke into a broad grin. 'Hey. I've just been hearing...'

He broke off as a minibus edged its way into the space next to his car, brushing one of the wing mirrors so that it snapped forward. Alex heard Belinda Chalmers' sharp intake of breath.

'Oh, really. There's plenty of space on the other side...'

'Looks as if he's missed me.' Leo tried to divert her, but Belinda Chalmers was already marching across towards the car park, no doubt intent on giving the driver a piece of her mind.

'All the same. Your car's blocking the side door of the minibus, and it's easier for the children to get off that way. You might not be so lucky when he realises that and tries to back up again.' Alex squinted at the gap between the minibus and Leo's car.

'Yeah. You've got a point…' Leo pulled his car keys from his pocket and turned to stride towards the car park.

It seemed that the minibus driver had the same idea. He moved back a couple of inches then thought better of it and switched the engine off. Then the back doors of the minibus opened, and he jumped out and began to unload sports bags. There seemed to be some jostling going on inside the minibus and Leo suddenly increased his pace from a brisk walk into a run.

A boy jumped down from the back of the minibus while the driver's back was turned. 'Sit down everyone…' The driver's instruction came too late and another boy tumbled out after the first.

A high scream floated through the cold air. Then another. Alex dropped her bag and started to run towards the bus. She could see Leo kneeling beside the fallen child, who seemed to be fighting him off, and Belinda Chalmers climbing into the back of the minibus to restore order amongst the children who were still inside.

'Andrew… Andrew.' The boy who had fallen was almost hysterical and Alex knelt down beside Leo, trying to calm him.

'Get off me…' Andrew pulled himself up to a sitting position and aimed a punch at Leo's face. Apart from a sharp intake of breath, Leo didn't react.

'Andrew.' Leo took his cue from Alex and used the boy's name. He couldn't possibly know what the problem was, but he seemed to sense that there was one and held his hands up in a gesture of surrender. 'Listen… Listen. I'm not going to hurt you. I just want to make sure you're all right.'

He sat back on his heels, still holding his palms forward for Andrew to see. The boy stilled, staring at him intently.

'Not too keen on doctors, eh?' Leo smiled at him.

That was the understatement of the year. When Andrew had first come to the training sessions, he'd insisted that the doctors had stolen his left foot, and he hated them for it. He was working through that with his own doctors, who were slowly gaining his trust, but an unexpected injury and an unknown doctor were too much for him.

'Andrew, this doctor's like your doctor at the hospital, Dr Khan…' Alex shot Leo a glance, wondering if he'd play along, and he nodded. 'He's not going to touch you unless you tell him that he can.'

A rush of tears spilled suddenly down Andrew's cheeks. From the way he was holding his right leg, it looked as if he'd injured it when he fell, and it must be starting to hurt now. And the boy was reacting to the pain, trying to protect himself in the only way he knew how.

'Tell him… I don't want him.'

'Tell me yourself.' Leo's voice was gentle, seeming to understand everything. 'Loud and clear. Make sure I hear you…'

'I don't want you!' Andrew turned his head, shouting the words straight at Leo.

'Okay, that's fair enough. But will you let me just watch? I won't come any closer.'

Venting his feelings at the top of his voice seemed to have calmed Andrew, and he nodded silently. Leo slowly started to take his parka off and Alex caught the significance of the gesture. Taking it from him and laying it down on the icy ground, she sat down on it.

'You must be cold. Come here, eh?' Andrew let her lift

him gently onto the warm down of Leo's jacket and she put her arm around him, hugging him close as the shivers of cold and fear subsided.

'That better?' Leo ventured a question.

Andrew nodded in reply, and Leo tried another. 'If you've hurt yourself…' He shrugged as if it wasn't completely obvious that Andrew had hurt his ankle. 'You could just point, if you felt like it. Perhaps let Alex take a little look?'

Andrew pointed at his ankle and Alex reached for his leg, pulling the soft fabric of his tracksuit bottoms up a little. The boy nestled against her without protest and she carefully took his trainer off and then his sock. The ankle was red and already beginning to swell, and Andrew looked at it mournfully. Injuring one of your 'good' limbs was every amputee's worst nightmare.

Leo's brow darkened, just for a moment. He'd know as well as Alex did that the ankle needed attention, but quite how they were going to do it without distressing Andrew even more was another matter.

'That doesn't look too bad to me. If we put a little bit of ice on it and a bandage it'll be better in no time.' Leo was deliberately looking on the bright side and assuming that there was no fracture, but it was the right thing to say. Andrew brightened visibly.

'We're in the way here, though.' Leo glanced up at the minibus, where Belinda Chalmers and two other teachers were keeping the children inside quiet and in their seats. 'Would you like to sit in my car?'

Andrew's gaze followed Leo's pointing finger. Whether by chance or design, Leo had picked the right thing. Andrew loved cars and his face lit up when he saw Leo's.

'I'm not sure how I'm going to get out of that parking spot. You want to come and give the hands-free parking a shot with me?'

Andrew nodded, and Leo bent forward slowly. The boy let him pick him up and carry him over to the passenger door of the car.

Alex followed him, brushing the dirt off his parka, and she reached into the pocket and found his car keys, unlocking the doors. Leo got in carefully, with Andrew still in his arms, sliding over into the driver's seat before depositing Andrew back in the front passenger seat.

'All right. We'll just buckle you up.' He pulled the seat belt across the boy, taking the opportunity to surreptitiously check on his ankle in the process. Then he closed the car door.

'Smooth operator.' Belinda Chalmers had got out of the minibus and stood next to Alex, watching as the car slid slowly out of its parking space, Andrew staring open-mouthed as Leo rather ostentatiously took his hands off the steering wheel.

Alex had been trying not to think about just how smooth. The charm that had convinced Andrew to accept his help was exactly the same as the charm which got him up to goodness knew what after dark.

'Has someone telephoned Andrew's mother? It looks like a sprain, but there's the possibility it may be a fracture.'

'She's on her way. I'll get the other children inside if you want to stay here.'

'Yes. Thanks.' Now that the side door of the minibus could be slid open, Alex would rather get the children into the gym and start the training session. Leo didn't appear to need her any more.

But there were three sports teachers, all qualified to supervise that, and Andrew was hurt and her responsibility until his mother got here. Her issues with Leo were completely incidental right now. Alex opened the door of Leo's car and slid into the back seat.

'How are you doing, Andrew?'

'Fine.' The boy was engrossed with the dashboard, and it was Leo who turned and grinned at her.

'What about letting Alex take a look at your ankle now, eh, Andrew? Must be hurting a bit.' Leo caught Andrew's hand, guiding it away from the control for the fog lamps just before he managed to switch them on.

'You can, if you want.' Andrew innocently chose Leo over Alex. Why not? Everyone else seemed to fall for his charm.

'Okay then. Thanks.' Leo leaned over, inspecting the ankle carefully, watching Andrew's face for any signs of pain as he gently rotated it. 'Well, that doesn't look too bad. Few days' rest and you'll be right as rain. I've got something to put on it to make it a bit more comfortable, though. Just until your mum gets here to take you home.'

Leo was saying all the right things. Reassuring Andrew that he wasn't badly hurt and that he'd be going home. The boy nodded and Leo got out of the car, bumping around in the boot.

'Want to see how this works?' He'd had the sense to just bring what he needed, not letting Andrew see his medical bag. Andrew nodded, and Leo bent his own hand, putting it inside the inflatable ankle splint.

By the time Andrew's mother hurried towards them, accompanied by Belinda Chalmers, Leo had coaxed Andrew into allowing him to put the splint around his ankle. He got out of the car, motioning for Andrew's mother to take his place in the driver's seat.

'Andrew… Are you all right?'

'Yes. Are we going home, Mum?'

'Let me speak to the doctor first…' Marion looked uncertainly up at Leo. She must have been told that Andrew was with a doctor, and was clearly surprised at how relaxed her son was with him.

'*No!* We're going *home*!' Andrew's face reddened.

Marion's face contorted into an expression of helplessness. 'Andrew...wait just a minute...please, love...'

'Hey, there.' Leo stepped in again. Always there, always charming everyone into doing exactly what he wanted them to. Alex was beginning to tire of watching it. 'Give me a minute to talk to your mum, eh? It's okay, we're not going to do anything you don't want to.'

He waited for Andrew's nod and then turned to Marion. 'It looks like it's just a sprain. But I'd like to get it X-rayed, just in case.'

Marion's face took on a pinched look. Clearly she wasn't looking forward to waiting with Andrew at the hospital, but she knew that it would have to be done. 'Yes. Thank you.'

'My surgery has a walk-in centre next door, and we make use of it for our patients. We can take him there, get him seen straight away and then I'll bring you back here.'

Marion pressed her lips together. 'That must be a private clinic. We don't have any insurance...'

'It won't cost anything. We have an arrangement with them.'

'Are you sure?' Marion looked uncertainly at Alex.

'If that's okay with Leo, then I think that would be better for Andrew.' It was a good offer, and Marion should take it.

'I really appreciate it. Thank you, doctor.'

'Call me Leo.' He cut through Marion's flustered gratitude and turned to Andrew. 'Right then. Here's the deal...'

She wanted desperately to go with them, just to be there for Andrew and Marion whether they needed her or not. But it appeared that Leo was the only person that either Andrew or his mother needed.

Alex climbed out of the car, walking back to where she'd dropped her sports bag. The training session had already started and, although she'd organised this evening so that she'd be free to show Leo around, she might as well go along anyway. At least she wouldn't have to deal with having to watch the Leo effect.

Leo had reckoned that Marion would like some time to talk alone with Andrew and he'd left them in his car together. Alex had got out of the car without so much as a word to say where she was going.

This evening she was different. She'd done all the right things, said all the right things, but the change was as marked as if the sun had suddenly gone behind a cloud. He wanted to know why. He didn't have time right now to examine why he wanted to know; he just did.

'Aren't you coming with us?' He caught her up at the door of the sports hall.

'You don't need me.'

He was tempted to tell her that he *did* need her, quite desperately. That worked with most people, without any need to elaborate on exactly why. But Alex was different from most people and he wouldn't get away with it.

'Don't you want to come?'

She turned, and he caught a glimpse of scorn in her eyes. Not quite the emotion he wanted, but then any emotion was generally better than none.

'Of course I do. But I should stay here and help with the training...'

She still had a bit to learn about being in charge. 'You're the Chief Executive of the charity, right?'

'I wouldn't put it quite like that. Sounds a bit stuffy...'

'You're the one who makes things happen, which makes you a Chief Executive, whether you like it or not. Which makes you responsible for leading the way, showing what your core values are.'

She stared at him for a moment and then the penny

dropped. 'And one of our core values is that we never leave anyone behind...' Suddenly she thrust her bag into his arms and pushed open the door of the sports hall. 'Wait for me. I'm just going to tell everyone that Andrew's okay but that I'm going with him for his X-ray.'

As they walked behind Leo into the smart reception area Marion caught Alex's arm, whispering to her, 'This place looks very posh... We don't have health insurance—are you sure it's free?'

'Don't worry. It's okay.' It didn't look free to Alex either. But this was the part of Leo that she could trust.

He was carrying Andrew upright, rather than cradled like a sack of potatoes. Probably not quite as comfortable for the boy's ankle, but it was protected by the splint and it changed the dynamic. Andrew wasn't helpless in his arms; he could lean across the reception desk and see what was going on, and the receptionist responded by smiling and talking to him.

She filled out a form and held it out for Andrew to take. He grabbed it and Leo nodded to her, smiling. 'I can take him straight through?'

'Yes, room nine.' The woman gave Leo a brilliant smile, which was over and above the requirements of her job, and undoubtedly just for him.

There was a brief interlude when Leo pretended to lose his way in the quiet, carpeted corridor, but Andrew put him right, pointing to the correct door. Inside, he waved Marion and Alex towards a couple of chairs and sat Andrew down on the examination couch, keeping the curtains that surrounded it open so that he could see his mother.

A woman in a brightly coloured top came in with a cup of tea for Marion and she took it awkwardly, still obviously worried about the cost of all this. Leo grinned at her. 'My surgery's just next door. We have an arrangement to use the clinic's facilities.'

'It's so good of you. The hospital's been wonderful with Andrew, but his usual doctor won't be there at the moment and the Urgent Care Centre…'

Leo nodded. 'I know. They do a great job, but sometimes you have to wait a bit. This is a lot easier for him.'

'Yeah.' Marion nodded.

It was a great deal easier. Andrew hardly seemed to notice Leo's gentle and thorough examination, nor did he protest when he was left alone for the X-rays to be taken.

'Looks fine to me…' Leo had reviewed the X-rays and confirmed that there was no fracture. 'I'm going to give you a support for your ankle, and I'd like you to wear it for a week or two until your ankle's strong again. But after that you'll be as right as rain. So I expect to see you at the training session in a couple of weeks, when I visit.'

'Can I ring you up when you're on the radio?' Andrew seemed to have given up on the question about going home now that it seemed likely he was just about to do so.

'Yes, if you want to. You have to have your mum do it, though. What do you want to talk about?'

'Your car.'

'Nah, no one's interested in that. What about your training sessions with Alex?'

'Maybe.'

Marion nodded. 'We'll call. I listened to the programme on Monday when we heard that Alex was going to be on.'

Leo turned. 'What did you think?'

'I thought it was great. It's really good that you're giving this some airtime. I wish we'd known sooner; I could have told more of my friends about it.'

Alex quirked her lips downwards. 'It was all a bit last-minute. We weren't the first choice.'

His gaze found hers, and suddenly it seemed as if he

was talking only to her. The way he spoke to his listeners, as if each one was the only one. 'Alex stood in for us when someone else let us down. She's made everyone realise that we made a big mistake in not asking her first.'

She tore her gaze away from his, refusing to believe what he'd just said. It was just Leo making the best of things.

'I think you're being nice…' And she didn't particularly want him to be nice. She wanted the businesslike Leo who didn't tear at her heart whenever he turned his blue eyes onto her.

'I'm *never* nice.' He picked Andrew up, switching his attention back onto the boy. 'Come on then. Time to go home.'

He'd been able to do little enough for Andrew, simply called in a few favours to make things easier for him. But when they'd got back to the school, and the boy had given him a high five before his mother took him off home, it had warmed Leo. It was sometimes the little things that were the most rewarding.

'Thank you.' He was alone with Alex now, walking towards the car park after managing to catch the last ten minutes of the training session.

'You're welcome. Must be very difficult when the kids get hurt like that. They've already had a lot of trauma to contend with.'

'Yeah. Some of them take it in their stride, but others… Sometimes the ones you need to watch the most are the ones who just go quiet.'

'That's my experience too.' He wondered whether he should mention that Alex seemed to have *gone quiet* on him, but wasn't sure where to start.

He decided to try an experiment. 'Did you see the report in the papers this morning?'

'No.'

Gotcha. Her voice was bristling with discomfort, and she hadn't even asked what report. Leo stopped to face her and she pretended not to notice and kept on walking.

'Fast-track,' he called after her and she turned slowly.

'What?'

'Fast-track. I ask you to come along to a drinks party, you say no and then I'm in the paper, leaving with Evangeline Perry...'

'So what? You can walk down a set of steps with someone, can't you? I do it all the time.' She pressed her lips together, knowing she'd given herself away fully now.

'I had my arm around her. That was because half a dozen paparazzi had suddenly appeared out of nowhere and were in her face.' Leo usually left the press to come to whatever conclusions they liked, preferring to just rise above it all and get on with his job. But this time it mattered to him.

'What you do is none of my business, Leo.'

'No, I know it isn't. But, despite that, I have an irrepressible urge to explain that I've known Evie for years, and she and I were just talking about some of the issues that you and I have been covering on my show...'

'Oh, pull the other one, Leo...' At last, an honest response. This, he could work with.

'Evie's sister used to run for the American national team. She contracted meningitis last year and that's put a stop to her career for the time being. Arielle always said that she wanted to work with kids when she took a step back from competing, and this project's been bubbling under for a while now...'

'And you just happened to bump into her sister at this drinks do.'

'No, I'd arranged to see Evie there—that was one of the reasons I asked you to come. She was there with her partner—he's the guy behind us on the steps.' He paused for a moment to see whether Alex was going to come up with something in reply, but she just stared at him dumbly.

'Of course she lent a bit of much-needed glamour to what was otherwise quite a dry evening. But that was incidental…'

What was he saying? The one thing that never went down well with women was calling another woman glamorous. They wanted to know that they were the only person in the room.

'Is she the same in real life?'

'She's a nice person.'

'I meant is she as beautiful? I saw her last film…'

'Evangeline's a film star. It's her job to be beautiful. She doesn't get paid for being nice, but she's that too. She's promised to give me an interview for the show on Friday.'

'Right. Good.' Alex seemed lost for words, wrenching open the door of her car and throwing her sports bag onto the back seat.

'Are you going to listen in?'

'I'll try.' She got into the car and the engine growled into life. Then Alex reversed out of her parking space so quickly that she almost shunted into the back of his car. Leo grinned. She'd be listening.

CHAPTER SEVEN

LEO THE IMPOSSIBLE. Being with him was like standing in a hall of mirrors, unable to tell whether the man in front of her was the real Leo or just a reflection.

She guessed from the smug look that Leo had given her as she drove off that he knew she'd be listening on Friday, but she did it all the same. Evangeline spoke passionately about her sister's illness and how it had prompted them both to think about setting up a scheme for young athletes with disabilities. Alex was sorry she'd misjudged her. But she knew she hadn't misjudged Leo. Whether he was lost to her because of another woman or because he was a different person now didn't really matter. He was lost to her and that was it.

If she'd remembered that, it would have made life a good bit easier. But instead she'd been jealous of Evangeline and, worst of all, Leo knew that now. Monday was going to be difficult.

She arrived at the radio station early. She'd thought about this and if there was going to be an atmosphere between her and Leo the listeners would know it. She had to clear the air. Half an hour alone in the restroom preparing herself only made her more nervous, and then Leo breezed in.

'Ready to go?' He smiled at her.

'Leo... Leo, wait.' Better get it over with now. 'I'm sorry. About the picture in the paper and...'

He turned his bright blue eyes on her and she fell silent, feeling her cheeks flush.

'The paparazzi jumped to the same conclusion and so did everyone who read the paper. Why not you?'

'It was none of my business.'

'I put myself out there, Alex. I have to accept that what I do is sometimes noticed. I care about what you think, which is why I bothered to explain myself.'

That... That sounded suspiciously like a compliment. 'Are you being nice?'

His smile. That luminous look which seemed to hide no secrets. 'Nah. I'm never nice.' He looked at his watch. 'We've got to get going now. Do you have ten minutes afterwards? I just need to discuss a few details for next week.'

When they got into the studio, it all clicked. He smiled. She smiled. She managed to find answers for the callers' questions. She saw what nerves had obliterated last Monday—that Leo was feeding her all the time, never making statements, always leaving what he said open for discussion. The hour flew.

Justin was smiling when he walked into the studio, after they'd handed over to the next presenter. 'Fabulous. Both of you.'

Leo seemed suddenly a little off-key. 'Yeah, I enjoyed it.'

'Follow-ups?' Justin held up a manila envelope and Leo gestured in Alex's direction.

'Alex might like to take those.'

'Yes. Thanks.'

'There was something else...' Leo was on his feet before Justin could get the rest of the sentence out.

'Yeah. That's in hand, Justin. Is the car waiting?'

'No, it's not here yet. As we've got a few minutes…'

'Later.' The one word was so final that even Justin got the hint. Leo picked up Alex's coat, holding it out in an unequivocal intimation that she should put it on. Then he practically frogmarched her out of the studio.

'What's this all about, Leo?' This was one version of Leo that she hadn't seen in the hall of mirrors yet.

'Can we talk in the car?' He caught the attention of the show's production assistant, who was passing in the corridor. 'Jo, have you called the car yet?'

'No, Justin said to wait…'

'Yeah, I expect he did. Could you do me a favour and give them a call now?'

This was crazy. Leo obviously had something he wanted to say privately, and it seemed to be bothering him. So much so that he was prepared to spend almost an hour driving needlessly around London.

She tugged at his sleeve. 'I could do with some coffee first…'

He shot her a smile. 'In that case… Jo, forget about the car. I'll call them.'

'Sure thing, Leo…' Jo broke off and watched as Leo hustled her away.

It was beginning to snow outside, large flakes drifting past streetlights and car headlamps. Almost a picture book scene. Leo offered his arm and Alex took it, her gloved hand resting lightly on the inside of his elbow.

This was ridiculous. He talked about all kinds of intimate issues to all kinds of people for a good proportion of his time. Putting things clearly and without embarrassment was part of his job, and he was good at it.

They walked in silence for a few moments and then she

held her free hand out, catching snowflakes in her palm. 'First snow of the winter.'

'Yeah.'

'I like it when it's like this. Fresh and clean, ready for my footprints…'

'Me too.' It occurred to Leo that she was trying to put him at his ease. That thought was even more confusing because that was usually his job as well.

He opened the main door to his apartment block, standing aside to let her go first. Smiling to the security guard, he escorted her to the lift.

When he ushered her into the lounge, she gasped, walking over to the window. 'Oh, it's beautiful, Leo. Is it always like this when it snows?'

'Not always.' The sky seemed almost luminous, a pinkish-white bank of cloud hovering over London. Large flakes of snow drifted past the window and, further away, the falling snow gleamed on the rooftops. Maybe he'd just never noticed it before.

Leo walked over to stand next to her and she turned her shining face up towards his. 'I bet if you stood here on Christmas Eve you'd see Santa's sleigh up there somewhere.'

Maybe he would have, if Alex had been here. She was doing it again, trying to put him at his ease, but somehow that didn't matter quite so much now. He grinned down at her. 'I'll go and make the coffee.'

'The coffee was just an excuse. I don't really want it.'

In other words: *Just get on with it.* Leo couldn't have put it better himself.

'Justin wants us to talk about sex…' He grimaced. Surely there was a better way of putting it than that, but all the usual polish seemed to rub off when he was alone with Alex.

She raised her eyebrows. 'Really? I'd better take my

coat off then.' She slipped off her padded jacket, draping it over the back of the sofa, and then turned to face him. 'Go on then. I'm all ears.'

She was teasing him, and it wasn't helping. Leo felt enough like a tongue-tied teenager already.

'All right. Make it easy, won't you.' He shot her a warning look. 'Justin's been very pleased with the way that you've covered a lot of the wider issues, and he's come up with this. I told him that I had my reservations and that I'd talk to you about it.'

She thought for a moment. 'I think it's a good idea. We cater for young people up to twenty-one and the physical side of relationships can be an issue for them. What are your reservations?'

'The first is that you've been speaking very candidly about your own experiences. And that's been great, but I don't want to put you in a position where you feel railroaded into sharing things you want to keep personal.'

She nodded. 'Okay. Well, I think I'd rather take that one as it comes. In principle, I'm happy to talk about anything if it's going to help someone.'

'Fair enough. But I want you to remember that we're on the radio. I have a personal objection to having any guest talk about things they're not comfortable with.'

'Thanks. I appreciate that. What's the other thing?' Her gaze caught his suddenly, tangling him in its web. Alex's eyes had the power to leave him shaking, babbling all kinds of nonsense, and Leo tried not to look at them.

'I think this is a fine line to walk. I don't want to minimise the practical difficulties that a disability can cause, because I've seen a lot of those kinds of issues amongst my own patients. But, at the same time, it would be wrong to imply that having a disability means you necessarily *have* to have a problem with physical intimacy.'

Her face broke into a brilliant smile. 'Since you know

that without needing to be told, doesn't that make you the ideal person for me to try this out with?'

For one dizzy moment Leo thought that she meant *actually* try it out. Up close and deliciously personal.

'Why don't we do this?' She brought him back down from the furthest reaches of fantasy with a bump. 'We'll talk about the effects of losing a limb on body image. Then, if anything comes of that and a caller asks specific questions, we can answer them.'

That was probably the way that Leo should have put it in the first place, and the fact that he'd made a perfectly straightforward issue as embarrassing as possible wasn't lost on him. 'Yeah. That sounds good. As long as you're completely happy with that.'

She nodded, turning to him suddenly. 'I'm fine with it. And I really appreciate you asking. I think the only point I really want to get over is that someone who really cares about you will take you the way you are. And that communication's the key thing.'

'Which applies to all of us, I guess.'

'Yes. It does. Can we sit down now?'

She never would have believed it, but it was actually quite sweet. Leo, tongue-tied about sex. Yet another facet of the enigma which, despite all her efforts, became more pressing to solve every time she met him.

'What made you take up being a radio doctor?' She sat down on one of the large designer sofas and Leo sprawled opposite on its twin.

'I happen to think that being there for people is important. Many of the people who phone feel they've no one else to turn to. For three hours a week, I get to be the one that they can call.'

'And the rest of the time?'

There was a trace of sadness about his smile. 'I just

have to hope that the time I have might make a difference somewhere. It's not an exact science.'

'When we first met… You so wanted to be on the cutting-edge, saving lives…'

'When we first met, I was dressed as a spaceship captain. I changed my mind about that as well.'

'You did look very dashing. Ready to fly off into the unknown and take over new worlds.'

He shook his head. 'That was more my brother's style. I was always the sensible one.'

'You didn't say you had a brother…'

'We were identical twins, and he still managed to be a lot better-looking than me. I kept him under wraps.'

'Were…?' There was something about the way he said it. 'May I ask?'

'I wish more people did.' Maybe it was a trick of the light, the luminous sky banding the carpet with reflections which merged into the subdued lighting in the room. But when he turned his blue eyes up towards her, Alex thought she saw the young man she'd first met looking at her.

She swallowed hard, trying to dislodge the lump in her throat. She knew how hard it was when people tried not to mention things that mattered.

'What was your brother's name?'

She thought she saw a smile flicker on his lips. 'Joel. He died six months after we first met. Just before Christmas.'

'I'm sorry. Really sorry, Leo.'

'Don't be. No one talks about him all that much and…' He shrugged. 'Sometimes I wish that everyone would just stop trying to spare my feelings.'

'I imagine they mean well.'

He nodded. 'Yes. I imagine that they do. But Joel should have more than just silence.'

'I'm happy to make some noise with you.'

Leo nodded. 'Sounds good to me. Join me in a brandy?'

'No, thanks.'

He walked over to a cabinet beneath the huge swirling picture on the wall, opening it and taking out a glass.

'Joel suffered from depression. He didn't tell anyone, but I knew something was up and confronted him. I persuaded him to go to the doctor, and when we found it was months before he could get to see a counsellor on the NHS we put what money we had together and he went privately to see someone.'

He turned, amber liquid swirling in the brandy glass in his hand. 'Not that it did any good. Joel took his own life.'

'But you tried. You were there for him…'

'Not when it mattered. And I should have told my parents—maybe they could have done something. Joel asked me not to.'

'Then you were respecting his wishes, weren't you?'

'Sometimes you have to act, despite what people ask you to do.' He took a sip from his glass and then another larger one, as if the first hadn't done anything to offset the pain. Alex doubted the second would either.

'And that's why you volunteered to work on the student helplines? For Joel?'

'Yeah. I wasn't there for him and the only thing that made me feel any better about that was being there for other people…' He took another sip of his drink, as if to stop some deathly cold creeping over him.

Suddenly the hall of mirrors came crashing down. The charming Leo, the businessman, the cynic and the doctor. All of his inconsistencies suddenly made sense.

Leo was exactly what he appeared to be. A passionate, dedicated man who had been broken by guilt and regret. The fame, the ratings on his radio show—they were just a way of reaching people. And he'd sworn himself to that—dedicating his energy to people he didn't know because people you didn't know couldn't hurt you.

'I know what you're thinking.' He spoke softly. 'It's been said often enough to me. I should let it go.'

'You're good but you're not a mind-reader, Leo.' A force that was nothing to do with her own will, and everything to do with the look in his eyes, impelled her to her feet and drew her across the room to where he stood.

'A lot of people aren't that hard to read…' His gaze searched her face.

'Go on then, if you think you can.'

He laid his index finger lightly on the side of her brow, frowning as if some great mental effort was in progress. 'Huh…interesting. Very interesting.'

For a moment it was as if he *could* see what she was thinking. *Impossible. Snap out of it.*

'What's interesting?'

'I can't read you. I never quite know what you're going to do next. Fascinating.' The curve of his lips made it clear that was a compliment.

She knew that it was just Leo's charm, his way of turning a situation around and removing the barbs. But it was still compelling, and when she looked into his eyes she felt that he really did find her fascinating. Alex swallowed hard.

'You know what, Leo? Even if you could read minds, you still wouldn't be able to see into the future.'

'I think the universe has something to answer for there. We can see the past but it's too late to go back and do things differently. And the future…' He shrugged.

The one time frame that mattered the most was the one that Leo seemed unable to get to grips with. 'What about now, Leo?'

If she hadn't been so beautiful he could have shrugged *now* off. Leo could have forgotten her scent and dismissed the idea that he didn't have to reach very far in order to touch her.

'Now is…just a moment. Gone before you have a chance to even know what to do with it.'

She reached her hand out as if to catch snowflakes. Then she closed her fingers tight. 'There. Got it.'

Time really did seem to stand still, and it was the oddest feeling. One of complete warmth, absolute safety from a world that couldn't throw anything at him because it was suspended, waiting for Alex to allow it to start turning again.

'What will you do with it?' Alex turned her gaze onto him and Leo knew exactly what he wanted to do.

'I want to tell Tara that I'm sorry I didn't get to see her again. I want to tell *you* that I'm sorry…for everything. For not being there and…'

She laid one finger across his lips and it was all that Leo could do not to frame a kiss. 'I think *everything* pretty much covers it, Leo. If I tell you that you're forgiven, can we put that behind us? Where it belongs, in the past.'

Somehow that seemed possible. Anything seemed possible as long as it was contained in this one moment and couldn't spill out into their lives. He caught her hand, turning it in his to press a kiss against her palm.

Alex smiled. 'Captain Boone and Tara. Let them kiss goodnight and slip away into the universe? Leave us to get on with the things *we* have to do.'

Maybe she was right. Ten years ago he'd let the chance to kiss her slip away. He'd regretted it then and the thought of repeating that mistake now was unbearable.

'I'd like that.'

What harm could there be? If it could help Leo to let go, why not? One of the points of fancy dress was that you got to do things you might not normally do, and if anyone questioned them afterwards you could say you were just *in character.* Alex extended two fingers in a rough imitation of Tara's immobility gun, prodding her middle finger against the side of his ribs.

Leo grinned. 'So you've seen that episode, have you?'

The one where Tara held Captain Boone at gunpoint, then kissed him. She'd seen it. 'I watched an awful lot of TV when I was recovering from the accident.'

'And now you're putting it to good use...' He held out his hands, as if she really did have a gun on him. But his smile beckoned her. Grabbed her and dragged her in.

She brushed her lips against his.

'Nice. Very nice...' She felt his words form against her cheek and Alex drew back, teasing him for a moment. Then she kissed him, trailing her lips from his mouth to the side of his jaw.

'Even nicer...' He kissed her fingers when she put her free hand to his lips, and then waited. He knew that she'd come back for more and when she did she made it a proper kiss, her hand wrapped around the back of his neck, her lips parted as they met his.

Leo let her draw away again, the broad smile on his face showing that he liked giving her the upper hand for a while, but they both knew it was never going to last. Alex kissed him again, feeling the softness of his lips, the strong brush of his jaw. She felt hard muscle flex and suddenly he gripped her wrist, pulling her arm up, her fingers away from his ribcage. His other arm pulled her against him and he turned her around, crowding her backwards against the wall.

Then *he* kissed *her.* Tender at first and then with a mounting hunger which made her gasp. Leo knew just how to kiss a woman. Enough control to let her know that he could produce almost any reaction he wanted, and yet just the right amount of surrender.

His lips left a trail of fire across her cheek. She felt his teeth gently nip at the lobe of her ear and she gasped. 'Tara...'

The retreat to the character's name was no mistake. This wasn't real, and he was telling her so. Just something they both wanted to do before their real lives reasserted themselves. He kissed her again, this time soft and slow. She knew there would be nothing more. There was a trace of regret in his eyes, as if he was finally waving Tara goodbye.

'I'm glad we waited.' His body was no longer pressing against hers, and he let go of her wrist. 'If I'd done that when I was twenty-one, it would have totally blown my mind.'

'And now?'

'It's totally blown my mind.' He chuckled, whirling her around in a loose embrace and planting a kiss on her forehead. 'But I'm not going to make any promises to call.'

'Because...?' She knew why. However much she ached for Leo, he wasn't the man she wanted.

'It's a while since I gave anyone my full attention.'

And he wouldn't give it to her. For a while maybe, it would seem so, but Leo always had something else on his agenda. He was afraid of missing anything. He'd committed himself to watching and waiting because he'd missed the most important moments of his life, the moments in which he could have answered Joel's calls.

'And I deserve nothing less.'

He grinned. 'Right in one. Can I get you something else? A drink maybe?'

He was doing this well. Making it clear that she was welcome to either stay or go, and that even if the kiss had been just one moment in time it wasn't one he regretted. And that was why she had to go.

'I should probably get home. Will you call the car for me,

please?' She picked up his glass, imagining that she could taste his lips on the rim before the brandy hit her tongue.

He nodded and made the call. The car arrived within minutes and Leo escorted her downstairs, holding the door open for her and exchanging a quiet word with the driver, as if he'd just entrusted him with something precious. Then he watched as the car drew away.

Maybe she should text him, the way she'd done that morning, from the bus. She took her phone out of her bag, but that was as far as she got. That was something that had started a long time ago, but tonight had been the final ending.

CHAPTER EIGHT

LEO AS A FRIEND. A good-looking, charming friend who seemed to get just how she felt, and who might be around for longer than just a fleeting love affair. It was a thought. Stranger things had happened...

They could have lunch from time to time, talk about their lives and promise to see each other again some time soon. No pressure. No expectations. It wouldn't matter that Leo was so bound up with the past that he couldn't contemplate anything more than a slightly distant relationship with the present.

All of that assumed that Alex could forget about the kiss. It was just one kiss. How difficult could it be? Particularly when the need to think about Saturday's race meeting was so pressing.

The attendance of an outside broadcast crew had persuaded the manager of the sports centre they normally used to allow Together Our Way to take over the main track instead of being consigned to the cramped practice track. A lot was hanging on this and it *had* to go well.

There was still more than an hour to go before the start of the meeting but Alex saw his car in the car park outside the sports centre when she arrived. He was inside, fiddling with his phone, and when she rapped on the window he looked up.

His eyes. His smile...

Her skin began to tingle and Alex reminded herself yet again that she wasn't supposed to be thinking about the kiss. It had been an ending, not a beginning.

Leo finished typing a message on his phone and swung out of the car, reaching back inside to pull a bag from the back seat.

'You're joining in?' Or perhaps the sports bag was just for show.

'Thought I might just give the impression that I would, if asked.'

'Okay. What happens if I don't ask?'

'You'll ask.' He started to walk towards the sports centre and she fell into step beside him. 'You won't be able to resist putting me up against a bunch of skinny kids and watching them beat me.'

'You're thinking that you'll bravely suffer the humiliation of letting them win, are you?'

'I'm thinking that I'd be proud to run with them. And I respect them enough to give it my best shot. Are you running?'

'Yes. Think you can beat me?'

'I'll try…' His phone beeped and he pulled it out of his pocket. 'Ah. She's just arriving. I took the liberty of asking someone along, I hope you don't mind.'

'Of course not. But they're a bit early—it doesn't start for another hour.' Alex followed Leo's gaze to where a black SUV was manoeuvring into a parking space. 'Who is it—someone from the radio station?'

'Um…no.' He was looking suddenly awkward. 'I… Evie's sister's over from the States for a couple of weeks, and I asked them to come.'

'You did what? Evangeline Perry!' Alex looked over to the SUV, where a tall, slim woman was getting out of the passenger seat. Her hair was wound beneath a baseball cap and the peak obscured most of her face. 'You asked a film star to my race meeting? Leo, you might have mentioned it.'

'Why, so you could run around panicking? That's exactly why I didn't say anything about it. They're here because they're interested in what you're doing, and they'll keep a low profile.'

'Keep a low profile! Leo, didn't it occur to you that people might recognise her?'

'Of course it did. You said it would be good for the kids to have someone showing a bit of interest. And Evie's not high maintenance. Her minder will look after her.'

'Minder! For goodness' sake, Leo, if you're trying to disrupt things...' He'd lulled her into a false sense of security with his careful way of including her in every decision. 'I told you that you couldn't just swan in and take over. The kids are always the most important ones.'

'That's why Evie's here. Because the kids are important and she wants to show them some support. Give her the benefit of the doubt, will you...'

'I'm more than happy to give her the benefit of the doubt. You, I'm not so sure about.'

'Don't worry about sparing my feelings, will you.' He was grinning broadly, laughing as he turned to wave to the two women who were walking across the car park, followed by a man who sauntered behind them.

'Leo...' The woman in the baseball cap greeted him with a smile and they exchanged kisses. 'We made it.'

She turned to Alex, holding out her hand. 'Hi, I'm Evie Perry. You must be Alex.'

Close up, she was beautiful. Creamy skin, huge green eyes, with strands of Evangeline Perry's trademark red hair escaping her cap. Her jeans and warm jacket were casual but didn't look as if they came from the high street, and couldn't conceal her tall, willowy figure. If Evangeline Perry thought she needed to introduce herself then she was mistaken.

It was impossible not to feel somehow dowdy and lacking next to her, and that wouldn't have mattered so much if Leo hadn't been there. Alex took Evie's hand, trying not to tremble.

'Thank you so much for coming. I'm… I wish I'd known you'd be here—I could have…done something.'

Evie laughed. 'From what Leo said the other night, you're already doing a great deal. He couldn't stop talking about you.' She smiled at Leo and he winced, as if he'd been caught out doing something he shouldn't.

The thought that, in the presence of such a woman, Leo would have one thought in his head for her was… Well, it was something to think about. But Evie gave her no opportunity.

'This is my sister, Arielle. She's very interested in what you've achieved here and, as we're looking to set up a scheme something like this in the States, we're here to learn from you.'

'I… I'm sure there's not a lot I could teach you… But I'd love it if you'd come and meet some of the kids…'

'That's what we're here for.' Arielle's smile was just as warm as her sister's and Alex grinned back stupidly, not sure of what to say.

'Right, ladies.' Leo had picked up her sports bag along with his own and started to make for the entrance of the sports centre. 'No point in standing around here…'

For once, Leo's no-nonsense way of making things happen was a boon. Someone had recognised Evie on their way into the auditorium and word had gone round the small group of competitors and helpers who were already there, like a whispered shock wave. He gently made a path for Evie and Arielle down to the running track, and then pushed Alex forward to introduce them to the group that was beginning to crowd round.

She saw Hayley at the back of the group, her eyes shining. Alex leaned over, pulling her a little closer.

'This is Hayley—she's our best runner.'

'Not as good as you…' Hayley clasped Arielle's hand and didn't let go. Clearly she knew exactly who Arielle was.

'What distances do you run?' Arielle gave her a dazzling smile.

Hayley was too busy hero-worshipping and seemed to have forgotten. Alex prompted her.

'Hayley's best event is the thousand metres. But she's pretty good over shorter distances as well.'

'Ah, an all-rounder. So what's your best time over the thousand metres?'

'I… Not as good as yours.'

Arielle laughed. 'Well, I've been doing this a bit longer than you. Can I see?'

Hayley looked around wildly. Apparently she'd also forgotten the notebook she kept in her sports bag, noting all of her times, along with the dates.

'Hayley, go and get your book. Show Arielle your times.'

Hayley dropped Arielle's hand suddenly and pushed through the group to the side of the track. Arielle flashed Alex a smile and followed her.

The initial frenzied excitement at Evie and Arielle's arrival had subsided to an elated buzz. Rhona was dealing with the sound engineers and the seating area was beginning to fill up. The first competitors were beginning their warm-up routines and everything seemed to be working like a well-oiled machine. Alex had sat down by the side of the track, feeling suddenly surplus to requirements.

'Everything okay?' Leo sat down beside her.

She turned to him, smiling. 'Thank you. You were right, Leo.' He probably knew that already, but Alex wanted to be the first to say it.

He shrugged. 'Have you taken Evie's number?'

'No. Am I supposed to?'

He sighed. 'It would be good to think about these things. You're a good contact for her to make and she and Arielle can help you too.'

'That sounds a bit cold-blooded, doesn't it?'

'No, it's not at all. You both have the same priorities, don't you?'

'Yes, I suppose so. But it's so good of them to come; I can't ask any more of them.'

He rolled his eyes, taking his phone from his pocket. Alex averted her eyes. Probably a message from someone that Leo couldn't help but take. He typed for a moment and then her own mobile beeped.

'Done.' He put his phone away and Alex withdrew hers from her pocket. A text from Leo, to both her and Evie. She looked up towards the top of the stand, where Evie was sitting with a group of parents, and saw her turn, look at her phone and then wave down at them.

'Leo…' She felt herself flush awkwardly. Her phone beeped again and she looked at the text.

Making yourself useful, Leo? Please keep my number, Alex. Will call you.

'See…' Leo leaned in, looking over her shoulder.

Her whole body screamed at her to relax against him, and her mind told her to keep her distance. Good sense won out and she blanked the screen, feeling the pressure of his shoulder against hers relax.

'I'm not very good at this. Networking…' Leo seemed

to do it all so effortlessly, knowing exactly the right thing to do in any given circumstance.

'No, you're not. You're good at making the magic. Leave the rest to us lesser mortals.'

Hard truth, laced with a compliment. Or maybe the other way round; it was impossible to tell with Leo. Somehow he managed to make it sound real, the two twisted together in a complex, sparkling spiral that sent shivers down her spine.

She should be doing something useful, not spending her time sitting here, however good it felt. 'Do you have an interview schedule or something? Anything I can help with?'

'I expect there is one. What I really need is a mike, though.' He signalled to one of the sound engineers who came hurrying over, putting a microphone in his hand.

'Thanks.'

'And here's the running order…'

'Okay.' He had the grace to deliver a sheepish grin as he stuffed the paper in his pocket without even looking at it.

'We'll start over there, with an introduction…'

'Yeah. Would you mind giving me a minute…?' Leo got to his feet, making in the opposite direction.

'Is he always like that?' Alex heard Rhona's voice behind her, and the sound engineer nodded.

'Yeah. We give him a list, he ignores it and we end up following him around, not sure what he's going to do next.'

'And that makes good radio?' Alex couldn't help but ask.

'Yeah. It makes great radio. That's why he gets away with murder, and no one ever complains.' The sound engineer shrugged, walking back over to his colleague.

'Going to go try keeping him under control, then? Just

for the sake of appearances.' Rhona nodded at Leo's retreating back.

'Suppose so.' Alex got to her feet, walking over towards Leo.

Everyone had been persuaded to sit down, despite the air of excitement running around the auditorium. The place was packed, the usual parents and families joined by people who'd heard about the meeting from the radio. Leo handed Alex the microphone, showing her how to mute it, and when she spoke into it her voice sounded disconcertingly through the speakers that the sound engineers had set up.

'You do it…' She covered the microphone with her hand and feedback squealed through the speakers.

'Too busy.' He shot her his melting grin and left her to it. Alex took a deep breath and haltingly started to thank everyone for coming. A roar of applause greeted her mention of Evangeline and Arielle, and then another for Leo.

'And, on behalf of the young people who are competing today, I'd like to welcome you all. Please show them how much you're looking forward to this afternoon…' She was almost breathless, carried away by the noise and determined that the kids should have the biggest round of applause.

Evangeline and Arielle were both on their feet and Leo suddenly reappeared from whatever he'd been busy with, arms held above his head, clapping. Alex could almost feel the din of cheering and clapping vibrating through the air, and when she looked over towards the group of competitors waiting by the starting line their faces were shining.

They'd done it. Together, they'd made this moment. All the hard months of training, raising the money they'd needed, the teaching and the encouragement, had been down to her. But Leo had taken all that and given the kids something to remember.

She thrust the microphone back into his hand and hurried to her seat by the side of the track. Alex didn't want him to see that this thing, the huge, roaring wave of response that they'd created between them, had brought her close to tears. And she didn't want to think about all the other things that they might achieve together, because Leo wouldn't be here for long.

The races started. Personal bests were shattered as the crowd cheered all the competitors on. Alex kept herself busy by the track side, making sure that everyone was warmed up and ready for their races. It was a difficult line to walk, encouraging everyone to do their best but reminding them not to get carried away and injure themselves in the process, and she made sure that she spoke to each of the young athletes before their races.

Then the first interval. Leo was still at the side of the track, a group of competitors gathered around him. Little Sam, the boy whose photograph she'd thrust in front of him when they'd met at the hotel, was hovering on the edge of the crowd, watching silently.

He caught sight of him and leaned over towards him. 'What's your name…?' Leo bent down as everyone made way for Sam to get closer.

'Sam.'

'Hi, Sam. And what will you be doing today?'

Sam eyed him thoughtfully. Alex knew he was a child of few words and massive determination. 'Running.'

'Sounds good.' Leo rose to the challenge, clearly not about to give up just yet. 'And are you taking part in any of the events?'

'Yes.'

'Well, good luck. Let's hear a round of applause for Sam…'

Leo was working his way around everyone, and the spectators quickly got the idea of what was expected of them. Each child got a round of applause before Leo went on to the next.

'Thanks, Hayley.' He turned to the second of the two girls who stood clutching each other's hands, and Alice spoke up immediately.

'I'm Alice. I want to say something.' Alice's cheeks were flaming red but she had that determined look on her face that Alex had seen time and time again. Leo tipped the microphone towards her and she took it out of his hand, as if she was afraid she might not get to speak her piece.

'What is it you want to say, Alice?'

For a moment Alice wavered and Alex saw Hayley take her hand, squeezing it. 'My leg was amputated two years ago…' The stadium had fallen silent suddenly, in response to the urgency in Alice's voice. She looked around wildly.

'And then what?' Leo's voice, gently encouraging her. Alice focused suddenly on his face and he nodded her on.

'I used to run for my county, and I'm training again now with the charity. I want to tell everyone that…' Alice dried up suddenly.

Alex started to push towards them. Alice didn't talk much about how desperately she wanted to run again, but somehow she'd screwed up the courage to share it with all these people. But this was enough. Good radio, good publicity for the charity, it all came second to Alice's best interests and she didn't want Leo pushing her.

He'd reached out, taking the microphone back and muting it. 'That's great, Alice. Is there something more you want to say?'

Alice nodded.

'Okay then, take a breath and just look at me. Forget about everyone else and say it to me. Whenever you're ready…'

'I'm ready.' Alice leaned towards him. 'I want to say that you can do more than you think. If you just try.'

A ripple of applause ran around the spectators, and Leo held his hand up for silence.

'That's something I could do with remembering…' Alex heard Leo's voice catch suddenly, as if he had something lodged in his throat. 'What do you do during your sessions at Together Our Way?'

'I can't run yet; I need a blade for that. But while I'm waiting I'm improving my fitness by exercising and I can jog… And I like the climbing wall.'

'I'll be looking for some advice on that, when I check it out next week.' Leo shot Alice a grin and she beamed back at him, flushed with her own achievement. 'Ladies and gents…'

He didn't even have to say it. The audience was his, and he knew it. One movement of his hand and they roared their approval, while Alice and Hayley clutched each other, waving to the crowd.

CHAPTER NINE

'ALEX!'

She looked round and saw Hayley's father signalling towards the door, where a man and a teenage girl were standing, looking around uncertainly. Alex always made sure to welcome any newcomers herself and she took the steps between the seats at a run.

'Hello. My name's Alex Jackson.' She paused to get her breath back and the girl's face broke into a grin.

'Hi. I'm Carys.'

Alex had hoped that Carys would come today, and she'd said that her father would be bringing her. She wondered whether Carys had told him that they'd already spoken.

The man held out his hand. 'I'm Ben Wheeler. I hear my daughter's been phoning you.'

'Dad…' Carys started to protest and Alex smiled at the man. Traces of grey in his hair, and lines around his eyes. His smile seemed weary, as if it was something he had to remember to do.

'We're always glad to hear from young people who might be interested in joining us.' She decided to tread lightly at first.

'Well, I don't know whether she's ready. She's having problems with the fit of her prosthesis…'

'Dad!' Carys frowned, obviously feeling that her father was intent on undermining her.

'That's not unusual. It sometimes takes a while to get things right. We can give some help and advice on that, and in the meantime perhaps I can introduce Carys to some of our members.'

'Right. Yes, that's…' Ben rubbed his hand across his head in a gesture of helplessness. 'Will you be all right on the steps, Carys?'

'I'm a physiotherapist; I'll make sure she doesn't fall.' Alex put on her most persuasive smile. 'Why don't you sit and watch—we'll be having more races soon.'

She gestured towards a seat, which just happened to be in front of Hayley's parents, and Ben nodded and sat down. As she turned, she saw Hayley's father leaning forward to introduce himself.

Carys was looking uncertainly at the steps running down in front of her. 'Shall we go round the other way? It's a bit further to walk, but there are no steps.'

'No. I think I can manage them.'

'Good girl. We'll do it together. Left leg first.' Alex tucked Carys's hand around her arm, ready to support her if she started to wobble, and Carys carefully lowered her prosthetic limb down the first step.

'I thought you were going to talk to him…' They'd got almost to the bottom of the steps, taking it slowly, one at a time, before Carys muttered the words at her.

Alex glanced over her shoulder. Ben had already swapped seats to sit with Hayley's parents, and a couple of the other parents had wandered over to introduce themselves. 'It's like we said on the phone, Carys…'

'Hi… You're Carys?' Leo was suddenly beside her, brimming with restless energy. Carys stared at him, momentarily forgetting all about the three more steps she had in front of her.

Alex waved Leo out of the way and he backed down the steps, giving Carys room to laboriously finish her descent. As soon as she was at the bottom, Carys turned to Leo, obviously deciding that she had a better chance of convincing him than she did Alex.

'I came for my dad. He's up there, talking to those people. Will *you* go and tell him?'

Leo was momentarily at a loss, glancing at Alex, who shook her head. 'I think it might be better to just allow him to talk to the people he's with for the time being.'

'But he'll listen to you—you're a doctor.' Carys was already treating him like a friend, venting her frustration at him. Alex supposed that a lot of people felt they knew Leo after listening to his voice on the radio, and that it must be something of a mixed blessing.

'What about showing him something? Show him that you can come here and make a few friends.' Leo was capitalising shamelessly on the artificial intimacy, moulding it into a real one.

Carys looked at Alex, clearly wanting her confirmation. This wasn't the time to indulge in hand-to-hand combat with Leo. Carys had told her that whatever her father said, her mother promptly took the opposite stance, and she must be pretty used to playing one off against the other. That was one of the problems she was facing.

'He's right.'

Leo shot her a surprised look and then warmed to his theme. 'Your dad's up there, talking to the other parents. They know exactly how he feels, and I think we ought to give him a chance to hear what they've got to say.'

'Yes.' Alex nodded her agreement, ignoring the amusement in Leo's eyes.

'Okay.' Carys shrugged. 'I suppose we could give it a go…'

'Yeah. Nice one.' Leo walked her slowly over to Hayley and Alice, making the introductions, and Alice shifted over one seat so that Carys could sit down in between them. Alex watched while the girls started to chat to each other. She'd get Rhona to keep an eye on Carys while she got ready for the next race.

Which reminded her… 'If you're going to take part in the adults' race, then you'd better go and get changed, Leo.'

'Yeah. Sure thing.' His smile took on a teasingly confrontational edge. 'Get ready to be looking at my back all the way round.'

'In your dreams.'

He feigned a look of surprise. 'What happened to "Yes"? I was thinking for a moment there that you'd finally got around to realising that everything I say is right.'

'That was in your dreams too. Go and get changed. And prepare to be watching *my* back…' Alex turned, leaving him standing alone, and made her way to the women's changing rooms.

The thought of being able to watch Alex's back all the way round the arena, with no one to accuse him of staring at her, was tempting. Almost tempting enough to make him throw away any thoughts of making a race out of it and slot himself in nicely behind her. But then Alex seemed to see right through him, and she'd probably guess. And if she thought for one moment that he was letting her win, she'd be furious.

He consoled himself with watching her walk away now. Leo knew that each step using a prosthetic leg took more energy than one with your own two legs. Just a little, but over the course of a day it all added up. The controlled, graceful sway of her body showed both the kids and their parents how much they could achieve, what they were working so hard towards.

Everything she did was a delicious reminder of their

kiss. That tangled web of so many delights, which even the sharp tang of guilt couldn't drive from his mind.

It was his own fault. If he hadn't surrendered to the moment, he wouldn't be plagued by it now. Nor would he have to keep telling himself that it mustn't happen again.

'Leo, Evangeline asked me to come and find you.' He turned and saw Evie's minder standing next to him.

'Yeah? Anything the matter?'

'Arielle's not well.'

'One of her headaches?' Evie had told him that, since the meningitis, Arielle had suffered from debilitating headaches and dizzy spells, which seemed to come on with no warning.

'Yep. She's in the first aid room.'

'Right. Where's that?'

Arielle was lying on the bed in the first aid room, her eyes closed, Evie at her side. When Leo opened the door, she ushered him backwards into the corridor, closing the door quietly behind them.

'How is she?'

'Done for this afternoon. She needs to go back to the hotel and sleep this off. Will you have a look at her though, Leo? We've got the name of a doctor here but I've never met him, and I trust you…'

'Would you like me to come back to the hotel with you?' The words fell heavy from his lips. This afternoon had been special in so many ways, and it felt suddenly as if he was ripping himself away.

'Oh, Leo, would you? I'm not sure whether the flight over here might have affected her…'

'Of course. I've finished everything I need to do here.' The lie sounded convincing enough to his ears, and Evie accepted it immediately. He'd been spending too much time with Alex lately. She was the only one who would have questioned him on it.

'I feel so bad about leaving now. So does Arielle—those kids have so much heart.'

'Why don't you stay? I'll take care of Arielle and stay with her until you get back.' It was the obvious solution. Leo's place was with anyone who needed him, not with Alex, however loath he was to admit that.

'Would you mind? Arielle asked me to stay, but I can't have you going with her while I'm here…'

Leo laid his hand on her arm. 'It's not a problem. These kids deserve all the support we can give them. Does Arielle have a copy of her medical records with her?'

'Yes, it's on the dresser in her room. Along with her medication.'

'I'll find them.'

Evie took the microphone from his hand and wound her arms around his shoulders, kissing him on the cheek. Leo hugged her. She was acknowledged as one of the most beautiful women in the world and no man in his right mind could fail to notice that. Only all he could think about was that she wasn't Alex.

'Do me a favour, would you, Evie?'

'Of course.'

'The little guy, Sam. Red hair and freckles—he's been following you around all afternoon.'

'He's such a cute kid. What about him?'

'Alex told me he loves being in the races, even if he always comes last. Make sure he gets a cheer when he runs, eh?' Leo knew he'd get one anyway but he'd so wanted to be there, cheering for Sam himself.

'Of course I will. You're not the only one who can work a crowd, you know.'

'I know. Now, get out of my way, will you. I've got a patient to see.'

* * *

Alex was eating a sandwich at her desk, in lieu of Sunday lunch, when her phone rang. That was Leo all over. She'd waited up last night, hoping he would call after leaving so abruptly, and he hadn't, and now that she'd managed not to think about him for five consecutive minutes he'd called.

'Hi. Where are you?'

'At my office.'

'Had lunch yet?'

'Yes, I've just eaten. How's Arielle?'

'Much better. Some people do suffer from headaches after they've had meningitis. It's a concern, of course, and Arielle naturally gets worried by it, but it's unusual for meningitis to recur. I called in this morning and she was fine.'

'That's good. I was wondering… I'd like to send her something, just to say thank you for coming and that I'm glad she's feeling better. I did think of flowers, but I guess she and Evie probably have whole roomfuls already…' Perhaps Leo could suggest something. Alex hoped he could because she had absolutely no idea what would be appropriate.

He chuckled. 'Yeah, it's a bit like Kew Gardens in there. I don't know how Evie stands it; I was sneezing all evening.' He paused for a moment to think. 'Do you have any photos from yesterday? I saw Rhona brandishing a camera.'

'We should have. Hold on, I'll look and see whether she's uploaded them onto the server yet.' Alex opened the images folder and saw a new folder with yesterday's date on it. 'Yes, they're there.'

'Why don't you pick out some nice ones and send them with a personal note? That's something I'm sure they'd both really appreciate.'

'It's not very much…'

'It'll be perfect.' Leo's tone suggested that the matter was dealt with and that he was already moving on. 'You'll be there for a while?'

'I think I'll pop out now and get a card to send with the photos. And I'll need a thumb drive too. I'll be back in half an hour.'

'In that case, I'll see you then.'

That question also appeared to be dealt with in Leo's mind because he didn't wait for an answer before hanging up. Alex stared at her phone.

'Yes, half an hour's convenient for me, Leo.' She dropped the phone back onto her desk. It really didn't matter if it wasn't, because it appeared that Leo would be coming anyway.

The card for Arielle sat in front of her on the desk and Alex was holding her pen, ready to write something as soon as inspiration struck her, when a quiet knock sounded at the door and it swung open.

She was getting used to the fact that all doors were open to Leo, and didn't bother to ask how he'd got into the building without pressing the night bell. Probably a couple of the people downstairs, who were busy preparing for a case in court tomorrow.

And who wouldn't let Leo in anywhere? He always looked as if he belonged, wherever he went. He'd made some concession to this being a Sunday, dark jeans and a charcoal sweater, his blond hair slightly more rumpled than usual. Of course, it was all artifice. Leo was never really off-duty; it just suited him to look as if he was from time to time.

'I thought you might need something to keep you going. Ready for a Tellurian cocktail?'

So he remembered. She couldn't attach too much importance to that, because she'd then have to attach an equal importance to the fact that she remembered too. And that particular episode of their lives was over now. They'd kissed it goodbye.

'I'm not sure I'll be ready for another one of those for at least another ten years.' It was tempting, though. Leo was tempting.

'They've improved a great deal.' He sauntered over to her desk, revealing what he'd been holding behind his back. Two crystal glasses that shone in the feeble afternoon light and a cocktail shaker.

'I seem to remember that pouring them down the sink was about the only thing that anyone could have done to redeem them.'

'Harsh, Alex.' He laughed. 'Don't you think that anything can be redeemed with a little work?'

Maybe. But Leo was working on all the wrong things.

'I'm not sure blue's my colour…'

'Blue is everyone's colour. Particularly yours…'

He opened the cocktail shaker and poured a measure into each glass. Maybe it was her imagination but the blue liquid was slightly less vivid than the original Tellurian cocktails. It actually looked quite intriguing.

Leo put a glass into her hand and sat down in the chair next to her desk. 'We should make a toast. To all we can achieve.' He tipped his glass towards hers.

'Yes. All we can achieve.' It sounded like a good toast. Alex took an exploratory sip from her glass.

'Oh! That's quite nice.' She took another sip. 'Actually, it's very nice.' Not too much sweetness, but just enough to temper the bite.

He smiled. 'Want to take a guess?'

'Hmm. Blue curaçao, obviously.' She took another sip. 'I'm not sure what else, though…' If there was another spirit, it had to be colourless. 'You haven't laced this with vodka, have you?'

He arched one eyebrow. 'No. I'm going for taste, not trying to get you drunk.'

'That's good to hear.' Alex took another sip, just to show him that she could handle it. 'So what *are* you here for, Leo?'

'Would you believe Sunday afternoon cocktails?'

'No. You said it yourself, Leo. There's no such thing as just drinks. What are you here for?'

'To apologise for rushing off like that yesterday.'

'You don't have to apologise. I know you had to go. I'm just happy that Arielle's all right.'

'Yeah. I guess it was my loss. There's something else.' He reached into his back pocket and brought out a folded envelope. 'I was talking to Alice yesterday.'

'Yes?'

'She says that running blades aren't automatically supplied on the NHS, and that her family can't afford to pay for one. You've been helping her to put applications in for funding, but she's not been successful yet so she's got herself a job.'

Alex quirked her mouth downwards. 'Yes, that's right. She stacks shelves in the supermarket a couple of evenings a week but that's not going to cover it. I'm going to have to think of something…'

Leo leaned forward, handing her the envelope. Alex opened it and drew out a folded sheet of notepaper. When she opened it a cheque fell out.

She read the letter carefully. Leo's donation to the charity was to be anonymous, and it was to be used to buy Alice's running blade. Alex caught her breath, blinking back the tears.

'Is that enough?'

'It's more than enough. This would pay for her blade and the upkeep for a couple of years.' It was what Alex had been praying for. Her fingers shook as she put the cheque down on the desk.

'This is…' She thought carefully about what she wanted to say. 'This is a wonderful act of generosity, Leo. Thank you.'

'It's my pleasure.'

'And you've tied my hands. I have to accept it.'

A flicker of doubt showed in his face. 'I sense a *but* coming.'

Alex took a deep breath. She owed it to Alice to accept the cheque, but she owed something to Leo too. 'But I want you to think about why you're doing this, Leo.'

'Why would I have to do that? You said yesterday that Alice has a lot of potential, and she's never going to be able to fulfil that without help.' His lip curled in disbelief. 'What more do you want?'

'We have a lot of people who support us, and we ask a lot of them. I have a duty of care to them as well as our clients.'

'You think I can't afford this?'

'I know you can from a financial point of view. My worry is that…that it's not going to buy you…' The word stuck in her throat.

'Buy me what?'

'Forgiveness.'

The shock in his eyes was palpable. For a moment Alex thought he was going to snatch the cheque up from her desk and walk out. What had she done?

Then he leaned back in his seat, rubbing his face with his hands. 'Why do you have to make everything so damn difficult, Alex?'

'Because…' Because she cared about Leo. If this money was all it took to allow him to forgive himself, it would be a bargain. But it wasn't, and he'd just keep on giving until he was too worn out to give any more.

'Because if I don't say this I'd be letting Alice down. And myself.' Alex reached forward and took his hand. Felt his fingers curl around hers in a delicious artifice of an embrace.

'Say it then.' His gaze was dark, suddenly. Entirely hers.

'I want you to know that this gift is not because you have some kind of debt to pay; it's because you're a good man and you have a good heart.'

'You don't understand, Alex.' Something about the way he said it told her that he might just be coaxed into explaining.

'Then tell me.'

He leaned forward, raising her hand to his lips in the parody of a kiss. For a moment Alex thought this was his way of letting her go, but he kept hold of her, clasping her fingers tightly between both his hands now.

'This is between you and me. No one else must know.'

'Yes. I understand.' What could be this bad? Alex swallowed hard, trying to prepare herself.

'My parents think that Joel overdosed by mistake. It's a possibility that gives them some comfort and I can't take that away from them. But it was no mistake. He called me.'

'But…you didn't speak to him, right? You don't know what he was going to say.'

Leo shook his head wearily. 'He called me five times, Alex, and I missed all of those calls. If that isn't a cry for help I don't know what is.'

She stared at him, numb with shock. Alex couldn't imagine how that must feel. How he must constantly be going back to that, wondering whether he could have saved his own twin brother's life.

'It was the last weekend before I went home for Christmas, and my girlfriend wanted to go away somewhere. I switched off my phone, and left my brother alone on the one night he really needed me.'

'But… Leo, people miss calls all the time…'

'I know. And usually it doesn't matter all that much but…' He shrugged. 'All I want is to give Alice the opportunity to run. I'm not looking to buy forgiveness because there isn't any.'

There was nothing she could say. It was too cruel, too heartbreaking and there were no answers to it. Alice came to her rescue.

'What Alice said…'

'I know. I heard her. If you just try hard enough you can do anything. It's a great thought and, coming from a kid like her who's had so much to contend with already, it's inspirational. But she doesn't know everything, Alex. You and I know that there are some things you can't do, and we just have to learn to live with that.'

'Won't you think about it?'

He shook his head, letting go of her hand. 'No, I'm not going to think about it. Because I can't change anything and if I thought about it too much I'd just be a mess. And there are things I have to do.'

She was losing him. He poured the rest of the contents of the cocktail shaker into her glass and drained his. Then he got to his feet.

'You're going?'

'Like I said. Things to do. Paperwork.'

'Can't you do it another time? We could go for something to eat, or catch a movie…'

He smiled. That relentless, charming smile which hid so much. 'Can I take a rain check? I really do have to work.'

He'd obviously forgotten that he'd asked her out to lunch first. Perhaps it was something that had suddenly come up, but Alex doubted it. Leo was drawing back, resorting to the tried and tested formula of not having time to think about anything.

'Yes, okay. Rain check.' She wondered what freak of nature was going to have to occur before the weather changed enough to induce Leo to change his mind.

'Fantastic. See you tomorrow...' He threw the words over his shoulder and walked out of the door.

CHAPTER TEN

IT WAS AS if nothing had happened between them. Leo was smiling and relaxed when he arrived at the radio station, taking the receipt for the cheque that she handed him with a nod but without saying anything.

If shaking him hard would have worked then Alex was quite prepared to do it. But it wouldn't. Leo's urbane charm wasn't a reflection that everything was right in his world. It was a fallback position, and he hung onto it just as grimly as anyone else might hold onto anger.

Their hour on-air together flew. Leo was the ultimate back seat driver, supportive when he needed to be and letting her talk when she was on a roll and knew what she wanted to say. His gaze connected with hers as they said their goodbyes for tonight and went off-air and they both heaved a sigh, flopping back into their seats in unison.

'Fabulous!' Justin burst into the studio. 'Great hour, both of you.'

Leo gestured towards Alex, chuckling. 'Nothing to do with me. That was the Alex Jackson Medical Hour you just heard.'

'You handled the sex beautifully…' Justin was in full flow, and Leo raised his eyebrows.

'Actually, we were talking about body awareness issues. You must have been listening to something else, Justin.'

'Sex, body awareness… It's all the same thing…' Justin stopped short as Leo shot him a frown. 'Okay, well, perhaps it isn't. Great body awareness, then. And it was a fantastic hour, just *like* sex on the airwaves.'

Alex had felt that too. A meeting of minds instead of bodies, but nonetheless a lot like sex. But Leo, gentleman to the last, wasn't having it.

'Do me a favour and save the sex on the airwaves for the Jazz Hour, will you? Have you got the call-backs?'

Justin produced an envelope from the file he was carrying. 'Here you go. Rather a lot of them, I'm afraid…'

'That's good. We want a lot.' Alex spoke up and Leo chuckled.

'Want to go halves?' Leo opened the envelope, drawing out a dozen sheets of paper, stapled together.

'Yes, thanks. I don't think I can get through all of those tomorrow.'

He nodded, counting the sheets out and dividing them, pulling the back half from the staple and putting them into the envelope.

'How's the piece going for the Community Affairs programme?' Leo asked Justin.

'Very good. We've put together what you did, along with a few bits from the second half of the afternoon. It'll be a fifteen minute slot.'

'That's great. Thanks.'

Leo waited for Justin to leave, and Alex saw him switch the voice link to the control room off. 'Despite all appearances, Justin's one of the best radio producers around. I'm lucky to be working with him.'

'But you don't tell him that. Just to keep him on his toes.'

'I told him. We were both a bit drunk at the time, and he told me I was radio gold and I told him he was the kind of producer that could turn a sow's ear into a silk purse. We don't mention it, of course.'

'Of course not. That would be kiss and tell.'

Leo chuckled. 'I wasn't drunk enough to kiss him. We're a good team though, and he knows it.'

'He keeps you focused and you keep him honest?' Alex wondered whether Leo would admit to being the heart behind the show.

'There you go again. Making out I'm better than I really am.' He got to his feet. That way of his, of closing a conversation before it got too uncomfortably close to reality.

Leo walked over to the door and waited and, when she didn't follow him, he raised his eyebrows. 'What?'

'Nothing.' She smiled back at him innocently, her heart pounding. This time, Leo wasn't going to walk away, not before she'd done what she'd decided to do. And then maybe *she'd* be the one to walk away.

He heaved a sigh and threw himself back into his seat. 'All right. I'll wait.'

Alex rummaged in her bag, and pulled out the thumb drive. Leaning over, she put it into his hand. 'The photos…'

'For our website?'

'No, I gave a set to Justin, before you arrived. These are for you.' She rose, planting her hands on the arms of his chair. He looked up at her steadily, obviously waiting for her to make the next move.

'I thought the show was great tonight. Thank you.' She met his gaze, staring him straight in the eye as she said it. Then she leaned in. 'So was the sex. Really enjoyed it.'

'Does that mean you're coming back for coffee?'

Alex straightened. 'Thanks, but no. I've got to go, and I asked your production assistant to make sure my car was waiting as soon as the programme ended.' She turned, grabbed her coat and bag and walked away from him.

It was snowing again, the light flakes taking on the shape of the wind, outside his window. Leo had taken a shower and was sprawled on his bed, his laptop in front of him, looking at the photographs.

He could almost taste the day again. Hear the cheers as Hayley passed the finishing line. See Alex running up to Alice and hugging her, ready for them both to smile into the camera. And there were snapshots of what had happened after he'd left. Little Sam, lagging behind the rest, the winners of his race turning to egg him on towards the finishing line. Evie, picking the little guy up, his arms held aloft, in front of a crowd that had risen to its feet and were applauding him.

He rolled over onto his back, staring at the ceiling. Alex had given him these photographs because she knew they'd touch his heart and in the stubborn belief that there was something of value there.

But their kiss had told him all he needed to know. It would be so easy, so sweet, to lose himself in her arms. But then the guilt would kick in and tear it all apart.

He'd work it out. Somehow strike a balance, learn to love her as a friend, and that would be enough. He'd start tomorrow, because tonight he wanted to look at the photographs, one more time.

'Hey. What are you doing on Saturday?' As usual, Leo launched straight into what he was intending to say without bothering with any preliminaries.

'Nothing very much. I was going to drive down to my parents' and stay the night, ready for the climbing wall on Sunday.' Almost twenty-four hours without having heard from Leo forced Alex to ask, 'You are coming on Sunday, aren't you?'

'Wouldn't miss it.' He neglected the obvious, not mentioning that he could be called away at any time. 'I've got a couple of tickets for a media do on Saturday evening; the radio station's got a table. Will you come?'

'I'm… What sort of do?' Alex thought furiously for some kind of excuse. It sounded much more like the kind of function that Leo would go to, and Alex suspected that she'd be like a fish out of water.

'It's a dinner dance. A lot of the right people are going, and it'll be good to get your name out there.'

'Out where…?'

Leo chuckled. 'Figure of speech. You get to meet people; they get to meet you. It's a great opportunity.'

It was a great opportunity to make a complete and utter fool of herself. 'I don't know, Leo. I'd have to drive all the way down to Sussex afterwards.'

'Not necessarily. It's being held in South London, and I can come and pick you up and take you there. Then afterwards we'll go to my place, down in Surrey, and grab a few hours' sleep. We can get up early on Sunday and drive down to Sussex then.'

That would work… Alex shook her head. She couldn't believe that she was even thinking about it.

'It'll be fun. Chance to dress up a bit…'

That was exactly what was bothering her. 'Well, to be honest, I'm not sure I have anything suitable to wear. This do is black tie, is it?'

'Yeah. Well, if that's all that's bothering you, then that's perfect. We can go shopping…'

Oh, no. She could see it now, having to try about a million different dresses on while Leo waited outside the changing room. He'd probably talk her into something that she normally wouldn't wear and then offer to pay for it, so she couldn't change her mind later.

'No, on second thoughts I can probably find something lurking at the back of my wardrobe.'

'Great. Last year it was quite formal—most of the women wore long dresses. You can't go wrong with black…'

'I'll bear it in mind. And… Well, thanks for the invitation. And I guess I'll see you on Saturday.' That was another five days, and Alex could say the words with only a minor murmur of panic.

'Something lurking in the back of your wardrobe?' Rhona looked up from her desk as Alex put her phone down. 'Going somewhere nice?'

'Leo's asked me to a dinner dance on Saturday. He says it would be good to meet some people.'

Rhona nodded. 'He's right.'

'Yes, I know he is. What am I going to wear, though?' Rhona had been through the contents of Alex's wardrobe often enough. Some summer dresses, a few smart separates and a suit; the rest was all casual wear. None of that was going to do.

'Looks as if you'll be hitting the shops. Or Mum can run something up for you, if you like.' Rhona's mother had been a seamstress and still made most of her own and her daughter's clothes. Rhona would bring a bolt of fabric into the office, and a couple of days later would appear in something that was entirely unique and usually stupendous.

'Thanks. I don't want to put her to any trouble.'

'You know it's no trouble. Why don't you go and have a look around at what's in the shops now, and if there's something you like that's fine. If not, you've got some clue about what you *would* like.'

What Alex really would like was to look effortlessly glamorous, the way Evie did. Have Leo gasp and compliment her dress. 'I think I'll settle for just not looking out of place.'

'Whatever. Just go. Once you've got a few ideas you'll feel better.'

Alex didn't feel any better. She'd been into three or four of the big stores in Oxford Street and picked up a whole string of black dresses, putting most of them back down again. The ones she'd tried on all had something wrong with them—too fussy, too revealing. And black just didn't seem to suit her.

She flopped down on one of the comfortable sofas next to the entrance of the changing room. This was all a disaster. She was going to be scouring the shops for the next three days, then she'd panic and get just anything. Then feel even worse because Leo would undoubtedly look immaculate and good enough to eat.

Alex looked at her watch. An hour before closing time. She could either look at everything again, to make sure there was nothing she'd missed, or give up and go to the in-store café. Maybe if she came back tomorrow evening, after work…

Then she saw it. Alex got up wearily, walking over to the mannequin and looking at the price ticket. That wasn't too much. If it fitted…

She caught up the dress and walked to the changing room. It wasn't going to fit. The neck wouldn't look right. There was going to be something the matter with it, the way that there was something the matter with all the others.

But it *did* fit. It was simple, plain and, when Alex left her cubicle to try walking up and down a little, the skirts were wide enough and didn't cling around her legs. She stopped in front of a long mirror by the entrance to the changing room and one of the sales assistants looked up from the desk.

'That looks nice…'

'I'm…not sure.' Alex stared at herself in the mirror.

'No, it's lovely.' A woman on her way into the changing room stopped, laying an armful of clothes on the counter. 'It really suits you. Understated but it looks classy.'

Classy was just what she wanted. Alex nodded her thanks and went back to the cubicle, pulling out her phone.

'Rhona… I need your help…'

* * *

Leo couldn't deny that he was looking forward to Saturday evening. By the time he'd showered and dressed, he could almost taste his excitement. He took one look in the mirror and gave himself a nod of approval. He'd do. Neat and unremarkable, his attire designed to allow the woman on his arm all the attention.

Not that Alex needed him for that; she dazzled all by herself. She looked great in anything because it was her smile that everyone noticed. Alex was one of those women who outshone anything that she could possibly be wearing.

He picked up the keys for his SUV, parked next to his saloon car in the garage downstairs. The past few days had been wet, drizzle alternating with snow, and the track which led to his house in Surrey was likely to be muddy. Patting his pockets, checking that he had everything, he let himself out of the flat and called the lift.

He found Alex's name on the console by the main entrance to her block of flats and pressed her buzzer. It was oddly gratifying that she answered almost immediately, buzzing him inside. He walked up the stairs and found her door. He'd been fantasising about what she might wear all the way here, and had decided that Alex would go for the understated. Black probably, figure-hugging without being showily tight, and classy. Definitely classy.

She opened the front door wide and he felt his mouth suddenly too dry to utter the compliment that he'd had waiting. His feet were rooted to the spot and only his eyes seemed to have any power of movement.

'You look…' Completely and utterly dumbfounding.

She flushed pink, a trace of awkwardness on her face. 'Too much…?'

Far too much. How on earth did she think that he was going to wrench his gaze away from her and talk coherently to anyone else tonight?

'You look stupendous.' He took one step towards her, almost afraid to go any nearer.

She was a deeper pink now, but the uncertainty had given way to a smile. 'You like it?'

Like it? Was she entirely mad? Her dress was jewel-green, simply cut, with sheer fabric at the neckline and covering her arms. Shimmering, iridescent sequins spilled from the right side of the neckline, spreading out across her shoulder and down her sleeve, with another trail meandering down across her breast and disappearing in the soft folds of her skirts. Her hair was swept up, and he could see silver pins anchoring the soft curls. Not quite Tara's silver dagger pins, but reminiscent of them. She stepped back from the doorway and as she moved the sequins glimmered blue and green and the silver tracery on the cuff bracelets she wore sparkled.

Many women had dressed up for him before, but no one had ever done anything like this. This was a shared secret, a nod to their past, which only he got. Everyone else would simply think she was the most beautiful woman in the room.

'It's stunning.' *She* was stunning. Leo stepped into the hallway, leaning towards her. 'If you tell me you have an immobility gun strapped to your leg, I think I'm going to faint.'

She laughed. 'No, it would spoil the line of the skirt. I am armed, though.'

'And ready to go?' He'd been wondering whether he'd get to see her flat, but now Leo didn't care. All he wanted to look at was her.

'Yes.' She picked up her coat, along with a small silver clutch bag, and indicated a large zipped bag. As he bent to pick it up, Leo caught a subtle breath of her scent.

He held out his arm and she took it. 'Armed how?'

'That would be telling…' Her eyes flashed with mischievous humour, and another layer added itself to the fantasy. 'The first strategy is always surprise.'

Leo wondered whether he should have thought to bring a weapon as well. Every guy in the room was going to be fighting for her attention tonight. But he had the advantage. He'd bet everything he had that Alex was the kind of woman who always went home with the guy she came with.

CHAPTER ELEVEN

He liked the dress. What had started out as a bit of fun had turned into uncertainty over whether the idea was really going to work. Rhona and her mum had egged her on, and the three of them had spent an evening laughing over the application of sequins to the dress that Alex had bought. Then the terror had set in. But when she'd seen approval in Leo's eyes she'd been able to breathe again.

It was an hour's drive to the hotel where the dinner dance was being held, and Leo seemed to know that she was still nervous. He always knew how to calm her though, and when she walked into the enormous banqueting hall, hanging on tightly to his arm, it seemed less daunting than she'd thought it would be.

He found their table and Alex was relieved to see Justin there, along with a few other faces she knew. Leo was on good form, quietly attentive but at the same time laughing and joking with everyone, and she began to enjoy herself.

A meal was served and then came the speeches, which were mercifully short. Then the diners began to meander away from their tables, circulating and greeting friends. Leo seemed to know almost everyone here and he was clearly on a mission, steering Alex from one group to another, introducing her and working her charity seamlessly into each conversation.

'What a nice man…' Alex had spoken for a while to

a white-haired man who had asked a number of perceptive questions about her work and listened carefully to her answers.

'He's on the board of one of the biggest publishing organisations in the country.' Leo leaned in towards her, whispering the name into her ear.

'Really?' Alex's hand flew to her mouth and she felt her ears begin to redden.

Leo grinned. 'Just as well I didn't tell you before. You would have clammed up, and smiled and nodded instead of being your usual interesting self.'

'Well…yes. I'll give you that. I *would* have clammed up.'

'And he didn't get where he is by standing grinning at people.'

Alex wrinkled her nose. 'Do you think I was too…?'

'You were perfect. Would you like to dance?'

Yes. She'd really like to dance with Leo. Have his arm around her waist, feel his body moving against hers. Maybe that was asking just a little bit too much of an already great evening, though.

'I'd like to find the ladies' room first…'

He gestured over his shoulder. 'That way.'

She moved through the press of people, finding herself in a large, comfortable lobby. Two women were already there, standing by the mirrors, gossiping. Alex paid no attention to them until she was about to leave, and walked over to the mirror to check her lipstick.

'I glimpsed Leo on the way in. Looking as mouthwatering as ever.' The woman in the blue dress was talking rather too loudly to ignore.

'Is he? I'll have to go and strike up a conversation!' the black dress replied.

'Fancy a threesome?' Blue dress laughed unattractively.

'I don't mind sharing, darling. Leo's never struck me as the type for that kind of thing, though.'

Alex pressed her lips together, staring at her reflection in the mirror, willing it to be impassive. Going across to the women and reminding them that Leo was a person and not just a pretty face probably wouldn't be all that tactful. She was meant to be putting on her lipstick, not listening to their conversation.

'Did you hear his show on Monday? I was playing it in the car on the way down here. Marvellous chemistry. Apparently he's brought her along tonight.'

'Really?'

'Yes—' Blue dress broke off, but Alex could see her reflection in the mirror, mouthing to her companion. *She's only got one leg. Fancy bringing her to a dance.*

'Poor thing.' Black dress shuddered ostentatiously. 'Are you still thinking of making Leo an offer?'

'I tried. Not interested. I offered him twice whatever he's getting at the radio station and he turned me down flat. Said that he wanted to concentrate on serious medical issues, whatever that means, and that he was happy working with Justin. *Justin*, for goodness' sake…'

'Shame. With his ratings, he could do anything.'

'Yes, and, between you and me, I need something. We're already having to fight for our advertising revenue…'

Alex glared at the women's reflections but they didn't notice. It wasn't the first time she'd heard any of the barbs they'd thrown at her and it wouldn't be the last, but they still rankled. How dare these women call her a *poor thing*? How dare they think that having had part of her leg amputated was so shameful they couldn't even say it? And how dare they assume that she couldn't dance with Leo if she wanted to?

They weren't worth her time, or her anger. She repeated the words over in her head a couple of times, looking at herself in the mirror. Then she put her lipstick back into her bag and made for the door, even returning the smile that blue dress aimed in her direction as she walked past them.

She turned the corner which led to the door and heard one of the women speak again. 'Don't you just *love* that dress? I wonder where she got it.'

'And did you see her shoes? So pretty.'

'I must get a pair like that. She looks so graceful, and I can hardly walk in these heels…they're killing me…'

Leo turned when she put her hand on his arm, smiling down at her. Alex reached out, running her fingers down the side of his lapel, not caring how unmistakably possessive the gesture was.

'Do you still want to dance?'

He grinned. 'I'd love to dance.'

He took her hand, leading her towards the dance floor. She felt suddenly both too warm and too cold, her fingers almost icy in his hand, her cheeks hot. Alex wondered how many other people here were looking at her, thinking exactly the same as the women in the ladies' room.

When he laid his hand on her back she smiled up at him, but her whole body felt stiff and tense. Leo took a couple of steps and she moved with him, like an automaton.

'What's the matter?' The tenderness in his gaze seemed to bore into her.

'Nothing.'

'Really?' He was guiding her over to the very edge of the dance floor. He was going to stop and go and sit down. And then everyone would be looking at her, thinking she couldn't dance.

'No, Leo. I want to stay here…' She heard the pleading tone in her voice.

'Okay. But what's up?'

'I… It's nothing. People just say things without thinking.' Leo wouldn't understand this. He was a doctor and he took it so much for granted that she was more than her disability that he probably didn't even imagine that people could be that cruel.

'Okay, so it's nothing. Care to share it, all the same? In the interests of research.'

'Research?'

'Yeah. Crass things that people say. I'm always interested in that kind of thing.'

She couldn't help smiling up at him. 'You won't like it...'

'Well, clearly you don't either, so we can not like it together. Call it a bonding exercise.' His hand had been resting lightly on her back but suddenly he drew her in, trapping her against him. His other hand curled around hers.

'It was just two women, talking in the ladies' room. They started off by saying they wouldn't mind a threesome with you.'

She felt his chest heave against hers as he choked suddenly. 'Tell me you managed to knock that idea on the head. Please.'

'I couldn't. They weren't actually talking to me. I overheard.'

'Okay, I get it. You're staring in the mirror, fiddling with your hair, and they're off in a corner somewhere gossiping.' His lips twitched into a smile. 'Nice bit of undercover work there, Lieutenant. Did you get them with the hairpins?'

'No. They're actually not very sharp.' Leo had this knack of making her feel better. Or maybe it was the way he was holding her. Almost an embrace, moving slowly along with the music.

'So they've escaped for the time being. Never mind; we'll get them later. Continue with the surveillance report, please, Lieutenant.'

Alex couldn't help laughing. 'They'd heard the programme. They called me a *poor thing* and wanted to know why you'd brought me along tonight, when I obviously couldn't dance with you.'

Anger flashed in his eyes, and she felt his body stiffen against hers. Then he puffed out a breath. 'And you didn't kick them?'

'I felt like it. But one of them said she'd made you an offer, for twice what you were earning now…'

Understanding dawned in his eyes. 'I know who you mean. Trust me, Alex, Clara Goodwin is seriously bad news. Three-quarters of the industry wouldn't even give her the time of day, let alone work for her. Anyway, it makes no difference, even if she'd made me the best offer in the world, you still should have kicked her.'

'It might have been a bit unfair. A prosthetic leg can give you a bit of a wallop, you know.'

'All the same. I'm disappointed in you.' He leaned in, his lips touching her ear. 'You are the most gorgeous woman in this room. You're intelligent and kind, and you dance beautifully. And even if you didn't, I'd still be proud that you agreed to come here with me tonight.'

Alex felt herself relax against him. 'That's nice of you.'

'I'm never nice, you know that.' He increased the rhythm of the dance a little, and Alex felt herself follow. 'What *is* nice is that you've finally loosened up. Any chance of letting me lead now?'

'I didn't realise I wasn't…' He raised his eyebrows, and Alex grinned back at him. 'Okay, maybe you're right. Take the helm, Captain.'

'My pleasure. Hang on, we have incoming on the starboard bow.'

His sudden turn almost lifted her off her feet, making her skirts float out behind her. It was like letting go without there being any danger of stumbling, because Leo was there.

They danced in silence for a while, their bodies moving together, staring into each other's eyes. Leo was good at this. He made it feel like sex should be, and very seldom was. A pure indulgence. Lost in his arms and yet there, right with him. Letting him lead and yet feeling him react to each movement of hers.

'So…' He pursed his lips thoughtfully, mischief flashing in his eyes. 'Am I correct in thinking that you're using me?'

'Absolutely. I'm showing the whole room that I can dance all night if I want to.'

'Good. Go for it.'

'But of course you're using me too.' He raised his eyebrows and she grinned at him. 'Those two women are out there somewhere, looking for a threesome…'

'Don't! You're going to have to stay right where you are until I manage to *un*-think that. And I warn you, it might take a while.'

'Good. Go for it.' She could do this all night. And then sleep for a while and do it all over again. But, since that wasn't going to happen, she'd make the best of it while she could.

Leo had tried to hide his anger, but he couldn't. How *dared* Clara Goodwin make Alex feel that she was anything less than perfect? Raising his hand to any woman was out of the question, but he might be persuaded to hold her still while Alex punched her.

And what made him angriest of all was that it wasn't the first time, and it was unlikely to be the last. Maybe it had been a good thing that he was unable to hide how he felt about that. She was so protective of the kids in her charge, so positive and encouraging on the radio, that it was sometimes easy to forget that she had feelings too, and that the careless cruelty of others still hurt her.

There was a measure of safety here, on the dance floor. Alex was nestled against him and the world seemed right. As if nothing could touch them for a while.

Not long enough, though. After two dances he found that a number of the people he'd introduced her to earlier wanted to continue their conversations with Alex on the dance floor, and he gave her up. This was what she was here for, to make new contacts.

Finally he got her back. 'Do you want to sit for a while?' He wondered if she would admit it to him if she did, but she did so without hesitation.

'Yes, I wouldn't mind. Shall we give this one a miss?'

'Good idea. There's always the next one.'

But there wasn't a next one. As they walked together over to the drinks buffet, he saw a commotion at the corner of the room. A couple of people looked around, and then someone pointed straight at him. A man dressed in the dark red jacket which was the livery of the hotel started to push his way towards him.

'Dr Leo Cross?'

'Yes?'

'There's been an incident in the kitchen, sir. We need a doctor. It's an emergency.'

'All right. I'll come now.' Leo shot an apologetic look at Alex and she nodded, disappointment showing on her face. He followed the man through the crush of people, cursing whatever twist of fate had called him away from her a second time. Last Saturday had been unfortunate. This Saturday was beginning to look as if some malevolent force of nature had it in for him.

It couldn't be helped. This was what he'd signed up for when he became a doctor. Alex would understand. She had to.

The man led him from the banqueting hall and along a service corridor. 'What's happened?'

'One of the cooks, sir. He's cut his finger off. I've got someone calling an ambulance, but we can't stop the bleeding.'

'You have a medical kit?'

'Yes, there's one in the kitchen. Gets used quite a bit so we keep it well stocked.'

'And you have Health and Safety procedures for dealing with blood spillage?' It sounded as if there was going to be a fair bit of blood, and there was no way of knowing whether there was a risk of infection.

'Yes, they're in place. I'll get everyone out of there and cleaned up.'

'Good.'

They rounded a corner and then hurried through a door, which led to a large kitchen. Even though it was late, there were still half a dozen people here who were currently all gathered around a man who was sitting on the floor in the corner. A trail of blood led from one of the nearby work benches, and was beginning to pool around his legs.

'Everyone move back, please.' Leo took off his jacket, rolling up his sleeves and grabbing a pair of gloves from the large medical box which stood open on the counter. The group around the man scattered, everyone craning to see what was happening.

The man was doubled over, cradling his injured hand and moaning loudly. Leo knew that he must be in a great deal of pain, but there was nothing he could do about that. He carried a medical bag in his car, but that didn't include the drugs he needed now.

'Alan…' The man's name was sewn onto his tunic, above the breast pocket. 'Alan, I'm a doctor. Let me see your hand.'

Leo reached for Alan's arm but he batted him away,

rocking back and forth, blood leaking from the towel that was wound around his hand.

'Alan… Look at me.' Leo put his hand on the side of Alan's face, tipping it towards his. 'I'm a doctor. I know it hurts, but you need to show me your hand.'

This time, Alan didn't resist when he reached for his arm. Gingerly, Leo unwound the towel and saw that the first phalanx of his index finger had been completely severed, leaving only a half-inch stump. Blood pulsed from the wound, dripping onto the floor.

'Alan, I need you to hold your arm up.' Leo elevated the man's hand and Alan swore at him, moaning with pain. Finding the position of the main veins in his wrist, Leo pressed hard, and the flow of blood began to slow.

'Can someone get me…?' He looked up and saw six pairs of eyes staring blankly at him. He needed someone to help him and it didn't look as if any of this lot were going to volunteer. Then he saw a flash of green by the door and a seventh pair of eyes, honey-brown. Alex was hurrying towards him.

CHAPTER TWELVE

'I NEED SOME water and plenty of gauze. Put a pair of gloves on first. And be careful—there's blood on the floor; don't slip on it.'

Leo bit his tongue. Alex worked at the hospital, she knew all about procedures for blood spillage. But he couldn't help saying it.

'Already seen it,' she reproved him gently and turned towards the medical box. Collecting what he'd asked for, she scooped up the hem of her dress, picking her way carefully across the blood-spattered floor and laying a basin of water and a large wad of gauze down next to him.

'Thanks. I'll need a small bandage in a moment.' Leo set about cleaning as much of the blood off Alan's hand as he could, and then packed the gauze around what was left of his finger. Then he ran out of hands. This was the trouble with medicine outside a hospital or surgery; he always seemed to get to the point when two hands wasn't enough.

'Here, let me.' Alex was there, the hem of her dress gathered in a makeshift knot at the side, to keep it out of the way. She bent over, winding the bandage over the gauze to keep it in place, and secured it with a safety pin.

Leo carefully relaxed his grip on Alan's wrist. Good. He didn't want to use a tourniquet unless absolutely necessary, and it looked as if the bleeding was stopping now.

Alan was quieter now and Leo turned to him, trying

to give a little reassurance. 'You're doing really well. The ambulance will be here soon and we'll get you something for the pain…'

'Where is it?' Alan was looking round, trying to get up now, and Leo pressed him gently backwards. Now that the bleeding was dealt with, he could think about finding the finger. But he needed to stay here with Alan.

And he wasn't quite sure how Alex might react to being asked to find a missing body part. But the one thing he did know was that just assuming she couldn't do it without even mentioning it would hurt her even more.

He smiled at her. 'Tough question. For me to ask, that is…'

She grinned back. 'I know. Easy answer for me…' She laid her gloved hand on the side of Alan's face and his gaze focused on hers. 'Alan, I'm going to find your finger. Can't have you going off to the hospital without it, eh?'

'Please…' Alan tried to move again but she shook her head.

'It's okay. You need to stay here and do what the doctor tells you. I'll find it.'

No one could have resisted the warmth of her smile, the reassuring certainty of her tone. Even Leo felt better. Alan relaxed back against the wall with a small nod, and Alex got to her feet.

'Can you see if you can find something to splint the hand with first?' Alan was still moving fitfully and he should keep his hand as still as possible.

She nodded, opening a couple of drawers and pulling out a flat wooden spatula. 'This do?'

'That's perfect.'

Alex delivered the spatula and another bigger bandage to him and Leo set about immobilising Alan's hand. When he glanced up again, Alex was standing at the counter top, moving the bloodstained knife carefully out of the way and sorting through the pile of peelings and chopped vegetables.

A slight shake of her head told Leo that it wasn't there, and he hoped that it hadn't rolled onto the floor. He'd been watching where he put his feet, but there had obviously been a bit of panic in here when the accident first happened. Alex was obviously thinking the same thing because she stopped, standing still, looking carefully around her.

Then she moved, one step towards the sink, and reached in. 'Got it. It's got some vegetable peelings on it.'

'Okay, get as much as you can off, but don't put it under water. Leave anything that isn't easy to remove for the surgeon at the hospital. Then wrap it with some moist gauze.'

She followed his instructions and then looked in the medical box, breaking open a plastic bag and tipping the contents back into the box. Alex slid the precious gauze-wrapped package into the bag, securing it carefully with some plaster.

'Great. Now the ice, but make sure it's not in contact with any tissue.' Leo decided not to say *finger*. Alan was calmer now and he didn't want to upset him any further.

'Gotcha.' She walked over to the fridge and found a bag of crushed ice. Tearing it open, she tipped half into the sink and then put the package with Alan's finger in it carefully into the bag, packing the ice around it and resealing the top.

She walked back over to them and bent down next to Alan. 'Here, I've got it. It's undamaged and on ice.'

'They'll be able to sew it back on?' Alan reached for the bag and Alex caught his hand, allowing him to touch it but not grab hold of it.

'There's a good chance they will.' She curled her hand over Alan's. 'They'll have to make an assessment, but these days the surgeons can do what seems like the impossible.

We've done all the right things, and they'll explain everything to you when you get there.'

It was just the right mix of truth and reassurance. And there was no trace in her manner of the stark truth that the surgeons hadn't been able to do the impossible for her. He'd never met anyone who was quite so generous with hope as Alex was.

'Thank you… What's your name?'

'Alexandra.' The use of her full name seemed just right at this moment. Something beautiful, a reassurance to Alan that even now there was time to appreciate the extra syllables.

'P…pretty name.'

'Thank you.' Alan moved restively and Alex caught hold of the bag a little tighter, steadying it without taking it away from him. 'I know it hurts. The paramedics will be here soon and they'll be able to give you something for the pain.'

Voices and movement at the other side of the kitchen confirmed her statement, almost as if she'd magicked them. A paramedic walked towards them.

'Not much for us to do here, then?' His practised eye took in Alan's bandaged hand and the bag of ice.

Leo supervised the administration of pain relief and Alan was settled into a portable wheelchair. Alex entrusted the bag to the paramedic's care and gave Alan a little wave and a brilliant smile as he was wheeled out.

'How do you do that?' Alex had turned to him.

'Do what?'

'Look at you.' She gazed at his shirt, inspecting it carefully. 'You have one tiny spot on your sleeve, but apart from that you're as clean as a whistle.'

Leo laughed. 'I worked in A&E for a while, when I was training. You get an instinct for avoiding all kinds of spatter.'

'And there was me thinking that you'd picked the knack up from your tailor.' She giggled.

'Nah. He'd be delighted if I went through a few more shirts. Better for business.' Leo stripped off his gloves, throwing them into the bag he'd put to one side for the bloodstained towel and dressings, and Alex followed suit. He walked over to a sink at the far end of the room, lathering his hands with liquid soap.

Suddenly she was next to him, holding her fingers under the tap. He tipped a little of the soap onto her hand, working it round with his fingers, expecting her to draw away from him at any moment, but she didn't. She just stayed still, her face tilted downwards so that he could only see the top of her head, allowing him to lace his fingers with hers then rub her palms and the back of her hands.

If he'd strayed over the line, made a touch into a caress, Leo felt sure that she would have drawn back. But in his head he was way past practical, heading through sensual at breakneck speed and making for sexual. Before thoughts turned into actions, he reached for the dispenser, putting a paper towel into her hands.

Letting his gaze trace her arms and ankles wasn't sexual either. It was strictly practical. 'You've got a smudge on your leg…there.'

'Oh…my prosthesis…' She leaned over to scrub the dried blood with the paper towel, but her dress seemed to have other ideas, choosing this moment to slip from the knot she'd tied to keep it clear of her ankles. She grappled with it, pulling it away from her legs.

'Here…' Leo put his hands tentatively around her waist and she didn't wriggle free, so he lifted her, perching her up on the counter top. She pulled her dress up, exposing her knees.

'Some soap and water…' She bent down, removing the

prosthesis and examining it, the remaining part of her leg covered with a thin white sock and hanging unnoticed.

She'd talked about practically every issue that she faced in front of him, and he'd seen amputees remove a prosthesis many times before. But, watching her now, he was no doctor. He was her date for the evening, someone that she'd dressed up for. It was warming that Alex seemed to trust him on that level too.

'I'll get it…' He pulled one of the towels from the dispenser and dribbled some soap and water into it. She held the prosthesis away from her dress and he wiped the blood away, making sure that there was no mark left on the silicone skin-toned covering.

'That's it… Oops, no, there's some on my shoe.' She unbuckled the pretty silver sandal and examined the dark stain covering the inside of the sole. There was a corresponding smear on the heel of her prosthesis, and Leo wiped that away.

'Rhona's going to kill me.' She was balancing the prosthesis on her lap.

'They're hers?'

Alex nodded. 'Yep. Four ninety-nine from the market. She sprayed them silver…' She ran her nail along the straps and silver paint flaked off onto the floor.

'We'll get her another pair. I think I can spare four ninety-nine.'

'No, we can't. She got them from some stall that does recycled stuff. They're a one-off.'

'We'll think of something. Do you want to go? The evening's probably winding down by now.' And Leo couldn't bear to give her up to the other people in the room. Not now.

'Yes. I'm ready to go now.'

'Okay. Take your other sandal off.'

'Why—is that stained too?' She swung her leg up to inspect her foot.

'No.' Leo leaned in close, planting his hands on the counter on either side of her. 'But there are three public relations options here.'

'As many as that?' The subtle curve of her lips in an otherwise solemn expression told Leo that she was teasing him.

'Yep. If I carry you out of here and into the car—'

'What would you want to do that for?'

'Because if you put your shoe back on you'll stain your heel. And you can't go barefoot over the gravel in the car park.' She pressed her lips together, nodding. 'So I can carry you out and everyone will think you're a poor thing who can't walk. I don't think we'll go for that option.'

'No.' She grinned. 'I don't think we will.'

'Or...they can think that I'm sweeping you off for a night of passion and I can't keep my hands off you.' At that moment, that sounded pretty much perfect to Leo.

'No. Probably not...'

She was right, of course. 'Or...you hold your stained shoes in your hand, and everyone thinks I'm just carrying you because you can't wear them.'

She nodded. 'Wisest choice, I think.'

'We'll go for that one then. Where's your evening bag?'

'I left it with that terribly important, terribly nice man. His wife's looking after it for me.'

'Right. I'll go and fetch that, and our coats, and make sure they're sending someone up to clean up this mess.' He let his hand stray to her right leg, brushing her knee with his fingers. 'Will you wait for me here? I won't be long.'

She grinned. 'That's fine. I'll yell if I need you.'

Leo made a show of rolling his eyes. She was more than enchanting. And they'd broken through a barrier. Alex's independent streak usually made her cautious about taking help, but she'd let her guard down with him tonight.

He turned away from her, pulling the sleeves of his shirt down and refastening his cufflinks before he put his jacket back on.

'Wait…' She beckoned him back over and she reached up, untying his bow tie and leaving it to drape around his neck, then unbuttoning the top button of his shirt.

'And what's that for?'

'If we're worried about how things look, then I think you should seem a little less neat. You can't battle for someone's life with your tie done up.'

'It's practical. Keeps it out of the way.' He grinned at her.

'Yes, I know, but we're thinking image here.' She reached forward, flipping open the second button on his shirt, and Leo felt a tingle run down his spine. 'That's much better. Makes you look very dashing.'

Leo was back in less than five minutes, accompanied by the hotel's cleaning crew. He *did* look enormously dashing.

He didn't just look the part. He'd saved her from the monstrous blue and black dresses in the ladies' room, and made her feel as if she was beautiful. If he hadn't saved Alan's life, he'd come pretty close to it and sent him off to hospital strong enough to undergo the complex surgery needed to reattach his finger.

He leaned across, gathering her up in his arms. 'You're heavier than you look.'

'Muscle weighs more than fat. You must be weaker than you look.' He was having no trouble carrying her at all. She picked up her sandals from the counter top and curled the other arm around his neck.

'Door…'

She reached down for the door handle, pulling it open,

and he manoeuvred through and along the concrete floor of the corridor, setting her back on her feet when they reached the carpeted area in the lobby. Smiling at the group who had gathered in the lobby, ready to go, he caught sight of Justin and shook his hand. A hotel employee was waiting with their coats and her bag and walked towards the entrance doors.

'Leo…' The woman in the blue dress had appeared suddenly from nowhere and was making determinedly for him.

'Clara. Nice to see you. Be a darling and get the door for me, would you.'

Leo swung back to face Alex, grim satisfaction burning in his eyes as he picked her up again. This wasn't one of Leo's charming jokes; he'd meant to put Clara firmly in her place.

Her dress brushed against Clara's arm as he whisked her through the door and out into the night. The cold air made her shiver, and she instinctively clung a little tighter to him.

For once, Leo was tight-lipped and silent, almost as if he'd been hurt by Clara's remarks as much as she had. 'It doesn't matter, Leo. She's not important.'

'Yeah.' He didn't sound all that convinced. 'Car keys. In my pocket.'

She made a bit more of a meal of feeling in his jacket pocket than she strictly needed to, and Leo finally smiled. 'Stop that. Or I'll throw you over my shoulder.'

CHAPTER THIRTEEN

TWENTY MINUTES ON the motorway and then they started to meander along narrow roads, through pretty villages. Then he turned off the road entirely, the car bumping slightly on a muddy track. To the left of them, the moon reflected in a long, shimmering trail across a stretch of dark water.

'Oh, look, Leo. Is it a full moon?'

'Tomorrow, I think.'

'Your house is near here?' She couldn't see any buildings ahead of them, just fields.

'Over there.' He pointed across the water and Alex saw the shadow of a house, nestling amongst the trees, overlooking the millpond. There must be a bridge up ahead of them.

But he slowed the car, backing it onto an area of hardstanding which was surrounded on three sides by stone-built walls and covered over by a small pitched roof. He got out, walking to the back of the parking space, and suddenly she was in wonderland.

Lights led all the way to the building. Along a paved path to a bridge, which stretched across the mouth of the stream that fed into the millpond. Across the bridge and then up a sharp incline, with steps set into it, to the front door of a solid two-storey timber-framed house.

The only way to get there was to walk. Alex had her trainers packed in her bag, ready for tomorrow, along with her sports leg. But suddenly the idea of being carried across, snuggling in Leo's arms as the night breeze caught her dress, seemed unbearably tempting.

He walked around the car, opening her door. 'You can walk, can't you?'

'Yes. I just need my trainers from my bag.'

He nodded. Without a word, he lifted her out of the car, settling her in his arms. She curled her arm around his neck, feeling his warmth.

'This is lovely. It's all yours?'

'I own the land but there's a public footpath which runs from the road, along this side of the millpond and through to the village. It's a bit of a tradition that people come and fish here during the summer and I wouldn't want that to change.'

'That's nice. A hideaway with plenty of people passing back and forth on the other side of the water.'

'Yeah. That's what I like about it. I lent the place to Evie for a couple of weeks last summer, and when the paparazzi stopped at the village pub and asked how to get here, they pointed them thirty miles in the other direction.' He chuckled quietly.

'Did they ever find her?'

'No.' He stopped halfway across the bridge, turning so she could see across the millpond. 'This is one of my favourite spots.'

'It's beautiful.' The water stretched out in front of them, moving gently. There were trees and a clear, dark sky, studded with stars. It was like being in the arms of a handsome prince, who was carrying her across a gilded lake to his castle.

Leo climbed the steps to the front porch, setting her down for a moment while he opened the door and flipped the light on. When she stepped inside, the hallway was bright and warm.

'Make yourself at home. I'll go and get the coats and bags and lock the car…' He left her alone in the hallway.

Her prosthetic foot was angled slightly to accommodate the heel of a shoe, and Alex had to walk on her toes. It somehow felt right to be tiptoeing through Leo's house, exploring it, like a lost princess. The kitchen was straight ahead, modern and utilitarian, much as she would have expected. But the sitting room came as a revelation. A stone fireplace, obviously used, from the pile of wood in the hearth. Large squashy sofas in powder blue and oak cabinets, full of books and ornaments which looked like an eclectic collection, made over the years.

The dining room was just as welcoming, wood-framed French windows with patterned curtains and a distressed wooden table. It was stylish but it felt like a home, and it was light years away from his London flat.

She heard him in the hallway and went back out to meet him. 'So it's your alter ego who lives here?'

'Not really. I'm the same person here as I am in London.'

It was another piece in the puzzle. Just as Leo's secrets had filled in the blanks, made sense of a complex and seemingly disjointed personality, this house did too. There was the Leo who loved the bright lights and the excitement of London, but that Leo needed a home and this was it.

He took her bag upstairs, showing her to a comfortable, elegant room with French windows opening onto a balcony and an en suite bathroom. It was clearly appropriate that he should make cocoa, since it seemed cocktails were reserved for the London flat. He took off his jacket, sitting down on one of the sofas while Alex curled up on the other.

'I'm really sorry about tonight.' A shadow passed across his brow. 'Didn't really go to plan, did it?'

'I suppose not. But what were you going to do—let the man bleed to death?'

'No. But if he *had* to chop his finger off, I wish he'd done it some other time. This Saturday was intended to make up for rushing off last Saturday.' His phone was on the arm of the chair and he was turning it over and over restlessly.

'You don't have to make anything up to me, Leo. Is life usually so eventful with you, though?'

He laughed, shaking his head. 'No. I seem to be having a busy period at the moment. Usually, I can go for weeks on end without people keeling over in my vicinity.'

'That's good to hear. I was beginning to worry that I might be next.'

'You won't be.' A pulse beat suddenly at the side of his brow, as if he was going to prevent anything from happening to her by the sheer force of his will.

'I know. I was just joking.'

'Yeah. I wasn't.'

How could she explain to him? She'd been proud to be part of the difference that Leo had made tonight. And somehow, when they were working together with a shared aim, it felt as if their connection was strongest. Work was his way of forgetting the incessant tug of the past, and living only in the present.

She drained the last few mouthfuls of cocoa from her mug. Leo was the best man she'd ever met. And the one she could never have because his attention would always be somewhere else.

'It's late. I should go to bed.' There was nothing more that she could say.

'Yes. I'll be turning in soon. Sleep well.' He reached for the slim leather laptop case that he'd brought in with the bags, and left on the coffee table.

If it wasn't a patient, it was his phone. And if it wasn't his phone, it was emails to read or papers to review. Leo just couldn't switch off.

'Hasn't your battery run down yet?' Alex suppressed the urge to snatch the laptop from him and pour the rest of his cocoa into the keyboard.

His lips twitched into a smile. 'I always carry a spare.'

'Too bad. Goodnight.' As she walked up the stairs, she heard a quiet tone from the sitting room as his laptop booted up. However late it was, it seemed there was always one more thing that couldn't wait until the morning.

Alex always knew when she was in the country as soon as she woke up. Even with the windows tightly closed against the chill of the morning outside, she could still hear the faint chirrup of birds, and still smell the clean scents that reminded her of home.

She'd left the curtains open, knowing that she'd wake with the dawn. As light began to filter through the windows, she rolled to the edge of the bed.

This was the time in the day when she felt loss. A new day, new challenges, the sun rising outside her window. But, instead of rising to meet it, she had either to crawl or do as she was doing now, lean down to reach the collapsible crutches that were stowed in her travel bag and snap them into rigid supports. Soon enough, she'd go through the morning ritual of rubbing cream into her residual limb, checking it for any skin abrasions or blisters and pulling on the thin fabric sock which acted as a liner for her prosthesis.

But, for now, there was something missing. She couldn't tumble straight out of bed to face the bright morning that was outside her window without pausing for a moment.

It was a small thing. At first, she'd mourned her leg in the same way that she would have mourned a death. But that had eased, and if each new day brought a moment of remembrance then perhaps that was what it was supposed to do. A moment when she could remember how things were and how she'd turned that around.

She swung her body between the crutches, over to the window. The shadows she'd seen outside last night were now a deep balcony, big enough to sit on and have breakfast in the summer. When she craned round she could see that it ran along the whole of the back of the house, and that there were doors leading onto it further down. Leo's bedroom, maybe.

She could imagine him walking along the balcony to tap on her window. Climbing up with a rose between his teeth. Alex grinned at the thought. Maybe not between his teeth—that was a little makeshift for Leo. It would have to be his buttonhole.

And on summer mornings maybe he sat out here, watching the sun rise. Coffee and orange juice, alone with the sounds of the countryside.

She stared at the frost-sprinkled fields on the horizon, allowing the balcony to drop into soft focus. Morning was the time when loss might be touched and then left behind. But she couldn't touch Leo and then leave *him* behind.

The view from her window would still be here when she was washed and dressed. Alex made her way into the shining, white-tiled bathroom and opened the door of the shower enclosure, ready to contemplate her next move.

A non-slip mat. Good. A couple of grab rails. Not all that common in a private house, but even better. She leaned forward to test the rigidity of one of them, finding it firm and in exactly the right place. Then a little sprinkle of dust fell from it, red on the white tiles.

She leaned down to inspect it. Brick dust. The grab rail was solid and secure enough, though…

These were new. They were for her.

It wasn't what he'd done, but the motive behind it. Leo had never shown any doubt as to her independence. This was his practical version of chocolates on her pillow. Freshly squeezed orange juice in the morning, or thick towels left on her bed. He'd taken the time to come down here and install a pair of grab rails. They didn't have red ribbons tied around them but it was the sweetest thing he could have done.

Leo had hoped that working until his head swam with exhaustion would guarantee unbroken sleep when he finally did go to bed. But still he woke in the night, aware of Alex's silent presence in the house.

He couldn't allow himself to contemplate the short walk along the balcony, the idea of tapping on the glass and finding Alex awake and waiting for him. It might be below zero out there but he had a feeling that being packed in ice couldn't cool the heat which seemed to draw him to her.

Breakfast was easier because he had something to do, to divert his attention from her smile. And this morning she *was* smiling, obviously enjoying the bright morning as much as he was.

'Ready to go?' Alex's holdall was in the hall, the ruined silver sandals in a plastic bag on top of it. She was dressed in a warm fleece top and leggings, her hair scrunched into a ponytail. The one delicious reminder of last night was the delicate shine of clear polish on her fingernails.

'Yes. You've got the coordinates?' Alex had given him a set of coordinates instead of a postcode to enter into the satnav. Clearly, her father's farm was relatively remote.

'Yep.' Leo decided that asking whether he could carry her over the bridge to the car was one step too far in wanting to recreate last night.

The morning was cold and crisp, seeming to hold all the potential of a new day. As he drove, the busy patchwork of villages and towns gave way to the more open landscape of the countryside.

'Is this right?' They'd reached the brow of a hill and, in the clear morning, he could see a smudge on the horizon which looked like the sea. In between there were just fields, dotted with clumps of trees and criss-crossed by narrow roads.

'Yep. Turn off right there.' She pointed to a track which wound around the edge of a field, leading to a large brick-built barn.

'You climb in a barn?'

'It's been converted. Wait till you get there.' There was a hint of pride in her voice which told Leo that the barn had been subjected to Alex's endless ingenuity and energy. This he had to see.

As they drew nearer, he could see a battered truck parked outside. He stopped next to it on the hardstanding area and Alex jumped out of the car, obviously eager to show him inside.

Two sets of doors acted as an air lock. It was still chilly inside the barn but a good few degrees warmer than outside.

'Dad…' Alex ran over to a man who was sweeping the floor, greeting him with a hug. 'This is Leo.'

Leo stepped forward, taking the man's outstretched hand. Although his hair was salt-and-pepper grey, he had the same thoughtful brown eyes as Alex.

'Howard Jackson. I've been listening to the programmes that Alex has been doing with you. I'm delighted to get the chance to meet you.'

A little shiver of embarrassment hit Leo. It felt as if he and Alex had been carrying out a very public exercise in intimacy over the last three weeks, and that had been okay up till now. Better than okay—it had made callers feel at ease and allowed everyone to talk freely. But at this moment it felt as if he needed to apologise for it.

'We've been… Alex has been great. She's a natural…'

'Nice of you to say so.' Howard smiled at his daughter. *His* daughter. 'I detected a fair bit of guidance on your part.'

'More than a bit, Dad. Leo's taught me a lot.'

'It's just a matter of…' Leo shrugged. This wasn't just an exercise in seeing who could compliment who the most; it was suddenly important. 'Alex gave us a lot of direction about what issues to cover. We helped her present them in a way she was comfortable with.'

Howard chuckled, apparently unfazed by the idea of his daughter discussing sex, thinly disguised as body issues, on the radio. 'I like to call it *direction* as well. Even if she doesn't compromise about exactly which direction she's going in.'

Alex rolled her eyes, nudging her father in the ribs. 'Where's Mum?'

'She's descaling the urn. Should be finished by now; I was just about to go and collect her.' Howard pulled a bunch of keys from his pocket and Alex took them from him.

'I'll go. You can show Leo around.'

And then she was gone, in a flurry of smiles and activity, leaving Leo standing alone with Howard. Somehow he got the impression that this had been some kind of plan.

Leo looked around the space, aware that Howard's gaze was on him. The whole of one side comprised a set of climbing walls, ranging from very easy to what looked like pretty difficult. There was a play area for younger children and thick crash mats were stacked in the corner, ready to transform the area into a safe space where kids could try things out without fear of hurting themselves.

'This is impressive. How often do you use this place?'

'Only a couple of times a month in the winter, because of the cost of heating it. We put in a false ceiling, and partitioned the space to make it viable. This area's about a third of the internal floor area.'

'It's a good size, though. And it's warm enough in here.'

'Yes, we have infrared heaters and they take the chill off. Once we get twenty or thirty people in here it's fine for activities. And in the summer we can take the dividing partition down and do more.'

'What kind of things?' This was obviously very well thought out.

'There's a riding stable close by, and they come and do lessons from time to time. We have a picnic area, and Alex organises family days and different activities. She's even got an eye on laying a proper running surface, but that's all pie in the sky at the moment.'

'At the moment…' Leo grinned. That sounded expensive but, if he knew anything about Alex, it wouldn't be pie in the sky for too much longer. She'd find a way.

Howard chuckled. 'Yes.'

'Do you get many down from London? It's a fair drive.'

'Two, maybe three cars full; the London parents take turns with the driving. There's local demand as well, and we never have any spare places for our activities. Safety considerations limit how many people we can have here at once.'

'This must all have taken a while.'

'Nine years.' Howard stuffed his hands into the pockets of his jacket, looking around as if suddenly he couldn't quite believe they'd done it all. 'We started small. The barn was on some extra land that I'd bought, and surplus to requirements. Alex's brothers and I built her the first climbing wall, in the summer after she lost her leg.'

A lump formed in Leo's throat. 'So this is where it all started?'

'Yes. The number of times I saw her fall off that damn thing, and then get right back up and try again…' Howard shrugged. 'I don't know where she gets it from. Her mother, probably.'

Leo doubted that was entirely true. He could see the same tough determination in Howard as he saw in Alex, and he couldn't help liking him. Which made him feel like a fraud for hiding the way he'd failed Alex from her father.

'I… I met Alex a while ago. At a party.'

'Yes, she told me. Some fancy dress thing…'

'Yes. It was actually the night before she had her accident.' This was turning into a confession but it was one he should make. 'We spent the night…just talking.'

Howard laughed. 'Alex always did have a lot to say for herself.'

'I meant…' He felt like a teenager, telling his date's father that he respected her and that he wouldn't dream of doing anything more than holding her hand.

'I know what you meant. I'm her father, not her gatekeeper. Alex made that very clear to me from a very early age.' Howard turned as if that was an end to it.

'I walked her to the bus stop in the morning. I didn't take her all the way home… I'm sorry.'

Howard nodded, facing him quietly. 'Do you know what *I* did? Alex used to call us every Sunday morning. I was busy on the farm and when she didn't call that day, I didn't think anything of it. When my wife got the call from the hospital, she had to run across the fields to find me.'

Leo stared at him. There were no words, but Howard seemed to be able to find some.

'When Alex was born, her mother put her into my arms and I counted her fingers and toes. Then I promised her that I'd always keep her safe.' Howard leaned towards him. 'You only found out about the accident recently?'

'I called her that day, but she didn't answer. I thought she…' Leo shrugged. 'You know. You call, and they've thought better of it and don't answer.'

Howard chuckled. 'Yeah. I've been there a few times too. Look, you can't blame yourself for something like this. Give it time.'

Leo wasn't convinced of that. But somehow it was as if Alex had spoken to him. He wondered whether she'd put him alone with her father for exactly the same reason that she'd put Carys's father with the other parents. He wouldn't put it past her.

'Thank you.'

'Don't thank me.' Howard seemed just as aware of their places in Alex's master plan as he was. 'But you can come and give me a hand with those crash mats...'

CHAPTER FOURTEEN

IT HAD TAKEN a couple of hours' work before the space was ready, but the transformation was complete. There was enough time for soup and sandwiches at noon, before the first cars started to arrive.

He recognised some of the people. Hayley was there with Alice, and Sam broke free from his mother's hand, tugging at Leo's jacket to tell him that today they were going to climb. Carys's father hovered by the doorway and Howard marched up to him, shaking his hand and taking him and Carys on a guided tour of all the facilities that the barn had to offer. Alex was busy, making sure she spoke to everyone and that the helpers were all in place before anyone started to climb.

At three o'clock refreshments were served, and Alex brought him coffee. 'Enjoying yourself?'

'You need an answer to that?'

She grinned up at him. 'Nah. I saw you at the wall with Sam. He doesn't give up, does he?'

'Incorrigible. Like someone else I know.'

'Can't think who you mean.' She looked around to make sure they weren't being overheard. 'The last of the trustees called me just now, so I can finish the paperwork on Alice's grant in the morning. I've asked her mother if I can pop in for a chat tomorrow, before the radio show.'

'That's great. Thanks.' Leo knew what Alex was asking.

'I don't suppose you want to change your mind and come along with me?'

'No. I don't suppose I do. This is your forte. I prefer to stay at arm's length.'

She shot him an incredulous look. 'How can you say that? You connect with people all the time, as a doctor and on the radio.'

'That's different.'

Alex flushed pink. That was generally a sign that she wasn't going to accept his stonewalling tactics. 'So it's okay to commit emotionally to people you don't know, but not to people you do…' She pressed her lips together. Perhaps she'd said more than she meant to.

He should walk away. Before they got onto why he couldn't commit to her. Because he had a feeling that this was where this was leading. 'Hey. Do me a favour, will you?'

'Of course.'

'Give me a break?'

She laughed suddenly, shaking her head. Maybe she was as relieved as he was to just steer away from a question that ultimately didn't have any answer. 'Yeah. Always.'

'Thanks.'

'Anyway, I think someone's got a job for you.' She pointed over to the most difficult climbing wall and he saw Sam standing at the bottom of it, gazing fixedly in his direction.

'He has *got* to be kidding…'

'I don't think he is. Go and use that charm of yours to talk him out of it.'

The last words that Leo said on-air to her were the ones that mattered the most to him. The ones he really meant. There had been so many callers that they'd been almost overwhelmed and hardly had time for anything else. But he made sure there was time for this.

'This last month has been both inspiring and life-changing for me. It's been an honour to make that journey with you, Alex.'

'Thanks, Leo. I've really enjoyed it.'

'We must do this again, soon.' He held her gaze, trying to show her that this wasn't just a hollow courtesy.

'I'd love to.' He thought he saw the glint of a tear in her eye, and he turned to a commercial before anyone noticed the lump in his throat.

She watched him silently as he took off his headphones and switched off the sound link to the control room. Then she puffed out a breath.

'So this is it…'

'I never say anything I don't mean on the radio.'

'Too many witnesses?'

Leo shook his head. 'Nah. It's just too important to me.'

She gave him a hesitant smile. 'You could…call me. I promise I'll get back to you this time.'

That was all he wanted to hear. 'I know where you live now. If you don't get back to me I *will* find you.'

'That's it.' Rhona put the last of the thank you letters into an envelope and added it to the pile. 'How are you doing with the cheques?'

'They're all ready for the bank.' It had taken all morning and half the afternoon to deal with all the letters and cheques that had been received in the post since last week. Alex was grateful for every word, every penny, but it presented a whole new set of challenges for the charity.

'Growing pains…' Rhona rested her chin on her hand, staring across the desks.

'Yeah. It's going to be a lot of work, spending all this

money wisely.' Alex traced the tip of her pencil across her writing pad.

'I blame Leo. And you, of course.'

'Thanks. Nice to know I'm the architect of my own difficulties.' She stared at the complex doodle in front of her. Boxes in boxes in boxes. That was how she'd felt for the last week. She'd known that Leo wouldn't be in touch until after the weekend; he'd been busy filming for a TV special. And today he'd be at his surgery and then the radio station for his Monday evening show. Maybe she could start hoping for a call tomorrow evening.

'We'll work it out.' Alex added a couple of optimistic curlicues to the doodle and then jumped as a loud rap sounded on the door and it swung open.

Leo. The tip of Alex's pencil broke, lead spinning across the desk. Instead of breezing in, the way he normally did, he was standing stock-still in the doorway. And he was smiling.

'Anyone for cake?' He had a box from the cake shop around the corner balanced on top of three takeaway cups in a cardboard holder.

'Leo! Don't be ridiculous—of course we want cake.' Rhona pulled him into the office, slamming the door behind him to prevent any possibility of escape.

He grinned, and Alex's heart lurched dangerously. Had he somehow become more handsome in the last week, or had she really missed him that much?

'Sit down.' Rhona pushed a chair up for him and grabbed the box from his hand, opening it. 'Ah, Leo. You know the way to a woman's heart...'

He chuckled, putting a cardboard cup down in front of her and a second on Rhona's desk, keeping the smaller cup for himself.

'Espresso?' It was all Alex could think of to say. Still

she couldn't stop staring at him, but that was okay because his gaze had never left her face.

'Yeah. I need to stay awake. I've been busy.'

He probably had been. But *busy* was Leo's excuse for everything. All the same, he was here, and all the reasons why she shouldn't miss him were crushed under the weight of his smile.

'I'm just off to the bank. Don't eat my cake...' Rhona snatched up the pile of cheques from Alex's desk.

'It's my turn.' Alex shot her an apologetic look. She supposed that she and Leo had made Rhona feel as if she was the third person who made up a crowd. 'I'll go later.'

'I don't mind. You and Leo stay here...'

'Actually...' Leo put a stop to the discussion. 'I have something I wanted to discuss with you both. What are you doing on Saturday?'

Alex looked at her watch. Twelve thirty, and the barn was already filling up. They'd decided to use the larger area because of the number of people coming today, and she had taken the previous day off work to help clear the space. Early this morning, a group of men had turned up with a van and erected a stage, messed around with amplifiers and microphones until everything was exactly to their liking and then left again. And now nothing seemed to be happening.

'Where is he? Suppose they don't turn up?' she whispered frantically to Rhona.

'You said it yourself—Leo's never early. We've got another half an hour.'

'Yes, but...' They'd brought all of these people down here on the promise of an unspecified music performance, after Leo had pointed out that making what they were planning public was likely to bring an influx of outsiders that they couldn't cope with. They had a sound stage and equipment, but there had been no word from Leo.

She pulled out her phone and looked at it. Nothing. And it was impossible that Leo didn't have his phone with him. He'd call if there was a problem.

'You just want to see him,' Rhona observed sagely.

'No...' Yes, actually. 'At the moment I'd just like to see someone on that stage...'

Suddenly the door at the far end of the barn, next to the stage, opened. Her father ushered Leo through it and Alex's heart thumped in her chest. Then a young man walked through the door, climbing up onto the stage.

Bobby Carusoe. The name was passed around the scattered audience like a brush fire. Six number one hits in a row. The young star who had taken both America and Europe by storm and who was in the UK for six weeks between tours. Every teenage girl's dream.

Every head turned towards him, mouths gaping open. Bobby picked up a microphone and addressed the stunned crowd.

'Is everyone here yet?'

'No...' Rhona shouted at the top of her voice, from where she and Alex were standing at the back. 'It's supposed to start at one o'clock...'

'Then there's time to meet everyone.' A communal gasp went up. 'But first I'd like you all to meet a good friend of mine.'

'Friend?' Alex hissed at Rhona, 'What's he done now? Leo didn't say anything about a friend.'

'Oh, my giddy aunt...' Rhona nodded towards the stage, where Leo was helping a young woman in high heels and a shimmering dress up the steps. She ran towards Bobby, smiling up at him when he put his arm around her shoulder. 'It's Aleesha.'

Bobby and Aleesha waved and everyone waved back.

Then Aleesha put her finger to her lips, and everyone fell silent.

'Bobby and I have a new album, due to come out next week. And we thought you might like to be the first to hear some of the songs.'

A deafening *'Yes!'* sounded through the barn, and Alex nudged Rhona in the ribs.

'I didn't know that. What on earth are they going to sing together?' Bobby was known for his soulful love songs, but Aleesha's style was more upbeat. It didn't seem as if they had an awful lot in common.

'Who cares? They're here, aren't they?'

Bobby jumped down from the stage and lifted his arms to swing Aleesha down next to him. Alex moved forward, afraid that there might be a crush around them, but Leo was there with another man and the carefully calculated child to helper ratio meant that everyone kept relatively calm. Bobby and Aleesha split up, obviously intent on getting to speak to everyone, however briefly.

Alex was trembling. She'd been unsure about Leo's idea at first, knowing that it might be difficult to control a barn full of teenagers in the presence of a pop idol. But they'd talked it through and Leo had answered all of her questions. Bobby's people would be instructed to stay back, and treat the kids with care and respect, and there would be enough adults there to make sure that there was no risk of injury to anyone. And he'd been right. Although everyone was excited, the event was well under control.

Leo was making his way over to her, stopping briefly to exchange a few words with some of the teenagers and their parents. The thought that Bobby and Aleesha were here, in her dad's barn, and that they were going to sing, paled into insignificance. Leo was here, and he was making straight for her.

'You made it.' She smiled up at him.

'Always do.' He grinned back.

'What are they going to sing? I can't imagine that they'd find anything that they both liked, let alone could sing together.'

'The new album's all oldies. Some rock and roll, a few ballads, done in their own way. It's interesting.'

'You've heard it?'

'They played it in the car on the way down.'

'How did you swing this, Leo? Bobby *and* Aleesha?'

'I told you. Friend of a friend. And, anyway, they're pretty much inseparable.'

'They're…going out?'

Leo nodded. 'Yep. For about a year now, only it's been a big secret. This album's a big risk for both of them; not only are they trying out some different kinds of music but they're going to go public with the fans. How many more people are you expecting?'

'Well, we've got forty kids and the same number of parents and helpers now. I reckon about another twenty of each.'

Leo nodded. 'Sounds good.' His fingers brushed the back of her hand. Then again, lingering a little longer this time. She took his arm, smiling up at him.

'Anyone remember this?' Bobby sang a couple of chords and Aleesha nodded and joined in.

'I do…' Alex's father shouted from the side of the stage.

'Help us out with the words, then.' Aleesha grinned down at him, and he laughed.

The two of them were just perfect. Keeping everyone under control so that parents and helpers were able to stand back and enjoy the performance too. The chemistry between them was obvious, and they talked with the audience almost as much as they sang.

'Dad loves this one. He used to sing it to us when we were kids.'

Her father was singing now and Aleesha walked over to him, bending down to share her microphone for a couple of bars. Bobby's hand went to his heart in an exaggerated expression of loss and then he beckoned Aleesha back and she strutted across the stage, into his arms.

'Never mind, Howard...' one of the helpers shouted above the music, and her father laughed uproariously.

'Glad you did this?' Leo leaned towards her.

'Yes. It was a risk, but... Yes, I'm so glad we did it.' She moved a little closer to him and felt his arm light around her shoulder. Then tighter, more possessive. That was another risk, but one that suddenly seemed worth taking.

Bobby and Aleesha stayed for three hours, far beyond what anyone expected, singing, talking to everyone and posing for photographs. Alex tried to think of words to thank them enough and failed, but they both seemed to get the message. Then they were whisked away in a convoy of three black SUVs.

It was the tidiest concert crowd that Alex had ever seen. Bags were filled with rubbish and taken away. Chairs were folded and stacked neatly and the floor was swept. Alice's mother even attempted to clean the sound stage before Leo bounded up the steps and coaxed her away from the electrical equipment.

'Home?' Leo murmured the word as Alex waved the last of the cars off.

'Yes. Which one?'

He chuckled. 'Any one you like. Lady's privilege.'

She had her overnight things with her, after staying with her parents last night, and they could go anywhere. 'The country, maybe?'

'Give me your car keys. I'll programme your satnav.'

CHAPTER FIFTEEN

SHE LOST LEO behind a large truck, blocking the road through one of the villages. It was dark by the time she swung off the road and onto the track which led to his house, and Alex manoeuvred onto the hardstanding and found the switch for the lights.

He'd dropped his front door key in her hand before climbing into his own car, and all she had to do was follow the trail of lights. Alex hauled her bag out of the boot, carrying it across the bridge and dumping it in the front hall.

She could see headlights, coming towards her along the track. It could only be Leo, and he must see the lights on the bridge ahead of him by now. Pulling the front door to behind her, she walked down the steps and onto the bridge.

His car swung onto the hardstanding next to hers and the headlights almost blinded her. When he switched them off the darkness seemed deeper, and then he came striding out of the gloom towards her.

'Is this a metaphor?' His hands rested lightly on her waist, his lips just an inch away from hers.

'Now you mention it... Maybe.' It had just seemed appropriate to meet him here. Suspended above the water, each reaching out for the other, unsure whether this was anything but a brief moment in the darkness. But, however brief, it was worth any amount of risk.

'I haven't been with anyone in a while.' He seemed

to want her to know that what the papers said about him wasn't true and that this was something special. Leo was finally allowing someone to touch him.

Alex reached up, tracing her fingers across the side of his face. 'I'd be happy to help you out with anything you're unsure of…'

Leo grinned. 'I said it's been a while. I still know what to do.'

Then he kissed her, his lips warm and very tender. She wrapped her arms around his neck, pulling him close. Something wild broke through the last vestiges of doubt and then there was only Leo, his body hard against hers in the cold evening air.

He pulled the zip of her jacket in a movement that was urgent, almost wild. His hand found her breast and, even though there were layers of clothing between them, she imagined she could feel his touch. Alex heard her own whimper of longing, smothered by his kiss.

'I want you *now*…' She nipped at the lobe of his ear and felt his body jolt, like an engine being jerked from first gear straight into overdrive.

'I want you every place and every way.' He backed against the stone parapet, lifting her against him. For one delicious moment she thought that *this* place and *this* way was going to be the start of it all, however unlikely and impractical. Wrapping one arm around his neck, she found the fastening of his jeans with her other hand.

'Forget the metaphor, Alex. It's far too cold. And uncomfortable.'

'I don't want comfort. I don't want pretty words.' She wanted him. Not his practised charm, which would leave her smiling but unchanged. She wanted that raw edge, the one that would respond only to need and be satisfied only with taking everything.

'Hold on tight, then.' He settled her weight against his

and she wrapped her legs around his hips. Striding across the bridge, he climbed the steps to the front door, kicking it closed behind him.

He paused in the hallway and she felt him reach into his pocket. Then he put something on the hallstand. 'I'll leave this here…'

She twisted round to look. It was his phone. Alex kissed him, and he suddenly seemed to lose interest in who might or might not be calling him and started to stride up the stairs.

She caught the frame of his bedroom doorway with one hand as they passed through it, jerking them to a halt. 'Lights, Leo.'

'Yeah…' He slammed one hand against the wall and she squeezed her eyes closed as the bedroom was bathed in bright light. Felt him move, and then tip her backwards. Her hands instinctively clutched tighter around his shoulders as she felt herself falling with him onto the bed.

'Open them…' She felt his lips brush her closed eyelids. 'Open your eyes.'

It was almost a command—that she see him, and he see her. Nothing hidden. She blinked and Leo's smile snapped into focus for one brief moment, before he kissed her again.

Her whole body was trembling, aching for him, and it seemed like a criminal act to break the spontaneity. But facts were facts and Leo would find a way to make things all right. 'My bag, Leo…' She felt her lips twist into a grimace. 'I need my crutch, for the bathroom.'

The sweet touch of his hands never faltered. The melting blue of his eyes suddenly made her want to cry.

'If that's what you want, I'll get it.' His fingers found the side of her face, caressing gently. 'Whatever you need, Alex. But I don't need to smell soap when I have your scent. And what's mine is yours. We can manage.'

We can manage. Tonight was all about what they could do together, not whether she could do anything on her own.

'I guess… Three legs is enough for anyone.'

'Yeah. Three legs, four arms…'

'Four eyes, eight fingers.' She used one of those fingers to caress his lips. 'One of me, and one of you…'

'*That*, I'm planning on changing.' He sat up on the bed, drawing her along with him, holding her close. 'Very soon.'

The rhythm didn't break. Urgent, and yet there was time to trade kisses along the way. It never faltered, not when he unbuttoned her shirt, or when she unbuttoned his. Not when she took off her prosthesis, or when he reached for the condoms in the drawer beside the bed.

'Hold me…please…' His eyes were dark and, stretched out under him, she could feel his erection nudging against her. Waiting. Drawing out this last moment until it was a confection of feverish anticipation.

She wrapped her arms around his neck and he reached down. They gasped together as he slid inside. Just a little way.

'Please, Alex…' His fingers gripped her right thigh, then traced down to her knee. Without thinking, she'd kept her right leg away from his back, not sure how he'd react to feeling her foreshortened limb against him, but now she curled both legs around his hips, holding him tight, pulling him further inside.

They both cried out together. Staring into each other's eyes, breathing hard. Tilting her hips, she pushed against him, feeling him slide deeper.

One moment of stillness, to sink into his gaze, and then Leo moved. His gasp was more than pleasure. It was triumph and need, helplessness and mastery.

'Are you going to make me wait, Leo?'

'No, honey. We've waited long enough.' He started to move and the trembling excitement turned into a roar.

She didn't have to reach for the orgasm—it was just there, building inside until she came in his arms.

'Again?' He kissed her neck, and she shivered at the touch of his lips against her skin.

'Again?'

He changed position slightly, angling his hips to set off a shower of new sensations. 'Again.'

After she'd come the second time, her body straining against his so hard that Leo had almost lost himself, she'd rolled him over onto his back and climbed on top of him. His sweet Alexandra. Taking him until all he knew was that he'd surrendered to her completely, and all he wanted to do was to shout her name out loud.

Perhaps he had. He thought he might have done, but then she'd pushed him further than he'd ever been before. She was strong and athletic, and yet soft at the same time, and when she pinned him down he could watch each movement of her body. Feel each corresponding sensation.

He didn't even properly remember what the orgasm had felt like. Just that he was being pulled into it by an overwhelming force. And that by the time she was done with him all he could do was to curl up with her on the bed, still craving her touch, but more content than he'd thought he ever could be.

They'd slept a little, and then talked a little. Then Leo had gone downstairs to fetch a bottle of champagne. Just the right thing at the right time. Leo, who charmed his way through every situation so adroitly. Only at the moment he seemed deliciously clumsy, spilling half the contents of his glass on the pillow when he pulled her close again to kiss her. And, when he ran a bath, climbing into the hot, foaming water with her, half of it slopped all over the floor and he had to get out and mop the mess up.

Even that was bliss. Lying back in the water, watching his strong body. Each flex of muscle, every square inch of perfect flesh, was capable of giving pleasure. And he was all hers for the night.

And she was his. When the sun rose, he caught her up from the bed, carrying her over to the window, and they watched the flaming sky together. Then breakfast in bed, tangled in each other's arms. And then they made love again. Lazy, sensual, not driven by the urgency of last night, but time enough to explore each sensation together.

When Leo opened his eyes, the sun was high in the sky and Alex was still sleeping. He watched her for a while, wondering vaguely what time it was. It didn't matter. There was nothing that he could think of to do today, except share it with her.

A quiet beep sounded from downstairs. Must be her phone. Only…

His phone wasn't on the nightstand, where it usually lay. Suddenly he was on the move. Rolling out of bed, grabbing his underwear and running down the stairs. When he'd left his phone downstairs he'd reckoned on retrieving it later in the evening but, wrapped in the warmth of their lovemaking, he'd forgotten all about it.

He picked it up, letting out a sharp curse. Three messages, two missed calls. He scrolled through the messages. Justin's could wait. Evie had texted to say that she and Arielle were leaving London for a few days and they'd catch him when they got back. And there was one from Aleesha, saying that she and Bobby had enjoyed their day yesterday and that they'd have to do it all again some time.

He smiled, walking into the kitchen as he flipped over to the missed calls. Two from his mother. Suddenly the past reared up and smacked him in the face and his hand shook as he pressed the icon to return the call.

'Come on… Come on.' The call switched to voicemail and he ended it. No, he didn't want to leave a message.

He called again and this time his mother answered.

'Mum… Everything okay?' He heard the tremor in his voice.

'Yes, of course it is, darling. I was just calling to remind you about dinner on Tuesday. With Carl and Peter.'

'Oh…yeah. I've got it in my diary. Thanks, Mum.'

'Leo. Whatever's the matter?'

There was seldom any way of fooling her acute radar when it came to her son.

'Nothing…' That wasn't going to wash. She'd only start worrying about him. 'I had a long day yesterday, and I didn't sleep much last night. I've only just got up and there are a load of messages on my phone.'

'Oh, for goodness' sake, Leo. It's Sunday. They can wait, can't they?'

'Yeah. Okay, Mum. Look, I'm standing in my underwear in the kitchen.'

'That I *didn't* want to know. Go and put some clothes on.'

'Okay. See you on Tuesday evening, then. About seven-ish?'

'That'll be fine. And don't bring any wine this time; your father's just gone out and bought two cases, and he's left them in the kitchen for me to trip over. My only hope of getting them out of the way is to drink as much of it as we can.'

Leo ended the call and put the phone down on the counter top. There was nothing to worry about. Everything was okay, so why did it still feel as if his heart was trying to pound its way through his ribcage?

He knew why. He'd finally let go with Alex. Forgotten about everything else and surrendered himself completely to her. It made no difference that the fears which had propelled him downstairs this morning had been unfounded. His guilt was that of a watchman who had deserted his post.

A bump from upstairs disturbed his reverie. Now what? He took the stairs two at a time and when he reached the bedroom he found Alex sitting on the bed, wrapped in his dressing gown and rubbing her knee.

'Are you okay?'

She tipped her head up towards him, smiling through the tears in her eyes. 'Yes, I'm fine. Just took a tumble.'

She must have got out of bed when he was downstairs. He'd made sure to pick up their discarded clothes from the floor when he'd got up yesterday evening and, without thinking, he'd moved her prosthetic leg away from the bedside and into the corner, where they couldn't trip over it.

'Did you hurt yourself?'

'No. You have nice thick carpet.'

Leo suddenly realised that she was looking at the phone in his hand. In his panic, he'd broken his promise to her. *We can manage*. He'd put all the things that kept her independent out of reach, and then left her on her own.

He dropped the phone onto the floor and walked over to her, kneeling in front of her. 'Alex, I'm so sorry.'

'It's okay.' One tear trailed down her cheek and she brushed it away. 'I'm used to thinking about these things. You shouldn't have to.'

That wasn't the way it had been last night. But he'd messed up badly and he couldn't expect her to allow him the precious trust that she'd shown last night. 'I'll get your bag.'

'Yes, thanks. I'll go and have a shower in the other bathroom, if that's okay.' She smiled up at him. 'There are grab rails.'

He wanted to say that she didn't need grab rails—that she could hold onto him. But the truth was that she did—because he couldn't be relied on, couldn't be the man she deserved.

'You've finished your calls?' She nodded at the phone, lying on the floor.

'Oh. Yeah. Nothing urgent.' Another layer of misery folded around his heart. That was the real reason for her tears. He'd got out of bed so hurriedly that he couldn't have failed to wake her up, and she'd heard him downstairs. It felt almost as if he'd been caught being unfaithful to her. Leo was under no illusions that he'd betrayed her trust.

He stood, catching up his jeans from the washing basket and pulling them on. It was suddenly chilling to be this naked in front of her. 'I'll bring your bag, and then I'll go and get us something to eat.'

She nodded. 'Thanks. That would be nice.'

Alex had gulped down the coffee he'd made and pushed the banana pancakes around on her plate, in a gesture towards eating them.

'What are you doing today?' Maybe she'd stay and they could try to work this out. Although Leo couldn't think how they were going to do that.

'I should get home. I…' She shrugged.

'You're not coming back, are you?' He'd seen women decide not to come back before, and he knew the signs. Maybe time had softened the memory, but he didn't recall it hurting quite as much as this.

'No, I need… With my leg, Leo, I need to…' She lapsed suddenly into silence.

'If you want to give me a reason then give one. If you don't, that's fine. But the one thing I won't take from you is that it's because of your leg, Alex. That's not a reason and we both know that.'

'Yes, we do.' She gave a sudden, all too brief, smile. 'I need to feel that you might be able to…that for just some of the time you can forget everything else and be with me, without regretting it afterwards. I don't think that's going to happen.'

He could tell her that it would. He could tell her he'd make it happen, but he'd be lying. The panic he'd felt this morning, the tearing regret that he'd been so stupid as to lose himself with Alex, had been a gut reaction but it had been there. She deserved a great deal more than that.

'No, it's not. I'm sorry, Alex.'

'We took a risk and it didn't work out. That's okay.' She looked up at him suddenly. 'Would you do something for me, please?'

'Of course.'

'I want you to delete my number from your phone. And I'll delete yours. I don't want us to be…' Alex gave a little shrug.

She didn't need to explain. The sudden impulse to beg her not to was almost too much for Leo, but he knew this was the right thing to do. 'You don't want me to be looking at my phone, wondering if you've called, do you. Because you're not going to.'

'No. I'm not.'

It seemed so final, but at least this was real. In some ways this was the most compassionate thing she could have done, in a situation that was tearing him apart. Leo took his phone from his pocket and, with shaking fingers, he found her number and deleted it. When he looked up, he saw that Alex was doing the same.

She stood up, seeming to shed whatever she felt about that, suddenly brisk. 'I should get going.'

He fetched her bag from upstairs, trying not to look at the rumpled bed. Trying not to smell the faint scent of their lovemaking, which still perfumed the air. By the time he got back downstairs, she was in her coat and looking for her car keys in her handbag.

'I'll take your things to the car…'

Alex shook her head. 'I can manage. Thank you.' She took her bag and turned, opening the front door. Leo watched her go. Across the bridge, alone this time. Then she put her things into the car and the engine choked uncertainly into life.

He wanted to shout the words after her, but he could only whisper them. Because shouting them might elicit some response from her, and he knew that he should just let her go.

'Be happy.'

CHAPTER SIXTEEN

HER KNEE STILL throbbed a little from when she'd crashed down on all fours. She'd woken with a start when Leo had got out of bed, and realised almost immediately that she'd lost him. Swinging herself out of bed and across the room should have been easy—she'd managed enough times before—but she'd been so shaken by grief that she'd fallen.

Somehow, she made it down the track without either driving into the millpond or crashing into a tree. But any further and tears would have blinded her. Alex pulled off the road into an entranceway to a field, switched off the engine and then crashed her fist into the steering wheel.

This might feel a little better if she hated Leo. If she could convince herself that he wasn't a good man. If he hadn't made love to her that way last night. He'd meant it. She knew he'd really meant it.

But none of that mattered. Leo had just been on loan to her. For one gorgeous night she'd thought that he could live for the moment, in the here and now, and then the past had clawed him back again. Alex couldn't forget the guilt and regret on his face when he'd appeared in the doorway. Last night had meant something to both of them and that look had taken it all back, soured and destroyed it.

She pulled a tissue from the glove compartment. She was going to cry. She could feel it welling up inside, an insistent and wordless agony. All she could do was to get it over with. She'd fallen down and, however much it hurt, she was going to have to get back up again.

Getting back up again hadn't been so easy. Alex missed Leo every day. Every time she walked past the cake shop on the way to the charity's office. Every time someone wrote to her or phoned her, saying that they'd heard her on the radio.

The dark days of March trickled away and became the slightly less dark days of April. It would be summer soon. Alice had been fitted for her running blade and was beginning to learn to run with it. She'd asked Alex to put a photograph up on the charity's website, in the hope that the anonymous donor might see it and know how much it meant to her. Perhaps Leo would. Perhaps he'd see it and smile.

'Look at these!' Rhona came flying into the office, a bunch of yellow roses in her hand, her face flushed with pleasure.

'They're lovely. You and Tom had a good weekend, then?'

'It was a great weekend. But Tom doesn't send yellow roses—he sends red ones. And not two dozen long-stemmed ones either; we're saving for the wedding.' Rhona put the flowers down on Alex's desk. 'These are for you.'

'Me?' Two dozen long-stems sounded suspiciously like Leo. Or maybe he was just the first person who sprang to mind because she'd been thinking about him again, on her way to work this morning.

'You. Yellow roses. That's for friendship, in case you were wondering.'

'Who are they from?' Alex didn't dare touch them. If they weren't from Leo then it meant they must be from someone else. And receiving roses from someone else felt somehow disloyal. Even if there was nothing between her and Leo any more.

'How do I know?' Rhona rolled her eyes and plucked a small envelope from the side of the wrapping. 'It's knobbly...'

'Well, what is it?'

'Oh, for goodness' sake.' Rhona opened the envelope and took out a thumb drive. 'Here. Roses and electronic media. And...'

She handed the card to Alex. Leo's firm, flowing handwriting.

Thank you.

She dropped the card onto her desk as if it had just burned her fingers.

'So they are from Leo?' Rhona raised her eyebrows.

'Yes.'

Rhona slumped into her chair. 'What do you want to do about it, honey?'

'I... I don't know. I can't do anything about it.' She and Rhona had been through all this. She'd taken a risk and it hadn't worked out. That had hurt so badly that she couldn't take another.

'What do you say I put the flowers in water and go down and get a couple of coffees from the shop? Then we'll think about the thumb drive.'

'Okay. Thanks.' Alex pushed the flowers away from her as if they might burn her.

The flowers were arranged, coffee was fetched, and she and Rhona sat in front of Rhona's computer.

'Sure you want me to see this?' Rhona slotted the thumb drive into the USB port.

'Yeah. It's okay. Yellow roses, right?' The message was friendship. It was probably photographs from the radio station, something like that.

Rhona clicked on a folder and then on the icon inside. A sound file. A familiar jingle sounded through the speakers and the two women looked at each other. It was Leo's medical hour.

'You want me to turn it off...?'

'No. Listen with me.' She'd come this far and she couldn't go back now.

Then Leo's voice. At first, all she could hear was the smooth, sexy sound and then she began to focus on what he was actually saying.

'We've tackled a lot of very difficult issues here on the medical hour, and we pride ourselves on making this a place for people to talk. I've come to understand that sharing our experiences is not just a way of healing for ourselves, but for others, which is why I've decided to talk about this very personal issue. My twin brother took his own life when we were twenty-two. I'm pleased to welcome Dr Celia Greenway, who is a consultant psychologist...'

'He's talking about Joel...' Alex turned to Rhona, her hand over her mouth, tears streaming down her face.

'Who? Never mind. Are we sticking with it?'

'Yes... Yes.'

A woman was talking now...

'Leo, I've spoken at some length with both you and your family, and I want to make it clear to everyone listening that Leo and his family have given me permission to speak about some of the personal issues that came out of our discussions. What would you say was the most difficult emotion for you?'

'Guilt... I wasn't able to talk about some of the things which happened on the night of my brother's death for many years.'

'In fact, not until you and your family talked to me?'

'No...'

He was going to crack up. Alex could hear it in his voice. But somehow, through an obvious effort of will, Leo was holding it together. He spoke to each caller in turn, encouraging them to talk and answering all of the questions that were put to him honestly. With the usual jingles and the break for the news edited out, the recording lasted three-quarters of an hour, and Alex and Rhona listened in silence.

Finally, he wrapped the programme up.

'I want to thank Celia for being with us—with me—tonight and, as I said, the lines will be open for another hour so that anyone who'd like a call-back can leave their number. And finally I want to thank the very special person whose own courage inspired me to take this first step tonight. Goodnight, everyone.'

Rhona let out a long breath. 'That whole programme was *the* most moving thing I've heard in a long while.'

'Yes.' Alex felt almost numb.

'What does it mean?'

'It means…' She shrugged. 'He means exactly what he says. Leo always means what he says on the radio.'

'He wants…you and him?'

'No. It's what he said. He's taking the first step on a long road. It takes a long while to turn a life around.'

'So what are you going to do?'

'I don't know.' Alex thought hard. 'Yes, I do. Those pictures of Alice you took the other day, with her blade…'

'Alice?' Light dawned suddenly on Rhona's face. '*He* was the anonymous donor?'

Alex nodded.

'That's generous.' Rhona nodded in approval. 'You know, I thought he was a bit of a rotter at first, but he's not such a bad guy at all.'

'No. He's a very good guy. Just not *my* guy.'

If anything, Leo's message had given Alex some closure, and she guessed that maybe that had been his intention.

She was getting back on her feet again. Bruised and still feeling broken, but she was getting there.

Justin's voice on the phone didn't make her heart leap, hoping that he had some news of Leo. She knew what Leo was doing, and he wished her well, and she could put those thoughts away now.

'Alex, how are you?' Justin didn't stop for an answer. 'I want to ask you a favour.'

'What is it?' As long as it had nothing to do with Leo, she'd be happy to do whatever Justin asked.

'Will you listen in at ten tonight? Just for fifteen minutes.'

'Ten o'clock? That's the music hour, isn't it?'

'Yes, on Friday nights it's two hours. But that doesn't matter. All I'm asking is fifteen minutes. I need you to promise.'

Whatever this was, Justin was being a bit overdramatic. But that was Justin. 'Okay. Fifteen minutes, at ten o'clock. What do you want me to do then?'

'Feedback. That's all. Do you promise?'

'Yes, I promise.'

'Fantastic. I'll put you on the list. Got to go…'

Alex settled down on the sofa with a cup of tea and a pencil and pad, and switched on the radio at exactly ten o' clock. She'd listen for fifteen minutes, give her feedback and then go to bed. There was going to be a climbing group going down to Sussex tomorrow and she had to be up early.

'And this is Clemmie Rose, with two hours of music for you to keep you cool and relaxed on a Friday evening. If there's someone out there you want to send a message to, then just call in. But first…'

Alex picked up her pencil. This must be it.

'Hi, Clemmie.'

What? When Leo's voice sounded on the radio Alex

threw her pencil back down in disgust. What was Justin playing at?

'You want to say something, I gather?'

'Yes. This is a message for Lieutenant Tara—'

'*The* Lieutenant Tara?' Clemmie interjected.

'No, not *the* Lieutenant Tara. *Me*. He means me,' Alex shouted crossly at the radio.

'The lady in question knows who I mean, and this is my message to her.'

'Go ahead, Leo.'

'Well, stop interrupting him then…' Alex had really liked Clemmie when she'd met her. Now she was beginning to get on her nerves.

Leo spoke, his voice clear and impassioned. 'There's no reason on earth why you should even listen, but I'm begging you to think about what I have to say. I love you and I want you to take me back. I promise I won't let you down this time.'

'What? Leo, you can't be serious…' Could he? He sounded serious.

Clemmie's voice again. 'Well, I can tell you that this guy surely looks as if he means it. So if the lady in question has an answer and would like to phone in we'll put her straight through. And, in the meantime, as it's you, Leo, I'm going to let you choose the next track.'

'Thanks. It's a song from Bobby and Aleesha's new album.'

'Ooh—*love* that. It's a new direction for both of these two, but it's been selling like hot cakes.'

'Yep. They took a risk, but it worked out. Here's Bobby and Aleesha.'

'No, Leo…' Tears started to roll down Alex's face. How could he do this?

She knew exactly how he could do it. She'd asked him to take her number out of his phone, and she'd taken his out of hers because she wanted no part of Leo's guilt. When he spoke to her, she wanted it to be real. And for Leo, saying it on the radio was about as real as it got.

She got to her feet, her heart thumping and her lungs straining to breathe. He loved her. He wouldn't let her down. Leo had promised.

'Okay. Take a breath. Count to ten.' That didn't work. She started to pace up and down, listening to the radio, wondering whether Leo would come back on.

It seemed not. The song had finished and there were more messages. From Darren to Claire. From Emma to Pete. Her head was spinning, and she still didn't know what to do. Dared she trust Leo?

'And we have Marion from Hampstead on the line. Marion, who's your message for?'

'My message is for Leo. I hope the lady says yes, but if she doesn't then just pass my number on. *I'll* say yes, Leo.'

'No, you won't!' Alex yelled at the radio, picking it up and shaking it hard.

Then she knew. Alex grabbed her phone, staring at it.

She didn't have his number. And, despite the fact she'd heard it about a million times, she couldn't remember the number of the radio station. She waited impatiently for the next piece of music to finish, and then Clemmie obligingly read it out.

She dialled and waited. She knew that if she hung on the call would be answered, but it might take a while. Then she heard the operator on the other end.

'Hello… Hello, it's Alex Jackson…'

'Alex. I have a question for you. What colour was that gorgeous dress of yours?'

'My what?' Suddenly she realised. They were making sure that it was her. 'Green. It was green.'

'Right. Hold on for just one moment. Don't go away—I'm putting you through to Leo.'

A couple of clicks on the line, and then Leo's voice. 'Alex?'

She closed her eyes, wishing that she could see him. 'Leo… Leo, are we on the radio?'

'No. It's just you and me.' Alex jumped as her doorbell rang. 'Is that your bell?'

'Yes, forget it. They'll go away. Leo…'

'I don't think so.' The bell rang a second time.

'Is that you?'

'Yes. I was hoping you might let me in…'

Alex ran to the intercom, slamming her hand onto the door release.

He was coming up. She tugged at the long cardigan she was wearing, pulling it straight, and looked in the hall mirror, pulling her hair out of its ponytail and shaking her head so that it fell around her shoulders. Then her panic subsided. Leo loved her. He'd always taken her just the way she was.

There was a quiet rap on the door and she flung it open. Leo.

He looked amazing. Dinner jacket, bow tie, white shirt. Beautiful, beautiful blue eyes.

'Leo…' She hardly dared breathe. Didn't dare touch him in case this was a dream and he'd suddenly evaporate.

'May I come in?'

She stepped back from the door and he walked into the hallway. 'You heard what I said on the radio? Can you believe me?'

'Yes. You always tell the truth on the radio.'

'I hoped you'd know that.' He seemed suddenly nervous, that easy charm stripped away from him. 'Will you hear me out, Alexandra?'

She swallowed hard. He'd unnecessarily and quite deliciously taken the time to use all four syllables of her name. 'Always.'

'I've done a lot of thinking, and a lot of talking. I'm letting go of the past and that's allowed me to take hold of the present.'

'Live for the moment?'

'I'm living for this moment, right now.'

She could feel it, see it in his eyes. The way she had when they'd made love.

'What you did…that hour on the radio, talking about Joel. It was amazing, Leo. It must have been so hard for you.'

'It wasn't as hard as losing you.' He reached out, taking her hand. 'I love you, and I know we can make this work. Will you take me back?'

Her heart thumped in her chest. But everything was suddenly crystal-clear. Alex cradled his hand between hers, raising it to her lips. 'I should never have left you, Leo. I should have believed in you—you always believed in me, and you took me just the way I am…'

'You *did* believe in me. You never could accept the way I used to be because you knew I could be a better man. That's how I came to believe it too.'

'I love you, Leo. I won't ever let you go again, I promise.'

He let out a sigh, as if finally he could start breathing again. They both could. 'Forever is a long time.'

'We're going to need it. We have a lot to do together.'

Suddenly he grinned. Leo fell to one knee in front of her, taking the red rose from his lapel and putting it into her hands. 'I love you, Alex. And I won't let you down.'

'What are you doing? Leo…' She felt suddenly breathless with joy.

'You know what I'm doing.'

'But… I'm such a mess. And you look so wonderful.'

'You're the most beautiful woman I've ever seen. I'm just overdressed.' He tugged at his bow tie, leaving it to drape around his neck, and pulled open the top two buttons of his shirt. 'Better?'

'Yes. Much better.' They could make this happen. Together they could do it.

'Will you marry me, Alexandra?'

She knew the answer to that too. One word that promised everything. 'Yes.' She reached forward to pull him to his feet. 'I love you so much, Leo, and I really want to marry you. Please, kiss me…'

But Leo had something else on his mind. Reaching into his pocket, he drew out a ring. A solitaire diamond, which flashed in the light. Alex gasped, covering her mouth with one hand.

'Leo, that's beautiful. It's too much.'

He grinned. 'I could take it back and get a smaller one, if that's what you want.'

'Don't you dare.'

He laughed, slipping the ring on her finger, and then he did the one thing she'd been wanting him to do. The only thing that could make her completely happy. He got to his feet and kissed her.

EPILOGUE

Two years later...

LEO WAS NO longer able to exactly pin down the happiest day of his life. When Alex had told him she would marry him, he'd thought that had to be it. Until the day she *did* marry him. And then the night they'd spent at the secluded beach house on their honeymoon.

As he'd learned to build a life that wasn't bound by guilt he *had* stumbled along the way, but Alex had always been there, stopping him from falling. Helping him find his feet, and love her a little more each time. And he'd been there for her too, encouraging her to take the step of working full-time for Together Our Way and to extend its services. The night she'd collected a Charity of the Year award, he'd thought his heart would burst with pride.

When she'd whispered in his ear that she was going to have his child, Leo had thought nothing could ever make him happier. Then came the moment that he held his newborn daughter in his arms, counting her fingers and toes, and promising little Chloe that he'd always be there for her.

There were the little things too. When Alex told him that she loved him. When she reached for him in the night, and when he caught her up from their bed to watch the sun rise. When he looked into her eyes and saw joy.

It was a summer's morning and Chloe, ten months old

now, had slept in the car all the way down to the house in Surrey. He parked the car and Alex walked on ahead with Chloe, her dress flapping in the warm breeze, and stopped at the middle of the bridge to wait for him. As he walked towards them in the sunshine, Chloe stretched out her arms towards him.

'Daddee…'

Alex caught her breath. 'That's right, sweetheart. That's Daddy. Say it again.' She hugged their daughter and Leo dropped the bags he was carrying, hurrying towards them.

'Daddy.'

Alex laughed with delight and he caught the two of them in his arms, hugging them tight. 'Have you been teaching her to say that while my back's turned?'

'No. It's the first time. I've been trying to get her to say, *Daddy, can I borrow the car keys?* But I don't think she's up to that yet.'

'I'm working on, *Mummy, let's go and make Daddy breakfast in bed.* She nearly managed it the other day.'

'I can think of much better things to do with you in bed than feed you breakfast.'

Leo laughed. 'Are you being nice?'

Alex brushed a kiss against his lips. 'I'm never nice.'

If he hadn't known better, and that there would always be more, Leo would have said that *this* was the happiest day of his life.

* * * * *

If you enjoyed this story,
check out these other great reads from
Annie Claydon

RESCUED BY DR RAFE
SAVED BY THE SINGLE DAD
DISCOVERING DR RILEY
THE DOCTOR SHE'D NEVER FORGET

All available now!

WEEKEND WITH THE BEST MAN

BY

LEAH MARTYN

Published in Great Britain 2016
By Mills & Boon, an imprint of HarperCollins*Publishers*
1 London Bridge Street, London, SE1 9GF

ISBN: 978-0-263-92628-6

Our policy is to use papers that are natural, renewable and recyclable products and made from wood grown in sustainable forests.
The logging and manufacturing processes conform to the legal environmental regulations of the country of origin.

Printed and bound in Spain
by CPI, Barcelona

Dear Reader,

Thank you for waiting so patiently for my new story. This time we're back in Casualty, with Dante and Lindsey.

It's true that your soulmate does not have to be perfect—just perfect for *you*. And I have to tell you that Dan took a bit of prodding to let his star shine in this story. His past failed relationship has left him wary of looking for love. He wears aloofness like a cloak. Then along comes Lindsey, my gorgeous heroine. Perceptive and smart, she sees a different Dan. She beguiles him, challenges him. Slowly Dan opens the doors to his heart. He tastes heaven with Lindsey. But his past keeps getting in the way. Lindsey puts him on notice and Dan realises he's been hovering in the shallows. Now he'll have to make the swim of his life or lose her.

I'm delighted to present for your reading enjoyment *Weekend with the Best Man*.

Leah x

For BRISROM—Brisbane Romance Writers—
where it all began.
I hope you're all still out there. And still writing.

Books by Leah Martyn

Mills & Boon Medical Romance

The Doctor's Pregnancy Secret
Outback Doctor, English Bride
Wedding in Darling Downs
Daredevil and Dr Kate
Redeeming Dr Riccardi
Wedding at Sunday Creek

Visit the Author Profile page
at millsandboon.co.uk for more titles.

Praise for
Leah Martyn

'A sweet story about a single mother trying to juggle kids and work… I highly recommend this book!'

—*Goodreads* on
Daredevil and Dr Kate

CHAPTER ONE

FRIDAY MORNING IN Casualty was the last place Senior Registrar Dan Rossi wanted to be.

And not with this patient—a seventeen-year-old drug-addicted youth. He'd arrested. And now the fight had begun to save his life. A life this skinny kid had valued so cheaply. How dared he?

Dan's thoughts turned dark. 'Start CPR!' He bit the words out as the team began the familiar routine, working in concert around the senior doctor, responding to his clipped orders.

Expectations rose and fell as they treated the patient. Rose and fell again. Dan glanced at the clock. They'd done all they could but he didn't want to call it. Not yet. Not today of all days. And not with this patient. What a waste of a young life. 'Ramp it up!'

He felt the sweat crawl down his back, his heart like a jackhammer against his ribs. He shouldn't be here. He'd lost his mental filter. Lost it.

Lost it. Lost it…

'OK, he's back.'

Thank God. Immediately, Dan's chest felt lighter as if a valve had just released the pressure building inside him. He woke as if from a nightmare.

'Pulse rate sixty,' Nurse Manager Lindsey Stewart relayed evenly. 'He's waking up.'

Yanking off his gloves, Dan aimed them at the bin, missing by a mile. 'Do what you have to do,' he said, his voice flat.

And walked out. Fast.

Lindsey's eyebrows hitched, her green gaze puzzled as she watched his exit.

'That was a bit odd back there,' Vanessa Cole, Lindsey's colleague, said, as they watched their patient being wheeled out to ICU. 'What's biting Rossi?'

'Something's certainly got him upset,' Lindsey agreed. 'Dan's usually very cool under pressure.'

'He hasn't been here long.' Vanessa shrugged. 'And we don't know much about him yet. Perhaps it's personal—girlfriend trouble?'

'Does he have a girlfriend?'

'Please!' Vanessa, who seemed to be at the sharp end of all the hospital gossip, gave an exaggerated eye-roll. 'With that dark, smouldering thing happening?'

'That's a bit simplistic,' Lindsey refuted. 'Dan Rossi is a senior doctor. He wouldn't bring that kind of stuff to work with him. I'd better try to speak to him. If it's a work-related matter, it'll need sorting.'

'Oh, Lins.' Vanessa's voice held exasperation as she pushed the privacy screen open. 'Don't start taking the flak for Rossi's dummy spit. We run—that is, *you* run an extremely efficient casualty department. It's my guess he'll take a long lunch and snap out of whatever's bugging him.'

Lindsey's instincts were not quite buying that scenario. She recognised mental stress when she saw it, and Dan Rossi had been far from his usual self since the beginning of the shift. She frowned a bit, wondering just where he'd fled to.

'Dan's usually pretty good to work with.'

* * *

Dan knew he'd been discourteous to the team but today, for very personal reasons, he'd had to get out.

Had to.

In a secluded part of the grounds he sank into a garden seat, taking a deep breath and letting it go. Every sensible cell in his brain told him he shouldn't have brought his personal problems to work today. In fact, he shouldn't have come to work at all. If he'd thought it through, he'd have taken a mental health day available to all staff. Instead, he'd come to work in an environment where emotions went from high to low in seconds.

He made a dismissive sound in his throat. Having to treat that last patient had been the trigger that had shot his ability to be objective all to hell.

Addiction. And a foolish boy, abusing his body with no conception of the amazing gift of life. A gift Dan's own babies had never had. No chance to draw one tiny lifesaving breath. Two perfect little girls.

It was two years ago today since he'd lost them.

At the memory, something inside him rose up then flattened out again, like a lone wave on the sea. The grief he felt was still all too real. Grief with nowhere to go.

A shiver went right through him and he realised he'd rushed outside without a jacket. Lifting his hands, he linked them at the back of his neck. He needed to get a grip. Once he'd got through today, he'd regroup again.

Flipping his mobile out of his pocket, he checked for messages and found one from his colleague and closest friend, Nathan Lyons. The text simply said: Grub?

In seconds, Dan had texted back.

Leo's in ten.

* * *

With things in Casualty more or less under control, Lindsey decided to take the early lunch. She needed to get her head together. In the staffroom she collected the minestrone she'd brought from home and reheated it in the microwave. Ignoring the chat going on around her, she took her soup to a table near the window and buried her head in a magazine.

Halfway through her meal she stopped and raised her head to look out of the window. She'd have to say something to Dan. She couldn't just pretend nothing had happened. But how to handle it?

It wasn't as though they had any kind of relationship outside the hospital. What did she really know about him anyway? She knew he'd worked in New York and, more recently, he'd left one of the big teaching hospitals in Sydney to come on staff here in this rural city of Hopeton. But beyond that? Except for the fact that Dan Rossi kept very much to himself—and *that* alone was an achievement in an environment where you were thrown together all the time—she knew next to nothing about his personal life. But she remembered his first day vividly.

She'd sneaked a quick peek at him as the team had assembled for the start of the shift. Her quick inventory had noted his hair was dark, very dark and cut short, his eyes holding a moody blueness, the shadows beneath so deep they might have been painted on. His shoulders under his pinstriped shirt were broad. She had taken a deep breath and let it go, realising as she'd done so that she'd been close enough to smell he'd been shower-fresh. In the close confines where they worked *that* mattered to Lindsey.

Then he'd caught her looking. And it was as if they'd shared a moment of honesty, a heartbeat of intimacy. His mouth had pulled tight then relaxed. He'd almost smiled. Almost but not quite.

And for what it was worth the vibe was still there between them. But it seemed to Lindsey that for every tiny bit of headway she made with Dan Rossi on a personal level, he took off like a world-class sprinter in the opposite direction.

She blew out a long breath of frustration, slamming her magazine shut as she got to her feet. Why was she even bothering to try to find out what made Dan Rossi tick? After her last boyfriend had cheated on her so spectacularly, she'd questioned her judgement about men. How did you work out which of them to trust and recognise those who were into game-playing? And right now, after the rotten morning they'd had, it was all too heavy to think about.

Leo's was five minutes away from the hospital, the unpretentious little café drawing the hospital staff like bees to puffy blossoms. Chef Leo Carroll kept his menu simple. And he'd done his market research, opening at six in the morning to accommodate the early shift who just wanted a coffee and a bacon roll. Lunch began at noon and lasted until three. Then Leo closed his doors, cleaned up and went to play guitar at a blues bar in town.

Dan settled into one of the comfortable side booths and stretched out his legs. Already he could feel the tension draining from him. Nathan's continued support had steadied him in ways that were incalculable. Dan recalled the day he'd flown into Sydney from the States. He'd been standing feeling a bit bemused in the passenger lounge, getting his bearings, when he'd heard his name called. He'd spun round and found himself looking into a familiar craggy face lit with a lopsided grin.

'Nate!'

Before Dan could react further, he'd been thumped across the back and enveloped in a bone-crunching hug that had almost undone him. 'Glad you made it back in one piece, dude,' Nathan had said gruffly.

Dan had swallowed. 'How did you know I'd be on this flight?'

'I have my ways.' Nathan had tapped the side of his nose. 'Now, come on, let's move it. I'm short-term parked and it's costing me a fortune.'

Dan had booked into a boutique hotel near the harbour, intending to stay there until he could find an apartment. As they'd driven, Nathan had asked, 'Do you have some work lined up?'

'Starting at St Vincent's in a week.'

'Still in Casualty?'

'It's what I do best. You still in Medical?'

'It's what *I* do best.' Nathan had shot him a glance. 'Uh—not going to see your folks, then?'

'Not yet.' His family lived in Melbourne and while he loved and respected them, he just wasn't up for receiving their sympathy all over again.

A beat of silence.

'I've met a girl.' Nathan's embarrassed laugh eased the fraught atmosphere.

Dan spun his friend an amused look. 'Serious?'

'Could be. Think so. She's a flight attendant. Samantha Kelly—Sami.'

'Get out of here!' Dan leaned across and fist-bumped his friend's upper arm. 'Tell me about her.'

'She's blonde.'

'Yeah?'

'Funny, sweet, smart...you know...'

'Yeah. And she's got you wrapped around her little finger. Nice one, mate. I hope it works out for you and Sami.'

'Uh—if it doesn't pan out for you in Sydney,' Nathan said carefully, 'you could come across the mountain to us at Hopeton District. Get some rural medicine under your belt. We're always looking for decently qualified MOs.'

'Mmm—maybe.' Dan gave a dry smile. Nathan went on to enthuse about the vibrant country city a couple of hours from Sydney across the Blue Mountains.

'And would you believe you can still fossick for gold around Hopeton?' Nathan concluded his sales pitch emphatically.

And six months later Dan had taken everything on board and made the move and now here they were, with Nathan's and Sami's wedding just a week away and *he* was Nathan's best man.

Dan looked at his watch just at the moment Nathan burst through the door.

'Sorry I'm a bit late,' he apologised, sliding his big frame onto the bench seat opposite. 'Would you believe I've just had to cannulate three old coots on the trot—no veins to speak of, dehydrated as hell. Why don't old people drink water, for God's sake?'

'Because it's a generational thing,' Dan said patiently. 'They drink tea. Probably have done so since they could hold a cup.' Dan turned his attention to the short menu. 'We need to get a wriggle on. What are you having?'

'If there's pasta of some description, I'm your man.'

'There is,' Dan said. 'And I'll have the steak pie.'

Leo was there in a flash to take their orders. 'Won't be long, Docs,' he promised, batting his way back through the swing doors to his kitchen.

Nathan sent a narrowed look at his friend. He was well aware of the significance of the day in Dan's life. 'How's it going?' he asked quietly.

Dan's mouth bunched into a tight moue. 'Getting there, as they say.'

Nathan wasn't so sure and he knew his friend well

enough to ask, 'It's got to be hard for Caroline as well. Have you tried contacting her again?'

'What would be the point? She couldn't wait to dump me and our marriage—such as it was.'

'Yeah—well.' Nathan decided it was time for some straight talking. 'I don't want to be brutal, but it was never going to work after the babies died, was it?'

'Probably not.' Dan frowned. 'But she wasn't even willing to try!'

Nathan shook his head. They'd had this conversation before—or one similar. 'Listen, Dan, I've known you for a thousand years. It's in your DNA to be decent and, to use a very old-fashioned word, honourable. But you and Caroline weren't in love and, believe me, that's the only reason you should get married. And stay married. For your own sanity, you can't keep second-guessing all the what-ifs.'

Dan knew what Nathan said made sense and, God knew, he'd tried to let it go. His mouth gave a wry twist. 'The last time I spoke to Caroline, she said she'd *moved on*.'

'Then maybe it's time you did as well,' Nathan said frankly. 'Hey!' He injected an air of enthusiasm around them and beat a little drum roll on the table. 'It's Friday and Sami's decided we need a night out. There's a new club in town. Why don't you join us?'

Dan's insides curled. He could think of nothing worse than tagging along with a completely loved-up pair like Nathan and Sami. 'Thanks, mate, but I'll be fine. You and your bride-to-be have better things to do—or you should have.'

'Speaking of brides…' Nathan picked up the pepper mill and spun it between his hands. 'Sami wants us to wear cummerbunds.'

Dan snorted. 'I'd rather shove my head in a bucket of prawns.' He took a mouthful of water, very carefully replacing the glass on its coaster. 'I'd probably walk through fire to save your butt, Nathan, but I am *not* wearing a cummerbund at your wedding.'

Nathan gave a bark of laughter and confided, 'Sami reckons it's *modern vintage*.'

Dan looked unimpressed. 'Tell her the menswear shop in Hopeton have never heard of cummerbunds, let alone stocked them.'

'She said she'd order them online—but don't panic.' Nathan held up a hand in a staying motion, deciding to let his friend off the hook. 'I've talked her out of it.'

'How?' Dan's interest picked up. From what he'd seen, Sami was one determined lady. In the nicest possible way, of course.

'I had a mental picture of us with bulging satin waistlines and fell about laughing. Sami wasn't amused. She wrestled me to the sofa and belted me with her slipper. Then she saw the funny side and laughed too.'

And then they'd probably gone to bed, Dan thought. It was great Nathan was so happy, so...loved. He deserved to be. Dan wondered how long it would be before he had someone special to call his own. Someone to love and who loved him back the same way. Unconditionally. *And that was what had been missing with Caroline.*

'So it's sorted, then?'

'It is. When are you coming up?'

'The day before, on the Friday, if that's OK?' The couple were being married in Sami's home village of Milldale, some thirty miles north of Hopeton. The wedding reception was to be held at Rosemount, one of the historic homes in the district that had been revamped into a functions venue.

'Friday's fine,' Nathan said. 'Sami's booked us into the local pub. My folks are staying there as well.'

'Your meals, gentlemen.' Leo slid plates the size of cartwheels down in front of them. 'Enjoy.'

'This looks good.' Nathan rubbed his hands in anticipation. 'Dig in.'

Halfway through their meal, Dan said, 'When is Sami leaving her job?'

'She has already. She's going to start up her own business here, a travel agency cum tourist thing. She's had mega hits on her website already.'

'That's fantastic. You're going to settle here in Hopeton, then?'

'Yep.' Nathan twirled a length of spaghetti around his fork. 'It's a good fit for us at the moment. And my job's safe—well, as far as any job can be these days.'

Dan's throat closed for a moment. Nathan's future seemed secure and...*good*. If only his own future had a semblance of the same simple expectations attached to it. He shook his head. God, he'd better lighten up, or he'd be like a wet blanket at his friend's wedding.

As if he'd tuned into Dan's thoughts, Nathan said, 'Have you written your best man's speech yet?'

'Not yet.'

'Don't say anything too incriminating that'll get me hanged, will you?'

Dan's mouth twitched. 'Like the after-rugby parties when we were at uni?'

'You were there too, matey,' Nathan reminded him. 'Let's not forget that.'

A swirl of emotions juxtaposed in Dan's head. They had been good times. Uncomplicated. Until *life* had happened. He swore inwardly. He had to release this choking collar of useless introspection. But it was the day, he justified. The date. The memories. 'I suppose I could talk about your peculiar eating habits.'

'Like what?' Nathan gave an offended snort.

'In all my travels, I've never seen anyone consume food as quickly as you.'

'It's a gift.' Nathan gave a Gallic shrug. 'What can I do?'

Dan chuckled. 'Ratbag.'

'So,' Nathan asked, suddenly serious, 'how was it this morning in A and E?'

'I wish you hadn't asked me that.'

'You didn't kill anyone, did you?'

Dan shook his head. 'Probably worse. I dumped all over the team in Resus and walked out.'

'Crikey. I'll bet Lindsey Stewart was impressed—not!'

Dan grimaced.

'Did you apologise?'

'Not yet.'

'Lins has the respect of the whole hospital.' Nathan looked serious. 'You'd better do a real grovel. Ask her for a drink after work and do it then. Properly.'

Dan felt worse and worse. He'd apologise, of course. But ask her for a drink? She'd probably turn him down flat. And he wouldn't blame her. In the short time he'd been at Hopeton he'd hardly put himself out to get to know her or anyone else. Out of nowhere, Lindsey Stewart's flashing green eyes seemed to challenge him. And he realised on some basic level that he *wanted* to get to know her. To break away from the past. He had to turn things around. 'I shouldn't have come to work today.'

'Possibly not,' Nathan agreed. 'Just fix it, mate. Hopeton's not so big that bad behaviour goes unnoticed.'

CHAPTER TWO

BACK AT THE STATION, Lindsey glanced at the clock and sighed. She couldn't wait for the shift to end. And thank heaven she had some leave coming up. And where was Dan? She scanned the precincts with a practised eye. Probably, as Vanessa had supposed, enjoying a long lunch. Except he wasn't late back, she admitted fairly. It was her own fault she'd taken only the briefest lunch break. But she'd got sick of her own company and her mixed-up thoughts had been driving her nuts. She needed to be busy.

Dan made his way slowly towards the station. There she was, sitting with her back towards him, her dark head with its subtle streaks of auburn bent over some paperwork. He silently thanked all the gods she was on her own. He couldn't do this in front of an audience. His breathing faltered, his stomach churned and he went forward. 'Lindsey…'

She spun round and looked up. 'Dan…'

Dan rubbed at the back of his neck, feeling his muscles bunch but not release.

For a few seconds there was an awkward silence as they both took stock.

'I owe you an apology,' Dan said eventually.

Lindsey stood up. She'd feel better able to sort this standing eye to eye. She sent him a cool look. 'Do you have a problem with the nursing back-up in the department? Or a problem with me?'

'Of course I don't.' Dan felt a spark of anger. Where had she got that idea? He gave a tight shrug. 'I was out of line earlier. I'm sorry. It won't happen again.'

Lindsey felt her whole bearing soften. His ownership of his lapse was more, much more than she'd expected. She lifted her chin and met his gaze, suddenly aware they were close, too close for comfort. What was he thinking? She couldn't tell. His eyes were clouded with uncertainty. Out of nowhere, Lindsey felt a twist of uncertainty herself. She hated being out of sync with any of her colleagues. Hated it. 'Stuff happens in Casualty.' She gave an open-handed shrug. 'Don't beat yourself up.'

'Thank you.' Dan felt the ton weight lift from him. He gave a tight smile. 'Put it down to an off day. We all have them, don't you agree?'

'I guess we do,' Lindsey said carefully. And if she was any judge of the human condition, he was still having an off day. He seemed a bit...*desperate*, for want of a better word. Edgy. And there were shadows beneath his eyes. Again. If anyone needed a hug, it was Dan Rossi. But that would be totally out of order. Unprofessional. And embarrass the socks off him. She looked away quickly. In seconds, the tenor of her day had changed completely. What was going on here had no rhyme nor reason. It was just... happening. And she felt she was jumping fences ten feet high and couldn't stop. It was an extraordinary sensation.

Dan swallowed through a very dry throat. She had her hair twisted into a topknot and flyaway strands were coming loose. He wondered what it would look like if she were to let it tumble down, releasing the scent of the flowery shampoo she used. It wasn't going to happen. In an almost reflex action she reached up, pushing the wayward strands back in. Dan fisted his hands, resisting the urge to do it for her. 'So, what's on the agenda?'

Lindsey put her nurse's head on quickly. 'We have a little kid waiting for sutures. Michelle and Andrew are presently treating a youth with burns, the result of walking barefoot on coals after a bush barbecue. If you'd rather take over there and have one of them see the child…?'

'No, no.' Dan frowned a bit. 'Our junior doctors need to gather experience. I'll see the child. Point me in the right direction.'

'I'll come with you,' she said, as Vanessa took over the station.

'Fill me in,' he said, as they walked towards the cubicles.

'Preschooler, Michael Woods. He was chasing a ball out of bounds, tripped and hit his chin on the edge of a brick garden bed. Fair bit of blood. Panic stations and the school rang mum. She's with him.'

'Good. She'll be a calming influence.'

Lindsey chuckled. 'You hope.'

'Are you saying it's the mothers we have to be afraid of, Lindsey?'

Lindsey turned her head and caught his gaze. She blinked a bit. Unless she was mistaken, there was actually a curve happening to one corner of his mouth. On impulse, she sent him a full-blown smile in return, urged on by a feeling of oneness with him she couldn't explain. 'I've met a few.'

Five-year-old Michael was sitting on the edge of the treatment couch, his small legs swinging rhythmically back and forth. He didn't look overly upset, Lindsey noted thankfully, although the blotches of dried blood on his T-shirt indicated it had been a heavy bump to his chin.

Dan smiled at the mother. 'Mrs Woods? I'm Dan Rossi. I'll be the doctor looking after Michael.'

'I'm Stephanie.' Michael's mother kept her arm protectively around her little boy's shoulders. She gave a wry smile. 'He's a bit of a tornado in the playground.'

'So, you like playing footy, Michael?' Dan asked.

'I can kick the ball as high as the house,' Michael declared, aiming upwards with one small arm.

'Fantastic.' Dan looked impressed.

Lindsey gave him a tick of approval for keeping things light and thereby gaining their small patient's trust. Unobtrusively, she gloved and said quietly, 'I'll pop that sticking plaster off Michael's chin, shall I, Dr Dan?'

'Let's do that.' Almost casually, Dan hooked over a mobile stool and snapped on gloves. He sat in front of Michael. His eyes narrowed slightly. The removal of the plaster had revealed a gaping hole underneath. The mother's gasp was audible. 'Easily fixed.' Dan's tone was gently reassuring. Tilting Michael's chin, he examined the damage more closely. The edges of the wound were uniform. They would align nicely. It would be a neat scar.

'Is he OK?' Stephanie asked anxiously.

'His bite seems even,' Dan responded. 'And his baby teeth all seem in place. I'll put a stitch or two in his chin and he should be as right as rain.'

Gently, Lindsey positioned Michael for the suturing procedure, laying him back with his head at the end of the bed.

Dan rolled across the trolley containing the instruments he'd need and switched on an overhead light. 'Now, Michael, this is where you have to be as brave as the best footy player in the world,' Dan said, flicking up the syringe of local anaesthetic.

Michael's blue eyes lit up. 'Like David Beckham.'

Dan huffed a laugh. 'That's the guy. Now, if you lie very still for me while I make your chin better, I'm sure

I can find an amazing sticker you can wear on your shirt tomorrow and show the kids at preschool.'

'My shirt's all dirty,' Michael said with childish logic.

'Honey, we'll find you a clean one to wear.' Stephanie smiled at her son and held his hand tightly.

Dan looked up. 'Lindsey, if you would, please?'

She nodded. The injection of the lignocaine would sting and be a shock to the little one. 'Squeeze Mummy's hand hard, Michael,' she said, placing herself gently across the child's body in case he tried to wriggle free.

In a few seconds the local had been injected and they waited a couple of minutes for it to take effect. Dan prodded the wound gently in several places. 'Can you feel anything hurting, Michael?'

Eyes squeezed shut, Michael said, 'No...'

'Good boy. Keep holding Mummy's hand and we'll be finished in no time.'

In a short time Lindsey watched Dan snip the last suture close to the skin. 'There you are, sweetheart.' She gave the little shoulder a gentle pat. 'All finished.'

'Can I get my sticker now?'

Dan looked a question. He'd promised one to his small patient. He just hoped they had some in the department.

'They're in a box at the station,' Lindsey said right on cue. 'Won't be a tick.'

'Gorgeous little boy, wasn't he?' Lindsey remarked lightly as she went about tidying the treatment room.

Dan was parked at the mobile tray, writing up his notes. He lifted his head in query. 'Sorry?'

'Michael,' Lindsey said. 'He'll probably be a real heartbreaker.'

'Yes, probably...' Dan went back to his notes, finishing them swiftly.

'Thanks.' He gave the ghost of a smile and left quietly.

Lindsey bundled the soiled linen into a bin with a vengeance. What was with this guy? Would it kill him to indulge in a bit of normal conversation?

Dan was amazed how quickly the rest of the shift passed. The ache in his shoulders had disappeared. Cautiously, he began to feel, as a result of the sudden turnaround with Lindsey, he might have a chance at some kind of normal life here at Hopeton. A chance he couldn't afford to ignore.

Deep in thought, he began collating paperwork at the station. There were some end-of-shift letters he needed to write to several GPs. In Dan's opinion, their respective patients would need referral—

'Still at it?' Lindsey stopped at the station, her brows raised in query.

Dan's mouth tipped into a rueful smile. 'Still a bit of tidying up to do. You're off, then?' His fingers curled round his pen. Idiot. It was the end of her shift. Of course she was *off.* Gone were the hospital scrubs; instead, she was wearing soft jeans that clung to her legs and a long-sleeved silver-grey top, a silky scarf in a swirl of multi-colours around her throat.

And knee-high boots.

Dan felt his heart walk a few flights of stairs. He couldn't think of a single thing to say to the beautiful woman standing in front of him. And how pathetic was that?

'It's Friday, you should give yourself an early mark.' Lindsey looked more keenly at him. The lines of strain were still there around his eyes. He needed to relax. But whether or not he'd allow her to help him do that was another matter entirely.

But for some reason she couldn't fathom, she had to try.

'Most of us are going to the pub. Few drinks, a game

of snooker, a pizza or five later. You're very welcome to join us.'

Dan's heart suddenly came to a halt. *Thank you, God.* 'Sounds good. Uh—which pub?'

'The Peach Tree. Ancient red-brick place at the top of the main street. See you there, then?'

'You bet.' He nodded enthusiastically. 'Thanks for the invite.'

'Welcome.' Lindsey hitched up her shoulder bag and turned, moving off quickly to catch up with Vanessa.

A fleeting frown touched Dan's eyes as he watched the two women make their way towards the exit. He took a long controlling breath and let it go. Thanks to Lindsey's invitation, he'd taken the first steps towards his new life.

With the thought still humming in his head, he went back to his office to type up his referrals.

Letters completed, Dan swung up from his desk, looking up in question when Martin Lorimer, the senior doctor on take, poked his head in. 'Ah—Dan. You're still here. MVA coming in. Pile-up on the highway, two vehicles, all teenagers. Can you hang about?'

Dan felt his gut contract. Did he have a choice? *Hell.* Lindsey would think he'd bottled out or just been plain rude. And he didn't need that kind of misunderstanding after today's debacle. He'd text her if he could but he had no idea of her mobile number. He swore under his breath. If the injuries to the kids were not too serious, maybe he'd still make it to the pub. Holding that thought, he made his way towards the ambulance bay.

'I got you another OJ.' Vanessa placed the glass of juice in front of Lindsey. 'And what's with you tonight, Lins? We could have won the snooker if you hadn't been so not into it. Now I owe Andrew ten bucks.' Vanessa pleated a strand of her blunt-cut blonde hair behind her ear. 'Um… do you think Andrew might be a bit keen?'

'On you?' Lindsey took a mouthful of her drink. 'Maybe. Every time he needs a hand with a patient, he makes a beeline for you.'

'So, do you think he's ever going to get off his butt and do something about it?'

'Why wait for him? Van, you live in the same building. Surely you run into him about the place. Just ask him in for a coffee or something.'

'But if he said no, I'd feel stupid,' Vanessa moaned. 'And I have to work with him.' She ran her finger around the rim of her glass. 'Did he seem to miss me while I was on leave?'

'Not that I noticed,' Lindsey said drily. 'But he's coming over now. Perhaps you're about to find out.'

'You bet I will.' Full of resolve, Vanessa whirled to her feet. 'Are you off home?' She gave Andrew a pert look and a very warm smile.

'Think I'd better. I'm back on a late tomorrow.'

'Oh, me too.' Vanessa grabbed her bag. 'Let's share a cab. I'll put the ten bucks I owe you towards the fare. Deal?'

'Deal.' Andrew's white smile gleamed. The two took a few steps away then turned and chorused, ''Night, Lins.'

Lindsey dredged up a smile and fluttered a wave. Ten minutes later her eyes did another tour of the lounge. Still no Dan. Inwardly, she gave a philosophic little shrug. She'd invited him and he hadn't shown. And yet he'd seemed keen enough. Perhaps he'd thought better of it. Her mouth turned down. And perhaps she'd come across as being too pushy. Well, whatever, she wasn't going to hang about, wondering.

Outside, the night was clear and crisp. Lindsey looked

up. The moon looked so pretty, hanging there like…a silvery seahorse…

'Lindsey!'

She spun round. She'd know that voice anywhere. Her heart jagged into overdrive. 'Dan?'

Dan emerged out of the shadows and into the filtered lighting at the pub's perimeter. 'You waited,' he said, and looked at her. 'I got caught up.' Briefly he filled her in.

'When will kids realise speed can be a potential killer?' Lindsey shook her head. 'They'll all be OK, though?'

'Should be, in time,' Dan replied, fisting his hands into the side pockets of his bomber jacket. 'I'm whacked,' he admitted frankly. 'Are they still serving meals here?'

'Long finished,' Lindsey said. 'The club scene's taken over now.'

'Uh, OK. Thanks for hanging about,' he said, hunching his shoulders in a shrug. 'I thought my not turning up might have ticked you off. I didn't want that.'

'I guessed you'd had an emergency,' Lindsey said, forgiving herself the small untruth. 'It's a bummer when that happens right at the end of a shift, isn't it?'

His blue eyes regarded her levelly. 'Well, this time it certainly was. I had no way of letting you know.'

Lindsey flipped a hand dismissively. 'We can fix that now, if you like.' She reached into her bag and pulled out her mobile and in a few seconds they'd exchanged numbers.

'So, we're good, then?' Dan's head came up in query and he returned his phone to his back pocket.

Lindsey swallowed unevenly. Running into him like this had been unexpected. And now it all seemed a bit surreal. And why on earth were they standing here? It was freezing. 'What are you going to do about some food?'

'I'm sure I'll find somewhere to get a takeaway if I look hard enough.'

Lindsey bit the edge of her bottom lip. She had the sudden vision of him going back to his place, sitting alone, eating alone. After the kind of brutal day he'd appeared to have had, the mental picture was awful. The fact that it bothered her so much took her by surprise. She lived only a few minutes away. She could offer to feed him. An invitation hovered on the tip of her tongue…

'Do you have the weekend off?' Dan asked.

Lindsey snapped her thoughts back to reality. 'Yes. You?'

'Back on an early tomorrow.'

Lindsey made a face. 'Make sure you eat, then.' She cringed inwardly. She'd sounded like his grandmother.

'Thanks for caring.' His eyes held a penetratingly blue honesty.

'Mmm…' Lindsey's mouth went dry.

'I haven't exactly been fun to work with.' Half turning, he dragged a hand through his hair, leaving a few dark strands drifting across his forehead. It gave him a faintly dissolute air.

Lindsey scrunched her fingers through the folds of her scarf, suddenly shaken by the intensity of emotion that just standing next to Dan generated throughout her entire body. 'Maybe we should appoint a laughter coach for the ED.'

Dan felt disconcerted for a second. Her mouth was smiling. Just. More a tiny upward flick at the corners. He smiled back and, for just a moment, a blink of time, there was a connection of shared awareness. Sharp. Intense. And then it was gone, retracting like the sun under cloud. 'Take that idea to the board.'

'Would I have your backing?'

Was she serious? 'You bet. Laughter in the ED sounds… remedial.' And ridiculous. In fact, the whole conversation was verging on the ridiculous. Which only went to prove how out of touch he was with the ordinary stuff, like social interaction. Especially with beautiful women. The atmosphere was fraught again.

'If you're looking for a takeaway, the Chinese should still be open,' Lindsey offered.

He gave a one-shouldered shrug, moving restively as though he wanted to be away. 'Maybe I won't bother after all. I've food at home. I can whip up something.' *Or I could ask you to come and have a coffee with me.* His thoughts churned with indecision. He took the easy way out and said, 'You're OK getting home, then?'

'I'm parked just over there.' Lindsey indicated the small sedan the same make as a dozen others in the car park. 'Where are you?'

'Near the exit.'

Lindsey burrowed her chin more deeply into the roll collar of her fleece. This was bordering on crazy, standing here like two puppets waiting for someone to pull their strings and activate their mouths. She felt like chucking all her doubts and insisting he come home with her for a meal. Instead, she lowered her head and began fishing for her car keys in her bag.

Dan's jaw tightened as her hair fell forward in a shimmering curtain and it was all he could do not to reach out and draw it back and hold it while he pressed a slow, lingering kiss on her mouth…

'Got them.' Lindsey held up the keys triumphantly. Her gaze held his for a long moment. Expectant. Something… 'I guess I'll see you at work, then.'

Dan managed a nod. Whatever chance he'd had to further their…*friendship* outside the hospital had gone now. He'd stuffed it. 'Guess so.'

'Make sure you eat,' she reinforced, and they both took off in different directions.

'Hey, Lindsey!'

She turned. He was walking backwards and smiling. 'In case you were wondering, I *can* cook.'

'Never doubted it.' Lindsey's own smile carried her all the way home.

Wednesday, the following week...

'Told you he'd shape up.' Vanessa's voice held vindication, as they completed handover for the late shift.

'Andrew?' Lindsey feigned mild interest.

Vanessa gave an eye-roll. 'Our Dr Rossi. He's been exceptionally co-operative and I detected quite a nice sense of humour lurking somewhere there.'

'I've hardly seen him this week.' Lindsey made a pretence of checking the list of patients waiting in cubicles. 'His shifts have obviously been all over the place.' And she'd noticed his absence. Oh, boy, had she noticed.

'Well, if you're happy with everything, I'm out of here.' Vanessa hauled off her lanyard and scattered a handful of pens into a nearby tray. 'Andrew and I are going to a movie.'

'Well, fancy that...' Lindsey drawled. 'He's finally asked you out on a date.'

'Well, actually, I asked him. But he was all for it,' Vanessa added quickly.

'Good for you, Van.'

'Well, the opportunity kind of just presented itself,' Vanessa said modestly. 'But it just goes to show, doesn't it? Some men merely need a shove in the right direction.'

Was there a message somewhere in there for her? Lindsey's eyes were thoughtful as she set about triaging the patients on her list.

CHAPTER THREE

LINDSEY TURNED UP the music and did a rhythmic little rock with her shoulders as she drove. It was Friday at last and she was on leave. *Going home*. It was a good feeling. And perhaps back among the vines and the majestic blue hills she'd be able to sort out her feelings about a certain doctor. Was she wasting her time, though? Maybe. Maybe not.

She shut her music off. It was time to concentrate on her driving. Even though the country road was bitumen and usually well maintained, it was narrow. And it was just on dusk, visibility questionable to say the least, but she hadn't wanted to hang about in Hopeton. With the thought of home beckoning, she'd just wanted to be on her way.

Automatically, she concentrated her vision on the road ahead. The headlights of an approaching car were illuminating the horizon. Lindsey adjusted her own headlights in preparation. She noticed there was a vehicle behind her as well. But so far it was obeying the road rules and keeping a safe distance.

Dan's thoughts were very mixed as he drove. He hadn't managed to catch Lindsey much over the past week. And that had been a frustration. He'd wanted to reinforce the little progress he'd made in getting to know her. But his hours at work had been manic, only because he'd made himself available so as to accumulate a few days' leave after the wedding. The wedding was tomorrow. He hadn't prepared a speech so he'd speak off the cuff. He and Nathan had so much shared history, it shouldn't be difficult.

Abruptly, Dan was jolted out of his thoughts of weddings and speeches as he noticed the lurching drift of an oncoming car. *What the hell?* All his reflexes sprang into action. He reduced speed instantly, preparing to brake. For a split second he forgot to breathe, following the speeding car's trajectory as it plunged out of control, crossing the centre line and placing it on a collision course with the car in front of him. He felt every nerve in his body tense.

Surely, a crash was inevitable.

Lindsey hissed an expletive, all her defensive driver training coming into play. This couldn't be happening! Who was this lunatic of a driver? Her heart pounded, echoing in her ears. *Please, no!* She pulled hard on the steering wheel, feeling she'd dodged a bullet as the sports car shot past in a blur. She was safe. The relief was instant but short-lived as the vehicle clipped the rear section of her car, pushing her off the road. Her head snapped forward and then back, slamming into her headrest as her car spun and spun again.

Dan's jaw went rigid. This was a nightmare. He watched in horror as the sports car rolled before coming to rest right side up in a mangled mess of metal and broken glass. One headlight remained working, shining brokenly on the prostrate figure lying in the middle of the road.

It took a few seconds for the nurse in Lindsey to react. All thoughts of her own welfare fled. Pushing out of the car, she set her feet on the road. She felt woozy as she stood, swallowing back sudden nausea. She had to get to the injured person. She began running.

* * *

The sight of the female figure running towards the accident wrenched Dan out of his quagmire of disbelief. He brought his Land Rover as near as was safe to the accident site, switching his headlights to high beam. In seconds, he'd lodged a call for an ambulance. Seconds after that, he was out and grabbing his medical case, complete with oxygen and suction. He had a feeling he was going to need every last item in his kit. He took off at a run, noting the woman was already at the scene, crouching over the injured man. Dan frowned. Should she even be there? He'd seen how her vehicle had copped the impact of the sports car. 'Are you hurt?'

Lindsey startled at the brisk demand, raising her head. She blinked uncomprehendingly. 'Dan…?'

Sweet God. Dan let his breath go in a stream. 'Lindsey?'

For a mini-second they stared at each other in amazement and total disbelief. But the whys and wherefores had to wait until later. They had a life to save. 'Are you OK?' Dan rapped.

She frowned slightly. 'Think so…'

'Then let's see what's going on.'

The injured man looked in his sixties. Possible causes for the accident ran through Dan's head. Had he fallen asleep? Suffered a stroke or heart attack…? He was wearing bike shorts, T-shirt and hiking boots. Dan threw open his medical kit, snapping on a pair of gloves. Who was this guy—some kind of fitness nut? First things first, he decided, placing an oxygen mask over the man's face.

Lindsey hunkered down beside Dan. 'Ambulance coming?'

'Yep. They've diverted one. Let's hope it gets here in time.' Dan shook his head at the carnage. 'Glove up, please, Lindsey. I need your help here.'

She swayed a little then gathered herself, taking a deep

breath and then another, pulling on her gloves over shaking hands. 'Is he still breathing?'

'Just. Obviously he wasn't wearing a seat belt to be thrown out like that.' Dan did a quick head-to-toe check. 'Multiple contusions, by the look of it, fractured tibias.' He ripped out an expletive. 'Arterial bleed from his groin.'

Lindsey felt her stomach turn upside down, the sight of bright blood pulsing from the femoral artery almost making her gag. She took quick, shallow breaths, swallowing down the bitter taste of bile. Working like a robot, she grabbed whatever she could find in Dan's bag to absorb the flow of blood and pressed hard against the site. Pressure. They needed pressure. A tourniquet. An ambulance. A and E back-up. Her brain fogged. This was bordering on her worst nightmare. She'd attended dozens of accident scenes. What on earth was wrong with her...?

'Sure you're OK?'

Suddenly Dan was butted up against her. Lindsey felt the warmth of his hand anchoring hers. Her teeth began to chatter. 'Bit s-sick...'

'You're in shock!' God, why hadn't he noticed?

'I'll...be all right.' Lindsey forced herself to slow her breathing. In and out.

Dan scanned her face. Even in the dim light he could see she was as pale as parchment. 'Do you hurt anywhere? Lindsey, I need to know.'

She shook her head and winced as a spasm in her neck caught her unawares. 'Bit of...whiplash. I'll be OK. Just... get on.'

Dan hissed a non-reply. Within seconds, he'd wound a tourniquet into place.

Freed from the task of providing pressure on the wound, Lindsey pulled back. 'Do you have a collar?'

'No, damn it.' He shook his head at his lapse. Made a mental note to include one in his kit ASAP. 'We've got to stop that racket somehow,' he grated. They both knew their patient's airway was seriously compromised, his tortured breathing rattling into the stillness. He'd have to improvise. Dan's responses were running at top speed. He moved forward, kneeling so that the injured man's head was between his thighs. It was the only kind of stability he could offer for his patient's head and neck. Using gentle pressure, he extended the chin. The man's breathing improved marginally. It had to be enough until the paramedics got there.

Lindsey rallied, giving Dan the back-up he needed. She passed him the portable suction unit, automatically pushing the mask aside so he could place the sucker inside their patient's mouth. She felt black nausea pool in her stomach as blood tracked down into the tubing. Turning away, she retched onto the road.

'That's enough, Lindsey,' Dan ordered. 'I can manage from here.' He motioned backwards with his head. 'Go and sit in my car and wait for me. There's bottled water in an Esky on the floor. Drink.'

Wrapping her arms tightly over her stomach, Lindsey walked a bit unsteadily to the Land Rover. Opening the passenger door, she stopped, breathing away the coil of utter wretchedness. The few seconds' hiatus gave her some relief and she scrambled inside. Letting her head rest back, she closed her eyes and steadied her breathing.

It took only a few minutes for her stomach to settle. Feeling more in control, she leaned down and took a bottle of water from the Esky. She began sipping, feeling better after each mouthful. But now she was beginning to feel cold.

Dan's jacket was draped across the back of the driver's seat. Guardedly, aware she could overstretch her already sore neck muscles, she reached over and slowly managed to unhook the coat, draping it across her body like a blanket.

She felt herself relax, snuggling into its warmth, breathing in the faint scent of sandalwood and seasoned leather.

And him.

Out of nowhere, Lindsey felt a warm sensation down low, sensual tentacles humming through her whole body. She burrowed more deeply into Dan's coat. And felt connected to him in a way she could have only imagined.

Her mind flew ahead to something much more intimate and she snuggled deeper, as though taking his body warmth into herself.

Gradually, she became aware that the ambulance had arrived in a blaze of lights and a blaring siren, the police vehicle and a tow truck not far behind, the multi-coloured strobes looking like a weird kind of stage show. Lindsey watched through the windscreen, glad to be away from it all. Her tummy had settled but the feeling of it all happening to someone else persisted. Unfortunately, the reality was there in the ache of her neck muscles.

She could only hope the injured man would recover. And if he did, it was all down to Dan's skill as a doctor. He had been amazing.

Twenty minutes later the ambulance had gone. Lindsey registered the activity up ahead. The police had redirected the oncoming traffic. She wondered why there seemed quite a bit for this rather quiet road. But, then, it was Friday and lots of folk liked to get away for the weekend for wine tours and the B&B comfort offered by several of the vineyards around Milldale.

'How're you doing?'

Lindsey startled. The driver's door had swung open and Dan was there beside her. 'Much better.' She gave a wan smile. 'I borrowed your coat.'

'Good. I'm glad you had the sense to keep warm.' He sent her a perceptive look. 'I take it Milldale doesn't have a hospital?'

'Not even a GP. Why?'

'Why?' Dan frowned. 'Because I think I should take you straight back to Hopeton and get your neck X-rayed.'

'Oh, Dan...please, no.' Lindsey squeezed her eyes tightly shut in rebuttal. 'I'll be fine, honestly.'

'You can't know that for sure, Lindsey.' He seemed unconvinced. 'But I had a feeling you'd be stubborn so I managed to snaffle a collar from the paramedics.'

'No collars.' Lindsey was adamant. 'Look, it's whiplash, resulting in a bit of muscle strain. I have some massage oil that works miracles. I'll attend to it the minute I get to where I'm going.'

Dan quirked a brow. 'And where is that?'

'Milldale. Home.'

'Home,' Dan repeated. 'I thought you lived in Hopeton.'

'I do, for work. But home for me is Lark Hill, the vineyard where my parents live. Where I grew up. I'm starting a bit of leave.'

It took Dan only a few seconds to process all this. She still had some way to drive to Milldale before she could get relief for her neck pain. Was she fit to drive? Was her car even drivable? He came to a decision. He was a doctor, for God's sake. He could treat her. Here and now. 'Do you have your *miracle* oil with you?'

Lindsey looked uncertain. 'Of course I have it with me.'

'In your luggage?' Dan was slowly opening the driver's door. 'Tell me where to look and I'll massage it in for you. The sooner it's done, the sooner some relief will kick in for you.'

Lindsey's hands clutched the collar of his coat, pulling it higher as if to ward off the idea. She couldn't let him do that. It was too intimate...too...everything. She moistened her lips. 'If you get me the oil, I can rub it on myself.'

He snorted. 'And how high can you lift your arms without it hurting?'

Emotions began clogging Lindsey's throat. If she was honest, she was aching all over and suffering the aftermath of shock. It would be so lovely to let go of all her scruples and let Dan take care of her. 'My car keys are still in the ignition.'

'And your luggage in the boot?' Dan swung one leg out of the car.

Lindsey managed a small nod. 'Just bring my beauty case. It's black with—'

'Lindsey, relax,' Dan broke in gently. 'I know what a beauty case looks like. I'll find it.'

Lindsey closed her eyes. He'd told her to relax so she'd try. He'd taken over anyway. And right at the moment the idea sounded heaven-sent.

Dan was back. Not only did he have her beauty case but he'd brought along her shoulder bag as well. And her long woolly cardigan was draped over his forearm.

'You've thought of everything.' Lindsey managed a trapped smile.

'And I have something for your neck pain as well.'

'What are they?' She looked dubiously at the foil-wrapped tablets he handed her.

'They're standard painkillers,' Dan said. 'Nothing to send you off to la-la land.' He watched as she broke open the foil and then handed her a bottle of water. When she'd swallowed the tablets, he asked, 'Now, how are we going to do this?'

Lindsey blinked. He was obviously referring to her massage. She unzipped her beauty case and handed him the bottle of oil. 'I could probably just manoeuvre myself so my back's to you,' she said throatily.

'Or we could fold back the rear seat so you could lie down.'

'That's not necessary.' Lindsey was firm. 'Just take your jacket back, Dan, and I'll get my shirt off.'

Dan's eyes widened. His heart gave a sideways skip. 'OK...'

Lindsey undid the buttons and shrugged off the loose-fitting shirt to reveal a snug little vest top beneath. She sent him an innocent look. 'What?'

'Nothing.'

She managed a soft chuckle. 'Had you going there, didn't I, Daniel?'

'A guy can live in hope,' he countered, his mouth lifting at the corners. 'Now, give me that oil and we'll get started.'

Lindsey felt her body relax its tension as Dan's fingers began the gentle kneading of her neck muscles. It felt good, so good, and she wanted it to go on for ever...

Dan let his hands drift over the smooth column of her neck and then tease out the tense muscles at its base, almost hypnotised by the feel of her satin-smooth skin under his hands. 'It's Dante, by the way.'

'Really?' Lindsey's voice went high in disbelief.

'Really.'

'From the Italian poet of the Middle Ages?'

'At least you have the origin right,' he said. 'My sisters used to tell everyone I'd been named after a middle-aged poet.'

'Oh, poor you. Were you teased a lot?'

'Sometimes I felt like quietly enrolling at another school.'

'I think Dante suits you.'

'Hmm.' Dan was noncommittal.

'Is your mother a romantic, then?'

'No.' He sounded amused. 'It's an old family name. Apparently, it was just my turn to be lumbered with it.'

'That's pathetic,' Lindsey said mildly. 'It makes you different...*special*.'

He didn't reply.

'How does that feel now?'

Lindsey heard the guarded tone in his voice. Had her remark embarrassed him? Probably. And she wouldn't have continued with the banter if she hadn't been feeling so relaxed with him. Her mistake. 'It's much better, thanks. I'll be OK now.' She swivelled round to face the front again.

'If you're sure?' Dan recapped the bottle of oil and handed it back to her.

'I'm fine.' She stowed the bottle back in her beauty case then reached for her cardigan and shrugged it on.

Well, he'd stuffed that up. Dan locked his hands around the steering wheel and looked blindly out into the night. He'd stomped all over her light remarks and shut down. Now she'd be back to thinking he was some kind of unsociable cretin. God, he felt like an infant trying to stand upright and walk.

His jaw tightened. He had to fix things. 'I've…made things awkward again, haven't I?'

Her throat constricted. 'I wasn't coming on to you.'

'I know that. You were being sweet and funny…' He paused painfully.

'I've—been out of circulation for a while.'

Lindsey glanced at him, taking in his body language. Obviously, he'd been through something that had knocked him sideways. Something it was taking him time to get past. She felt a river of empathy run out to him. 'Do you want to talk about it?' As soon as she'd said the trite words Lindsey wished them back. Whatever it was that was bugging him, he'd probably *talked* about it until he was blue in the face. 'Sorry, scratch that.'

He blew out a controlled sigh. 'It's just stuff that's a bit hard to…revisit.'

'I get that, Dan,' she said softly.

His head swung towards her. Even in the subdued lighting in the car, the force of his undivided attention was like a mini-riot inside her. They breathed through several beats of silence. Until… Dan bent, his lips grazing hers. It was the lightest of kisses but heady with the taste of promise. For a long moment they stared at each other. 'That was a bit…' Lindsey's voice faded.

'Unexpected?' Dan moved closer, so close she had to tilt her head up to look at him. So close she could feel the heat radiating from his body. 'Nice, though?'

His softly spoken question danced across her nerves, creating a new wave of warmth to cascade through her. She nodded, words simply escaping her.

Dan stroked her cheek with the backs of his fingers, his body drenched in emotions he'd almost forgotten.

A gossamer-thin thread of awareness seemed to shimmer between them, until they drew back slowly from each other, breaking the spell.

Lindsey began pulling her cardigan more tightly around her. 'Um, do you think we could find a hot drink somewhere?'

'Oh, God—sorry!' Dan hit the heel of his hand on his forehead. 'You're probably still shocky. I'm an idiot—'

'Dan, it's OK.' Lindsey bit back a half-laugh. 'I didn't expect you to have a Thermos of tea with you. There's a service station a few clicks further on. We could stop there.'

'Right. Good. We'll do that. But we'll need to do something about your car first. From what I saw, it's not drivable.'

'Oh—are you sure?' Lindsey looked pained.

'I'm no mechanic but looks like you had a pretty big whack. The back wheel seems out of alignment and I had trouble getting the boot open. I could have a word with the tow-truck guys for you?'

'No, it's fine.' She waved the idea away. 'I'll get on to

my insurance company.' She flicked out her mobile and found the number on speed dial. 'All sorted,' she said after a few minutes of intense negotiation. 'They'll arrange for my car to be towed for repairs and if I need it I can pick up a replacement vehicle from the garage in Milldale.'

'I'll drive you home, then,' Dan said.

'I don't want to take you out of your way.'

'You won't be. I'm going to Milldale myself. I'll get your personal stuff from the car, shall I?'

'I'll help.' Lindsey volunteered, making to get out of his vehicle.

'Hang on a tick.' He stayed her with the lightest touch on her wrist. 'I'll come round and give you a hand. Don't want you falling.'

'Dan, I'm fine,' she remonstrated.

'Humour me, all right?'

Lindsey gave a contained little sigh but waited until he'd come round to the passenger door. He opened it and offered a steadying hand. She took it gratefully. He'd been right. She did feel a kind of light-headedness.

'When did you last eat?' Dan asked, keeping his hand firmly on hers.

'Sandwich at lunch.'

'Then the sooner we get some hot food into you the better.' He reopened the boot and retrieved her suitcase and a canvas backpack.

'And would you mind getting that large plastic bin as well?' Lindsey asked. 'It has a lid so you won't spill anything.'

Dan hefted the bin out by its handle, almost staggering at its solid weight. 'What the blazes do you have in here—body parts?'

Her mouth crimped at the corners. 'Clay.'

'I…see.' Although clearly he didn't.

'It's potter's clay,' Lindsey explained, following him

back to the Land Rover. 'I have a wheel and kiln at home. I aim to make some pieces while I'm on my holiday.'

Dan tried to get a grip on his wayward thoughts, imagining *Lindsey the potter* with her dark hair wild and flowing, perhaps her feet bare, her body lithe and swaying as she threw her pots. A compelling new awareness, sharp and insistent, stirred within him. An awareness that hadn't been stirred in a long time. An awareness that he'd stomped all over on that first day when Lindsey Stewart had smiled at him.

'Do you think you should let your folks know what's happened so they won't be worrying?' Dan asked as they settled back into the car. 'I imagine it'll be a bit late by the time we get you home.'

That sounded so thoughtful. Lindsey turned her head, slowly taking in his profile. It was almost sculpted. He'd make a perfect model. Her fingers began to tingle and she imagined carving out his features from a block of clay, pleating, smoothing, working her thumbs to form his cheekbones, a slow sweep to define his jaw, the touch of a finger defining the cleft in his chin. Definitely that. She pressed her thumb and forefinger together, almost feeling the slide of wet clay as she fashioned the curve of his mouth…

'Lindsey?'

'Uh—' She came back with a jolt.

'Do you need to ring home?'

'Actually, my parents are in Scotland, visiting my brother and sister-in-law. They've just had their first baby. Mum and Dad are away for a few more weeks yet.'

Dan started the engine and they began moving. 'So, who's at home for you, then?'

'I don't need looking after.'

'You've been through a trauma tonight, Lindsey. What if you need something—or someone?'

Heck! Was he offering? Lindsey pulled back from the flight of fancy. 'I should explain,' she said. 'We have managers for the vineyard, Jeff and Fiona Collins. Their cottage is quite close to the main house. Knowing I'm coming, Fi will have aired the place, stocked the fridge and left the lights on. I'll phone her when I arrive and she's around if I need anything.'

'I guess that's all right, then,' he said, as the bright lights of the roadhouse came into view.

'That was lovely, thanks.' Lindsey forked up the last of her omelette and then sat back, replete. 'So, why are you heading to Milldale?'

'Nathan Lyons's wedding.' Dan finished off his steak sandwich and casually swiped his mouth with the paper napkin.

'Of course. I can't believe I'd forgotten for the moment. It'll be a big do. Sami will have all the trimmings.'

Dan raised a dark brow. 'You know Sami?'

'For ever. Our parents' properties adjoin. We lost touch a bit when she relocated to Sydney but we've caught up again now she's back.'

'I'm Nathan's best man,' Dan said.

'I knew from the hospital grapevine you were mates.' Lindsey rested her chin in her upturned hand and looked at him. 'Are you looking forward to the wedding?'

'Yes, I am...' he said slowly, and realised it was true. 'They're a great couple.'

Lindsey gave a soft laugh. 'They're in love. It shows.'

'I suppose it does. Have *you* ever been in love, Lindsey?' he asked abruptly.

Wow! That was out of left field. 'In love. Out of love,' she sidestepped lightly. 'You?'

He gave a tight shrug. 'Same.'

They picked up their mugs of tea, each silently assessing the weight of their answers, each guessing that they hadn't exactly been lies but that they hadn't been quite the truth either.

'You're not Sami's bridesmaid, by any chance?' Dan asked after a minute.

'No. Her sister Caitlin's filling that role. She's just back from a modelling assignment overseas. Cait's the face of Avivia.'

'Which is...?'

Lindsey chuckled. 'Avivia is an international cosmetic company.'

'Ah.' He nodded sagely. 'But *you'll* be at the wedding?'

'Yes. I'll save you a dance,' she ventured daringly.

Dan's eyes flicked wide. The thought of dancing with her, *holding* her, sent a new chain of awareness shooting up his spine.

'I take it you *can* dancc?'

'Yes, I can dance.' He gave a guarded kind of smile. 'In fact, I used to love dancing.'

'Used to?'

'It's been a while.'

'Oh.' Lindsey drew back in her chair. Out of nowhere, her body felt tingly with electricity. 'We'll have to catch you up, then.'

His chuckle was a bit rusty. 'Don't plan ahead too much. I think I'm supposed to dance with the bridesmaid a bit.'

'Well, only the first dance, perhaps.' Lindsey's eyes gleamed. She was enjoying this. 'Cait's engaged. She'll have her bloke with her.'

'So...' Dan considered. 'After the first dance, I'm off the hook?'

'Unless Nathan expects you to work the room.'

'Unlikely.' His mouth curved into a crooked moue that was almost a grin.

'That's good, then.' Suddenly Lindsey's breath felt fluttery. What was it about being with Dan that made her feel as though she was flying through space without a parachute?

And loving it?

CHAPTER FOUR

THE NEXT MORNING Dan was awake early. He got up, embracing a new sense of purpose, a kind of upbeat feeling, as he threw himself into the shower and then dressed in faded jeans and a long-sleeved navy T-shirt. He'd arranged to meet Nathan for breakfast.

He slipped quietly down the stairs from the upper floor of the pub and stepped out onto the street. So this was Milldale, Lindsey's family home. He could imagine her growing up here, he thought. A leggy country kid, bright as newly minted gold, a bit sassy, self-reliant… He shook the image away and continued along the quaint village street.

He checked his watch. He had time to spare for a walk and gain his bearings. Hope for something he couldn't quite define was springing up in his heart as he continued on his walk. The main street gave way to a few houses, a park and an unexpectedly steep hill. Full of energy, Dan climbed the hill to a viewing platform that overlooked the surrounding countryside. He leaned on the safety rail and looked out. The view seemed never-ending, timeless, stretching from the early spring greenness of the vineyards to the gentle rise and fall of blue hills beyond. Houses were dotted through the vineyards, a wisp of smoke drifting from one of the chimneys.

He took a cleansing breath so deep it almost hurt. Today was the first day of the rest of his life. He couldn't wait to see what it might bring.

'You're almost a married man,' Dan addressed Nathan as they sat over their traditional English breakfast.

'Can't wait.' Nathan added a curl of bacon to his egg. 'I'm sorry it didn't work out for you, mate,' he said quietly.

Dan gave a rough laugh. 'Well, the circumstances were hardly ideal, were they? Not like you and Sami. Even Lindsey remarked how "in love" the pair of you seem.'

'You mean it shows?' Nathan's face was lit with a goofy grin.

'Just a bit. Make sure it stays that way,' Dan said.

'Oh, man.' Nathan lifted his gaze briefly to the ceiling. 'You're not about to give me a *talk*, are you?'

'No. But I need to say something before we get caught up in all the hoopla. I can't count the number of times you've had my back, Nathan. You've been the best mate. The best. I hope you and Sami have the most amazing life together.'

'Thanks,' Nathan responded, a bit gruffly. 'That means a lot, Dan. But friendship is a two-way street. I'd like to think we've both had each other's backs over the years. Right, I could go another round of toast.' He broke what could have been an awkward male moment and hailed a passing waitress. 'Speaking of Lindsey...' he gave Dan an enquiring look '...how is she after last night's MVA? Have you called her?'

'It's a bit early yet.'

'And the injured guy?' Nathan asked.

'Induced coma. That's all they're prepared to say.' Dan placed his knife and fork neatly together on his plate. 'Uh—did you know Lindsey's into pottery?'

'Yeah. Lins is a seriously talented artist. When the

new maternity wing opened last year she gifted a mother-and-child sculpture for the foyer. You should take a ride to the fourth floor and poke your head in some time.'

'Maybe I'll do that,' Dan said, knowing he wouldn't. But that was his business. He poured a second cup of tea and gave himself permission to relax, to shuck off the negative thoughts Nathan's suggestion had set running.

Today was about new beginnings.

The wedding was wonderful, the best man's speech a triumph. Dan's remarks were warm and lively, with just the right amount of wit, nicely balanced with sincerity and in keeping with the significance of the occasion.

Lindsey joined in the applause as Dan resumed his seat. For some reason she couldn't define, she felt inordinately proud of him.

The remainder of the speeches were heartfelt but brief and the newlyweds took to the floor for the first dance. Almost as if her eyes were hotwired in Dan's direction, Lindsey saw him incline his head towards Caitlin. Caitlin smiled and they rose together. Obviously, they were about to join Nathan and Sami on the dance floor. Lindsey made a dry little swallow. Dan seemed very much at ease as he whirled Caitlin into an old-fashioned waltz. They looked stunning together. And Lindsey was swamped with jealousy. Taking up her glass, she took a gulp of her champagne and pretended not to care.

'Dance, Lindsey?'

Lindsey brought her head up sharply to find Eliot Swift, one of Sami's cousins, hovering. He'd come to Milldale for holidays when they'd all been in their teens. He'd had a bit of a crush on her then. Her eyes widened. 'Hi, Eliot. I didn't know you were here.'

He grimaced. 'Big crowd. You on your own?'

She nodded. Well, she *was*, wasn't she? Eliot held out

his hand and she took it and let him guide her across to the dance floor.

'Been a while.' He sent her a wry smile.

'Yes. What have you been up to?'

'Selling IT to the masses. Travelling a bit. You?'

'Travelling a bit as well. Presently nursing at Hopeton District.'

'Ah.' His eyes held a glimmer of humour. 'Found your niche, then.'

'I believe so.'

'Great summers back then, weren't they?'

'Mmm. But now we've all grown up. Are you married?'

'Nah.' He shook his head, and they took to the floor. 'Sorry, was that your foot?'

'One of them.' Lindsey laughed. She couldn't help herself. They could have been seventeen again and she could have been back on the Kellys' veranda, trying to teach Eliot to dance.

'I still can't waltz,' he apologised. 'But we can shuffle about until they change the tempo. Shouldn't be long. Ah, good.' He sounded relieved as the music changed into something slow and torchy and he gathered her in with style.

Dan frowned a bit, catching sight of Lindsey as she danced past. She was wearing a red dress, one smooth shoulder exposed, her hair loose and shiny. She looked... beautiful. Dan's interest intensified as he checked out her partner. They looked pretty cosy. And he was holding Lindsey far too close. Dan felt his gut curl into an uncomfortable knot. *He* was the one who should have been holding her.

For the next while Lindsey danced and mingled. She stopped to chat with Sami's mother, Marcia, and assured her it was a marvellous wedding. And, yes, she, Lindsey, was having a fine time.

'Oh—excuse me, love.' Marcia turned in response to some urgent hand gesturing from one of the catering people and took off.

Lindsey took a relieved breath. This was her cue to slip outside for some air.

It was a cool evening, and because much of the gracious old home's beauty lay in its outdoors, the verandas were spectacularly lit, fairy-lights peeped out of boxed hedges arranged beside the door, and glossy-leaved potted plants were decorated with love hearts and sparkly bows. Lindsey's mouth tipped into a wry smile. It seemed Sami had indeed got her trimmings.

Descending the shallow flight of stairs to the sweeping lawn beyond, she looked up and gave a little breath of delight. The fairy-lights sprinkled around in the trees gave a storybook feel. It was the perfect setting for a wedding, she decided, sitting down on one of the old-fashioned garden benches.

She rested her head back on the wooden slats, looking up to the clear sky and the twinkling necklace of stars.

The light strains of the music floated out on the night air. After a while she heard the change to the thump, thump of an upbeat rhythm. Was Dan still dancing with Caitlin? She'd heard a discreet whisper that Caitlin's engagement was off. Perhaps Dan would feel obliged to partner her for most of the evening. But from what she'd seen, it hadn't seemed much of a hardship for him. She shivered slightly. Obviously, he'd forgotten about *their* dance.

She closed her eyes.

'Hey…'

Lindsey's eyes snapped open. 'Dan!' She swallowed jerkily.

He sat beside her. 'I've been looking for you everywhere. I meant to call you but I got caught up. It's been like a circus all day and then the wedding...'

'Well, you had to expect that.' Lindsey gave a little shrug. 'You are the best man.'

'Last night was pretty rough.' Dan paused and looked at her. 'Did you manage to sleep all right?'

'Yes.' Lindsey turned her face up to his. Even in the half-light she could see the concern in his eyes. It unsettled her to realise how relieved she felt. She hadn't imagined the closeness of last night. It seemed he did care. 'In fact, I slept in. And Fiona's been like a mother hen all day.' She sent him a guarded smile. 'I'm fine.'

'You look amazing.' He lowered his head slightly, so close his chin was almost dusting her cheek.

Her breath caught on a stilted laugh. 'So do you.'

'I take it, then, we're both pretty amazing.' His eyes gleamed with intent.

Her stomach curled. He'd taken off his suit jacket, loosened his tie and rolled his sleeves back over his forearms. She took a breath, the subtle scent of his aftershave filling her nostrils. 'I thought you'd forgotten our dance.'

'Was that likely?' His mouth went to where her neck met her shoulder in the softest caress.

Lindsey's eyes drifted shut and she shivered.

'I had to have a couple of duty dances,' Dan said, 'with Nathan's mum and his Aunt Tilly.'

'The large lady in the purple pants suit? She looked formidable.'

'But a great dancer,' Dan proclaimed, his lips twitching. 'She runs a pub in Sydney.' His gaze went to Lindsey's mouth and lingered. 'Why are we having this crazy conversation? When we should be doing this...'

Lindsey swallowed, her heart banging out of rhythm. Racing. He was bending towards her, his blue eyes capturing hers with a magnetic pull. 'Dan...?'

'Don't talk…' In an almost imperceptible movement he slid his hands beneath her elbows and they rose as one.

Instantly, Lindsey felt her nerve ends tingling, her breathing uncomfortably tight. She lifted her head, searing her gaze with his.

'I need to do this again…' Dan reached up, sliding the tips of his fingers over her face, feeling the gentle throb of heat under her skin, the feminine, fragile line of her jaw. Even as his thumb lifted her chin his fingers were seeking her nape, drawing her to him.

He lowered his head slowly, giving her the chance to end it, if that's what she wanted. But she didn't, and her lips gave a tiny sigh of welcome as his mouth brushed hers, settling over its softness with touch-and-retreat little sips, feeling the instant response and teasing her lips into a more open kiss.

Lindscy was drowning in feelings she hadn't experienced for the longest time. Dan's mouth on hers felt right, their kiss pure and perfect. So dazzlingly perfect. He drew her closer and she opened her mouth as though to savour and hold onto the magic of his kiss, walking her fingers to the curve of his neck and into the soft strands of his hair.

And she didn't let herself think for one second whether any of what they were sharing had a future. She was just amazed that they should be kissing at all and that she'd so longed for it without even knowing why…

'You have the sweetest mouth,' Dan murmured much later, moving his hands to her shoulders and then cupping her face in his hands.

She licked her lips. 'Do I?'

'Mmm.' He bent to her again, pressing his forehead to hers. It seemed a lifetime later when Dan drew back. He took her hands, absently running his thumbs across her knuckles. 'I suppose we should get back in there.'

'Yes, I suppose we should.' Lindsey reluctantly withdrew her hands, swiping a fall of hair back over her shoulder. 'I imagine the bride and groom will want to get away soon.'

'Come on, then.' Dan held out his hand and they were linked again. As they made their way back indoors to Rosemount's beautiful ballroom, they saw the crowd gathering for the farewells. 'I'd better have a word with Nate,' Dan said. 'He looks like a rogue bull caught in the headlights.'

Nathan's relief when he saw Dan was almost palpable. 'Sami and I want to split. Any ideas for a quick getaway?'

'I'll alert the limo driver.' Dan pulled out his mobile, his eyes assessing a possible exit route. 'Have you said your private farewells?'

'All done. And, mate...' Nathan slung his arm around Dan's shoulders. 'Thanks. And I mean for the classic speech and, well, for everything.'

'It's been a great day.' Dan's jaw worked a bit. 'You and Sami have a fantastic honeymoon. Where is she, by the way?'

'Just here.' Sami materialised beside them and linked her arm through Nathan's. 'Are we heading off, babe?' She turned a very sweet smile on her new husband.

'As soon as Dan can find us an escape route.' Nathan bent and pressed a kiss into his wife's hair.

'Dan.' Sami let go of Nathan's arm and turned to Dan, kissing him on both cheeks. 'Thank you so much. You've been the best best man! Oops!' She put a finger to her smiling mouth. 'I think I've had a bit much champagne. But you know what I mean.'

'It's been fun, Sami,' Dan said. 'Take care of this big guy.'

'Take care of each other,' Lindsey chimed in, and hugged them both.

'Oh, Lins.' Sami whisked Lindsey aside. 'Keep an eye

on Cait, would you? She's a bit emotional about…well, you know…'

Lindsey nodded. 'Don't worry, Eliot's taken Cait under his wing.'

'Good old El.' Sami sent Lindsey an arch look. 'He still has a thing for you, you know?'

Lindsey just grinned. 'In your dreams, Samantha. Oh, look, Dan's beckoning. Grab Nathan and scoot.'

'Thanks for everything, guys!' Sami threw back over her shoulder as Nathan took her hand and urged her swiftly through the blaze of farewells and good wishes to the white stretch limousine in the forecourt.

Lindsey smiled softly as they watched the car drive out of sight. 'Wasn't it the loveliest wedding?'

'Yes, it was…' Dan's thoughts winged back to another time, another wedding…

'You OK?' Lindsey asked, realising he'd gone quiet.

Dan blew out a breath that untied the sudden knots in his stomach. 'Bit nostalgic,' he admitted, and threaded his fingers through hers.

'You and Nathan go back a long way, don't you?'

'First day at uni. Shared a house through our training…'

'Parties and girls,' Lindsey surmised, and smiled at him.

He gave a half-shrug. 'All that. I'm immensely happy for him.'

'So, you believe in marriage, then?' she said casually, although her antenna was tuned for his answer.

His look became shuttered. 'Well, people seem to be still doing it.'

And that, decided Lindsey, was no answer at all.

They headed back inside. 'My duties as best man are all done,' Dan said. 'The band is on a break, so perhaps we could find somewhere less noisy and have a drink? I believe the champagne is still flowing.'

Lindsey made a small face. 'I think I'd actually prefer some tea.'

* * *

They made their way through to a kind of garden room where a helpful waiter organised their pot of tea. Lindsey poured, saying, 'I'm assuming you have the rest of the weekend off?'

'Actually, I have a few days' leave.' Dan took the cup she handed across to him. 'I pulled some extra shifts to make it happen.'

'Oh.' The tip of Lindsey's tongue roved her bottom lip. So that was the reason she'd kept missing him at work. He'd been off when she'd been on. 'You must be running on empty, then, with the wedding on top of everything.'

He shrugged. 'I'll recharge quickly.'

Lindsey's heartbeat picked up a notch and an idea began forming. 'So…what are you doing with your time off?'

'I haven't quite decided yet. I have the use of an apartment at the Gold Coast whenever I want it. Maybe I could catch some waves. A bit of sun. A bit of fun.'

Fun? Lindsey dropped her gaze. Did that mean a holiday fling while he was at the coast? That idea didn't gel at all. She tilted her head back to look at him properly. 'Do you have friends at the coast?'

'No.' Dan's eyes seemed to track over her features one by one before he went on. 'I'm used to being on my own. It doesn't bother me.'

Well, it should. Lindsey's fingers spanned her teacup. Was Dan Rossi a loner by choice? She didn't think so. She'd seen how much he'd enjoyed the social interaction at the wedding. And he hadn't been faking it. He'd been warm and funny. And sexy…

However hard she tried, she couldn't remain detached. That assumption had been shattered like eggshells under a heavy boot the moment they'd tasted each other. She'd loved the way he'd kissed. So many men didn't know how to kiss, she thought. But Dan had it down in spades. Or maybe it was simply that their bodies were totally in tune, their chemistry perfect for each other. She felt her skin prickle at the thought. Suddenly she straightened in her chair. Like a spark on tinder, the idea turned into possibility. 'I have a much better idea. You could spend your days off here in Milldale. With me.'

Dan looked up, startled. 'With you,' he repeated.

'Well, not exactly *with me*,' Lindsey explained. 'What I meant to say was that we have several holiday cabins at the vineyard. You could have one of those—if you wanted to, of course.'

'Uh-huh.'

Oh, God, she thought as her heart began pattering. She couldn't believe what she'd just done. It was so unlike her. She'd jumped in boots and all and had probably put Dan on the spot. But he was a grown-up, she justified. He could say no. 'There arc hiking trails if that appeals, heated pool and spa up at the house. Soft blue sky days and the quiet just seem to settle around you. There's no feeling quite like it. It kind of all ties together; the peace and the feeling you can let go and just...*be*.'

Be. Dan's breath jammed in his throat. One tiny word with a thousand connotations. Her eyes had turned almost silver. Here I am, they seemed to say. So why on earth was he hesitating? Unless his instincts were leading him astray, Lindsey Stewart was the real deal. Lovely, exciting. Sexy. He felt a wild heat in every part of his body.

And he hadn't had a feeling like this about a woman for the longest time.

Somehow their hands had met across the table, their fingertips touching.

'That sounds excellent,' he said almost formally. 'I'll be happy to accept your invitation, Lindsey.'

Lindsey watched as his mouth quirked with humour and acknowledged the almost painful lurching of her heart as it thundered out the heated rhythm of physical attraction. 'Oh, ha-ha.' She took her hand away, realising she'd worried about nothing. 'You're taking the mickey, aren't you?'

His grin unfolded lazily, his eyes crinkling at the corners. 'You looked so earnest selling me your idea, Lindsey, when in reality you didn't have to sell it to me at all.' Reaching across, he took her hand again, slowly interlinking his fingers through hers. A tiny pulse flickered in his cheek. 'I'd love to spend my days off with you.' He fiddled with the gold filigree ring she wore on her middle finger. 'Perhaps we could just *be* together?'

Her eyes slanted, their expression sultry and soft. 'Perhaps we could.' She reclaimed her hand gently. 'Now I'm going to call it a night.' Picking up her clutch bag, she held it against her chest. 'You know the way to Lark Hill so I'll see you tomorrow, shall I?'

Dan was immediately alert. 'How are you getting home?'

'Cab. I imagine all of Milldale's taxi fleet is on duty tonight.'

'My car's here. I'll drive you.'

'Dan.' Lindsey shook her head. 'It's not necessary. You've had a long day—'

She watched his mouth firm.

'I'll drive you home.'

CHAPTER FIVE

LINDSEY WOKE WITH a start on Sunday morning. She grabbed her phone off the bedside table and fell back against her pillow. It was just eight o'clock. Dan probably wouldn't be here for ages yet.

A smile touched her mouth and widened to a full-blown grin. The good Dr Rossi thought he'd played the cool card but she knew her invitation had rattled his composure. She was still a little amazed that she'd asked him to spend his leave with her. But the invitation had bubbled out from somewhere deep within her.

And just maybe it was all meant to be.

When her phone rang she was still hugging the thought. Checking the caller ID, she felt a thrilling reality. 'Dan, hi.'

'Ms Stewart, I presume. Are you up?'

'Of course.' She hastily levered herself upright and swung to the side of the bed. 'Are you?'

'Yes.' He didn't tell her he'd already been to Hopeton and back to collect some extra clothes for his impromptu holiday.

'Are you still at the pub?'

'Actually, no,' he said easily. 'I'm only a few minutes away from you.'

'You are!' Lindsey almost squeaked. Abruptly, she ended the call and sprinted to the bathroom.

What to wear? Back in her bedroom, she shuffled

through the clothes she still hadn't unpacked from her suitcase. She took out her soft jeans, a white T-shirt and, because she felt a lingering chill of winter in the air, she shrugged into a little cropped-style cardigan. Now shoes—

As the sound of the old-fashioned door knocker echoed along the hallway, she spun to a halt. He was here! And she felt only half-dressed. Hastily, she shoved her feet into ballet flats, finger-combed her hair and went to let him in.

'Dan…' She blinked out into the early-morning sunlight and felt a soft shiver like a slipstream of desire feather all the way down her backbone. He looked so early-morning sexy with the beginnings of a dark shadow along his jaw and the simple male thing of the collar of his check shirt all askew under his navy jumper. She made a little sound in her throat.

Just the sight of her curled a wild kind of excitement through Dan's gut. She had no make-up on. No lingering smell of perfume. But she exuded a kind of femaleness that was…intoxicating. A bubble of pure want exploded inside him. He took a step forward.

In a second they were leaning into each other.

Dan's mouth moved against hers, shaping her name as their bodies aligned. And then he kissed her, a gentle, sweet, slow kiss that tingled all the way down to her toes, before he let her go. 'Good morning,' she said softly.

He lifted a strand of her hair and wound it around his finger. '*Now* it is,' he said.

She gave him one of her wide smiles, activating the dimples beside her mouth. 'Come through. Have you eaten?'

'I had a coffee earlier.'

'Let's see what the pantry can yield up, then,' she said, leading the way along the hallway to the kitchen.

Dan took a quick inventory of the timber benches and

the navy blue and white tiles. 'Big workspaces,' he commented. 'Do you cater for your guests as well?'

'The cabins allow for self-catering,' Lindsey said, 'but sometimes we provide breakfast baskets if anyone requests them. I'll fix something for us now. What would you like?'

'Anything is fine. Surprise me.'

She flipped him a cheeky grin. 'I think I have already.'

She had. And his mind still couldn't quite grasp the fact that he was here with her. In her home. About to share breakfast with her. His gaze jagged across her face. 'I can't believe I'm actually here.'

'Of course you're here.' Her lashes swooped, eyeing him from head to toe. 'Otherwise who have I just kissed?'

Dan gave a gravelly laugh and looked around the room, his gaze lighting on the sun-catcher crystal that dangled from the window in front of the sink. 'Nice *feng shui*.'

Lindsey raised an eyebrow at the abrupt change in conversation. 'You a follower, then?'

He shrugged. 'Parts of the philosophy appeal to me.'

Who'd have thought? Now he'd surprised *her*. Lindsey loaded crockery and cutlery onto a tray and set them on the bench.

'What can I do to help?' Dan asked.

'Let's eat outside on the back deck,' she said, handing him the tray. 'Could you set the table?'

'I think I can manage that.'

Male distraction gone for the moment, Lindsey set about preparing breakfast. She juiced oranges and deftly arranged portions of melon and a variety of other fruit on a glass platter. That would do for starters, she decided, picking up the plate.

Dan was leaning over the railing, looking into the distance. He turned to Lindsey as she came to stand beside him. 'This is God's own country,' he said, a faraway look in his eyes. ‘How can you bear to leave it and go to work in a casualty department?’

She sent him a pained look. ‘Now you’re talking like a tourist. Running a successful vineyard is extremely hard work, Dan. You can’t sit around, admiring the scenery.’

His mouth quirked. ‘And that’s what you do in Casualty?’

She made a face at him. ‘That’s the creek down there.’ She pointed out an unbroken line of willows. ‘Sami, Cait, my brother James and I had some fun times there when we were growing up.’

‘I can imagine.’ Dan sent her a soft look. ‘James is your brother who’s in Scotland, right?’

‘Yes. He and his wife, Catherine, are physiotherapists. Their baby daughter, Alexandra Rose, is just three weeks old.’

‘Nice name.’ Dan felt an uncomfortable tightening in his gut and breathed it away. ‘And the cabins?’

‘There are four. See, over there to your left.’ She indicated the weathered timber structures nestled into the side of the hill. ‘You can get settled in later.’ She touched his forearm. ‘Shall we eat, then?’

‘So, how come the name Lark Hill?’ Dan asked, as they each took a selection of fruit. ‘As far as I know, we have no larks as such in Australia.’

‘Long story short,’ Lindsey said, popping a sliver of golden kiwi fruit into her mouth, ‘my great-grandparents came from England. When they came to Milldale to begin farming, the bird calls reminded them of the larks back home. But of course they were our magpie larks, better known as peewees. But they’d already registered the place as Lark Hill so it just stayed.’

‘Fascinating,’ Dan said. ‘So your family are literally pioneers of the district.’

Lindsey lifted a shoulder. 'It just feels like we've always been here, I suppose. What about the Rossi family, then?'

Dan's mouth puckered briefly. 'I don't think we're pioneers of anything—except maybe passing down old names.'

Lindsey *tsked.* 'I really meant whereabouts are you from?'

'Melbourne.'

'You mentioned sisters. Any more siblings?'

Dan shook his head. 'I suppose you want a rundown.' He gave a resigned lopsided grin.

'Of course. Then I'll know where to put you in your family.'

Dan lifted an eyebrow and helped himself to a sliver of melon. 'My dad is a linguistics professor at Melbourne Uni. Mum is a director of early childhood education.'

'Wow.' Lindsey lifted a hand, casually swinging her index finger through a long curl as it fell against her throat. 'I'll bet some interesting conversations happened there.'

'Mmm.' Dan sucked the sweet juice of the melon deeply into his mouth. 'They're both pretty passionate about learning. I think the girls and I could read before we could walk,' he joked.

'And your sisters,' Lindsey asked interestedly. 'Younger? Older?'

'Younger.'

'And what are they—lawyers, doctors?'

'No.' He gave an amused chuckle. 'Juliana trained as a teacher-librarian but now she runs a combined bookshop and coffee corner in downtown Melbourne. Reg—Regina—is married to Christoph. They're both professional musicians, violinists with the Melbourne Symphony Orchestra.'

Lindsey drank the information in. 'So, you're rather an arts-related kind of family, then. Rich in good conversation, music, books and so on.'

'I suppose.'

So, in fact, quite similar to her own background, Lindsey thought. 'But you obviously broke the mould and opted for the sciences and medicine. How did that happen?'

'My uncle Robert, Dad's brother, is a physician,' Dan explained. 'He arrived late in their family so to us kids he was more like a big brother than an uncle. I hung out with Rob a bit. And with his skeleton,' he added with a smile. 'I was always fascinated with the idea of becoming a doctor.'

'You weren't daunted by the study involved?'

He shook his head. 'Couldn't get enough of it.'

'It's a real calling for you, then.'

'Becoming a doctor? I guess it was.' Dan chased the last piece of fruit around his bowl and thought with something like amazement that it had been an age since he'd talked so freely about himself. But then again Lindsey seemed to have that effect on him. There was an openness about her that called to him to respond in a similar way. He leaned back in his chair, eyeing her thoughtfully.

'What?' Lindsey flicked him a startled look. His gaze had gone all smoky.

'Just thinking. This is good, isn't it?'

'This?' Her eyes widened and lit.

'This. Us. Here.'

Lindsey tipped her head on one side and looked searchingly at him. His voice had held slight wonder. 'Yes, it is,' she said, and thought that on a personal level they probably still had a few mountains to climb. But what was a mountain or two when Lark Hill was beginning to work its magic already...

'Well, come on, Ms Stewart.' Dan broke into her thoughts. 'That's me done. What about you and nursing?'

Lindsey batted the question away. 'There's not all that much to tell. I actually thought seriously about medicine but I'm a hands-on kind of girl. I figured it would be ages before I could do anything useful as a doctor, whereas nursing offered the chance to get stuck in fairly quickly,' she summed up with a smile. 'And here I am.'

Dan's gaze softened. 'Indeed you are.'

Deflecting his scrutiny, Lindsey hurriedly got to her feet and began collecting their used dishes. 'Shall we make some toast? Fiona's left one of her special wattle-seed loaves.'

'Sounds interesting.' Dan pushed himself upright and took the tray from her and they made their way back to the kitchen.

An hour later they were on their second pot of tea and still talking. About anything and everything. And it had all seemed as natural as breathing, Lindsey thought. In fact, so engrossed had they become, neither heard the sound of the front door opening and closing or the soft footfall along the hallway until, 'Yoo-hoo. It's only me. Are you there, Lindsey?'

'It's Fiona.' Lindsey put a finger to her lips. 'Be prepared to be well looked over. On the deck, Fi,' she called.

Fiona, cropped greying hair and with the suntanned complexion of her outdoor lifestyle, came out onto the deck and stopped, her clear blue gaze running assessingly over them. 'Not interrupting, am I?'

'Of course you're not.' Lindsey sought to put the older woman at ease. 'This is Dan Rossi. He's a friend from the hospital.'

Dan rose courteously and they shook hands. 'Nice to meet you, Fiona.'

'And you, Dan.' Fiona's gaze widened as something clicked. 'You're the doctor who kindly brought this one home after the accident, then?'

'That's me.' He shot a slightly mocking look at Lindsey. 'I think she'd have tried to walk home if I'd let her.'

Fiona shook her head. 'Independent to a fault. Always has been.'

'Hey, you two,' Lindsey protested. 'Do you mind?' She beckoned Fiona to a chair. 'Tea's still fresh.'

'No, thanks, love.' Fiona sat. 'I really just popped in to tell you I've let the last cabin.'

'Oh—OK… Who are the new people?'

'Young couple, Scott and Amy Fraser. Having a few days' holiday before the birth of their first baby.'

'A babymoon.' Lindsey smiled. 'That's so sweet.'

'They arrived last night,' Fiona said. 'Just saw them a while ago. They're off picnicking.'

'Well, it's a beautiful day so let's hope they enjoy the peace and quiet.' Lindsey looked at Dan. 'We should get out and stretch our legs too.'

With Fiona gone, they went inside, washed up and put the kitchen back to rights. Dan shoved the last of the cutlery into the drawer. 'I'll go back and stay at the pub tonight.'

'Why would you do that?' Lindsey hung the damp tea towel near the AGA to dry.

'Fiona said she's let the last cabin.'

'Stay here, then,' Lindsey countered practically. 'There's a guest bedroom you can have. It has its own en suite so you can be as private as you want to be.'

'Ah…' Dan swiped a hand across his cheekbones.

Watching his body language, Lindsey gave a little huff of disbelief. 'Surely you're not obsessing about propriety?'

He frowned through a beat.

'That's so sweetly old-fashioned.' Leaning back against the benchtop, she let her eyes rest softly on him. 'You're so well brought up, aren't you?'

Dan snorted. 'Give me a break. It's a small community. You and your family obviously have a certain…status.' And he hadn't missed Fiona's overt curiosity in his presence.

'Dan…'

'What?'

She stepped closer to him, her green eyes almost translucent as she met his gaze. 'We're grown-ups, aren't we?'

'I'd say so,' he murmured gruffly. 'Very grown-up…' he added, as he wound her hair loosely around his fingers, using the impetus to draw her closer and find her mouth.

They kissed long and hard until Dan let her go with a last lingering touch to her lips. 'Ah, Lindsey…' His fingers lifted her chin, his mouth only a breath away as he said her name again. 'Lindsey…'

'That's me.' She reached out to stroke his face, feeling his skin faintly, deliciously rough.

'I'll stay here then.'

Watching his mouth, so sexy in repose, Lindsey felt her heart pick up speed. 'I'm glad you've decided that. Now I won't have to put my fallback plan into action.'

He raised a brow in query.

'I was going to wrestle you for your car keys.'

'What's with you Milldale women?' Dan shook his head. 'Nathan said Sami was prone to wrestling *him*.'

'Must be something in the wine we grow,' Lindsey challenged, laughing, as Dan spun her away, as if they were about to dance. She shimmied back to him and locked her arms around his waist.

Dan's gaze heated. 'Now what…?'

She lifted her hand and traced the outline of his lips with her finger, recognising there was a new awareness beating its wings all around them. 'A walk perhaps?'

Or seventeen cold showers, Dan thought darkly, his mouth achingly sensitised by her touch.

Or he could give in to the avalanche of emotions engulfing him. And take her to bed.

Suddenly, making love with Lindsey seemed a natural progression from where they were now. The last step in intimacy. But perhaps he was fantasising. It had been so long since he'd been this close to a woman.

Had wanted to be this close.

So…all things considered, a walk, preferably a long one, would probably be a better option.

'Go get your stuff from the car,' Lindsey said, her gaze alight. 'I'll sort out some bed linen.'

CHAPTER SIX

'THIS IS GOING to be magic,' Lindsey said, as they walked through the vines, and then she showed Dan the creek and the rock pool. 'Next time you come, we'll swim here,' she said.

'So, I'm coming again…?' Dan held her loosely, looking deeply into her eyes.

He'd spoken quietly, his voice so husky it had made Lindsey shiver. 'Of course you are.' Wrapping her arms round his neck, she stepped closer to him so that they were hard against each other. And they kissed.

'So…' he said, when they'd broken apart.

'So…' she echoed.

'Funny how things turn out.'

'Mmm.'

They linked hands and continued on their hike. 'Should we be on the lookout for snakes?' Dan queried.

'Only elephants,' she deadpanned.

'I see.' Dan did a little sidestep away from her then pulled her back in. 'I've taken up with a joker.'

Further on, she challenged him to walk across the old bush log that spanned the deepest part of the creek. Dan obliged, easily and gracefully, arms held out like a tightrope walker to keep his balance. He gave a bow when he reached the other side and she made a face at him, before stepping lightly across the length of the log and joining him on the other side.

'Now where?' Dan asked as he gathered her in and spun her round.

'Up there.' Lindsey pointed to the highest point of the paddock. 'It looks steep but it's really a steady climb and then you get a great view.'

'And survey your domain,' he teased as they wandered off again.

'This is as far as we go,' Lindsey said when they reached the top of the hill.

Dan stopped and wheeled her round, linking his arms around her from behind. 'Ah...*bella vista*.'

'Pretty special, isn't it?' Eyes half-closed, Lindsey placed her hands on his forearms, almost absently stroking her fingers over his skin. She tipped her head back to look at him. 'Makes you feel good to be alive, doesn't it?'

'That—and being with you,' Dan added, a throaty edge to his voice.

They sat in a patch of dappled shade beneath a leopard tree, easing back against the trunk, their shoulders touching. For a long time they did little else other than absorb the gentle landscape and breathe in the air that was heady with the scent of wattles that edged up the hill and along the walking tracks.

'So, why New York, Dan?' His head jerked up as if she'd activated a string and she added quickly, 'Am I being too nosy?'

'No...' He pulled off a blade of grass and began shredding it with his fingers. 'I'd been there a couple of times on holidays, loved the buzz. When the chance came to work there, I grabbed it. The rest, as they say, is history. What about you?' He changed conversational lanes deftly. 'Travelled much?'

'Quite a bit.' Lindsey smiled up at him. 'The UK, of

course, seeing that James and Catherine live in Scotland. That was brilliant. We did some of Europe together. And last year I went to Japan for the snowboarding.'

'You're a snowboarder?' There was admiration in Dan's voice.

'Did you travel with a group?'

She shook her head. 'It probably would have been better if I had. I went with my boyfriend at the time.' She pulled her knees up to her chin and looked out into the distance. 'The day after we arrived he hooked up with one of the tour guides.'

'Ouch.'

Lindsey rolled her eyes in disdain. 'He described her as *cute* and said it was just a holiday fling. That it needn't change anything between us. The awful part was that it was all going on under my nose. How dumb was I?'

'I wouldn't call it dumb,' Dan said quietly. 'You trusted him and he let you down.' He brushed his fingers down her cheek. 'His loss, I think.' A long beat of silence until, 'I got married in New York.'

Married. The word fell like the thud of a stone into a deep pool. Lindsey's stomach began turning cartwheels. If he'd been going for shock value, he'd got it. She hesitated before asking, 'Are you still—?'

'No.' The word was snapped out. And then more or less on a sigh, 'We crashed and burned.'

Lindsey raised her gaze to look at him. That sounded awful. But he couldn't drop a major detail like that into the conversation and expect her to leave it there without comment. 'Do you want to tell me about it?'

Dan eased his back against the trunk of the tree, unaware his eyes had assumed a bleak look. He clamped his jaw and agonised over whether now was the time to tell Lindsey everything, but his gut did a somersault at the thought of resurrecting it all. He rubbed a hand across his cheekbones, feeling the familiar tightening in his throat, but he realised that if there was any chance of deepening his relationship with Lindsey, he had to plough on. 'Caroline and I met at a party. She was from out of state, an attorney, new to the city as I was. We began dating, doing stuff together...'

'OK. Fast forward all that. Obviously, you fell in love and got married.'

Dan averted his eyes quickly but not before she saw the pain in them.

She held out her hand to him. 'Sorry...that was glib.'

He took the hand she offered, pressing her fingers tightly as if to gain strength from the contact, then let it go. 'I imagine you've heard of the expression about your life turning on a dime?'

'Is—is that what happened to yours?'

'More or less.' There was silence as if he was searching for the words and then he began to talk very quietly and measuredly. 'When we met, we were both in crummy apartments so it seemed reasonable to move into something better and share the rent.'

'As a couple?'

'Well, it didn't start out like that and it wasn't something we'd planned.'

Lindsey frowned a bit. That didn't sound like the love affair of the century so why had they got married? Unless...?

'Caroline got pregnant.' His voice flattened. 'Down to a glitch in her contraception. She was panic-stricken. Her parents were...protective, ultra-conservative in their outlook, so totally proud of their only child when she'd got a place at one of the city's prestigious law firms, convinced she'd make partner in a few years. She was fearful of telling them about the pregnancy, distressed she'd let them down in some way. She said if she could tell them we were getting married, it would lessen the shock.'

Lindsey could hear the thudding of her own heart. She paused and frowned. 'And you married her?'

Dan registered her look of disbelief. 'It was my child too, Lindsey,' he justified. 'And I thought...well, if we put our best into the relationship, we could make it work. Then life began throwing us curveballs. We found out Caroline was carrying twins and that was scary enough but then we discovered they were mono-mono.'

Lindsey's breathing faltered. She interpreted what he was saying, that the babies had shared the same amniotic sac and the same placenta within the mother's uterus. 'That's extremely rare, isn't it?'

'Only in one per cent of pregnancies.' Dan looked out into the distance. 'The survival rate is not great. Cord entanglement can happen at any moment.'

Which meant the babies' oxygen could be cut off. Lindsey tapped into her medical knowledge, fearing what Dan was about to tell her. 'Do you want to stop now?'

He gave the ghost of a smile. 'What would be the point? You need to know and, God knows, I need to start gaining some perspective about it all.'

'OK...but I imagine, as a doctor, you knew the scenario you were facing and obviously you tried to shield Caroline about the extent of your fears.'

He dipped his head. How did she know that's exactly how it had been? 'I tried to keep positive for Caroline's sake but it was like living with a time bomb. At sixteen weeks the scan showed they were girls. Their heartbeats were strong and they appeared to be growing well. Caroline was being monitored by an ob team, of course, and they had protocols in place for the babies to be delivered by C-section at the earliest viable date. We dared to hope...' He stopped, his jaw working. 'They died in utero at twenty-two weeks.'

Lindsey heard the pain in his voice and tears welled in

her eyes but she said nothing, just sat with her arms locked around her middle and waited until he carried on.

'We had amazing support from the hospital and my family flew over. And Nathan.' His throat moved convulsively as he swallowed. 'Seeing Nate was hard. Brought it home the reason we were all there. I'd kept it together until then... But I was so damn glad to see him.'

Lindsey felt drenched in emotion, breathing harder as if a thumb pressed on her throat. 'Dan... I'm so very sorry this happened to you.' She looked at him, blinking away the scattering of tears. 'How on earth did you move forward from such heartache?'

'In a fog mostly.' He made an attempt at a twisted smile. 'I'm certainly in no hurry to experience fatherhood again. In the end, you do what has to be done. Caroline didn't want to be around me.' He shrugged. 'She was hurting.'

'And you weren't?' she queried softly.

'Caroline maintained there was nothing holding us together any longer. She quit her job and went home to her parents. I completed my contract at the hospital and then went to Florida. Did some training with a search and rescue team. After that, I came back home to Australia.'

'And you're not in touch with Caroline at all?'

'I tried a few months after I'd got home. She said she'd moved on and she hoped I'd do the same.' He paused. 'It's been two years now.'

Lindsey let the revelation hang for a moment. 'I imagine it's been pretty hard—trying to let it go, I mean.'

'I'm slowly getting there.' He gave a hard laugh. 'Except when it's a significant memory—like on the day I lost it in Resus.'

'I wondered...' She bit her lip. 'You said you were having an off day. But it wasn't the day, was it?' she stated with some perception. 'It was the *date*.'

'Yes, it was,' he said, his voice hollow. 'It was the date I met my babies. And the day I said goodbye to them.'

For a long time they stayed sitting under the tree. Dan had his arm around her, her head buried against him. Finally, he said, 'Thanks, Lindsey—for listening.'

'I hope it helped a bit,' she said, her voice scrappy.

His arm tightened and he pulled her closer.

And he figured only time would tell whether that was true and whether he could start taking more steps forward than backwards from now on.

'Hey.' He gave her a little shake. 'Want to race me home?'

She pulled back. 'I don't know about that.' Raising her arms, she lifted her hair and let it tumble down. 'One of us would probably break our ankle.'

'If it was you, I'd be on hand to patch you up,' he declared manfully.

'Then you'd have to carry me.'

Dan looked unfazed. 'You look like you don't weigh much. I think I could manage to hoist you over my shoulder in a fireman's lift.'

Her mouth turned down. 'I'm too tall for that. I'd be all dangly.'

He gave a deep-throated laugh. 'Dangly you would never be. A gentle jog, then,' he suggested, unwinding upright and taking her with him. 'Let's go.'

When they got home, Lindsey declared, 'You must be starving. What about a club sandwich?'

'Sounds good.' Dan got lemon squash from the fridge and poured them both a tall glass.

Lindsey began setting out the ingredients for their sandwiches. 'Perhaps, later, we could go into Milldale. The country markets are on all day on Sunday.'

'Again, that sounds good. But don't think you have to entertain me, Lindsey.'

She sent him a look of dismay. 'Is that how it seems?'

'Of course not. It's been the most brilliant day I've had in the longest time. And just *being* with you…' He shook his head, still poleaxed by the complete wonder of it all.

'Oh, Dan.' She sent him a misty kind of smile. 'Me too.'

'I think I'll change,' Lindsey said as they finished their impromptu lunch. 'The weather's warmed up.'

'So it has.' Dan hauled off his jumper. He sent her a quick smile. 'Don't be long.'

In her bedroom, she divested herself of her cardigan and T-shirt and stepped out of her jeans. She had managed to hang up a couple of dresses yesterday and she pulled one off its hanger. It was dotted with tiny flowers.

Longish and floaty. I feel like spring, she thought happily.

It was only a ten-minute drive to the village.

'You know, I haven't been to one of these for years,' Dan said as they roamed the market stalls, picking up and putting down various items.

'You should get out more, Dante.'

'Cheeky.' He sent her a lazy grin. 'So, are we looking for anything specific?'

'We are.' Lindsey urged him towards a stall decorated with flags from many nations. 'I like to support this group. They donate to several primary schools in one of the developing countries. Oh, recycled paper!' She pounced on the pale green and speckled box. 'It's Mum's birthday soon, she's a compulsive letter writer. And I must get some of this herbal mixture that helps to heal bruises.'

Dan looked bemused. 'Are you expecting some—bruises, I mean?'

'I work in Casualty, Dan,' she reminded him drily.

'I'm learning so much here,' he said.

Not sure whether he was being serious or not, Lindsey sent him an eye-roll. 'I just need to get some of the fair-trade tea and coffee and I'm done here.'

'I'd like some of that too.' Dan stayed her hand as she was reaching for her purse. 'I'll get this.' He handed over a note of a large denomination, waving away the change.

'That was a nice gesture.' Lindsey swung her carry bag lightly as they strolled on.

'Hardly philanthropic,' he mocked himself. 'But perhaps it might go towards funding some story books for the kids or a bit of sports equipment.'

'Happy thought,' Lindsey said. 'But the hard reality is it might help to pay for someone to keep the kids safe on the way to and from school.'

His mouth tightened at the bleak thought. 'We take so much for granted, don't we?'

'Not always,' Lindsey countered gently. 'I like to think most of us do what we can for others less fortunate. But for some folk it could never be enough.'

Dan looked at her with something like awe. 'You're such a wise woman.'

'So better not mess with me, then.'

He returned her grin. 'I think we need some ice cream.'

'Now let's have a wander through the art gallery,' Lindsey suggested, as they finished off their ice-cream cones. 'Check out the work of the local artisans.'

'Are you among them?' Dan asked.

'I've had a few pieces shown from time to time but nothing lately. I need inspiration.' She paused, her bottom lip puckering, considering. 'Would you sit for me, Dan?'

'No.'

They entered the gallery with its clean lines of black and white space and a striking mullioned window through which the afternoon sun was streaming.

'Just—no?' Lindsey stopped to look at a painting.

'I'm not that narcissistic, Lindsey.'

'That's pathetic reasoning.' She shook her head.

They continued their tour of the gallery and Dan held the door open for her as they left. 'I'd only need you for a couple of hours just to get the basics down,' Lindsey pleaded her case.

'It's not something I'd do. Count me as a firm no!' He softened his abruptness with a smile that spread his lips wide and Lindsey found she was biting down on hers. He looked so sexy, unshaven, a bit rumpled. So…perfect for her.

'Spoilsport,' she muttered, and stepped out into the street again.

Dan wound her fingers through his as they continued up the street. 'I saw a plant nursery when I took a walk yesterday. Would they still be open?'

'Probably. Sunday trading is the go in the village. Lots of tourists about. What do you need a nursery for?'

He squeezed her hand and swung it gently. 'Need to get some flowers for my lady.'

A few minutes later, Lindsey looked at the flowers she held. Dan had given her long-stemmed irises, their colour a rich and gorgeous violet, deepening to amethyst. 'Let's make tracks now,' he said, as they left the shop.

'Thanks for these, Dan,' Lindsey said when they were back and seated in his car. 'But why irises? Any special reason?'

He thought for a moment. 'Because they're extremely special and lovely…like you.' His fingers went to her nape and stroked. 'And brave-looking somehow, with their tall, straight stems.'

She turned to him, her heart beating so heavily she could feel it inside her chest. 'Today's been so amazing, hasn't it?' she said softly.

'Oh, yes…' His mouth lowered to her throat, his lips on the tiny pulse point that beat frantically beneath her chin. He looked at her, an unfulfilled yearning, as sudden as a lightning strike catapulting into his veins. 'I think we need to take this home, don't you?' His voice caught as he swallowed.

She nodded. No further words were needed.

Dan kissed her again before they got out of the car. Then, gathering up their parcels, they went inside. Somehow they found themselves back in the kitchen.

'We seem to end up here, don't we?' Lindsey gave a strained laugh, reaching up for a jug and putting her flowers in water.

'I like kitchens,' Dan said. 'They're friendly places.'

'The hub of the home.' Lindsey felt her nerves jangle, achingly aware of the almost tangible expectation hanging in the air between them. She turned to him, crossing her arms against her chest. 'Tea, then? Glass of wine, anything?'

A beat of silence.

'Dan…?'

He was very close. Unlocking her arms, he slid his hands down to her wrists, holding them gently. They waited there a moment, staring into each other's eyes. He took her wrist and raised it to his mouth. 'We haven't had our dance yet. Do you have some music?'

'I do—heaps of music.' Lindsey felt caught in a bubble. The world had faded and there was just the two of them. She could already feel the surge of heat between them. She swallowed drily.

They went through to the lounge. Lindsey slid a disc into the player and music, slow and smooth, filled the room. She looked up expectantly and saw that Dan had gone to the picture window and was looking out. She crossed to his side and saw what he did. Spears of red and orange shot across the western sky. 'Day's almost done.'

'We still have the night…' His voice was husky on the words as he turned and took her in his arms. Lindsey raised her face for his kiss, her whole body seeming to melt when their lips met. His hands stroked her back, encircled her hips, burning through the soft fabric of her dress as if his fingers were on fire.

Entwined, swaying together, almost lost in the throb of the music, they danced. And danced, wheeling and whirling around the room and all the way down the hallway to his bedroom.

They went in and Dan closed the door behind them. The curtains were partially drawn, the bed turned down. Dan pressed her to his side. 'When did you do this?'

'A bit earlier.'

'For us?'

The softest smile edged her mouth. 'Do you mind?'

He shook his head and paused. 'Ah, Lindsey…'

'What is it?'

'There's no chocolate on the pillow.'

'Silly.' She smiled mistily. 'That's for later.'

At her words, Dan's fragile control shattered and he took her in his arms. Then he stepped back, and without taking his eyes from her face slowly ran his fingers down between her breasts, unbuttoning her simple cotton dress, sliding it in one movement from her shoulders.

Then he was tugging off his own clothes and Lindsey was doing the same. 'This is us,' she whispered, as Dan drew her down with him onto the bed. She wrapped her bare legs around his, her arms reaching up to pull his head down, sighing deeply as she felt the slickness of his skin on hers, felt his body tensing with the effort to control it.

'This is us,' Dan echoed as his mouth ravished hers, hungry, demanding, tasting her everywhere.

Lindsey shivered, inhaling the scent of his naked skin, losing herself, returning his passion with her own kisses, hardly registering when Dan pulled back, pausing to protect her. 'Where were we…?'

'Don't stop…' She held onto him for dear life, his pleasure feeding hers.

Dan had no intention of stopping. Not until he had taken her with him all the way, higher and further, to a place beyond thought or reason. Only when release came, wave flooding upon wave, did they realise how very high and far they had climbed.

Together.

For a long time they lay replete, turned on their sides so they were facing each other. The soft light of early evening fingered the pale walls and ceiling. Outside the window a wood dove called to its mate and a burst of cicada drumming drenched the stillness.

Lifting a hand, Dan lazily combed his fingers through her hair. Something real was happening here. He could do nothing other than feel amazed. 'I'm lost for words…'

Lindsey sighed, sated, wrapping herself around him with the contentment of a purring cat. She gave him an indulgent look from under half-closed lids. She knew exactly what he meant. Freeing a hand, she ran a finger along his jaw and into the slight cleft in his chin. 'I've never wanted to be with anyone the way I wanted to be with you, Dan.'

He felt his heart contract. He could so easily fall for her—if he hadn't already. He could say, *Me too*, and mean it. But it was Lindsey and he needed to spell it out.

He brushed her lips once, twice. 'Without exception, this has been the happiest day of my life. It's been like a day out of time.'

'That's exactly how I feel.' Lindsey stopped and thought.

'It's a pure kind of happiness, isn't it? Like opening a mail-order parcel and finding everything just right.'

He gave a soft chuckle, his breath stirring her hair. 'I'll go with that.' He half spanned her waist with one hand, stroking a lazy pattern on her skin. 'I thought the spa looked pretty inviting earlier. Should we try it?'

'Perfect.' Lindsey rubbed her toes against his in anticipation. 'Then I'll fix us some dinner.'

'Uh-uh.' With exquisite sweetness, Dan claimed her lips. '*I'll* fix dinner.'

CHAPTER SEVEN

'CAN I DO anything to help with dinner?' Lindsey had arrived in the kitchen to find Dan well under way with his meal preparations.

He sent her a very sweet smile. 'A glass of your finest might be the go. I didn't know where to look.'

'Oh, that's easy.' Lindsey went to a door in a recess of the kitchen that led to a proper climate-controlled cellar. 'Red?' she called.

'Mmm, think so. I'm doing pasta.'

Lindsey took glasses and poured the wine and then watched as Dan expertly tossed onions, tomatoes and herbs in a pan. 'That smells wonderful.' She picked up her glass, lacing both hands around it. 'You really do know your way around a kitchen.'

'Would I lie?' He grinned, touching his glass to hers. 'Nathan would have cheerfully existed on takeaways if one of us hadn't cooked. I think he's a bit more interested these days. Sami has probably had some influence there.'

Lindsey made herself comfortable on one of the high-back stools and watched Dan at work. He was such a handsome man. With such an *air* about him. Perhaps it came from good breeding, she pondered. Or from a world of experience in so many ways. Her eyes took their fill. He was wearing a long-sleeved black cotton shirt outside his jeans and he'd shaved.

Her thoughts wandered off, unwinding the last hour. They'd had their spa and then instinctively gone to their separate bathrooms. Lindsey had been glad about that. Her emotions were in overload. She guessed Dan's had been the same. She'd had a long shower and shampooed her hair, spritzed perfume in the air and walked through it. Then, dressed in soft jersey pants and a ruby-red top with a crossover neckline, she'd come to find Dan. She took a mouthful of her wine.

'I took the liberty of lighting the fire in the lounge room,' Dan said. 'OK?'

'Very.' She parked her chin on her upturned hand. Her eyes lit softly. 'There's a little gate-legged table we can set up and eat our meal in front of the fire—if you like?'

'Of course I like.' He picked up his wine, his eyes caressing her over the rim of his glass. 'A perfect end to our perfect day.'

They erected the table and Lindsey set out the place-mats and cutlery.

'We should have some music.' Dan selected something from her collection, flooding the room with rich, mellow sound.

Lindsey was curled against Dan on the sofa. They'd ended their meal with Irish coffee and she'd raided the stash of dark chocolates her mother kept for special occasions.

'Are we fulfilling our brief to just *be*?' Dan smudged a kiss against her temple.

'Passed with flying colours.' Lindsey turned to meet his lips. They were still kissing when the phone rang, startling them apart. 'That's the landline,' she said, levering herself upright. She sent Dan a wry smile. 'Probably Mum from Scotland. She knew I'd be here this weekend.'

'You'll be a while.' Dan got to his feet as well. 'I'll sort this out and start the dishwasher.'

'Thanks.' Lindsey took off down the hallway to the room they used as an office and where their home phone was located. Contrary to what she'd expected, it wasn't her mother at all. 'Oh, Lord,' she murmured, after she'd ended the call and replaced the handset. She had to tell Dan what was happening. Full of misgivings, she hurried along to the kitchen. 'It was Fiona on the phone.'

Dan glanced at his watch. 'At this hour? What's up?'

Lindsey suppressed the urge to run to him. Hold him tighter than tight. 'It's the young couple from the cabin, Scott and Amy. They've just rung Fiona. They don't know what to do.'

'About what?' Dan felt his guts go into free fall. He had a fair idea. And he didn't need this. He really didn't. 'Is it the baby?'

'Amy's waters have broken.'

Dan let his breath out slowly. 'Well, there should be plenty of time to get her to Hopeton. Have they rung for an ambulance?'

'Fiona tried. And they'll get one to us as soon as they can. But there's been a major road trauma twenty Ks out of Hopeton on the Sydney highway, a semi-trailer and two cars. All the ambulances are there.' Lindsey felt her throat tighten. 'Amy's already getting strong contractions.'

In an instant Dan felt as if he was drowning in a sea filled with sharks, waiting to tear him to bits. And there was no escape. He saw the pleading in Lindsey's eyes and turned away, gripping the edge of the bench top until his knuckles turned white. And stared out into the night. He had to get it together. Be professional.

So, sort the logistics. The baby was probably well on the way. They had no history. What if the baby was breach? What if there was a bleed? *Sweet God, he hadn't signed on for this!* He spun back to Lindsey, a truckload of emotions churning through his mind. 'So, where have you left things with Fiona?'

'I've said we'll call her back as soon as we have a plan in place.'

Dan flexed a shoulder dismissively. 'We don't have much choice, do we?'

Lindsey shook her head. If there had been any other way around this, she'd have gone with it. She wouldn't have wished this emergency on Dan for the world. She just had to hope and pray everything would turn out all right for Amy and the baby. And Dan as well.

'The best plan would be to get Amy up here to the house and see what's going on.' Dan's voice was clipped and professional. 'The lounge room is probably the warmest. We'll set up as best we can in there. If you'll call Fiona, I'll get my bag from the car.'

They left the kitchen together, Dan striding ahead down the hallway to the front door.

'I don't suppose you have a birthing kit on board?' Lindsey called after him.

Was she nuts? Of course he didn't have a birthing kit! Without answering, Dan opened the door and stepped out into the crisp night air. He looked up at the tumble of stars and pulled in a deep breath that almost hurt. He had to centre himself.

Or go under.

Why on earth had she asked that damn fool question? Lindsey berated herself. She guessed Dan was feeling hijacked, pushed into a situation he'd rather have avoided. Delivering babies was certainly not on his agenda. And who could blame him?

Dan returned with his medical case and they began getting things ready. The sofa could be converted to a bed. That done, Lindsey went to search for some kind of plastic sheeting, resorting to a roll of garden bin liners she found in a utility cupboard. She came back with her booty plus sheets and cotton blankets. 'Amy could be a bit shocky,' she said, as Dan helped her prepare the sofa bed for their patient.

Well, he knew that. Dan's mouth tightened. Once the waters had broken, many women experienced a kind of delayed shock, shivering uncontrollably. 'I'll stoke up the fire,' he said.

'I'll warm some linen in the dryer,' she said to the back of Dan's head as he hunkered down at the grate. He grunted a non-reply and she shrugged and went off about her business. If the ambulance didn't get here in time…? She felt a curl of unease in her stomach. She'd delivered babies before but not away from the back-up of a fully equipped hospital.

When Lindsey returned to the lounge room, Dan was just putting his mobile away. 'I called Midwifery at Hopeton. Amy's not booked there.'

So no chance of any history. 'Fiona will have an address,' Lindsey said. 'I could check…'

'Bit late for that.' Dan swung round. 'Sounds like them now.' He managed a smile of sorts, softening the tension around his mouth. 'We'll just have to wing it.'

Dan flung the door open. The young couple stood there, Scott supporting his wife. Introductions were quickly made and they were ushered inside. Dan helped Amy onto the sofa bed.

'I feel so c-cold…' Amy was shivering, her teeth chattering.

Lindsey produced one of the cotton blankets warm from the dryer and tucked it over her. 'Try to relax now, Amy.' She placed a hand on the girl's shoulder and rubbed gently. 'Just breathe in and out. That's good.' Lindsey smiled. 'Bit better?'

'Mmm.' Amy blinked rapidly. 'The baby's not due for another three weeks.'

'That's neither here nor there,' Dan said. 'I'm sure your baby will be fine.' And, please, God, able to breathe, he added silently. Don't go there. He clamped his jaw, dragging his thoughts to the present. He turned to Lindsey. 'Could you get Amy ready and I'll see how she's doing.'

Lindsey quickly prepared Amy for Dan's examination. 'Scott, perhaps you'd like to sit over here close to Amy.' She smiled at the young husband, who was looking helpless and overwhelmed.

'We brought the bag Amy packed for the hospital.' Scott looked around awkwardly. 'Where should I put it?'

'I'll take it. And good thinking,' Lindsey said.

Dan bent to his patient. 'I'll be as gentle as I can, Amy.' His examination was painstaking. He was leaving nothing to chance.

'What do you think, Doctor?' Amy bit her lip and grimaced.

'I think your baby isn't waiting, Amy.'

Amy whimpered. 'Scott…?'

'I'm right here, babe.' Scott held tightly to his wife's hand.

Dan took Lindsey aside. 'She's fully dilated and the baby seems small.'

Small? Lindsey felt a lick of unease. 'We're not going to have a problem, are we?'

'Shouldn't think so. Foetal heartbeat is strong. I'd say she's been in labour most of today and not realised it.'

Lindsey stared into his blue eyes. She knew it had probably taken a Herculean effort but he looked in control. Confident. She gave a mental thumbs-up.

'Oh, help,' Amy moaned from the bed. 'I can't do this…'

As if they'd worked together in a birthing suite for years, Dan and Lindsey began talking Amy through each contraction. Dan checked his patient again. 'Not far now, Amy,' he encouraged quietly.

They had only seconds to wait before Amy began moaning again.

'OK, sweetie, big push.' Lindsey helped Amy into a more comfortable position as she bore down, eyes squeezed tight, her fists clenched.

'Head's crowning. We're almost there.' Dan looked down at his hands. The infant's head lay there, streaked and glassy, the dark, perfect curls pressed wetly against the tiny skull. His throat tore as he swallowed. 'Gentle push now, Amy—fantastic. And one more.'

Amy pushed and the rest of the baby slid into Dan's waiting hands. 'You have a daughter.' Dan had unconsciously steeled himself for a baby almost translucent, fragile, but little Miss Fraser was offering up an offended squawk, already pink and beautiful.

'Well done, you,' Lindsey murmured, handing him some cord clamps.

'Did I have these in my bag?' Dan looked bemused.

'Must have.' Lindsey unfurled one of her smiles. 'I didn't find them in the kitchen drawer.'

Dan felt his throat jag again as Lindsey handed him a warm towel to wrap around the infant. He passed the baby to her mother. 'Take great care of her,' he said, his voice not quite steady.

'Nice sound,' Lindsey said a little later, giving a nod towards the top of the bed where the young couple were clucking over their newborn.

Dan refrained from commenting. He felt stretched, hollowed out. 'I'm about to deliver the placenta,' he said. 'Can you find something to bag it? We'll send it to hospital with Amy. They'll need to check to make sure it's complete.'

'Plastic bags I can do.'

Lindsey went along to the kitchen, finding Fiona tip-toeing through the back door.

'Fi!' Her eyes went wide. 'You didn't need to come back. You OK?'

'I didn't like to intrude,' Fiona whispered. 'Is the baby—?'

'Delivered safely. Little girl.'

'Oh, thank goodness.' Fiona put a hand to her heart. 'I felt so responsible for all this. I should have checked how far along Amy was—perhaps recommended they stay closer to the hospital or something…'

'Fi, that's not your brief,' Lindsey said kindly. 'Scott and Amy made their own decision. And fortunately it's turned out fine. Mainly thanks to Dan. He was amazing.'

'Then what a blessing he was here,' the older woman said. 'That both of you were here,' she added, her gaze thoughtful and a little curious. 'Now, should I make some tea?'

'That would be wonderful.' Lindsey searched out the plastic bags Dan needed. 'And some toast as well, please. Amy, especially, must be famished. Oh, do you know if Mum still has Gran's cane-washing basket?'

'Hanging where it always has,' Fiona said. 'On the laundry wall.' She frowned a bit. 'What do you need that for?'

Lindsey smiled. 'It'll make a temporary bassinet for the baby.'

'Oh, bless.' Fiona was almost purring. 'What a sweet idea. Anything else you need me to do?'

'Perhaps you could check on the progress of an ambulance for us. But tell the base everything's under control here so the guys know they're not coming to an emergency.'

Laden with stuff, Lindsey went back to Dan. 'Ambulance has just left Hopeton for us.'

'Good. Placenta's almost out,' he said, continuing to massage Amy's tummy gently.

'As soon as we're finished here, I'd like to give Amy

a little tidy up,' Lindsey said quietly. 'Do you think you could organise a bit of privacy?'

Dan nodded. 'I'll need to write a few notes to send with the ambulance.'

'Use the office,' Lindsey said.

'OK. I'll take Scott with me. That do?'

'Nicely, thanks.'

Her basin of warm water at the ready, Lindsey passed Amy a sponge.

'Oh, that feels heavenly,' the new mother said.

'So, you're not from round here, then, Amy?'

'Further west, Shackleton. Scottie does contract farm work and we have a cottage in town.'

'We'll send you along to Hopeton District when the ambulance gets here,' Lindsey said. 'They'll check you and the baby ovcr and maybe keep you a day or so. Will that suit your plans?'

Amy nodded. 'It'll give Scott time to trade the ute for something more practical for a family before we head home.'

'That sounds like a great idea,' Lindsey approved. 'Now, I'll just raid your case here and get you feeling fresh and beautiful.'

'Come on, let's get this lot cleared away.' Lindsey was looking purposeful. The ambulance carrying Amy and the baby had gone. Scott would follow later when he'd packed up their things from the cabin.

'Damn!' Dan surveyed the chaos in the lounge room and gave a short hollow laugh. 'Do you believe any of this actually happened?'

'Yep.' Lindsey began bundling sheets. 'There's a new little member of the human race to prove it.'

She glanced up. Dan sounded tired and the eyes that lifted briefly to hers were guarded and shadowed. He'd spent the past few hours on an emotional roller-coaster. He must be feeling wrung out.

She made a quick decision. 'Let's leave all this for now,' she insisted. 'Dad usually has some decent Scotch around. Fancy a dram?'

'Lead on.' Dan's agreement was heartfelt.

They were back in the kitchen again, sitting side by side at the breakfast bar. Lindsey had dimmed the lights and the big clock ticked on the wall.

'You're quiet,' Lindsey said as they sat over their drinks. 'You OK?' Her eyes scanned his face, looking for clues.

'I'll do.' He gave a trapped smile. Just, he added silently.

'I'm sorry you had this emergency thrust on you to-night.' Her voice was low, hardly there.

'It was out of your control, Lindsey. Don't stress about it.' He lifted his glass and finished his drink in a couple of mouthfuls.

'Another?' Lindsey offered.

He shook his head. 'I'm good, thanks.'

Lindsey had barely touched her drink. Where did they go from here? she fretted. Where? 'Do you want to…talk?'

'No…not really.' He covered her hand with his. 'Shower and bed, I think.' His eyes locked with hers, dark in shadow, tender in their caress. 'Come with me. I don't want to sleep alone.'

They made love slowly and with great care for each other. The soft mingling of their sighs and murmurs sprinkled the silence until the fire of their passion reignited, driving them before it until there was no escape and they tumbled into a blinding oneness, wrapped in each other's arms.

Lindsey woke to find the room suffused with morning light. At once snatches of their lovemaking flooded her mind and she reached out to touch Dan, but he wasn't there. Her heart fell. Dragging a sheet off the bed, she wrapped herself in its folds and scooted along the hallway to her bedroom. Hastily, she pulled on track pants and a jumper and went to find him.

She headed for the back deck. She had a feeling he'd be there and he was, looking out over the fields, focusing on the clouds of early mist already pierced with gold from the first rays of the sun. He was still. Absorbed.

Almost as if he was looking at it for the first and last time.

'Dan?'

He spun round. 'Hey…'

'Hey…' she echoed. Her eyes widened and she frowned. He was dressed in dark trousers and a charcoal-grey business shirt, his hair still damp from the shower. 'Have you been called in to work?'

'No.' He shook his head. 'Let's sit down. I need to talk to you.'

'OK.' For the first time she noticed his laptop open on the table. They each pulled out a chair and sat opposite each other.

'I'm going to take off,' Dan said bluntly.

'Oh.' Lindsey linked her hands on the table in front of her. He looked jaded, the fatigue lines around his eyes and mouth in sharp relief. 'What's going on?' she asked, her voice catching in her throat.

'I'm flying to Melbourne to see my family—well, my parents at least. I haven't been home since I got back from the States.'

They breathed through a beat of silence.

'You feel the need to be with them,' Lindsey said with some perception.

He was silent for a long moment and then he let his

breath out in a ragged sigh. 'We haven't really had an opportunity to talk properly since the twins... Their grief was as real as mine. They lost their first grandchildren. We need to connect, talk about the babies. Share the loss.'

Which he *should* have been able to do with Caroline. Oh, the unfairness of it all. Lindsey bit hard on her bottom lip. 'Last night...the birth...'

'It sharpened everything all over again. Stuff I'd thought I'd come to terms with—' He stopped, his expression set hard as if anything else would weaken his resolve. 'I'm hoping talking to my parents will give me a way forward. They'll understand.'

Understand, as she'd been unable to. Was that what he meant? She pushed the thought away. 'Would you like me to come with you? Not to your parents' obviously—but just for support?'

He hesitated, as if thinking it through. 'I need to do this on my own, Lindsey. But thanks.'

'When are you going?'

'Soon.' He flicked a hand towards the laptop. 'I'm booked on a flight to Sydney at ten. That'll get me on a connecting flight to Melbourne pretty well straight away.'

And in his mind he was already there, the monumental intimacy they'd shared nothing but a pleasant memory. Lindsey got to her feet, her insides suddenly twisting with the sad truth. 'I'll make some coffee, then.'

'Don't on my account. I'm packed. I should get going.'

She shook her head. 'Why didn't you wake me so we could have had time to talk about this?'

His brows twitched into a frown. 'I'm not following you.'

Damn right you're not.

'You're just...disappearing.'

He looked taken aback. 'With respect, Lindsey, what is there left to talk about?'

Lindsey flinched as though he'd slammed a door in

her face. Suddenly the magic of their lovemaking seemed a figment of her imagination. The carefree, wonderful man she'd discovered had gone. The amazement of their connection all but broken. 'You should get moving, then.'

Lindsey did a frenzied clean of the lounge room after he'd gone. Something in her heart scrunched tight and lodged there. He should have held me this morning while he told me he was leaving, she thought sadly. He should at least have done that. I would have understood. But he'd chosen to walk alone. Well, I don't need you, Dan Rossi. She kicked the off switch on the vacuum cleaner with the toe of her shoe.

She'd go back to being her own person. Depend on no man for her happiness.

Dan's thoughts were in turmoil as he travelled the thirty kilometres back to Hopeton. He couldn't believe how badly he'd handled things with Lindsey.

He hadn't slept. But that was no excuse for the stuff-up he'd left behind. He could turn round and go back. Sort it quickly. Take Lindsey with him to Melbourne. He glanced at his watch and the faint hope that had flared died. If he did that, he'd miss his flight. And he was pushed for time as it was. He had to be back tomorrow to begin a roster of night shifts.

His thoughts flew back to Lindsey and the way she'd made him feel plain glad to be alive, the way she'd made him laugh. He swore under his breath, disgusted at his lapse this morning. He should have been more caring. But right now talking with his parents had to be his priority. For his own sanity. And if that didn't work, then he had nowhere left to go to feel whole again.

Lindsey spent the afternoon venting her anger and frustration on her clay. She moulded, spun pot after pot and then trashed the lot of them. A bad end to a bad day, she decided grimly, making her way up the stairs from her studio. As she came in from the deck, the home phone was ringing. Dan? Her heart spun out of rhythm and she hurried to answer it, her expectations crashing when the caller proved to be Caitlin Kelly.

'Hey, Lins,' she said. 'I wasn't sure you were still at Lark Hill.'

'I'm taking a bit of leave.' Lindsey perched on the corner of the desk. 'How're you, Cait?'

'Bored.' She gave a half-laugh. 'Actually, I'm driving back to Sydney tomorrow. Wondered if you'd like a change of scene and come with me.'

'To Sydney?'

'Mmm. My apartment's right on the beach at Bondi. It'll be like old times. We could do some galleries for you, some clubs for me and shopping for both of us—are you in?'

Lindsey paused only infinitesimally. To heck with Dan Rossi and his machinations. She owed him nothing. 'You bet I am. What time?'

'Is six too early for you?'

'Honey, I work shifts,' Lindsey pointed out drily. 'My body clock is in permanent disarray. I'll be ready.'

CHAPTER EIGHT

THE FOLLOWING SUNDAY, Lindsey sat up in bed and blocked a yawn. Checking the time, she groaned. It was already well into the afternoon and she must have slept almost the entire day away. But she'd been late home last night, after flying from Sydney then picking up her newly repaired car in Hopeton.

She threw herself out of bed and showered, dressing in jeans and a dark green top. Gathering her hair up, she let it fall haphazardly around her shoulders.

She blocked another yawn on her way to the kitchen, filling the kettle and setting it to boil. That done, she went out onto the back deck.

So much for spring, she decided, leaning on the railings and looking across the landscape, seeing jigsaw pieces of darkening sky between the trees. Unless she was mistaken, those were storm clouds scudding across the mountain-tops as if in a hurry to be elsewhere. But Lindsey knew about these kinds of storms. They came in fast and usually dropped their quota of rain and left just as quickly. She hoped it was one of those but even as she watched, the wind had begun whipping through the trees, swirling their foliage into a mad dance, while a streak of lightning snaked its way across the sky.

Lindsey felt a wave of unease. She'd better prepare in case there was a power cut later. She ticked off her to-do list—first locate the torches, make sure the batteries were viable. She'd just opened the cupboard where the lantern torches were kept when the front doorknocker sounded. Probably Fiona, she thought, come to check she was OK. She hurried along the hallway and opened the door.

'Oh—' Lindsey felt goose bumps break out all over her. Dan stood at the outer perimeter of the veranda, his hands jammed in his back pockets.

'I'm not taking anything for granted,' he said.

Lindsey's fingers tightened on the doorknob. You'd better believe it, she vented silently. Swinging the door wide open, she stepped back and with a small inclination of her head she said, 'Come in.'

For a second Dan's blue gaze faltered. 'Are you sure?'

'Sure I want you to come in?' Lindsey tilted her head in question. 'Of course. Lark Hill welcomes all strangers.'

Dan felt if she had struck him. Was that what he was now? A stranger? Well, he'd asked for it. The lady wasn't going to make it easy.

'I was about to make tea,' she said shortly. 'Come through.'

Dan stepped inside, noticing the carrier bags on the hall table and spilling onto the floor. His eye caught some of the big-name fashion brands, none of which were available in Hopeton. 'Been away?' he asked.

'Sydney, with Cait.' Lindsey sent him a look over her shoulder.

'Good trip?'

'Magic. Cait threw a huge party. Met lots of new people. Just what I needed.'

'Well, that's what holidays are about,' Dan felt compelled to say. But thought darkly that if she was sending a message that she'd moved on and that what they'd had was already history, then he'd got it.

'Looks like a storm coming,' Lindsey said, as she made the tea. 'Are you staying long?'

'Why?' he shot back immediately. 'Do you need to be somewhere?'

Lindsey looked taken aback. 'No…'

Dan's sigh was audible. Lifting his hands, he linked them behind his neck. 'You're still ticked off with me. And I understand that,' he added in response to her elegantly raised eyebrows.

'So at least you agree I have reason to be.'

'I was in overload.'

'And that's your excuse?' Lindsey snapped. 'For the whole weekend we were on fire for each other and then…' She palmed a hand and shook her head. 'You left me feeling…'

'I know… I wanted to turn round and come back but there wasn't time.'

Lindsey felt herself softening. She proffered the mug of tea.

'No tea, thanks.' Dan shook his head. 'I've been on nights. I'm in tea up to the gills.'

Lindsey swallowed. 'Would you like something else, then?'

A tiny pulse flickered in Dan's cheek. 'Just to talk—is that possible?'

She nodded, unable to speak. Every nerve in her body began tightening. What he had to say now would probably make or break them. She flicked a hand towards the kitchen table and they sat facing each other.

'I don't want you to think I'm some kind of messed-up loser.' Without warning his hand reached out and covered hers.

'I would never think that.' Lindsey stared down at the hand covering hers. She took a deep breath and let it go. 'But you do get the prize for behaving with the sensitivity of a block of wood.'

His mouth pulled down. 'Don't hold back on my account.'

'Dan, you all but dismissed me! That was pretty low after everything we'd been to each other.'

He tilted his head back and dragged in air. 'You're right,' he conceded without rancour. 'And I apologise. My only excuse is I wasn't thinking straight.' Abruptly, he pulled away, leaning back in his chair. 'I would never have wanted to leave you feeling hurt and questioning that what we'd had had been anything but entirely special. And *ours alone*,' he emphasised.

Lindsey took a shaky breath and asked the question that needed to be asked. 'Did talking with your parents help, then?'

'Their wisdom astounded me.' His voice roughened. 'I finally realised that I wouldn't be dishonouring my babies if I let them go.'

'Oh…' Lindsey's voice was a thread. 'Oh, Dan…'

'Yeah.' His smile was slightly wry. 'Took me a while to get there. But I have. I hadn't grieved properly. Hadn't said goodbye properly. It was as though there was a chunk of ice inside me that needed to thaw. And it was you who started the thaw, Lindsey. Only you.'

Lindsey's eyes pricked. 'I really just listened.'

'No.' He shook his head. 'You did a lot more than that. You brought something fresh and wonderful to my life. And I realised I had to break out of the mental straitjacket I'd put myself in. That's when I decided that talking to my parents might be the answer.'

Lindsey looked at him earnestly. 'So, what now?'

'For us?' Dan swallowed hard. 'I'd like it if I could hold you, if we could hold each other…'

He'd given her a look so warm Lindsey felt a quicksilver flip in her stomach. She swung up from her chair. 'So why are you still sitting there, then?'

Their kiss started gently but in a second they were desperate for each other. Dan lifted her hair, exposing the side of her throat. Lindsey felt his breath warm against her skin and then came the slight rasp of his tongue.

'Dan…' She gusted his name on a shaken breath and sighed when his mouth felt its way to the corner of hers.

'I've so missed you…' Dan made a muted sound in his throat. It was like the growl of a lion, shuddering through his whole length. 'Missed us.'

'I've missed us too,' she responded, shifting against him, her hands moving in a sweep under his T-shirt, taking him to her.

Where their kisses might have ended, they weren't about to find out. A clap of thunder ricocheted through the house, sending them springing apart. Lindsey put her hand to her heart. 'I don't like the feel of this, Dan.'

'Don't panic,' he said. 'A bit of thunder can't hurt us.'

'It's not that,' she countered. 'Around this valley, it's the wind. It can wreak havoc. The power lines can go down and knock out anything electrical. Is your mobile fully charged?'

He frowned. 'Ah—think so.'

'I'd better call Fiona.' Lindsey took off down the hallway. 'See who's at the cabins.' She was back in a few minutes. 'Thank goodness, there are no guests. The last ones left this morning.'

'One less thing to worry about, then. Do you have torches?' Dan asked.

Lindsey nodded. 'I was about to sort all that just before you arrived.' She got the torches and set them on the kitchen bench, testing them one by one. 'They seem OK.' She looked at Dan. 'When are you back on duty?'

'Late shift tomorrow.'

'So…' She bit her lip. 'You can stay tonight?'

He lifted his hand and stroked his knuckles down her cheek. 'If you'll have me…'

Lindsey pretended to think about it for a moment. 'Oh, I think I probably could.'

'Thank you.' He pulled her into his shoulder for a lingering hug. 'Now, what else do we have to do before the storm hits?'

'Just make sure the windows are secure, I guess. I'm so glad you're here, Dan.' Another crack of thunder sent her snuggling in against him. 'I think I'll make us an early dinner while we still have power,' Lindsey decided. 'Quick frittata, OK?'

'Fantastic. I'm starved. While you're doing that, I'll take a look outside. Might give us a clue if the storm is heading in our direction.'

Lindsey had no doubt it was. She went quickly about her task, sautéing onions, mushrooms and zucchini, fluffing eggs, and scattering fresh herbs and cheese across the top as she poured the mixture into the pan. In two seconds it was under the grill. She raised her eyes in question as Dan came back into the kitchen.

'It's really whipping up a frenzy out there,' he said. 'Actually feels a bit spooky.'

Lindsey punched him lightly on the arm. 'Not scared, are you, Dr Rossi?'

His mouth folded in on a dry smile. 'I thought perhaps you were, Ms Stewart.'

'Milldale girls don't scare easily.'

Dan felt a swell of desire as her lips made a soft little pout. Hell, she turned him on. In a reflex action he swept her up and swung her round and round, ending up in the centre of the room.

'Put me down, Dan,' Lindsey protested, laughing hard and hanging on tightly to his arms. 'That's if you want to eat tonight.'

They ate their meal, one eye on the weather as they glanced up constantly through the big kitchen window. The wind had now begun roaring, the rain falling sleet-like and icy. 'Glad we don't have to go out in this,' Dan said.

'Oh, me too.' Snuggling up in bed sounded like a much better idea.

Dan leaned across, his fingertips making long, shivery strokes down her forearm. 'We have a lot of making up to do, don't we?'

Lindsey made a tiny sound like a purr and felt a strange lightness as if love and desire had rolled into one high-voltage surge, sweeping through her body and out to the tips of her fingers. 'Should we do the dishes?' she ventured coyly.

'Are you serious?' Dan pretended outrage. 'Some matters are vastly more important than others. Don't you agree?'

Lindsey's laughter was sweet and clear. 'I agree.'

CHAPTER NINE

Wednesday, the following week...

FIRST DAY BACK from leave and Lindsey went in to work early.

She hadn't seen Dan since the storm but now she was back in town...the prospect of seeing him every day curved a smile around her lips, a flood of desire pooled into a warm ache inside her. It was a rainy, dreary morning yet she felt she was standing beneath a sunbeam.

It was good to catch up with her team, Lindsey thought as she stowed her bag and finger-waved around the staff lounge. Making a coffee, she joined Vanessa at one of the corner tables that looked out onto a rock garden. This morning the big succulent plants were dewy with rain-drops.

'Well, aren't you the chirpy one?' Vanessa said. 'I take it you had a nice break?'

'Fantastic.' Lindsey's hands spanned her coffee mug. 'But it's good to be back all the same.'

Vanessa gave an eye-roll. 'You *must* be on a high.'

Lindsey laughed good-naturedly. 'How're things with Andrew?'

'I think *cautious* must be his middle name,' Vanessa said darkly.

'Well, he's at a crucial stage of his training,' Lindsey

pointed out gently. 'Perhaps he's not into making commitments just yet.'

'Oh, *yawn.*'

Lindsey gave her contemporary a quick dry look. 'If you think he's worth waiting for, Van, cut him a bit of slack.' She glanced at her watch. 'Who's been the charge on nights?'

'Brooke Bartholomew.'

Lindsey's full lower lip pursed. Brooke was relatively new to the casualty department. She'd seemed nice enough during the casual encounters Lindsey had had with her.

'I don't get her,' Vanessa said frankly. 'She's not on for a chat when things are quiet—well, only with Dan. She kept bringing him cups of tea!'

'Well, that's not a crime.' Lindsey felt a lick of unease she couldn't explain, her pool of happiness shrinking ever so slightly. 'How come you were on nights anyway?'

'Anita Rayburn's little boy was sick. She asked me to swap a couple of shifts.'

Lindsey didn't wait to hear any more. She finished her coffee quickly and stood to her feet. 'I guess I may as well get a jump-start and take handover.'

'OK.' Vanessa helped herself to one of the mini-muffins someone had brought in. 'I'll rouse the team shortly and see you out there.'

'Oh, Lindsey.' Brooke Bartholomew looked up startled from the computer and blinked a bit. 'You're early.'

'I'll take handover, if you like,' Lindsey offered. 'Then you can get off. Are you OK?' She frowned as she looked at the other woman. 'You look a bit rocky.'

'Night shifts…' Brook's nostrils pinched as she breathed in. 'I hate them.'

'Have you been busy?'

'Swamped.'

'Right, who's still waiting for triage?' Lindsey's trained eye flew over the list. One name sprang out and rang warning bells. *Mia Roche.* She turned urgently to Brooke. 'Where is this child now?'

'I was about to get to her. We'd had an MVA and a gunshot wound…'

'Mia Roche is registered at the asthma clinic.' Lindsey was on her feet. 'You should have flagged it.'

'I know. She would have been next. I'll get to her now.'

'No.' Lindsey was definite. 'Page the registrar to Paeds Resus. And, please, Brooke, sign yourself off but don't go anywhere until I've sorted this.' Lindsey's request left no room for argument as she took off at speed to the waiting area. 'Erin!' She located the mother of the sick child and held out her arms for the toddler. 'How long have you been here?'

'A while… I tried to give Mia a drink but she vomited. She's so ill…'

Lindsey could tell that. Mia's little body was radiating heat through her cotton pyjamas. She pressed the back of her hand to the child's forehead, long experience telling her Mia's temperature was far too high for safety. 'Come with me,' she instructed, tight-lipped. With relief she saw her team assembling at the station. 'Vanessa, you're in charge. Jess and Gail, I'll need you both in Paeds Resus.'

Newly graduated, Jess bit her lip. 'I haven't done much paeds.'

'You'll be fine.' Lindsey hardly slowed her stride. 'Gail, you know what to do.' Gail Smith was one of their mature assistants in nursing, an absolute gem in this kind of situation.

The nurses all knew Erin from her attendance at the asthma clinic. Gail placed a guiding arm around the distraught young mother. 'It's OK, sweetheart. Mia's in good hands now.'

Lindsey quickly placed the toddler on the resus trolley. 'Erin, go with Gail now,' she said kindly. 'We'll take great care of Mia.'

'But...' Erin hesitated, her mouth trembling out of shape. 'Shouldn't I...?'

'Best if we leave it to the doctor and nurses now,' Gail said. 'You must be exhausted. Have you been up all night with the bub?'

Lindsey let out a relieved breath as Gail led the young mother from the room. She turned to Jess. 'Get me a Hudson mask, stat. We need Mia on a hundred per cent oxygen. Move!'

Jess moved. 'She's burning up, Lindsey.'

And they were running out of time. They could only hope the little one didn't start fitting. And where was the damned doctor when you needed him? 'Help me hold her, Jess.' Lindsey's calm request held nothing of her inner disquiet. 'I need to get some readings here. Come on, baby, hold still for me,' she pleaded. 'OK, all done... Thanks, Jess.'

'So, we'll give paracetamol next?' Jess had begun to step up into her role.

'Yes.' Lindsey placed what looked like a small piece of dissolvable paper under the little girl's tongue. 'Let's hope it'll start getting her temp down.'

Dan moved at speed through the casualty department. He'd barely pulled into the doctors' car park when he'd been bleeped. And by rights he shouldn't be here at all, but with Martin going home sick he was back on take for the early shift and straight into an emergency.

He pushed through the doors to Paeds Resus. 'What do we have?'

Lindsey spun her head up, expecting to see Martin

Lorimer, and went perfectly still for a beat. 'Dan!' She tamped down a slather of mixed emotions.

He gave a perfunctory nod. 'What do we have?' he repeated.

'Mia Roche, eighteen months old,' Lindsey relayed. 'Ongoing patient at the asthma clinic. Temperature forty-three, oxygen sats seventy-eight, pulse one-seventy. I've given oral paracetamol.'

Deep concern catapulted into Dan's eyes. One glance told him the child was rapidly becoming cyanosed. They'd need to move fast. 'Let's get an IV up and running. Smallest cannula, please, Lindsey. I'll need to crack a vein in Mia's foot.'

They sprang into action, Jess restraining the distressed toddler as best she could while Lindsey assisted Dan.

'Left foot, I think,' he said tersely, gloving quickly. 'I see a vein that might work for us.'

Lindsey's heart twisted. Tiny child, tiny veins. She prayed Dan's skill would be enough. 'I have a cut-down tray ready just in case.'

'We're short on time so let's hope not.' Dan's fingers were deft and sure. He secured the cannula on the first attempt, slapping down a dressing he'd stuck on the back of his left hand in readiness.

'Nice work,' Lindsey murmured, moving in to secure the site with a paediatric bandage.

Dan's expression lightened fractionally. 'Let's run five hundred normal saline and adrenaline five, please. We need Mia on a Ventolin nebuliser. And, Jess, keep checking the sats, please.'

'Yes, Doctor.' After a few minutes the junior reported, 'Sats up to eighty.' Jess looked up hopefully. 'That's a good indication we've got her in time, isn't it?'

Dan looked at the tiny, perfect fingertips. They were beginning to lose their blueness. 'A way to go yet but looking hopeful.' He flicked up his stethoscope. 'I'll have a listen to her chest now. See what that tells us. Left lobe a bit suspect,' he said finally, straightening Mia's little pyjama top. 'She's not allergic to anything, is she?'

'No,' Lindsey confirmed.

'Then we'll start with benzyl penicillin.' He picked up Mia's chart and began scribbling the dosage. 'Plus Maxolon to keep things settled down. Both delivered IV.'

Lindsey prepared the medication, relieved beyond words Mia would pull through this episode and that it had been Dan who had been around to treat this special little girl. Even if he wasn't aware of it, he had a natural affinity with kids. The thought made her happy.

'You did really well,' Lindsey said as she and Jess tidied up. 'Want to debrief later?'

'Thanks, Lindsey. That'd be awesome. Should I get back to the ward now?'

'Yes. Van will have need of you, I'm sure.'

'Excellent work, Jess.' Dan added his congratulations. 'Thanks for your help.'

Jess slipped out.

'I'll hang around until we can safely transfer Mia to Paeds ICU.' Dan pulled up a stool and parked himself beside the bed. 'Parents here?'

'Mum is—Erin,' Lindsey said.

Dan's eyebrows twitched into a query. 'Left it a bit late to bring the child in, didn't she?'

'No, she didn't.' Lindsey felt nettled. 'Erin is extremely up to speed regarding Mia's health. Very unfortunately, triage protocols were not followed here. Mia was kept waiting. I took over as soon as I got in. But I'm going to have to report it to the DON.'

Dan eyed her sharply. 'Who was the nurse on triage?'

'Brooke Bartholomew.'

Dan went very still, all his energies reined in. This

could have dire consequences for the department if he didn't speak up. 'Brooke is battling with some personal issues.'

Lindsey felt wrong-footed. 'How well do you know her?'

Dan hesitated briefly. 'We were thrown together on night shift. She needed to talk so I listened.'

Suddenly the air was taut with tension. 'So, what are you not saying, Dan?'

Dan was quietly monitoring his small patient. 'Brooke spoke to me in confidence, Lindsey. I advised her to ask for a transfer to another department urgently.'

Lindsey frowned. 'If she's not fit to work, she shouldn't be here.'

'You're right.' Dan's look was cool. 'But Brooke was competent on the shifts I worked with her. So what could I do except counsel her to act in her own best interests? Unfortunately, it appears she hasn't. I would have spoken to you about it but you were on leave. So do what you have to do.'

Lindsey shook her head in dismay. She hated having to report another nurse. 'Will you speak with Erin now?'

Dan didn't look up. Instead, he dragged in a weary breath and let it go. 'Yes, of course.'

With Mia finally transferred, Lindsey went back to the station. 'Everything OK here?' she asked Vanessa.

'Everything's under control,' Vanessa said shortly. 'How's Mia?'

'She'll be fine—eventually.' Lindsey paused, swallowing back the swell of emotion that rose in her chest. This was so unlike her. Normally, at work she was clinical and objective. But the thought that things could have just as easily gone drastically wrong for Mia… 'Keep covering for me, please, Van. I need to speak with Brooke.'

'Good luck with that,' Vanessa huffed. 'Don't get me wrong. I feel sorry for her. But the hospital's good reputation could have been put at risk. We all work too hard for that to happen.'

Lindsey's mouth tightened. She'd begun the day with such happiness in her heart. Now she was stuck with Brooke's mess to clean up. She looked at Vanessa. 'I asked Brooke to wait for me. Do you know where she is?'

'She disappeared pretty fast.' Vanessa picked up the phone as it rang. 'Staffroom perhaps?'

Lindsey decided she'd go there first. She just hoped Brooke hadn't cut and run. If only she knew the woman better. And why was Dan suddenly in the mix? she fretted as she pushed open the door to the staffroom. 'Brooke...' Lindsey took a steadying breath. She'd play this by the book. 'Thanks for waiting.'

Brooke took off the black-framed spectacles she'd been wearing and closed the magazine she'd been reading. 'How is the child?'

'She'll recover.' Lindsey pulled out a chair and sat down. 'You know I'll have to report this to the Director of Nursing, don't you?'

'Am I going to lose my job?'

'If there are mitigating circumstances, you won't lose your job. But it's not up to me, Brooke.' During the awkward silence that followed, Lindsey took stock of her contemporary. Brooke had changed out of her uniform into denim overalls and a simple white T-shirt. Her fair hair was out of its knot and flowing freely around her shoulders. She looked curiously vulnerable. 'Is there anything you want to tell me?'

Brooke's chin came up defensively. 'About what?'

'Did you feel ill during your shift? Headache—anything that would have clouded your judgement?'

Brooke worked her bottom lip as if searching for words. Words that wouldn't come.

Lindsey sighed audibly. 'Look, I'll do everything I can to advocate for you. But I'm in the dark here.'

'I was seconds away from getting to Mia.' Brooke tried to justify her actions. 'We were swamped.'

Lindsey kept her cool. 'You were on triage, Brooke. It means you're the first contact. You follow very set protocols.'

'Don't you think I know that, Lindsey?'

'OK.' Lindsey pulled back in her chair and said quietly, 'I'd urge you to be completely upfront with Clarissa. You'll be supported, Brooke, but sadly there may have to be an inquiry.'

Brooke pressed a hand to her temple.

'No one is ganging up on you here,' Lindsey said. 'But we have to follow the rules. Otherwise there'd be chaos throughout the hospital.'

The nurse didn't reply, yet somehow her silence was deafening. 'Are we done now?'

'Yes, we're done.' Lindsey got to her feet. 'Clarissa will be in touch.'

'I'm on days off.'

'But you'll be available on your mobile?'

'Yes.' Brooke stood abruptly. Snapping up her shoulder bag from the back of the chair, she walked out.

Lindsey's mind was churning as she made her way back to the station. As the song said, some days were stones. And today she felt like chucking her job and going to work in the scented serenity of a florist shop. 'Van, a word, please?'

Her friend nodded and came over. 'What happened?' she asked curiously.

Lindsey *tsked*. 'You know I can't talk about that, Vanessa. But I need some air. Can you keep holding the fort for a while longer?'

Lindsey left the hospital by the rear staff entrance. The rain had cleared and the sun was strafing pools of light and warmth across the car park. Leaning against the brick wall, she tipped her head back, breathing in the pure, crisp air. Ah, that felt better. Then she lowered her head and levelled her gaze.

And that's when she saw them.

Dan and Brooke standing beside a silver sports car—obviously Brooke's—their heads very close together, one so dark, one so fair, absorbed in conversation. At least Dan was the one doing the talking while Brooke seemed drawn towards him, her hand on his arm, listening as though her very life depended on it.

Lindsey felt the drum-heavy beat in her chest align with the sudden recoil in her stomach. She dragged in a shallow breath, hurt and anger in equal parts clogging her throat. Not again!

Sick with uncertainty, she spun on her heel and dashed back through the doorway.

Dan found her in the staffroom barely seconds later. 'Lindsey!'

Go away! she felt like screaming as she filled a paper cup at the sink. She took a gulp of water and then turned to face him.

He moved forward, wanting to take her by the shoulders, but caution held him back. Something in her face, her eyes. 'Don't go reading anything into what you just saw in the car park,' he attempted.

Lindsey shook her head. She wouldn't dignify any of this with a response. 'I have no idea what you're talking about, Dan.'

'Look.' Dan spread his hands in a plea. 'It's complicated.'

Lindsey's mouth felt stiff as she took another sip of water. 'What is?'

He frowned. 'Don't pretend you didn't see me with Brooke.'

Lindsey threw professional caution to the winds. 'Don't treat me like a fool, Dan. What the hell are you playing at?'

'I told you before, Brooke is dealing with some personal stuff,' he said, censure in the coolness of his tone. 'She needed a friend.'

'How touching.' Lindsey actually managed a jagged laugh. 'Dan the *go-to* man!'

A muscle at the corner of Dan's mouth pulled tight and flickered. 'This is all a bit juvenile, isn't it?'

'Let's get professional, then.' Lindsey swung round, tossing her paper cup into the bin. 'Are you protecting Brooke?'

'Oh, for God's sake.' In a gesture of a man almost at the end of his tether Dan jabbed his hands to the side of his head and hung on.

'Why can't you give me a straight answer?' Two spots of colour glazed Lindsey's cheeks.

'Oh—hey guys…' Vanessa popped her head around the door, her smile fading as she picked up on the thick tension in the room. 'I was just looking for… Is everything OK?'

'Everything is…fine.' Dan was the first to gather himself.

'Which one of us do you need, Van?' Lindsey swallowed, her throat aching from the brutal exchange with Dan.

'Well, Dan, actually,' Vanessa said carefully. 'We've a two-year-old with an inhaled foreign body. It looks a bit tricky. Andrew would like some guidance. If you wouldn't mind?'

'Where the hell are the paeds people when you need them?' Dan growled.

'Well, we've only one on staff and she's on her honeymoon. There are a couple of others in town but they're in private practice,' Vanessa supplied helpfully. 'No one is conducting a clinic here today. They usually do Monday and Thursday.'

Oh, Van, your timing is appalling, Lindsey gritted silently. Please, just stop the inane chatter and go away.

'Give me a minute,' Dan said. 'Tell Andrew not to do anything until I get there.'

With Vanessa gone, the tense atmosphere heightened again. Lindsey and Dan were left scoping each other. Dan was the first to speak. 'Are you saying I haven't been upfront with you, Lindsey?'

Lindsey felt sick to her stomach. The thought that he might have divided loyalties only increased her unease. '*You* work it out, Dan.'

Tension crackled between them as brittle as spun sugar.

Dan felt his heart surge to a sickening rhythm. God, he didn't want any of this. He felt racked with fatigue, having been dragged back on duty when he should have been on days off. Days he'd been looking forward to when he could spend some quality time with Lindsey after her shifts. Now it was all out the door like the garbage collection. But he had to try to salvage something. 'Look.' He pressed a hand to the back of his neck. 'If this needs to be sorted, let's sort it. But not here and not now. If I can get out of here at a decent hour, I'll come over to your place. And we'll talk.'

Lindsey lifted a shoulder indifferently. She didn't want to be patted down like some kind of recalcitrant child if that's what he was offering. Either they were equals or they were nothing. And right at the moment, she'd put her money on nothing. 'Please yourself.' She walked to the door and turned. She gave a sad little shake of her head. 'I thought I could trust you.'

For a second Dan felt poleaxed. 'You can,' he said. But his words were lost in the vacuum of her leaving.

Working alongside someone you had a personal relationship with was the pits when it all went wrong. Lindsey's throat constricted as she made her way back to the station. Or maybe she was just rubbish at relationships. She looked at the clock on the wall and sighed. It was still hours until the end of her shift.

Dan felt like ramming his fist through the wall. Being at odds with Lindsey felt as bad as having a cartload of gravel dumped into his guts. He swished back the curtains on the paeds treatment room, vowing he would sort things, whatever it took.

The day wore on and Lindsey couldn't believe how bad it felt to be offside with Dan. But there was no going back and she couldn't see a way forward. 'What is it, Jess?' Lindsey looked up sharply as the junior nurse approached the counter.

'Eighty-year-old male, Lewis Gaines,' Jess, who was gaining experience on triage, said. 'He's very frail, seems quite dehydrated and his pulse is thready. I've given him water and told him to keep drinking. But I think he needs to be seen.'

'Let's see what we can do, then.' Lindsey scooted down the list to see where she could juggle patients. 'Is someone with Mr Gaines, a relative?'

'No. He's on his own. He had to come to the hospital on the bus!' Jess was mildly outraged. 'Someone should have cared enough to be with him, Lindsey.'

'In an ideal world, you'd hope so. Right…grab Michelle. She's just back from lunch.'

'Oh. OK.' Jess hesitated.

A jaded sigh left Lindsey's mouth. She knew what this was about. Unfortunately, Michelle had a habit of being offhand with the junior nurses. It left them feeling unsure of their role and devalued as a result. Lindsey realised it was a personality thing with Michelle but they were *supposed* to be a team. 'Take your patient along to cube one, please, Jess, and wait with him. I'll ask Michelle to attend.'

As she made her way through to the cubicles, Lindsey let her pent-up breath go in a stream. It was turning out to be the shift from hell.

It was almost the end of the shift.

'Hey, Lins, want to come for a drink after work?' Vanessa came back to the station and propped herself at the counter.

'Sorry, not today.' Lindsey threw her pen aside and stretched. 'I just want to get home and have a long, long shower.'

'How did your meeting with the DON go?'

'Clarissa took her usual laid-back approach. If Brooke speaks up for herself, it will all probably blow over. I couldn't do anything more than tell it as I found it.'

'You're always scrupulously fair,' Vanessa declared supportively.

'I just want today over,' Lindsey said with feeling. And she still had to deal with Dan this evening. That's if he even showed up.

'Rotten first day back for you,' Vanessa commiserated. 'Why don't I do handover? Then you can take off and get that shower.'

'Oh, cheers!' Lindsey let her shoulders drop as if sloughing off a huge weight. 'That's the best offer I've had all day.'

* * *

Sweet God, how had all this happened? Slumped at his desk, Dan shaded his eyes with his hands. He had to fix things with Lindsey. She was keeping out of his way, delegating the other nurses to assist him.

He was still considering a plan of action when his mobile rang. Sitting back in his chair, he activated the call and then sat bolt upright as he listened.

'You've done what?'

Lindsey's thoughts were deeply focused as she made her way from the station to the staffroom.

'Lindsey…' Dan appeared out of nowhere and closed in beside her.

'Oh!' Lindsey drew to an abrupt halt. She brought her head up in question.

'Martin is back on deck.' Dan got straight to the point. 'He'll be in a bit later. I'll be off duty. We can talk. I'll come to you or we can meet somewhere neutral if you'd prefer.'

There was a wavering in her eyes, a sign of hesitation. Finally, 'My place is fine. Come when you get off.'

Dan felt relief course through him. 'I should be out of here by six. Could I bring a takeaway?'

Lindsey looked up and saw the sheen of appeal in his eyes. 'Thanks, but no need. I'll fix us something. Just one thing, Dan.'

His brow rose briefly. 'Name it.'

'We sort this. Truthfully. No double-talk.'

A tiny pulse flickered in Dan's cheek. His eyes softened, taking in the brave set of her head, the soft curve of her cheek, the sweet, very sweet fullness of her mouth. 'You've got it.'

'Do you have the address?' she asked, almost formally.

'You gave it to me on Sunday night. Remember?'

She did. Soft heat flooded her cheeks. She'd told him when they'd been snuggled up in bed during the storm and she'd foolishly thought that nothing or no one could touch their newfound happiness. Now they were both hurting and she hated it. In a gesture of fence-mending she put out her hand and he took it loosely. 'See you later, then.'

'As soon as I can make it.'

Lindsey couldn't keep still. When would Dan get here? She just hoped he hadn't had an emergency at the last minute. She had her stir-fry ready to just throw in the wok and she'd cooked rice to go with it. Taking a deep breath, she let it go. It felt like a first date all over again. She spun round from the kitchen bench, a little tumble in her stomach as the doorbell pealed.

Dan waited for Lindsey to open the door. Mentally, he was wiped. Today in Casualty had been one that took years from a health professional's life. Add the stress of that to the personal stuff that had gone down…the thought of that made him go cold. Everything between them had so nearly run off the rails today.

Lindsey opened the door. 'Hi…' She met his gaze almost hungrily. 'Come in, Dan.'

He nodded and stepped inside, realising he'd crack wide open if he didn't hold her. Properly. With no agenda. And she had that gleam in her eyes. The one that could send a sweep of sensation down to his toes, igniting all the parts of his body in between. He held out his arms and she melted into them, wrapping herself tightly around him, feeling his chest rise and fall in a broken sigh. 'God, I thought I'd lost you. Lost us.'

She reached up to bracket his face with her hands, her heart in her gaze. 'I hated what happened today.'

'Don't go back there.' Suddenly he looked uncertain. 'Tell me I'm not dreaming. I am actually holding you?'

'You're not dreaming, Dan.' Slowly she became aware of his palm resting warmly at her nape, the tips of his fingers playing gently with the strands of her hair.

'Could we delay *talking* and just go to bed?' he asked throatily. 'I need to put things right.'

CHAPTER TEN

'THAT WAS WONDERFUL.'

'I gathered it must have been.' Lindsey looked on indulgently as he forked up the last of the stir-fry from his bowl. 'You had two helpings.'

'Didn't eat much today,' he offloaded with a grin.

Lindsey looked across at him. 'Today was pretty bad, wasn't it? In all kinds of ways.'

'Just marginally,' he underplayed. 'For most of it I felt as though I had a knife jammed between my ribs. How about you?'

'No knife.' Soft humour shone in her eyes. 'But I wanted to just jump in my car and head back to Lark Hill and never set foot in a casualty department again.'

'That would be a terrible shame.' Dan swallowed the sudden razor-sharp emotion clogging his throat. Today could have all turned out so differently. 'You're an amazing nurse, Lindsey.' His blue gaze shimmered over her face. 'An amazing lover…'

She reached out her hand and they touched fingertips. 'Only with you…'

Her mouth suddenly dried. What they'd found together was still so new. And wonderful. *I think I love you.* Only she didn't voice that thought out loud.

She took her hand back and got to her feet. 'Coffee?'

'Oh, yes, please.' He looked up and thanked her as she took his bowl.

'How long have you had this place?' Dan asked interestedly. They were relaxing on Lindsey's big comfy sofa, their coffee and a plate of orange shortbread, compliments of Fiona, on the low table in front of them.

'I bought it ages ago. When I decided this was where I wanted to be.'

'For always?'

Lindsey looked startled. 'I hadn't thought about it like that. But my job is here. And my family.' She frowned a bit. 'Do you think that's…odd?'

'No.' He gave her a long, intense look. 'Knowing what you want, what makes you happy, sounds wonderfully… grounded.'

Lindsey felt a glitch of uncertainty. 'Not boring?'

'Is that even worth an answer?'

Probably not. 'The house was once a miner's cottage,' Lindsey went on. 'The structure was pretty sound when I bought it and I just refurbished it to my own taste as I went along.'

'You've certainly put your own stamp on it.' He looked around at the unmistakable *Lindsey* touches. 'Some of your work?' he asked, flexing a hand towards the table lamps with their blue and white ginger jar bases.

'Some of my early pieces.' She leant forward and poured their coffee. 'I found the fireplace at an auction. It was in an old post office they were pulling down.' She handed him his coffee. 'I offered twenty dollars to get the bidding started and came home with it.'

Dan gave one of his lazy smiles. 'I'm impressed.'

'You should come with me some time.' Lindsey pressed her head against his shoulder.

'To an auction?'

'I'm guessing you've never been to one. Am I right?'

'Guilty as charged.' His mouth tipped at one corner.

Lindsey took one of the tiny shortbreads and bit into it thoughtfully. 'Are you still in the hospital accommodation?'

'One of the flats. They're not bad and close enough to the hospital to make getting to work on time less hassle.'

'Nathan had a flat there as well, didn't he?'

'Still has. He didn't entirely move out before he and Sami were married. Living there suits me for the present anyway.'

And then what? Lindsey wondered. She knew he had a work contract with the hospital and Dan, being Dan, would honour his contractual arrangements whatever it took. But when his commitment to Hopeton District ran out, then what? Would he go elsewhere? *Then what about us?* she wanted to ask. But couldn't. Possibly because neither of them knew the answer.

Dan's chest rose in a long, uneven breath. The faint drift of Lindsey's distinctive floral shampoo was already escalating into the reality of her head on the pillow beside him earlier. And the completeness of their loving. It came as something of a shock to him that he'd never felt remotely like this before. The thought made him want to go forward with new purpose. Leave no room for doubt or misinterpretation. Lindsey deserved that. He expelled a rough sigh. 'If you're up for it, I guess we should talk about the elephant in the room.'

Well, no second-guessing there. 'Brooke?' Lindsey felt her heart beating in double-quick time. 'I heard back from Clarissa. They had a long talk. At the end of it Brooke decided to resign. She's left the hospital.'

'She's left town as well. She called me.'

So Brooke had his mobile number. Lindsey felt that sense of unease return. Suddenly her nerve ends were tingling, her breathing uncomfortably tight. She lifted her head, searing her gaze with his. 'Is she in love with you?'

'No.' In a kind of releasing gesture Dan raised his hands, ploughing his fingers through his hair. 'It's a bit of an involved story. But now Brooke's gone...' He stopped and considered. 'I don't think it would hurt if I told you. But before I do I want you to know there was nothing going on in the car park when you saw us.'

Lindsey was far from mollified. 'She was practically welded to your groin!'

He gave a reproving look before his mouth twitched into a transparently smug grin. 'I can't help it if women flock round me.'

'Oh, get over yourself, Dr Rossi,' she countered drily. 'I was probably mistaken anyway.' She spread her hands in a shrug. 'Go on with your story.'

Dan looked serious for a moment. 'It's off the record, Lindsey.'

'Of course. And before we go any further, I feel really sorry for Brooke. It was a rotten thing to happen but it did and there were consequences.' When Dan remained silent, she asked, 'Why did she come to Hopeton?'

'Spot on the map,' Dan said. 'As random as that. And there were vacancies advertised at the hospital. It had been a while since she'd nursed but she took a chance and applied. She was offered a position in Casualty. She hadn't wanted to begin there but she needed a job.'

'But it seems as though she was far from comfortable, working there. What kind of training did she have?'

'She was well qualified to work in Casualty. Brooke was in the ADF. She'd done two tours in Afghanistan.'

Lindsey frowned. 'She was an army nurse?'

'She was dedicated. And decorated.'

She blinked uncertainly. 'So, what are you saying?'

'In my opinion, Brooke is suffering from PTSD.'

'Oh—that's awful.' Lindsey felt a flow of sympathy. 'Because of her time in the Defence Force?'

Dan nodded. 'Her fiancé was a soldier. They were both attached to the same company when they were overseas. He was wounded. Brought in when Brooke was on duty.'

'Oh, Lord…' Lindsey squeezed her eyes shut. It got worse and worse. She swallowed heavily. 'Did he survive?'

'No. They airlifted him out but it was too late. Brooke went with him. Not that it counted for much in the end.'

'And Brooke told you all this on night duty?'

'We had long stretches when it was quiet,' Dan replied. 'I'm pretty tuned in to mental fatigue.' He didn't add he'd done advanced training in stress management as part of his search and rescue course. 'I sensed something about her. I put out a few feelers and she responded. I urged her to be upfront with Clarissa and ask for a transfer to another department. Anywhere but Casualty. I think she was getting around to it.'

'But not soon enough.' Lindsey looked thoughtful. 'Did she say what triggered her meltdown this morning? Why she didn't react when Mia was brought in?'

'The ambulance base had called and said there was a gunshot wound coming in. Brooke admitted she freaked.'

Lindsey shook her head. 'Where did all her training go, her protocols?'

'Lindsey, we can't have any real idea of Brooke's mental state at that moment. We hadn't been through what she'd been through. Obviously, she wasn't thinking straight. She spun out at the mention of guns. In any event, it turned out it was only a superficial wound. Some idiot out spotlighting feral pigs had misfired and shot himself in the side of the foot.'

'And in all the carry-on Brooke forgot about Mia.'

'Well—momentarily anyway.'

Lindsey felt her stomach churn. The incident could

have all been avoided if Brooke had just signed off and gone home and let someone else deal with the emergency. 'When did she tell you all this?'

'I watched for her to leave this morning and followed her out to the car park. I reiterated what I'd already told her. Suggested she get counselling as a priority.'

'Instead, she's left town.' Lindsey's eyes looked troubled. 'Where will she go?'

'When she called me she said she was going back to Sydney. She'll have family support there. And I've linked her up with a good shrink. She promised to follow through. Today has been a huge wake-up call for her. She'll get the help she needs now and life will get much better for her.'

'Oh, Dan…' Lindsey scooted up the sofa to him.

'I know.' He gathered her in and placed a soft kiss on her mouth. 'If we all had hindsight, the world would be a much better and kinder place.'

'Brooke kept to herself a lot. It was difficult to offer any kind of friendship.'

'Don't beat up on yourself,' Dan said. 'In our job we can only do what we can do. What people will *allow* us to do.'

'I'll scotch any rumours,' Lindsey promised.

'That'll be good.' He gave her a quick hug. 'You didn't really think I had something going with Brooke, did you?'

Lindsey felt his smile on her skin as he touched his lips to her throat.

'I admit to a smidge of jealousy.'

He looked into her green eyes. An intensity of emotion he'd never felt swamped him. 'You're all I need, Lindsey. So…with that in mind, am I staying the night?'

Lindsey drew in a shaken breath, feeling the sweet sting of anticipation tingle up her spine. 'Where else would you go?' A smile flickered around her mouth. 'But just so you know, I'm on an early tomorrow.'

'Ah.' His eyes caressed her tenderly. 'And I'm on a day off.'

'Then I'll leave it to you to make the bed and tidy the kitchen, shall I?'

He reached out a finger, his touch feather-like along her bottom lip. 'I think I can manage that.'

'Hey, I'm kidding.' Lindsey smothered a laugh. 'I wouldn't expect you to do that.'

'I'll do it anyway.' Carefully, he scooped up a wayward tendril of her hair and tucked it behind her ear. 'I'm really quite house-trained. I thought you knew that.'

'I probably did.' She snuggled closer. 'So, what are you going to do with your day off?'

His mouth quirked. 'I'm going to a talk on beekeeping.'

'Well, that makes sense—not.' Lindsey chuckled. 'Where are you going to do your beekeeping, may one ask?'

He sent her a pained look. 'It's good to have a hobby. And who knows, I may invest in acreage one day.'

Next morning Lindsey drove to work with a new resolve. Surely there had always been a sacred bond among nurses? Perhaps if Brooke had been more open… Lindsey turned into the car park. From today she'd make extra sure her team knew they were valued and supported.

It wasn't long into the shift when Vanessa pounced. 'Did you hear?'

Lindsey lifted her gaze in query. 'If this is about Brooke, Vanessa, yes, I heard. She's resigned.'

'I heard she got the sack.'

'Well, she didn't,' Lindsey said firmly. 'She decided Hopeton wasn't for her and she's gone back to her family in Sydney.'

'Will she be all right?'

'Let's hope so. Brooke was in the armed forces.' Abruptly,

Lindsey decided she'd tell Vanessa just enough to settle the wild supposition that was probably on speaker phone around the hospital already. 'She did a couple of tours in Afghanistan. Apparently, it was pretty rough.'

'Wow…' Vanessa sobered. 'What went down—personal stuff?'

Lindsey nodded. 'Very personal. Someone very close to her was killed.'

'Oh, that's awful.' Vanessa blinked quickly then straightened her shoulders resolutely. 'If anyone starts spouting rubbish about Brooke being sacked, I'll quash it.'

Lindsey's mouth kicked up in a resigned smile. 'Diplomatically, please, Van.'

'Of course I'll be diplomatic.' Vanessa looked wounded. 'By tomorrow it'll all be a non-event anyway.' She picked up the phone as it rang. 'Bound to be something more juicy come along.'

Continuing with her new resolve, Lindsey drew Jess aside when she got a chance later in the shift. 'How did things turn out with Mr Gaines yesterday?' Lindsey knew she could have pulled the notes and found out for herself but it would be helpful for the young nurse's professional development to let Jess debrief.

'Oh, Michelle admitted him,' Jess said earnestly. 'He was exhibiting early signs of pneumonia.'

'So, you made a good call, then.'

'Think so.' Jess's mouth curved, a tiny dimple showing in her cheek.

'Are you getting on all right with Michelle?'

Jess went pink. 'She can be a bit daunting. But yesterday she included me in Mr Gaines's treatment plan and that felt really professional.'

'Good.' Lindsey smiled.

'And Mr Gaines has a nice neighbour who brought some

pyjamas and things in for him,' Jess went on. 'And I got some toiletries for him as well. And some batteries for his little radio.'

'But I hope not out of your own pocket, Jess?' Lindsey pressed the point. Patient care only went so far. And while Jess was very committed to her role, shelling out for patients' extras was not part of it.

'Oh, no. Mr Gaines was very upfront with his money. And Michelle had a chat to him about his living arrangements and apparently his granddaughter from Sydney would like to come and live with him.' Jess continued enthusiastically, 'Grace, that's her name, has a little three-year-old, Liam, and her husband is a FIFO worker. Fly-in, fly-out,' Jess enlarged.

Lindsey hid a smile. 'I know what it means, Jess. So that would seem a good arrangement if they're both keen.'

'Well, Grace is a bit lonely and so is Mr Gaines and he seemed really chuffed to think it might all happen. Michelle's handed everything over to Declan,' she said, mentioning the hospital's social worker.

'Well, good outcome,' Lindsey approved.

'Um...' Jess looked a bit uncertain. 'Is it OK if I run up to Medical to see Mr Gaines now and again? In my break, I mean.'

'Of course.' Lindsey smiled. 'I imagine it would brighten Mr Gaines's day as well. Just realise, though, that in Casualty we're just the jumping-off point. We can't give holistic care, no matter how much we'd like to. You're really enjoying your nursing, aren't you, Jess?'

'More than I thought.' Jess considered. 'And it's nice when your patient says thank you and when you've made a positive impact on them.'

'Perhaps we could nominate you for Nurse of the Year,' Lindsey said teasingly. 'The local Lions Club gives an annual award with a cash prize.'

'Wow—I didn't know that.' Jess's hand went to her heart. 'That'd be so cool—to be nominated, I mean. But I guess one of the midwives would be sure to win.'

'They do seem to have all the fun,' Lindsey agreed. 'Next time we have a staff meeting, I'll run it past the DON.' She touched Jess briefly on the shoulder. 'You know I'm always available if you need to discuss anything work-related, Jess. Or anything personal, for that matter,' Lindsey added, thinking of Brooke again. 'Confidentiality guaranteed.'

'Thanks.' Jess bit her lip. 'Could I extend my time in Casualty, do you think? I really like being part of our team.'

'Just keep doing what you're doing,' Lindsey said. 'That's probably the best way to go.'

Lindsey leaned over the counter to replace a file, deciding that if yesterday's shift had been hell on wheels, today's had been relatively uneventful.

'How was your meeting?' Vanessa looked up from the computer.

'Quick for a change.' Lindsey gave a wry smile. 'Apparently, we're getting a new senior nurse for the department.'

'Mmm, I heard.' Vanessa stretched languidly. 'Charlie Weston, thirty-two, divorced, shared care of four-year-old Poppy.'

Lindsey shook her head. 'You take my breath away sometimes. How do you know all this?'

An imp of mischief danced in Vanessa's eyes. 'Oh, I have my ways. And I like to keep ahead of the game.'

Lindsey cast her eyes down. She wondered how long she and Dan had before their involvement was *out there*. She gave a mental shrug. They'd deal with it when it happened. As it undoubtedly would.

'It's ages since we've had a male nurse in the department,' Vanessa said chattily. 'Do you think he'll come on to our team?'

'We'll have to wait and see, I suppose.'

'We'll lose Annie Logan soon when she takes her mat leave.' Vanessa considered. 'So possibly we'll get Charlie to replace her.'

'Possibly.' Lindsey came round and joined Vanessa at the desk. 'I'll give handover. Take an early mark, if you like.'

'Ta, Lins.' Vanessa was already on her feet. 'I'm off to the gym.' She bit down on her bottom lip around a quick smile. 'Andrew kind of said he might be there.'

Lindsey watched her friend leave. Privately, she thought Vanessa was chasing shadows. If Andrew had wanted a closer relationship with her, he would have acted ages ago, not left her wishing and hoping for something he wasn't capable of giving.

Thank heavens Dan had known what he wanted and gone after it. Lindsey's gaze turned dreamy. She wondered whether he'd be there when she got home. Would he stay again tonight…?

'Afternoon, Lins.'

Lindsey's head swivelled round as charge for the late shift, Greta Ingram, joined her at the desk.

'Oh—hey, Greta.' Lindsey brought her thoughts smartly back to reality.

'How are things?'

'Pretty good, thanks. And with you as well, I imagine.'

Lindsey's eyes opened to questioning wideness.

'You and your new man? I heard you and Dan got off together after Nathan's wedding. Looking very much an item, according to my cousin Alison.'

When Lindsey remained speechless, Greta gave a chuckle and went on. 'You've obviously forgotten Ally works in Nathan's department. Her mum made the wedding cake.'

'Well, I saw Alison there, of course,' Lindsey flannelled. 'But there was a big crowd so I didn't...' She picked up some paperwork and held it against her chest. 'Who else knows?'

'Well, I haven't said anything,' Greta said calmly. 'But would it matter?'

Lindsey thought for a minute. 'I suppose not. You know, in all my years of nursing I've never become involved with someone I worked with.'

'Well, that doesn't make you *odd*!' Greta insisted. 'I didn't date work colleagues either.'

'Kind of ironical then, wasn't it?' Lindsey teased, 'That you actually met your husband-to-be in a hospital setting.'

Greta's husband, Harry, was a painter and decorator. When they'd met, he'd just started his own company and had won the tender to refurbish the entire Hopeton casualty department. 'I thought he needed looking after.' Greta sank onto a chair, looking amused. 'I kept bringing him big mugs of tea.'

'I remember.' Lindsey's laugh tinkled. 'Poor guy. No wonder he was in and out of the men's so much.'

'Oh, he never was!' Greta chuckled and flapped her lanyard in protest. 'Now, what do you have for me?' She moved closer to the computer.

When Lindsey arrived home from work there was no sign of Dan, but he'd left a note on the kitchen counter. It said simply that Nathan and Sami were due back that evening and he was meeting their flight. He'd see Lindsey at work tomorrow.

And he hadn't taken the spare key she'd left him. It was placed pointedly on top of the note.

Now, what was she supposed to read into that? Lindsey fretted as she stripped off and threw herself under the shower. Suddenly her mind was a whirlpool of jumbled thoughts and emotions. Well, obviously Dan didn't trust what they'd found together at all. She'd assumed. And *he* hadn't liked it. Vigorously, she washed her hair and let the shampoo puddle round her feet. Did they have yet another elephant in the room? It seemed so.

As Lindsey towelled dry, she gave a bitter little laugh. Where understanding men and their motives were concerned, she'd obviously been as naïve as Vanessa.

As soon as she saw Dan arrive at work on Thursday morning, Lindsey went straight to his office. There was a knot in her stomach and tension in her muscles as though she'd run a marathon, but she wasn't about to let him retreat to some place in his head and leave her outside.

Knocking briefly on his door, she popped her head in and then the rest of herself. Turning, she closed the door and looked across at him. 'Hi.' She managed a smile. 'Got a minute for me?'

'Of course.' Dan got to his feet slowly, meeting her where she'd stopped at the front of his desk.

He parked himself against the edge of the desk, folding his arms and crossing his feet at the ankles. He sent her a narrowed look, drawn by the intensity of her expression. 'You OK?'

'Fine.' Lindsey shoved her hands into the pockets of her trousers. 'How was your day off?'

'It was good.'

'And the talk?'

'It was interesting.' A tiny flicker of amusement appeared behind his eyes. 'I learned the queen bee mates with fifteen males in mid-air and then flies back to the hive to lay her eggs.'

'Wow! That's quite an impressive gene pool they have going.'

'Mmm.' Dan rubbed his chin. 'I felt a bit sorry for the males, though. They're history after they've mated.'

'That's nature, I guess.' Lindsey hardly gave the statement head room. She had to do what she'd come to do now or let it fester for the rest of the shift. She tilted her head higher and sent him a very frank look. 'So…the key. Too far, too fast?'

He frowned a bit. 'Sorry?'

'I left you a spare key to my home. Clearly, you didn't want it.'

Dan felt the wind taken right out of his sails. He'd hoped for opportunity and the right time to explain his motives but it seemed he wasn't going to get it.

'We hadn't talked about it and I didn't want to presume anything.'

'In other words, you thought *I'd* taken far too much for granted.'

'Hell, Lindsey…' He lifted his hands and scrubbed his fingers impatiently across his cheekbones. 'I don't know what I thought. It just seemed a bit…awkward.'

'Oh, Dan…' Lindsey shook her head. It appeared they still had a long way to go. A long way. 'I left the key as a kind of no-strings invitation,' she flannelled, going all-out to save the situation as best she could. 'I just thought you might have wanted to come back after your talk, relax a bit, even though I wasn't there.' She took a tiny swallow. Even to her own ears the whole scenario sounded less than plausible.

Dan felt the unease in his gut begin to unravel. How had he got it so wrong? Lindsey was everything he'd ever dreamed of in a woman. He'd accepted almost greedily everything she'd offered in the bedroom. Why had he got all stiff-necked about her offer of a damned key! It made his stomach twist. 'I'm an idiot.'

'Well, maybe the jury's still out on that.' She managed a smile of sorts and stepped away. 'Oh.' She turned at the door. 'How were the honeymooners?'

Dan cracked a crooked grin. 'Still in love, by the look of them. They had a great time.'

'Oh, bless. Where did they go?'

'One of the Barrier Reef islands.'

'Fantastic. Ever been?'

He looked a bit sheepish. 'Very remiss of me, I know. Never seemed to get the time.'

'Poor excuse.' Her green eyes lit briefly. 'We'll have to remedy that.'

Why on earth had she made that ridiculous comment? Lindsey gave herself a mental ticking off as she made her way back to the station. The way things were going between her and Dan, they had about as much chance of making a romantic trip to the Reef as being in Edinburgh for lunch on Sunday.

Back at her desk, she buried herself in paperwork.

'You OK?' Vanessa gave Lindsey an assessing look when the two caught up during a quiet moment.

'Yep.' Lindsey gathered her paperwork and tapped it into a neat pile. 'Oh, by the way, Greta left a flyer. Harry and the Rotary need some helpers for a community project. Working bee at the kindergarten. Could you bung it up in the staffroom, please?'

'Sure.' Vanessa scanned the bright yellow notice. 'Oh, it's at the kindergarten that caters for differently abled little ones. I'll be off that weekend, so I'll go along. Perhaps Andrew as well…'

'Did you meet up at the gym?' Lindsey asked casually.

Vanessa made a face. 'He didn't show. I hung around until I'd made myself dizzy on that stupid walking thing. And then I left.'

'Do you think—?' Lindsey stopped. How to be diplomatic here? 'Tell me to mind my own, but do you think it's really working with you and Andrew?'

Vanessa blinked a bit and shrugged. 'Obviously, *you* don't.'

'What do I know about men and their *ways*?' Lindsey snorted.

'Are you and Dan…you know?' Vanessa rocked her hand suggestively.

Lindsey sat back in her chair. Why keep up the secrecy? 'We've been seeing each other a bit.' And wasn't that the understatement of the year?

'You were into something pretty heavy yesterday when I walked in on you.'

'That was entirely work-related.'

Vanessa rolled her eyes. 'And if I believed that, I'd believe someone's just given us the rest of the day off!'

'Oh, hush up, Van,' Lindsey responded mildly. 'It's sorted, OK?'

'You know,' Vanessa said thoughtfully and with a seemingly new-found maturity, 'I'm starting to believe that trying to have a personal relationship with someone you work with is doomed from the outset.'

'Well, perhaps it depends on the *someone*,' Lindsey countered. 'But whatever, it's certainly a minefield,' she added darkly, picking up the phone as it rang. 'MVA coming in. Grab whoever you can and I'll meet you at the ambulance bay.'

He should be certified.

Dan gave vent to a groan of frustration as he drove home. And placed in lockdown, he gritted silently.

What the hell was wrong with him? Why couldn't he just have accepted the key to Lindsey's home with grace? Because deep down he knew it had been a loving gesture from her. And, however much she'd denied it, loaded with expectation. And that fact was what had almost brought him out in a cold sweat.

He made a sound of disgust at his pathetic handling of his relationship with Lindsey. She was lovely, her femininity enthralled him. And she was sweet and clever. And she made him laugh. Put simply so that even an idiot could understand, everything about her called to him. So why couldn't he have sorted things when she'd come to his office? Told her he wanted to take things slowly—for both their sakes. God, after his stuff-up with Caroline—

He shook his head. *But surely to God he could have just taken a step forward and wrapped his arms around Lindsey. Reassured her.*

His jaw tightened, the regret almost numbing him. And he didn't wonder any longer why all day his arms had almost ached with the thought of the lost opportunity.

His introspection was cut short when he responded to an incoming call on his hands-free mobile. 'Rossi.'

'Hey, mate.'

'Nate.' Immediately, Dan's mood lifted. 'How're things?'

'Yeah, great. Are you by any chance on your way home?' Nathan asked.

'Almost there.'

'Any plans for tonight?'

Dan grimaced. He could have had plans but he'd well and truly scuttled those. 'No, I don't have any plans. What do you need?'

Nathan chuckled. 'You know me too well. Actually, I need a hand to shift the last of my stuff out of the flat. Some other dude wants to move in over the weekend.'

'What kind of *stuff* are we talking about?' Dan asked cautiously. 'I don't need extra health cover for a broken back, do I?'

Nathan snorted. 'It's only a few books and things.'

'What books? Those massive medical tomes you've been carting around for years?'

'It won't be that difficult,' Nathan justified. 'I've hired a trolley thing. I just need you and your car boot. It'll be sweet.'

'What's in it for me, then?' Dan shot back.

'Hang on, I'm thinking.'

'Yeah, I can hear the cogs.'

'Fish and chips for dinner,' Nathan offered gallantly. 'Plus a very smooth bourbon.'

Dan cracked a laugh. 'Fair enough. I'm two minutes away.'

CHAPTER ELEVEN

Friday...

CASUALTY WAS BUSY. Lindsey thanked her lucky stars it was. It gave her less time to begin thinking. Analysing. Had she come across to Dan as too organised about their relationship? Too calculating? Pushing too hard? She shook her head. She hadn't meant to give that impression at all.

She wondered how he'd spent last night. Had he stayed home and thought about her? About them? Maybe he'd gone out on the town. Not that Hopeton had much of a night-life during the week but still…

'The police just brought in two old chaps, drunk as.' Vanessa came round the corner of the station and slapped her notes on the desk. 'They politely or impolitely vomited all over the floor and now the waiting room smells like—well, you know.'

'Get the cleaners in,' Lindsey said patiently.

'I tried.' Vanessa's mouth twisted comically. 'They're on a tea break.'

'What's wrong with your patients, besides needing something for their hangovers?' Lindsey asked.

'Cuts and bruises mostly. When the pub shut they spent the rest of the night in the park. A couple of low-lives rolled them this morning. Stole their wallets.'

'What's the place coming to?' Lindsey frowned. 'Are the police looking into it?'

'Dunno. Dan spoke to them.'

'I imagine their ID and social security details were in the wallets.'

'Declan's on it,' Vanessa dismissed. 'For the present, the old boys are *resting* in the side ward. I guess we'll do what we always do. Patch them up, give them something to eat a bit later and send them off.' She flopped into a chair. 'You can't help wondering how people's lives disintegrate so drastically. I mean, they must have been young and hopeful once. I wonder where they'll sleep tonight.'

Lindsey looked at her friend sharply. It was not like Van to be introspective. 'Perhaps Declan will be able to arrange some sheltered accommodation for them. Are *you* OK? You still have some leave due. Maybe you should take it? Get away from the place for a bit.'

'Maybe.' Vanessa managed a jaded smile.

'By the way, Annie finished last night. Her ob wants her to rest up. Our new man is starting on Monday on an early.'

'Oh, joy.' Vanessa brightened. 'On our team, then?'

'For the moment. Uh-oh.' Lindsey sighed as she picked up a call from the ambulance base. She listened to the report and then shot off a few questions of her own. Putting the phone down, she turned to Vanessa. 'Ten girls from St Faith's College coming in from a school camp, suspected food poisoning. ETA twenty minutes.'

Quickly, Lindsey found Dan and relayed the details of the emergency.

'Right, this is where the rubber hits the road, people. We'll need everyone on deck,' Dan said when the team had assembled at the station. 'We'll wait to ascertain the extent of the illness and go from there.'

'And be ready with basins, please,' Lindsey said. 'Some of the students could still be vomiting.'

Within minutes two ambulances had arrived, followed by one of the teachers who had helpfully offered his Land Rover to transport several of the young patients to the hospital.

'Let's get some triage happening, shall we?' Dan came in authoritatively. He half turned his head. 'Lindsey?'

Lindsey ran her eyes over the assembled group. 'This is going to need everyone's co-operation. Some of the students appear quite ill so, Gail, where you can, would you begin taking names, please? And liaise with the accompanying teachers about letting the parents know.'

'How do we work this patient-wise?' Andrew cut in, throwing the question at Dan.

'We'll see the kids on stretchers first. You team with Jess. Michelle, you team with Vanessa. Anything you're uncertain about, don't dither. Give me a yell. Now let's go.'

Accompanied by Dan, Lindsey went into the first cubicle. Their patient, a sixteen-year-old student, looked pale and clammy. Lindsey placed her hand on the youngster's shoulder. 'What's your name, honey?'

'Katherine Enders.'

'And when did you start feeling ill?' Lindsey smoothed the girl's long fair hair away from her cheek.

'Soon after breakfast.' She bit her lips together and went on. 'The other kids were sick too.'

'Katherine,' Dan said gently, 'I just need to feel your tummy.' His mouth compressed as he palpated. 'Right.' He stepped back and drew the sheet up. 'That's fine. Have you had any diarrhoea?'

'Some. Oh…'

Lindsey noticed the girl's sudden pallor. 'Do you want to vomit, Katherine?'

The girl blocked a tear with the tips of her fingers and sniffed. 'I feel so awful.' She swallowed convulsively and tried to sit up. 'My little sister, Alix, is really sick…'

'Shh… It's OK,' Lindsey hushed gently. 'She'll be looked after. Let's just try to get you settled.'

That wasn't going to happen.

'Oh, help!' Katherine gulped and gave a little moan. 'I want to be sick…'

Lindsey grabbed a basin. They were in for a morning and a half with this lot.

'Someone's head should roll over this.' Dan was grim-faced. 'Let's run ten milligrams of Maxolon stat, please, Lindsey. That should settle her nausea.'

Quickly Lindsey secured the drip and taped it down. 'Lomotil for the diarrhoea?'

Dan nodded. 'Start with two orally and cut back to one after each bowel movement. She's dehydrating. I'd like her on four per cent glucose and one-fifth normal saline IV. Sips of water only. Could you take her blood sugar levels as well, please? Anything below three, I need to know.'

And so it went on for the next couple of hours.

'I don't know about you, but I'm starving.' Dan followed Lindsey into the staffroom. They'd just done a round, re-checking all their young patients. And releasing most of them into the care of their parents.

'I have sandwiches, if you'd like to share?' Lindsey offered.

'Hmm…' Dan considered his options. 'I think I'd like something hot. Let's go to Leo's.'

'Oh.' Lindsey hesitated. 'OK. I'll just make sure Vanessa's around to mind the station.'

'What about Alix Enders?' Lindsey asked as they crossed the street to Leo's. 'How long will you keep her?'

'I'd like to leave her drip in a bit longer. She was seriously dehydrated.'

'Did you get any clue as to what may have caused the food poisoning?'

'Probably something dodgy they ate for breakfast, seeing they were ill so soon after. The guys from Health and Safety will suss it out, send whatever they come up with for analysis.' Dan pushed open the door to the café and they went inside.

'I'm not usually out for lunch.' Lindsey took the chair Dan held for her. 'I shouldn't be away from the hospital too long.'

'You're entitled to your break.' Dan had no such qualms. 'And we're only five minutes away if we're needed.'

'I suppose.' She ran her gaze over the short menu. 'I think I'll have the fish.'

'I'll have the beef stroganoff.' Dan placed the menu beside his plate. 'I had fish last night. An impromptu dinner with Nathan and Sami.'

So that's where he'd been. Lindsey looked up as Leo arrived to leave water and take their orders. How pathetic, she berated herself, waiting for any crumb that would let her a little further into Dan's world. While they waited for their food, Lindsey poured them each a glass of water. Suddenly she was aware the silence had extended for too long. 'So… Nathan and Sami settling into their new place all right?'

'New *old* place,' Dan countered drily. 'It's Georgian in design, huge garden, built in the eighteen thirties, according to Sami. She's already on a roll, talking in terms of topiary, stone walling and hedge laying.'

'How's Nathan feel about that?'

'Terrified.' Dan's eyes glinted with soft amusement. 'Sami's been to the historical society to get details of the house as it used to be. She found the front hedge was originally clipped into a whimsical line of marching elephants.'

'Are you serious?' Lindsey spluttered a laugh. 'That girl is totally priceless. But I don't know why I should be surprised. Sami has always known what she wanted and gone after it. I guess that's what Nathan loves about her.'

'I'm sure...' Dan paused. 'Oh, while I think of it, I've been given time off on Monday to attend a refresher training day in search and rescue. If you're pushed, Nathan's back on Monday. He'll come down. And Martin's in at noon.'

Lindsey nodded. 'Thanks for letting me know. Where do you have to go for your training?'

Dan lifted a shoulder. 'Locally.'

And that seemed to be that. Within seconds they were facing another wall of uneasy silence.

It was Dan who broke it.

'Would you like to go out for dinner tomorrow? Perhaps somewhere we could dance as well?' He'd made himself aware of Lindsey's roster, knew she was on an early tomorrow and then off on Sunday, and had decided he could work around that as well.

Slowly Lindsey raised her gaze. Her throat constricted. 'That would have been...good. But I'm heading straight out to Lark Hill after my shift. Mum and Dad are due home next week. I want to make sure everything's looking nice for them.'

It was on the tip of Dan's tongue to ask if she'd like a hand—his for preference—but it was clear she wasn't about to issue an invitation. It was also clear she was making a statement. She didn't want him there. He took a mouthful of water and placed his glass back on its coaster. 'Something's obviously bugging you, Lindsey. Why don't you just hit me with it?'

She didn't pretend to misunderstand him. 'I like clarity in my life. That's how I am. I don't seem to be getting it from you, Dan.'

They stared at each other.

'Let's be frank, then.' Dan's blue eyes glittered. 'You're still ticked off with me because I didn't accept the key you left for me.'

Lindsey hated confrontation but there was no backing down. 'I was hurt at your reaction,' she admitted.

'I acted like a jerk.' His mouth straightened into a grim line. 'Your leaving the key was spontaneous and sweet. I could have called you and sorted it, instead of leaving that pathetic note.' He gave a mirthless laugh. 'God, I can't believe I did that!'

Lindsey raised an eyebrow. 'But you did. And I was left wondering whether every move I make in the future is going to be the right one. If you want out of this relationship, then tell me. Let's end it cleanly.'

End it? Dan felt a cramp in his chest. Was that what *she* wanted? He let his breath go in a stream. He'd been the luckiest man alive, finding Lindsey. Lindsey with the generous spirit, the forgiving heart. But everything had its limits and her patience with him must be running low. 'Are you saying there's no hope for us?'

Lindsey drew back sharply. 'I'm not saying that at all.' She spread her hands in appeal. 'But I can't be myself around you any more.'

Dan felt his heart beating hard against his ribs. 'OK. I hear what you're saying. I don't want to lose you, Lindsey. Lose *us*.'

Lindsey could see the sudden tight set of his shoulders. She didn't want to put pressure on him. Push him to do things he wasn't ready to do. But they couldn't have gone on the way they had been, neither knowing what the other was thinking half the time. 'I don't want to give up on *us* either, Dan.'

'OK, we won't, then.' His blue eyes held an appeal. 'So this is the new, improved me, communicating. If I wouldn't be intruding, I'd like to come out to Lark Hill on Sunday. We could spend the day together.'

'That would be good,' Lindsey said guardedly. 'And definitely a step in the right direction.'

'More like thirty Ks in the right direction.' There was the slightest waver in his eyes. 'So we're back on track, then.'

'Come early on Sunday.' Lindsey tilted her head and reached out a hand across the table. 'I'll put you to work.'

Dan took her hand, shackling her wrist. 'I want to kiss you,' he said softly.

'No chance.' She ran her tongue along her lips. 'Here's Leo with our food.'

'Sunday, then?' Dan leaned back in his chair.

She nodded.

And so it was settled.

They ate quickly and went back to the hospital. As they approached the station Vanessa called out, 'There you are! We've an MVA coming in. Collision between a car and one of those double-cab utilities. Woman reversing out of her gateway into the main road. Guy in the ute didn't have time to swerve.'

'What kind of injuries do we have?' Dan asked calmly.

'Terry Ryan said the woman's pregnant, ten weeks or so. She's a bit shaken but nothing broken. Ute driver's an older man, shocky, possible ribs and seat-belt injury. It happened just out of town a bit so they'll be here directly.'

'Right.' Dan said, 'Anything else happening?'

'No.' Vanessa shook her head. 'We've been quiet.'

'OK.' He glanced at his watch. 'It's nothing Michelle and Andrew can't handle between them. I have a meeting with the board. Lindsey, will you deal?'

'Go.' Lindsey shooed him off. 'Do we have names, Van?'

Vanessa checked her notes. 'Rebecca Brannon and Graeme Ley. Did you have a nice lunch?' she sidetracked deftly.

'Yes, thanks.' Lindsey busied herself at the computer. 'Can't remember the last time I was at Leo's. OK.' She whirled off her chair. 'Van, would you grab Jess and make sure the resus room is ready, please? And check the radiographer's on hand. At some stage there'll need to be an ultrasound done on the pregnant woman.'

'Got all that.' Vanessa took off.

The ambulance siren could be heard outside as Lindsey briefed the junior doctors. She addressed Andrew. 'Which patient do you want?'

'I'll take the ribs,' he said emphatically. 'I've a bit to learn yet about pregnant women.'

'Better smarten up, then, if you're aiming to be a family practitioner,' Lindsey suggested, her tone dry. 'Jess will assist you. Michelle, I'll be with you.'

'Perhaps we should get the ob down?' Michelle looked a question at Lindsey as they made their way to Resus.

'You're the doctor,' Lindsey said. 'It's your call.'

'On the other hand, he'll be grumpy if we call him down for nothing untoward. We'll play it by ear and see how we go, I think.'

Lindsey shot her a discerning look. 'You're OK about treating this patient?'

'Mmm. Yes, of course.' Michelle gave an awkward little laugh. 'I know I've not been the easiest to work with but I'm finally getting the hang of working in Casualty. It's like running a marathon every day.'

'Maybe. But you'll learn a lot here.' Lindsey pulled back the curtain and they went into the resus cubicle. 'Hi, Rebecca, I'm Lindsey. This is Michelle. She'll be your treating doctor. How are you feeling?'

'A bit scared...' Rebecca was shivering, her eyes wide in trepidation.

'Have you felt any bleeding?' Michelle asked.

'No. Don't think so.'

'Well, we'll make sure anyway. Lindsey, would you check Rebecca, please?'

A few moments later Lindsey was able to report, 'So far, so good. But we'll pop a pad on you, Rebecca, so we'll be able to monitor any change.'

Rebecca took a shaky breath. 'I don't want to lose this baby.'

'We'll do everything we can to stop that happening,' Michelle interposed gently. 'Now, I want to check your tummy for any injury from your seat belt.'

Michelle's hands worked their way methodically across her patient's abdomen, palpating, checking and rechecking. Finally, she lifted her head and smiled. 'You seemed to have escaped any spleen damage. Now, let's see what the rest of you is doing.' She turned to Lindsey, her brows raised in silent query.

'BP and pulse within normal range.'

'Thanks.' Michelle shone a torch into Rebecca's eyes to check her pupils were normal and reacting. 'OK, that's fine,' she said. 'Now, I want you to squeeze my hand as hard as you can and then I'll check your legs and feet. Excellent.' She smiled. 'You're doing great.'

'Are you ready for the Doppler now?' Lindsey asked from behind Michelle's shoulder.

'We certainly are.' Michelle ran the special obstetric stethoscope over Rebecca's slight bump. For several seconds she concentrated, listening. Shifting the stethoscope slightly, she listened again.

'Is s-something wrong?' Rebecca's eyes flew wide in concern.

'Nothing at all.' Michelle gave a reassuring pat to her

patient's arm. 'Your little one's heartbeat is ticking away very nicely.'

'Oh, thank God.' Tears spilled from Rebecca's eyes and down her cheeks.

'Thank you so much, Doctor.'

'I don't think you've anything to worry about,' Michelle said. 'But to make absolutely sure, we'll do an ultrasound as well.'

'Are you booked here to have your baby?' Lindsey spread a blanket over the young woman.

'No…' Rebecca bit her lip. 'I'm from Sydney, here visiting my nanna. It was her car I was driving. It's a bit different from mine. I had trouble adjusting the seat belt and then I think I may have put on too much speed as I reversed. Is the driver of the ute all right?'

'We'll find out for you,' Lindsey said. 'In the meantime, could we contact someone for you—your husband perhaps?'

Rebecca shook her head. 'Dean's away on business. I'll call him later.'

'What about your nanna?' Michelle plonked herself on the corner of the bed.

'She's not been too well. I was actually on my way to get a scrip filled for her.' The young woman gave a funny little grimace. 'She's probably thinking I've gone shopping or something. I…suppose I should let her know…'

'That might be a good idea. I'll speak to her as well, if you like,' Michelle offered. 'Just to reassure her.'

'Thanks…both of you.' Rebecca's eyes flicked between the doctor and nurse. 'For being so kind to me and everything…'

'That's what we do.' Michelle scribbled quickly on her patient's chart. 'Now, if you give me the name of your doctor in Sydney, I'll make sure he or she gets your notes. And I'd like to keep you here for a couple of hours, just to make sure you and your bub are fine. We'll pop you on a saline drip and a little later we'll take some blood. That'll tell us whether your haemoglobin levels are where they should be.'

'OK…' Rebecca pulled herself higher on the pillow. 'Could I have my bag, please? I'll dig out my phone and call Nanna.'

'How's the side ward looking?' Michelle turned to Lindsey. 'Perhaps Rebecca would be more comfortable out there.'

'Should be fine,' Lindsey said. 'Most of our youngsters have been discharged.' She smiled at their patient. 'Now, what about a cup of tea?'

Rebecca gave a little tearful nod of appreciation. 'That sounds like heaven.'

Sunday at Lark Hill…

Hands resting across the railing, Dan and Lindsey were on the back deck, looking down at the patch of newly mown lawn. 'Thanks for doing this, Dan.'

'It's fine.' He sent her a wry smile. 'Anything else you'd like me to do?'

'Well…if you wouldn't mind, I'd like the wood brought in for the fireplace. Even though we're eventually heading into summer, the nights can still get quite cool. Jeff would have seen to all these jobs but he's a bit off-colour at the moment.'

Dan hooked a questioning brow. 'Should I look in on him?'

'Do you have your bag with you?'

'Of course. I'll get it.'

'Dan—stop!' Lindsey smothered an embarrassed laugh. 'I'm kidding. Fiona will have everything in hand.'

'Ah. I see.'

He lifted a hand, stroking the back of his index finger

gently over the curve of her cheek and across her chin. 'You're playing the joker again. Is this something you do only at Lark Hill, Ms Stewart?'

'Must be...' She tried to laugh again but the laughter caught in her throat. His body was very close, his mouth closer still. 'Got you in, though.'

'Payback, then,' he murmured as his mouth came down and closed over her tiny sigh.

While Dan brought in the wood, Lindsey prepared lunch. 'I've made burgers,' she said, when he came through to the kitchen. 'But not your usual kind.' She gave him a quick, hopeful look. 'They're sweet potato and quinoa. And don't look like that.' She flicked him playfully with the tea towel. 'I promise they won't be bland. I've made a chilli yoghurt dressing to go with them.'

Dan washed his hands at the sink. 'So we're on a vegetarian kick today, are we?'

Lindsey put her health professional's hat on. 'It's good to have a change from an all-meat diet.'

'Hey.' He held up his hands in mock surrender. 'Did I say anything to the contrary?'

'No, you didn't.' The dimple in Lindsey's cheek came into sharp relief as she smiled. She loved him like this. Light-hearted. Fun to be with. And the look in those glinting blue eyes sent her insides melting.

They assembled the lunch tray together. 'There's some feta to crumble over the burgers,' Lindsey said. 'Interested?'

Dan's mouth pursed as he considered. 'Think I'll pass. But I'll have some of those black olives, please.'

'And there's rocket from our own veg patch.' Lindsey separated the delicate green leaves from their stems.

'Mmm. Fantastic.' Dan hefted the tray. 'Are we eating on the deck as usual?'

'Why not?' She gathered glasses and a jug of water. 'It's kind of our special place.'

'And I love being here.'

And I love you, he could have added, and wondered why he couldn't voice it.

Because saying it would cause repercussions as wide and deep as the ocean. Was he ready to leave the safety of the shore, take Lindsey with him and set sail to an unfamiliar destination? He deliberately steadied his breathing, tightening his fingers on the edges of the tray and pulling himself back to sanity.

As they neared the end of their informal meal he asked, 'Would you mind if I ran a work-related matter past you?'

'Fire away.' Lindsey refilled their glasses and waited.

'Michelle's evaluation is due. She's about to move on to her next rotation.' He paused. 'Professionally, I wondered how you've found her.'

Lindsey considered her answer. 'Is that a reasonable request, Dan? Michelle's evaluation is surely down to you and Martin.'

'I know all that. But the fact of the matter is the nurses work day in and day out with the junior doctors. And I trust your judgement entirely.'

'Well, in that case…' Lindsey met his gaze, seeing the crease in his cheek as he smiled, the action activating the persuasive gleam in his eyes. 'Michelle's attitude towards the junior nurses has been off-putting for them. They need to gain confidence just as much as the junior doctors do. But things have improved markedly.'

Dan's lips twitched. 'Since you had a quiet word.'

Lindsey gave a shrug. 'She seems to have finally got the message that she's in Casualty as a member of a team. And, believe me, from the nurses' point of view, that's a whole heap of progress.'

'Clinically, she appears very sound. Would you agree?'

'Yes. I've made it my business to work with her a bit more lately. She seems confident in her diagnoses and treatment. And I should charge you for this consult, Dr Rossi,' she added drily.

'Oh, I'll see to it you're well compensated.' His voice was low, deeper than deep, whispering over her skin and right into her heart.

She looked at him mistily. Making love in the afternoon had a lot going for it.

'So, what are you thinking?' Dan's eyes were tender.

'That we have such a lot going for us.'

'We do. I think you're wonderful. And beautiful. And perfect. And damn,' he deadpanned, 'there's my mobile...'

Lindsey sent him an eye-roll, packed up their lunch tray and left him to his call. A few minutes later Dan joined her in the kitchen. He looked serious. 'Everything OK?'

'Hope so. That was the SES.'

Lindsey stopped what she doing and waited for him to explain.

'There's an emergency situation at Mt Rowan. It's near here, I believe.'

'A few Ks up the road. What's happened?'

'Apparently, it's an absciling group from one of the churches—seven young lads, one leader and one parent.'

'And?' Instinctively, Lindsey moved closer.

'The last of the boys to descend pushed out too far. He came back in at an angle instead of front-on to the cliff and appears to have slammed against some kind of projecting rock. And knocked himself out. Fortunately, his locking device has activated and that's saved him from further injury.'

'Oh, poor kid.' Lindsey looked uncertain. 'But why are the SES calling you?'

'Because I've made myself available this weekend. With my training in search and rescue, volunteering for the SES seems a natural fit. And as I'm relatively close to the accident scene, I said I'd attend. It might be some while before the base can muster a team.'

'Then I'll come with you,' Lindsey said. 'Just give me a minute to change.'

Dan clocked her quick response. 'You're not thinking of abseiling?'

'Of course.' She made a motion of brushing him aside. 'I've done heaps. What about you?'

'As you say. I've done heaps.'

'We're a team, then?'

'We seem to be.' Dan shrugged his acceptance, meeting her hand in a high-five salute. 'Now, get a wriggle on.' He tapped her backside. 'I'll close up the house.'

'Do you have your own ropes and things?' Lindsey asked.

'Yep. Luckily, as I've this training day tomorrow I put together what I thought I'd need for any emergency. See you outside.'

Toby Marshall, the team leader, was waiting for them at the cliff-top. 'Boy, am I glad to see you, Doc,' he said grimly as Dan shook hands and skimmed over the introductions.

'So, do wc have a name and how far down is the lad?' Dan asked, already beginning some warm-up arm and shoulder exercises for the physical task ahead.

'Riley Dukes, aged sixteen. By my estimation, he's about twenty metres down.' Toby looked keenly at Dan. 'Obviously he's going to need medical attention, so it's you for the drop, is it, Doc?'

'We'll both go,' Lindsey said firmly. 'I'm a nurse. I'm Dan's back-up.'

'And you've abseiled before?' Toby queried.

'Lots of times.'

'OK, then. The sooner we get this under way, the better

for young Riley. And, Doc, I realise you have your own gear, but I'll need to check what you're wearing. We don't need any more mishaps.'

'Sure.' Dan was compliant. 'No worries.'

'And I'll be your anchor at the top,' Toby said.

Dan showed Toby the special sit-in retrieval harness he'd be wearing, pointing out the sturdy shoulder straps and leg loops.

'You realise you're going to have to attach Riley's harness to yours to get him down?'

'These are the clip gates I'll use for that.' Dan's hands closed around the metal locking devices. 'This type is the best and easiest to operate in case I have only one hand free. And I have a sheathed knife to cut Riley's line away once I have him secured to my harness.'

'Right, you seem well equipped,' Toby said approvingly. 'Don't forget you'll have Riley's extra weight on your line so be aware of the sudden impact when you cut the line away. But I'll have you firmly anchored and it should be fairly smooth sailing down to the base. And hopefully by then the SES team and ambulance will be there. Meanwhile, take this radio. It'll connect you with me. Any problems, yell.'

Meanwhile, Lindsey had climbed into her own harness tightening the waist belt above her hips.

'You set?' Dan touched her shoulder.

'Yes.' She swallowed the dryness in her throat, checking the trauma kit's bulk, which she'd anchored at the rear just below her bottom. 'Let's do it.' Her eyes met Dan's and clung. She hadn't done this for quite a while, but she wasn't about to tell Dan that. What they had to do would be tricky, to say the least. He would, of necessity, have to keep focused. She didn't want him distracted and worrying about *her* safety.

* * *

Bouncing down the granite face of the cliff, Dan felt the familiar adrenaline kick in. The hard slog of his training in Florida had been well worth this feeling of achievement. Cautiously, he cast a look downwards, just able to glimpse their quarry in his bright yellow sweatshirt. 'We're nearly there,' he called to Lindsey, who was slightly above him and to his left. 'Slacken off.'

'I hear you.' Little by little, Lindsey began paying out her rope, moving on down the rock face until she was alongside him.

'Right—this'll do us.' Dan signalled and together they swung in as closely as they could to the boy. 'And Eureka…' His voice held relief as they landed on a ledge of rock and he began testing its viability. Finally, he managed to position his feet so that he was more or less evenly balanced. 'This should hold both of us, Lindsey. Close up now.'

'I'm with you…' She edged in beside him.

Dan's gaze swung to her. She looked a bit pale. A surge of protectiveness shot into his gut. 'You OK?'

'Piece of cake.' Her brittle laugh jagged eerily into the stillness.

Riley was hanging in space, quite still. But the top part of his inert body had drooped so far forward he was almost bent double into a U-shape.

Dan swore under his breath. Another couple of centimetres and the kid would have turned upside down. They had no time to lose. 'OK, Lindsey, let's reel him in.'

Lindsey looked doubtful. 'Can you reach him from there?'

'Just about, I think. I'll give it a good shot.'

She felt her stomach knot, fearing for Dan's safety as he edged perilously along the ledge, making the most of his long reach to grip the boy's waist harness and guide him in close to the cliff face. Riley's colour was glassily blue. Her nerves pulled even tighter. Were they already too late?

'Lindsey, listen,' Dan instructed firmly. 'I want you to position yourself to receive Riley's torso and support his head, OK?'

Lindsey was put on her mettle. She reached out her arms. 'Right, I've got him!' Immediately, she began to equalise the position of Riley's head and neck, which would automatically clear his airway. 'How's his pulse?'

Dan's mouth screwed tight. 'It's there but it's faint. And no breath sounds. Damn.' He dragged in a huge breath and in one swift movement bent to deliver five quick mouth-to-mouth breaths into their patient.

The silence was deafening; seconds felt like hours as they waited. And then they heard Riley's roughened cough. 'OK, he's breathing but still well out of it. Grab me the torch, Lindsey.' Automatically, he took their patient's weight so Lindsey could access the torch from the trauma kit.

Dan's face was set in concentration as he flicked the light into the boy's eyes. 'Equal and reacting,' he relayed, feeling the tightness in his temples ease fractionally.

So, no bleed to the brain, Lindsey interpreted silently. 'His knee seems at an odd angle.'

'I had noticed.' Dan began feeling around for the clip gates attached to the runner looped over his shoulder. Riley's injured knee was an added complication. The sooner they got the kid down and treated, the better. His gaze lowered to where Riley's injury was just visible below the coloured band of his shorts. The matter of the scraped skin was of little concern but Dan's instincts were telling him that the puffy state of the boy's knee plus the blood seeping from the wound from the rock were a worry. 'He's obviously hit the rock with some force.'

'Do you think he's banged his head and lost control?' Lindsey voiced her own concerns tentatively.

'Quite possibly. Whatever, I can't do much from here.

We'll need to get him down so I can look at him properly. Right, I'm about to try to anchor Riley to my harness.'

Lindsey felt unease crawl up her backbone as she realised the logistics. It seemed a very big ask. Dan was going to try to align Riley's body to his, chest to chest. 'In practical terms, how do you want to work it, then?'

'Slowly and carefully. We'll endeavour to manoeuvre Riley upright now. I'll help as much as I can but I'll have to concentrate on getting him adjacent to my own body so I can link our harnesses together. OK, let's do it.'

It was useless. Lindsey shook her head in despair. It was like trying to steady a ton weight balloon with a piece of string. Riley was a well-built young man, his unconscious state only adding to their difficulties. And in their precarious position, it was nearly impossible to co-ordinate the lift so the two harness belts were close enough to link.

'This isn't going to work,' Dan said concisely. His shoulders slumped and he shook his head. 'This was a hare-brained idea.'

Lindsey sensed his anguish but they couldn't give up now. Riley's young life could well depend on their teamwork. She pushed down her fears. 'Give me the clip gates, Dan.'

'That's ridiculous!' His brows shot up. 'Riley's way too heavy and you're not wearing the right kind of harness.'

'I didn't mean I'd try to take Riley's weight,' Lindsey pointed out. 'But we have to find a resolution here. What we're doing is not working—when you're steady, Riley's either too high or too low.'

Dan swore under his breath and slumped into his harness. 'We'll just have to wait until the SES guys get here. They can drop someone. Between us, we'll be able to attach Riley and get him down.' He reached inside his vest for the radio transmitter.

All that could take precious time. Lindsey thought

swiftly. It was time they didn't have. Her confidence in her own capabilities kicked in. 'Wait a minute. Could you try linking your hands under Riley's behind and lifting him to your waist level? Then I could make a grab for his harness and snap you together.'

Dan's jaw tightened so hard it felt like snapping. He hated not being in control. Hated and loathed it. Nevertheless, he did what Lindsey had suggested, gripping Riley and lifting him as high as he could, his muscles straining with the effort.

Lindsey's nerves were stretched like the strings on a bass fiddle. She had only the barest window of opportunity to hitch the two harnesses together before Dan's strength gave out and he'd have no choice but to abort his hold on the injured boy. She steadied her breathing, conscious of almost choreographing her movements.

'Do it now, Lindsey…' Dan gasped, pulling his torso back so Lindsey could use what little space there was between him and the boy. 'Now!' he yelled.

'Do it—or I've lost him!'

In a flash, remembering everything she'd been taught, Lindsey used her feet in a technique called smearing, where most of the climber's weight was positioned over one foot to reduce the overall load on the arms. Twisting slightly, she turned her upper body so that her arm closest to the rock face could counter-balance her movement and give her other arm maximum extension. It took barely seconds to execute.

But to Dan those same seconds felt like hours. The muscles of his throat and around his mouth were locked and sweat pooled wetly in his lower back. His mind was so focused he hardly felt the nudge of Lindsey's fingers as she secured one then two more clip gates to link Dan to his patient.

'Done…' Her voice was barely above a whisper.

* * *

Lindsey hardly remembered how they got down. She only remembered the relief she'd felt when Dan had cut Riley's rope and they'd been able to begin their descent.

And there were plenty of hands to help them once they were safely on the ground. A subdued cheer even went up. Riley was released from his harness and placed on the stretcher.

Lindsey divested herself of her own harness, vaguely aware her legs felt as unsteady as a puppet's. She swallowed back the taste of bile. Surely she wasn't about to disgrace herself and throw up here in front of all these macho men. Someone from the SES handed her a bottle of water. 'Nice work, Lindsey. You're a beauty.'

She managed a weak smile before swallowing several big mouthfuls of water. Her equilibrium steadied and she pulled her thoughts together. Removing her safety hat, she shook out her hair and began making her way across to where Riley's stretcher had been placed in the shade and Dan was bending over him.

Dan looked at her briefly. 'He's come round. You'll be fine, mate,' he reassured his young patient. 'Take it easy now. We'll get you on some oxygen.'

The portable oxygen unit appeared as if by magic. And a space blanket.

'How is he, Doc?' Toby Marshall hovered uneasily. He'd have some explaining to do to the kid's parents over this.

Dan folded his stethoscope away. Riley's breathing was a bit raspy but this wasn't the place to be passing that information along. It would right itself as the oxygen kicked in. 'Riley has a fractured kneecap and possible lower rib injury. We need to get him to hospital.' He turned to the paramedic and took him aside. 'I'll leave Riley in your capable hands, Terry. Cane it in, mate. His parents are probably wearing out the floor in the ED.'

'No worries, Doc. Scratch us a few notes to take and we'll be out of here.'

Late afternoon and the vivid sunset was rapidly being overtaken by the sweep of pearly grey evening sky and the wind that had risen had the sharpness of a whip crack. One of the SES crew had given Dan and Lindsey a lift back to the cliff-top and Dan was rapidly sorting his climbing gear and stowing it safely in his Land Rover.

Arms wrapped around her middle, Lindsey stood watching him. It had been the oddest kind of day.

Dan closed the tailgate on his SUV and turned, his gaze narrowing. He frowned a bit. She looked shattered. 'Why didn't you go and sit in the car?'

'I wanted to wait for you.'

'Aw…' He gave a goofy grin. 'Need a hug, then?' He opened his arms and she ran to him. She cuddled into his embrace and he held her. And held her. 'You were amazing.' He looped back a strand of hair from her cheek. 'I couldn't have done it without you. You had no fear at all, did you?'

Lindsey bit back a snort. If only he knew. But a girl was entitled to warm herself in his male look of admiration for just a little while. 'Climbing is practically a religion around here. We did lots of it when we were growing up and we were taught properly from the beginning. Today was the first time I've had to assist in an emergency situation, though.'

Dan frowned and then said slowly, 'Then I hope you never have to do it again, Lindsey.'

She pushed her hands up under his T-shirt, feeling the

clean sweep of his skin. And loving it. 'I didn't enjoy it much,' she admitted. 'But I was impressed by *your* skills.'

'You were?' His eyes glinted with dry humour. 'You're just saying that.'

Lindsey bugged her eyes at him. 'Stop fishing for compliments, Dante, and take me home.'

'I'm going to have to head straight back to Hopeton, I'm afraid,' Dan said as they neared Lark Hill. 'The training day starts at six a.m. tomorrow.'

'And you need all the sleep you can get. I'm heading back myself. I'm on an early tomorrow and we've a new member of staff joining us. I'd better look at least as though I'm awake and functioning.'

Dan picked up her hand and raised it to his lips. 'I would much rather have lain with you and held you all night.'

'That sounds really poetic…' Lindsey rested her head against his shoulder and smiled. 'Perhaps you do take after your namesake.'

He spluttered a laugh. 'And perhaps not.'

'And here we are,' Lindsey said as they pulled into the Lark Hill driveway and Dan coasted to a stop. Almost simultaneously, they released their seat belts and reached for each other. They kissed long and slowly, savouring every last stroke of the tongue, each lingering taste of each other.

'I won't come in.' Dan pressed his forehead against hers. 'Will you be OK?'

'Mmm. I just have to throw my stuff together and take off.' She moved to open the door. 'Just one other thing, Dan.' She bit her lip. 'I don't know what kind of crazy stuff you'll be expected to do tomorrow. But…please…be safe. For me?'

Dan felt his insides twist, the sudden swell of emotion

hitting him like the force of a king tide. His heart was overflowing with love for this woman. He reached out, slowly drawing her gaze up so it was level with his. 'I promise I won't do anything reckless. And I'll come back to you safely, Lindsey. For no other reason than I need to.'

CHAPTER TWELVE

LINDSEY LOOKED OUT at the landscape the next morning. It was raining lightly, the gentle, soaking kind that would have the farmers smiling and the mothers of young school children dredging up an endless supply of patience as they pushed reluctant little arms into raincoats.

She pulled a face, making her way slowly from her bedroom to the shower, her leg muscles protesting all the way. So much for the abseiling lark yesterday, she vented silently.

Arriving at the hospital, she went through to the staffroom.

'Well, get you!' From her table near the window, Vanessa looked up, her eyes wide in laughing disbelief. She rattled the pages of Hopeton's daily paper.

'You and daring Dan in a cliff rescue. What else did you get up to, Ms Stewart?'

'Oh, show me.' Lindsey gave a *tsk* and leaned over Vanessa's shoulder to read the report on the incident. 'Why on earth would they have thought this was newsworthy?' she dismissed.

'Because the kid you rescued just happens to be the grandson of Angus Whittaker, the local MP. He was here at the hospital only last week, doing what they euphemistically call "a guided tour". Ring any bells?'

'No.' Lindsey slammed the paper shut. 'He didn't come to the ED.'

Vanessa's mouth turned down. 'Bit too confronting for him, I guess. I heard he went to Midwifery. He wanted to tell them personally he'd got funding for a new birthing suite.'

'Well, bully for them,' Lindsey huffed. 'I could have given him a long list of things we need in Casualty.' She made a cup of tea and came back to the table. 'Riley's surname is Dukes,' she said, wanting to get things straight in her head. 'So his mother must be Whittaker's daughter.'

'Correct.' Vanessa pushed the newspaper aside. 'So, what's to prevent you from popping in on Riley at visiting time? I'm sure his mum would like to meet one part of the rescue team who got her son down from the cliff.'

Lindsey's eyes widened. 'Are you suggesting I should go armed with my list for the casualty department?'

'Well, not quite. But you could start opening doors, so to speak. If you get my drift? I mean, Mr Whittaker's bound to be visiting his grandson some time or other.'

Lindsey grinned. 'You should be working for the UN. But I'll definitely think about popping up to see Riley.'

'Now, what about the second part of my question?' Vanessa wasn't about to be put off.

Lindsey's shoulders lifted in a resigned gesture. There was no use prevaricating. When Vanessa sensed intrigue, she was like a terrier with a bone. 'Yesterday Dan spent the day with me at Lark Hill. He's volunteered for the SES. They called him about the abseiling incident. The rest, as they say, is in the local paper.'

'So…' Vanessa moved her head closer. 'You two are a couple, then?'

'Yes.' Lindsey took a mouthful of her tea and wondered what else you could call it. 'Your hair looks amazing, by the way,' she diverted skilfully.

'Oh, thanks, Lins. Mimi's had a cut-and-colour special.' Vanessa swung her new choppy style as if to emphasise the all-shades-of-blonde highlights. 'I thought I needed an update.'

'Well, it's gorgeous and it suits you.'

A beat of silence and then, 'Oh. My. God.' Vanessa's gaze was riveted on the doorway and the male who hovered there. 'Now, that's what I call a body…'

Lindsey swung round. And blinked a bit. *Wow.* 'That must be our new recruit.' She got swiftly to her feet. 'Let's make him welcome.'

'Wait for me.' Vanessa almost catapulted out of her chair.

'I'm in the right place, then?' Charlie Weston's sea-green gaze tracked between the two women after introductions had been made.

'And on time as well.' Vanessa took the lead cheekily.

'Awesome. I've brought muffins,' Charlie said, with a kind of eager-to-fit-in look.

'Apple and blueberry?' They were Vanessa's favourite.

'Tuna and mustard,' he deadpanned.

'Perfect,' Vanessa shot back, already on the same quirky wavelength. 'Come and I'll show you where to put your stuff.'

Lindsey just shook her head at the pair of them and went to take handover.

When the team assembled, Lindsey allotted jobs, adding, 'Vanessa, I'll leave Charlie's orientation in your capable hands. Yell if you need me.'

'Thanks, Lins.' Vanessa all but batted her eyelashes. 'I'm sure we'll be fine.'

Watching the two walk away, Lindsey noted that Charlie's longish sun-bleached hair was neatly tied back in a ponytail. And she'd already clocked his hands and nails were well kept and scrupulously clean. Good, she thought with satisfaction. He'd do nicely.

By mid-afternoon Lindsey could hardly keep her eyes open. She discreetly blocked a yawn. Yesterday's escapade had obviously taken more out of her than she'd realised. She wondered how Dan was faring.

Dan took some deep breaths, mentally clearing his thoughts for the umpteenth time. He could have done all this stuff standing on his head. But when in Rome…

They'd completed all the physical training and now he just had to sit in on a lecture about handling hazardous materials, dealing with oil spills, chemical leaks and more. Then he'd be out of there. Tonight he and Lindsey were going to dinner with Nathan and Sami. And on Saturday he was going to Lark Hill to meet Lindsey's family. It seemed they were *out* as a couple. Dan was amazed how good it felt.

Friday...

'Are you going to Greta's working bee tomorrow?' Vanessa propped herself on the counter at the nurses' station.

Lindsey glanced up. 'I'll come for a while. Dad's just turned sixty. We're having a celebration dinner for him at Lark Hill.' And Lindsey had invited Dan. It was time he met her family.

'From what I hear, it'll be a good turnout for the working bee,' Vanessa chirped. 'Charlie's coming along too. He's brilliant at DIY.'

Lindsey gave her friend a long look. 'And you know this how?'

Vanessa went pink. 'He's taken over Nathan's old flat. I've been helping him tart it up a bit before Poppy arrives. He's made such a cute job of her bedroom.'

'You and Charlie have really hit it off, haven't you?'

'He's fun.' Vanessa shrugged. 'And I can be myself around him. It's…nice. Uncomplicated.'

And he's so different from Andrew, Lindsey interpreted, happy for her friend. And for Charlie as well, for that matter. Van was a gem.

A week later…

OK, so this was crunch time.

Dan braced himself. He had clearance from the board. He was packed. Now he just had to tell Lindsey. He knew she'd hate it but it was something he needed to do.

He looked at his watch. Still early. But she'd be up and he didn't have much time.

The sound of her doorbell roused Lindsey. She sat up groggily. What the heck?

She sat for a second on the side of the bed and felt around for her dressing gown. Oh, why bother? She was decently clad in long pyjama pants and a T-shirt. Shoving her feet into a pair of slip-on sandals, she clacked to the front door. 'Dan…' She blinked, her gaze uncertain. 'Is something wrong?'

'Morning.' He gave a contained kind of smile. 'Nothing's wrong. May I come in?'

'Of course.' She stood back to let him in.

'Did I wake you?' He looked concerned.

Lindsey finger-combed a fall of hair from her forehead. 'I'm on a late. I just felt like a sleep-in. Come through. I'll make some tea.'

'I'll make it,' Dan offered.

He felt guilty. She looked whacked.

'Thanks.' She gave a wry smile. 'I'll wash my face and wake up a bit.'

After she'd changed into jeans and combed her hair, she felt more in control, more like herself. She headed into the kitchen, where Dan was making himself busy.

'So, what's up?'

He handed her a mug of tea and she saw he'd made toast as well. She took long mouthfuls and looked at him above the rim of her mug. Waiting.

'I have something to tell you.' Dan was hunched over his tea mug.

She forced her lips into a smile that felt stiff and uncomfortable. 'Better get on and tell me, then.'

Dan hesitated as if searching for the right words. 'Have you been watching the TV news at all over the last twenty-four hours?'

She shook her head. 'Why, have I missed something important?'

'A category-three cyclone has hit parts of New Guinea's coastline, and particularly a little island to the north. It's called Cloud Island. There's huge damage and their resources are poor. The ADF are organising to send supplies and personnel as we speak. They need MOs on the ground. I've volunteered. I'm flying out at noon today.'

'Oh.' She moistened her lips and took a long controlling breath. 'How dangerous will it be?'

Dan shrugged. 'It's hard to put a classification on it at this stage. But there'll be protocols in place. We'll just follow orders mainly and do what we're trained to do. In my case, I'll be helping to set up a field hospital and treat the incoming casualties.'

Her throat closed tightly. 'Are there many people injured... do you know?'

Possibly hundreds, he could have told her, but refrained. 'Well, the gurus at the weather bureau are calling it a natural disaster so I imagine there'll be a bit of tidying up in all directions.'

'How long will you be gone?'

'Don't know yet. Possibly not more than several weeks. Once the hospital is up and running, the army will start taking things over, bringing in more of their own personnel. But right now they need as many trained boots on the ground as they can get.' A muscle pulled in his jaw. 'And I *am* trained for this kind of emergency, Lindsey. I can't just sit on my hands and do nothing.'

Her heart did an odd tattoo. One part of her was inordinately proud of him but the other part… She looked at him, her eyes unguarded. 'I guess there's nothing to say other than take care of yourself.'

'Of course I will.' Dan reached out and took her hand across the table. 'You take care as well while I'm gone.'

She gave a jagged laugh. 'I'll be just going to work and coming home. I can't get into much trouble.'

'Will you come out to the airport and see me off?'

Lindsey stared at him for a moment, then suddenly and clearly, saw things from his perspective. He had to go. And she was glad and proud of his humaneness and the depth of his commitment to medicine and his willingness to use his skills in whatever way and wherever they were needed. 'Of course I will.'

'You're not taking much.' Lindsey saw he had only a carry-on bag. They were in Hopeton's airport lounge and holding hands tightly.

'We'll be issued with everything. I'll try for a video hook-up so you can see me in my army fatigues.'

'And handsome as all get-out.' Lindsey tried to joke but it was hard. She swallowed. 'So when you get to Sydney, what then?'

'I'll meet up with the rest of the contingent. We'll fly out in a Hercules later today, I imagine. Look at the TV news tonight. There's bound to be a camera or two recording our departure. I'll send you a wave.'

'And I'll be bound to see it,' she said drily, looking out through the glass wall of the passenger lounge to the airstrip, where the luggage was being ferried across for loading. She felt a wrench to her heart. He'd be gone soon. The line of her mouth trembled for a second.

Watching her, Dan took stock, finding it hard to believe the avalanche of emotion that swamped him. He, Dan Rossi, had fallen headlong in love with this beautiful woman. And what he had to say couldn't wait a moment longer. 'I love you absolutely, Lindsey Stewart. Will you marry me?'

Dazed, her mouth opened and closed. She couldn't speak. She just bit her lips together and nodded. Then smiled as if her lips might crack. 'Oh, Dan…'

'So that's a *yes*?' Dan's eyes locked with hers.

'Yes! Of course, yes! I love you, Dan. How could you think I didn't?'

Dan's heart began clamouring. He heaved in a long breath and let it go. Joy, clear and pure, streamed through him. Oblivious to the crowd around them, he pulled her close and kissed her—hard. 'When?'

Lindsey felt shaky and happy all rolled into one. She fiddled with the button on his shirt front. 'As soon as you like. As soon as you come back from your tour?'

'Yes.' He nodded eagerly. 'In the meantime, think about what kind of wedding you'd like and I'll do the same. And we'll do it,' he added softly, as if making a promise to himself, a promise to both of them. His eyes clouded for a second. 'And you don't mind all my baggage?'

She placed her fingers on his lips, her gaze clear and untroubled. 'What baggage? This is *us*, Dan.'

He took her hands and held them against his chest, as if reaffirming their commitment. 'It's about time I got that into my head. After I get back, I never want to be away from you again.'

'You won't have to be,' she said, knowing it as surely as she knew her own name. 'We'll be together.'

'Oh, my Lindsey…' Dan leaned into her, kissing her softly, tenderly.

'This is the best day of my life.'

Lindsey's smile was tremulous. 'And mine. Oh.' She lifted her head and listened. 'That's your boarding call. Do you have everything you need?'

His face worked for a minute. 'Everything but you.' He gave her one last, fierce kiss. 'That'll get me through the tough times,' he said, and picked up his bag.

Lindsey watched as he jogged across to join the end of the queue of boarding passengers. Suddenly, he turned. He began walking backwards and smiling. 'I love you!'

'And I love you,' she echoed, but he was already out of sight.

Two weeks later...

'Have you heard from Dan recently?' Vanessa asked as she and Lindsey met up in the staffroom before work.

Lindsey made a face. 'The mobile reception is pathetic. I've had a few phone calls. But Dan said the army techs are hoping to have a satellite up and running shortly so that will make communication easier.'

Vanessa propped her chin on her hand. 'You look a bit wan, Lins. You're really missing him, aren't you?'

Lindsey nodded and bit her lip. 'Every day seems like a month.' She paused. 'Dan asked me to marry him as soon as he gets back.'

Vanessa's mouth fell open. 'Get *out*. Oh, Lins—that's amazing! And you said yes? Of course you did. Oh…' Vanessa's hand went to her heart. 'A wedding. How could you have kept that kind of news to yourself? I'd have been doing a shout-out all over the ED. What plans have you made?'

'Well, none, really.' Lindsey was still feeling stunned to some extent. She needed Dan's presence to make things real.

'I'll help you,' Vanessa said promptly. 'We'll make a list. All you need is the date, time and venue. And your dress, of course. And the guest list. Oh, and flowers...'

Lindsey managed a shaky laugh. 'I need to think about it a bit more, Van. But thanks.'

Vanessa batted a hand. 'What kind of wedding does Dan want?'

'We left it open-ended. We'll decide on something when he gets back...'

'But you could get a jump-start,' Vanessa pointed out excitedly. 'Guys usually go along with whatever the bride wants anyway. I'll dash out on my break and get the latest bride books. Lace is so *in*. But you'll look stunning in whatever you wear,' she summed up happily.

Lindsey locked her arms around her stomach. Butterflies as big as doves were looking for a place to land. Vanessa's enthusiasm had been like an avalanche, drowning her in excitement. And the faintest trepidation.

Later in the day, Lindsey was surprised to receive a phone call from Sami.

'Is it OK to call you at the hospital?' Sami asked.

'Of course.' Lindsey swung away from the computer. 'If I'm elsewhere in the department, you can always leave a message and I'll get back to you. Is everything OK?'

'It's wonderful.' Sami gave a throaty laugh. 'Look, Lins, I know Dan is away and you're possibly a bit at loose ends so I wondered if you'd like a little catch-up after work—cup of tea or something?'

'What a good idea. That sounds just what I need. Where?'

'You know where my cubbyhole is in the main street? There's a tea room newly opened a few doors down. It's called Browne's. I'll pop along and keep a table. See you when you get there. All right?'

'Fantastic.' Lindsey smiled, glad for once she'd brought a change of clothes to work.

'Over here!' Sami's blond curls bobbed as she waved Lindsey across to the table. The two friends hugged briefly and settled themselves in the old-fashioned high booth. 'Now, what are we having?' Sami scanned the menu. 'Pot of tea?'

'Oh, yes, please!' Lindsey smiled and ran her tongue along her lips. 'I'm parched.'

'And something to go with it…' Sami made a moue of conjecture. 'Everything looks a bit buttery and I'm so off sweet stuff. What about cucumber sandwiches?'

'Lovely.' Lindsey tossed back her head and laughed. 'We can pretend we're having high tea at the Ritz.'

Sami cackled. 'Have you done that too?'

'A long time ago with James and Catherine.' Lindsey looked up as the waitress arrived to take their order.

'So, what news do you have for me, Lins?' Sami asked, placing the menu back in its folder.

'Dan's asked me to marry him,' Lindsey blurted. Once she'd told Vanessa, she'd been bubbling with a queasy kind of happiness all day.

'He did?' Sami gave a subdued squeal. 'That's brilliant!' She pressed her hands together in a praying motion under her chin. 'Oh, help… I feel a bit teary. Dan's so lovely. And you're so right for each other. So, are we invited to the wedding?'

'Of course, you dope.' Lindsey blinked a bit and thought

she may as well start making concrete plans. 'In fact, I wondered whether you'd be my matron of honour…'

'Absolutely! I'd be delighted. As long as it's relatively soon so I'll fit into my dress.' Sami's look grew misty. 'I'm pregnant, Lins…'

It was Lindsey's turn to look stunned. The outline of Sami's face went out of focus and then righted itself. 'Ooh…' She let her breath go in a sigh. 'That's so sweet. Congratulations!'

'Thanks. It's a bit sooner than we planned but…you know?' Sami looked coy.

Lindsey felt her own tears welling up. 'I'm so thrilled for you and Nathan. Are you feeling OK healthwise?'

'Pretty good, actually. Off the sweet stuff, as I said, but so sleepy I can't believe!'

Sleepy. Lindsey's stomach heaved alarmingly. Warning bells like the peal of a carillon resounded in her head.

'Mum said she could fall asleep at the drop of a hat when she was expecting Cait and me,' Sami went on happily. 'I've been so looking forward to getting our house in order and now we've a nursery to plan. And Nathan's on cloud nine. He'll be such a *dad.*'

It can't be. Lindsey clasped her hands on her lap, then unconsciously spread them over her tummy. *I'm imagining things. I have to be.* She'd had a period. But it had been lighter than usual. Much lighter, she corrected. It didn't mean anything untoward. She lifted her cup and swallowed a mouthful of her tea. She had to leave. But she couldn't, not yet. Instead, she half listened to Sami. Gave answers when she had to and Sami was on such a roll she hardly noticed anything amiss. Except when they got up to leave.

'You know, Lins, you're looking pale. Working in that hospital environment does absolutely nothing for your complexion.'

Lindsey laughed the comment away and felt as though her lungs had flown into her throat. Sami blew air kisses and they parted, promising to meet again soon.

As Sami had said, they had dresses to choose and a wedding to plan.

Would there even be a wedding now? Lindsey felt shaky as she reversed out of the parking bay. She'd go to one of the busy big chain pharmacies where no one would recognise her and buy a pregnancy testing kit. She swallowed. It was absolutely the last thing she'd expected to be doing when she'd got up this morning.

When she arrived home, she went straight through to the bathroom. Removing the box from the chemist's wrapping, she felt as though she was handling a time bomb.

And it may as well be. An explosion that would surely blow her and Dan's plans for their future to smithereens. He'd said that after the tragic outcome with his twins he was in no hurry to experience fatherhood again. She couldn't do it to him. Present him with a fait accompli like Caroline had done. No way I'll do that to Dan, she vowed, preparing herself for what she had to do.

The test was positive.

Lindsey felt all the strength drain from her legs as she sank down on the side of the bath. *I'm having a baby.* We're *having a baby.*

She sat there for a long time. Then, surprisingly calmly, she got up, had a shower and shampooed her hair. Out of the shower, she towelled dry and dressed in a pair of her softest cotton pyjamas, then went through to the kitchen and put the kettle on. She gave the ghost of a smile. Perhaps she'd have to stop drinking so much tea. She called in sick for work next day. She needed time to herself. Time to start planning hers and her baby's future.

Next day...

Lindsey was amazed she'd slept so soundly but as the day wore on she was aware of a slow crawl of panic overtaking her. She so wished Dan was there so she could have told him, got everything over and done with. And if he walked, so be it. She'd manage on her own. She could even go to Scotland, to James and Catherine. Have her baby there. Her thoughts flew wildly ahead.

The ringing of the doorbell startled her out of her introspection. She sighed, hoping it wasn't Vanessa with her wretched bride books! She went to the front door, flinging it open almost impatiently. And took a breath so deep it almost hurt. 'Dan!' She'd already begun steeling herself for when he'd get back, running over little speeches in her head, but seeing him standing there in the flesh, still dressed in his army fatigues, all her carefully prepared words flew away like leaves in the wind. 'When did you get back?' she croaked.

Dan gave the briefest smile. 'Flew into Sydney in the early hours this morning. Had to hang about for a debrief. There wasn't a flight to Hopeton until God knows when, so I got a cab.'

'You got a cab from Sydney!'

'Needed to see my girl.' He followed her inside to the lounge. 'I rang the hospital. They said you were home sick so I came straight here.' His gaze flew over her. She certainly looked under the weather, not like his bright, beautiful Lindsey at all. And surely she'd lost weight in the time he'd been gone. He put out his hands and took hers. 'Are you actually sick?'

'No—not really.' Just *worried* sick more like. 'I felt like a day to myself, that's all.'

'Ah.' His eyes burned like brilliant sapphires. He grinned. 'Well, you won't be getting that now, will you?'

Suddenly, like a dam breaking, Lindsey burst into tears.

'Hey…what's up?' Dan guided her down onto the sofa. Hell. He felt his heart beating hard against his ribs. What was wrong here? He held her until at last she took several shaky breaths and regained control.

'Oh, Dan…' She curled her face into his neck.

'It'll be OK, Lindsey.' He stroked her back. 'I love you. Whatever it is, you can tell me.'

That's just it, she thought despairingly. I don't know how to.

'Have you gone off me?'

'What?' That brought her to her senses in a flash. 'Of course not.' She sniffed, reaching for the box of tissues on the coffee table. 'This is so unlike me.' She gave a watery smile and made use of the tissues.

'Better now?' His eyes were so close she could see the faint specks of silver in the blue.

She nodded.

'OK, then.' Dan stretched his arm along the back of the sofa behind her. 'I can't keep guessing, Lindsey. Just spell it out. Please.'

His voice was gentle but it couldn't free her from the stomach-caving fear that this was all too difficult, and even now, when he'd told her he loved her, she still couldn't guarantee his reaction would be one of…gladness?

His fingertips stroked the back of her neck. 'I'm going nuts here, sweetheart. What the hell is it?'

Lindsey drew in her breath and let it go. 'I'm pregnant. We're having a baby.'

A beat of silence, absolute and prickling with awareness and disbelief.

A baby. Dan felt his heart double in size. For a second he felt his life spinning out of control and then it slowed and came right. And he was able to think. 'We always used protection.'

'Well, we obviously slipped up. It happens.'

Another beat of silence.

'Have I ruined your life?' he asked quietly.

Lindsey looked at him uncomprehendingly.

'Do you want to be pregnant?' he asked in the same quiet manner.

She jerked upright. 'Are you asking if I want your baby, Dan? *Our* baby? Perhaps I should be asking you if you want it. Because if you don't—'

His kiss cut her off. Rough. Then gentle. Sweeter than sweet. She felt his chest rise and fall in a broken sigh. 'Give me a break, Lins. I think I'm in shock. But I also think I'm ecstatic.'

'Really?'

'Did you think I wouldn't be? Our own baby.' His hand smoothed over her tummy as if he hoped there might already be changes. 'When did you find out?'

'Just yesterday.' She went on to tell him about Sami and Nathan's news and how she'd identified with some of Sami's symptoms.

Dan chuckled. 'Nathan a dad! What a stud, eh!'

Lindsey slid her hands around his neck. 'Our babies will grow up together. Won't that be a laugh?'

He pressed a kiss into her hair. 'What about you? Are you feeling all right?'

'Think so,' she murmured.

'Do you have an ob you prefer?' Dan's mind skipped to professional matters.

'Therese Gordon.' She paused. 'And don't take this the wrong way, Dan, but I don't want you hovering.'

'Oh.' Dan felt his throat suddenly dry. A thousand reasons why he *should* be hovering juxtaposed in his head. And who could blame him—after last time? But there was nothing to indicate that Lindsey's pregnancy would be anything but perfectly straightforward. He had to get that through his head. 'OK.' He took a deep breath and let it go. 'I promise I won't be neurotic about things. But I would like to be there for your scans and ultrasounds.'

'And I'll *want* you there,' Lindsey hastened to reassure him. 'Like any normal expectant dad.' She brushed a kiss across his mouth. 'I love you, Dan, but this is *us*.'

And thank heaven for that. Mentally, Dan kicked all his uncertainties to oblivion, resolving to leave them there.

Lindsey snuggled closer. 'I'm so glad you're back.'

'Me too.'

'How was it?'

'A bit taxing but we managed. Things are quickly getting back to normal. That's why they chucked out the civilians and got their own medics in. Have you thought what you'd like for our wedding?'

'Sorry, no.' She ground her bottom lip. 'I just couldn't seem to get my head around it and then when I found out about the baby…'

He cupped her face in his hands. 'Surely you didn't think I'd do a runner?'

'I hoped not…' She took a deep breath. 'Prayed not. But you were adamant about not wanting fatherhood again.'

His gaze deepened and darkened. 'I was still angry back then. And I hadn't realised I'd just met the love of my life.' He shook his head as if it still amazed him. 'Could we pull a wedding together pretty soon?'

Lindsey looked into his eyes, seeing the sheen of tenderness. 'I think we could. But we'll need a licence.'

He tapped his breast pocket. 'I already have one. Picked it up in Sydney this morning. It's amazing how fast you can get things done when you're in uniform.'

'Oh, Dan,' Lindsey chided. 'Did you let them think you'd been posted?'

He shrugged. 'I suppose I might have given that impression. I just looked a bit helpless and they fell over themselves cutting red tape.'

Lindsey fisted him on the chest. 'You couldn't look helpless if you tried. But back to the wedding. Where? Any preference?'

'Lark Hill? That's if it's all right with your folks. Something intimate and all about us. What do you think?'

'That sounds perfect. There's a wonderful spot amongst the vines where we can make our vows. Reception up at the house. We don't want a crowd, do we?'

He shook his head. 'Just your lot and mine, a few mates from the ED and Nathan and Sami to stand up for us. Easy. Can you take a couple more days off?'

'I guess so. What do you want to do?'

'I still have a few days' leave up my sleeve. I'd like us to fly to Melbourne tomorrow so you can meet my family. We'll take them all to dinner and you'll be wearing your ring.'

'Oh…' Lindsey reached out and placed her palm against his cheek. 'Are you buying me an engagement ring, then?'

'Absolutely. And we'll get matching wedding rings as well.' He smiled indulgently. 'I want to do things properly.' He added silently, this time.

CHAPTER THIRTEEN

A few weeks later, Saturday, a wedding at Lark Hill...

IT WAS MID-MORNING and a clear day. A bridal path had been especially prepared between the rows of vines.

A string quartet was playing softly.

Surrounded by a stunning display of old-fashioned bush roses and fruiting vines, Dan was waiting with Nathan. The guests were seated in bespoke chairs. It was an informal setting but the atmosphere was laden with dignity and purpose. And so much love for the happy couple.

Vanessa sat with Charlie. They were now officially *going out*. Or staying in, as Vanessa laughingly told anyone who would listen. Poppy was now living with her dad most of the time. She adored Vanessa and the feeling was mutual. Charlie leaned over and whispered, 'Is my tie all right?'

Vanessa gave it a quick straighten. 'It's fine. Why?'

'I looked everywhere for it this morning, then found Poppy had been using it as a lead for her guinea pig.'

Vanessa rolled her eyes. 'Why didn't you just wear another one?'

Charlie looked blank. 'I don't have another one.'

'Shh…the music's changing. The bride must be on her way.' On cue, the guests rose as one. Vanessa gripped Charlie's arm. 'Oh, bless…doesn't she look gorgeous? I knew she'd wear lace. And look! Dan's going to meet her. Oh…it's just too romantic.'

Daintily, Vanessa began tapping away the press of happy tears.

Charlie, wearing a goofy grin, handed her his big red hanky.

The newlyweds stepped into their reception, where the atmosphere was already bubbling with laughter and music.

'Dr and Mrs Rossi,' announced Nathan, who was doubling as master of ceremonies.

'I like the sound of that.' Dipping his head, Dan kissed his bride gently but thoroughly for all the world to see. 'You take my breath away, Lindsey Rossi.' His eyes held a gleam of teasing humour. 'I'm so glad you turned up this morning.'

Lindsey gave a shaky laugh, her heart cartwheeling with happiness. 'Of course I turned up,' she countered. 'This is our party. Our beautiful wedding day. Doesn't everything look amazing, Dan?'

It did.

The lovely old home was adorned with fresh garden flowers and a sumptuous buffet lunch was set out on the long table in the dining room. There was comfortable seating everywhere. Guests could wander out to the verandas or into the garden. The back deck had been cleared and the floor sanded and polished for the dancing later.

Lindsey directed Dan's attention to their wedding cake, lavishly decorated with meringue buttercream icing and a trail of blue forget-me-nots. A silver-spangled bauble on the top declared simply: *Love*.

'This is Fiona's gift to us.'

Dan looked smug. 'I knew she approved of me from the get-go.'

They wandered out onto the deck, where so much of

their courtship had taken place. Dan lifted Lindsey's hand and kissed her fingers and the sunlight caught her new rings, causing a beautiful rainbow of sparkles to reflect all around them. 'I love you,' he said for the umpteenth time. 'What about dancing with me?'

Lindsey looked at him through a haze of happiness. 'I think we're supposed to wait until after the speeches and we've cut the cake.'

Dan looked unimpressed. 'It's our wedding, we can do what we like.' He spun her away and she sashayed back to him, draping her arms around his neck.

His eyes lit with satisfaction. 'Happy?'

'I am.' Lindsey smiled serenely. 'You're a very nice man, Dan Rossi.'

Dan gathered her closer. His beautiful Lindsey had come to him today as his bride. He had no doubt their marriage would be good and true. He had to be the happiest man alive.

'And not a bad dancer,' he said.

EPILOGUE

'PANT THROUGH THE BREAK, LINDSEY,' Jenna Metcalf, the midwife, coached.

'I can't…'

'Yes, you can,' Dan encouraged.

'The lights are too bright,' she whined. 'Dan…?'

'Head's almost out,' Jenna said. 'One more push…'

'One more push,' Dan echoed. 'Come on, Lins, he's almost here.'

Lindsey gave a long sound of effort, one that thrust her head back hard against Dan's chest as he held her. They wanted pushing? Well, she'd give them pushing!

'That's it. You're amazing.' Dan kissed the top of her head. And prayed as he'd never prayed before.

'Gently now. Almost there,' Jenna called encouragingly. 'Looking good. Head's out. I'm delivering one shoulder. Wow.' She laughed. 'We have a strong little guy here. He's very anxious to meet his mamma and daddy, aren't you, gorgeous?' In seconds, she held the baby up, his little body all wet and slippery.

Dan made a noise that came from deep within his chest. *Born*. Their son was safely born. His eyes stung and filled as baby Rossi cried lustily and waved tiny fists.

'Oh, Dan, look…' Lindsey's voice cracked. 'He's so beautiful. And perfect.'

'Perfect,' he whispered throatily. Almost in a daze he

cut his son's umbilical cord. 'Jen, thank you.' He felt his throat clear and he swallowed. 'You were brilliant.'

'Uh-uh.' Jenna shook her head. 'Your wife was the brilliant one.' She expertly wrapped the baby and handed him to Lindsey.

Dan moved to sit beside Lindsey, his whole heart in his eyes. 'Put your hands beneath mine,' she said, pressing her cheek against his shoulder. 'And we'll both hold him.' She smiled mistily. 'He looks like you.' Gently, she unwrapped their infant son and they looked in wonder at the perfection of his tiny limbs, fingers and toes. 'Happy?' Lindsey looked at Dan, knowing how special this moment was for him.

Dan nodded, too full for any words—well, any that would make much sense. He felt a surge of love and protectiveness for his beautiful Lindsey and their little boy. They were a family. They had been truly and magnificently blessed.

Lindsey stroked the gentlest finger around the baby's cheek, watched as his little mouth moved instinctively in a suckling motion. Tipping her head back, she smiled at Dan and their gazes locked in sweet understanding.

Lindsey placed the softest kiss on her husband's mouth and then bent to look again at their son. Pride and a kind of triumph filled her. 'This is *us*,' she said.

* * * * *

If you enjoyed this story,
check out these other great reads from
Leah Martyn

WEDDING AT SUNDAY CREEK
REDEEMING DR RICCARDI
DAREDEVIL AND DR KATE
WEDDING IN DARLING DOWNS

All available now!

EXCLUSIVE EXTRACT

Kate Ashton's night with Sam Ryder leads to an unexpected consequence—but can he convince this nurse that their love is meant-to-be?

Read on for a sneak preview of
THEIR MEANT-TO-BE BABY
by Caroline Anderson

'You didn't tell me you were a nurse,' Sam said.

'You didn't tell me you were a doctor.'

'At least I didn't lie.'

Kate felt colour tease her cheeks. 'Only by omission. That's no better.'

'There are degrees. And I didn't deny that I know you.'

'I didn't think our…'

'Fling? Liaison? One-night stand? Random—'

'Our private life was anyone else's business. And anyway, you don't know me. Only in the biblical sense.'

Something flickered in those flat, ice-blue eyes, something wild and untamed and a little scary. And then Sam looked away.

'Apparently so.'

She sucked in a breath and straightened her shoulders. At some point she'd have to tell him she was pregnant, but not here, not now, not like this, and if they were going to have this baby, at some point they would need to get to know each other. But, again, not now. Now

Kate had a job to do, and she was going to have to put her feelings on the back burner and resist the urge to run away.

Don't Miss
THEIR MEANT-TO-BE BABY
By Caroline Anderson

Available February 2017
www.millsandboon.co.uk